Strange As

This Weather

Has Been

Strange As This Weather Has Been

a novel

Ann Pancake

Shoemaker & Hoard

This book is a work of fiction.
Nothing is in it that has not been imagined.

Portions of this novel have appeared in slightly different
forms in *Hunger Mountain, Kestrel,* and *Narrative.*

Library of Congress Cataloging-in-Publication Data
Pancake, Ann.
Strange as this weather has been : a novel / Ann Pancake.
p. cm.
ISBN-10 1-59376-166-X
ISBN-13 978-1-59376-166-0
1. Mountain life—Fiction. 2. West Virginia—Fiction. I. Title.
PS3616.A36S77 2007
813'.6—dc22
2007011838

Cover design by Gerilyn Attebery
Book design by Mark McGarry
Set in Plantin

Note on the cover art: *The Agony of Gaia* was created in response to
the devastation caused by mining techniques such as mountaintop
removal. Originating from the Greek, "Gaia" is the personification of
Mother Earth. The sculpture took over 1,000 hours to create, spanning
a period of over 16 years. The head and hands of the carving are of clay,
fired to achieve a rock-like hardness. The rest of the sculptural form is
of rigid Styrofoam. The surface textures are all natural materials
including moss, sand, rock dust, and twigs.

Printed in the United States of America

Shoemaker Hoard
www.shoemakerhoard.com

10 9 8 7 6 5 4 3 2 1

For the people in the central Appalachian coalfields who struggle against catastrophe daily. Nowhere have I seen courage and integrity like theirs.

Lace

WHEN I WAS eleven, I got it in my head I was going to a high school basketball game in Charleston. Mom told me I was not. Said I had no business going to some high school basketball game in Charleston, I wasn't even in junior high, but I had friends older than me and that's all they'd been talking about—the first time we've made it to regionals since 1962, everybody's going to be there, we're making banners, and Paula's mom's driving and taking us to Shoney's beforehand. My mom said she didn't care who was driving.

The game was on a Saturday night. The week leading up to that Saturday I made sure not to mention it again. Soon as I finished the supper dishes, I slipped on back into me and Sheila's room—Sheila and Dad busy watching TV, Buck and Roy and Grampa Jones, even at eleven I wouldn't be caught dead watching *Hee-Haw*—and I put on my clothes I thought made me look oldest. I ripped my jeans a little climbing out the window, but I told myself just don't take off your coat, and then I was running light and quiet and very, very fast down the Ricker Run in the March early dark. I stopped on the footbridge, stitch ripping in my side. I could hear Yellowroot Creek under the hoarse of my breath. The hardest part was next, trotting the whole mile down Yellowroot Road without anybody seeing me. Everybody knew everybody back then, and everybody knew I had no business running down the road on a Saturday night in the dark. But then three miracles happened, two for me and one for Mom. First, I made it to Route 9 and had my thumb out before a single neighbor saw me. Second, a man in a Lantz truck picked me right up and drove me all seventy-five miles to the Civic Center without a word about my age, my parents, or why I was hitching. And third, and least surprising, given the time and place, the Lantz truck man didn't do me any harm.

I didn't get to the game until the last quarter, but I was there. After we lost, Paula's mom took me home with everybody else, called Mom before we left once she figured out I hadn't ridden in with them. I was the last one they dropped off, and it wasn't until we were all the way down to just me and Paula in the van that I started thinking about what was going to happen once I got home. But I wasn't scared. And I sure didn't feel guilty. Just mad at Mom, it was her fault. If she'd let me go the regular way, I wouldn't have had to hitchhike. Right there I decided I wouldn't let her get me.

I trudged back up the Ricker Run in a dark so pure I could hardly see my feet at the end of my legs. Then I saw the porch light. Mom waiting there with her long wooden spoon. I stopped out in the yard, just beyond where the light fell. "Get your rear end up here. Now," Mom said, and there wasn't nothing else I could do.

When she went at it, though, something was different. Once I had that don't-get-me in my head, I dodged that whipping like a boxer who fought from his behind. I danced, swinging out on Mom's grip on my arm, I arched my back and fast-footed, I spun and I leapt, to where every lick either missed me or barely grazed. Mom wore out faster than me. Then we both stood there, her panting, me feeling the wind through the spreading rip in my jeans.

She ended up making me stay in my room except for chores and church every Saturday and Sunday for three months. I still do say it was worth it. I still do say I won.

By then I'd decided I was newer than all this here. Here was fine for Mom, Dad, and Sheila—you could take one look at them and see how they fit—but only outside of here would I, Lace See, live real life. Ages one to eighteen were just a waiting for that. Nothing on TV, nothing in books, nothing in magazines looked much like our place or much like us, and it's interesting, how you can believe what's on TV is realer than what you feel under your feet. Growing up here, you get the message very early on that your place is more backwards than anywhere in America and anybody worth much will get out soon as they can, and that doesn't come only from outside. Still, despite all those shows and pictures and stories and voices, I never was able to see what lay ahead for me as something solid. I saw it instead as a color, a sweet peach-pink. A color I could walk into, with its own temperature, own smell, and by the time I was a teenager, that color, temperature, and smell had put such a spell on me I didn't see much else.

So when I was in eleventh grade, and they brought in a guidance counselor from away from here, and I ended up doing work-study for her second period, it proved what I'd known all along about my own specialness and how southern West Virginia was just a holding pen for me. Mrs. Claylock always seemed nervous, and she only lasted two years, but in that time, she figured out not only was I smart, but really good at tests. Us cooped up in that supplies closet they gave Mrs. Claylock for an office, cloudy with her strange perfume. I never smelled that perfume again until a department store in North Carolina, and when I did, Mrs. Claylock came so clear I could see the acne scars on her chin. Mrs. Claylock told me how to apply for college, then she went even further and fixed me up with scholarships and grants, and the day I graduated high school, May 1983, I told myself once I got to WVU, I'd never look back.

Truth was, though, after a month away, I was feeling a kind of lonesomeness I'd never known there was. I'd start drinking in my dorm room most evenings, stretched out on my window ledge on the eighth floor of Tower Two, a rum and coke between my legs, or a bottle of Mad Dog 20-20, and if anybody asked, I'd say I was just warming up for that night's party, but really I'd be watching the ridges in the distance. It was like I was all the time feeling like I wasn't touching nothing, and wasn't nothing touching me back, and yeah, they had hills in Morgantown, but not backhome hills, and not the same feel backhome hills wrap you in. I'd never understood that before, had never even known the feel was there. Until I left out and knew it by its absence.

October made it worse. The sky never clearer any time of the year, keen mornings and warmish afternoons, sharp color in the hills, and the threat of winter making everything more precious. I'd be sitting in a lecture hall, in the library, trying to take notes, trying to study, and there'd come to me October things I'd thought I'd left behind when I left being a kid. The rich wild fur smell of squirrels in my daddy's canvas jacket pockets. The rough of a burlap sack for picking up hickory nuts. Persimmon taste. Searching for the prettiest of the pretty leaves for Mom to help me iron between wax paper. By the third week of the month, I couldn't hold off any longer. Just for a weekend, I told myself. There's no failure in that.

I left on a Thursday, and because I didn't have another way, I hitchhiked, but I'd gotten so turned around by those two months in Morgantown I headed east instead of south and was halfway to Cumberland, Maryland, before I realized something was wrong. Spent the night at a truck stop on Keyser's Ridge, head in my arms, and woke up with ketchup in my hair. I was in the restroom washing it out when the counter lady came in and asked me, "Where you trying to get to, honey?" The lady knew a lot of drivers coming through and found one heading my way.

Daddy was out in the garden twisting off pumpkins. He almost lost his balance when he recognized it was me. He took off stiff towards me, his legs loosening as he walked, then he clapped his arms around me and slapped on my back. Hollered for Mom, and even Mom looked happy to see me. People around here don't really want their kids leaving, doesn't matter for what. They don't have a lot else. With his arm around my shoulder, Daddy guided me on into a kitchen chair, Mom carrying my suitcase behind, and "Get us out a plate of them peanut butter cookies," she called to Sheila. Then we all four sat around the table, and they listened to the parts of college I knew they'd want to hear, Daddy saying, "Well now! Well now!" once in a while, slapping the table in surprise.

That evening Mom made fried chicken and good thick lumpy gravy, my favorite, and rice and green beans, birthday food, and mine wasn't until March. Afterwards, we sat in the living room while Dad and Sheila watched the one channel we picked up and Mom worked on one of her projects. It was breadbag rugs that year, her twisting the plastic into little ropes that she would weave together later. And for a while, I watched TV, too.

But by 9:30, how Sheila talked over top the show was starting to irritate me. So was the rustle of Mom's bread bags. I was feeling again the smallness of the room, how piled up we always were, and then I began to hear Daddy's breathing. It couldn't have gotten so bad so fast, had I just been used to it before? His three-fingered hand lay spread on his knee. He'd lost the other two in a mine before I was born, and when I was in junior high, how that gap'd embarrassed me. About ten o'clock, I stood up and told them I was going to bed, even though I wasn't tired. Then I lay there in the bed I'd slept in since I left my crib, my eyes wide open, and I should have been exhausted, but I couldn't sleep, and at first I thought it was because my mind was confused. Then I realized it was the tangles in my heart. Sweet and hurt.

The next morning I pretended to take my time drinking a cup of coffee with Mom and Dad, but all I was really thinking about was calling some friends. Most weren't home, and I tried four numbers before Missy McDaniel was. She said she was going to the away football game down in Watson that night. Did I want to come?

We got there a little late, and instead of heading for the bleachers, we took a circle around the field. I knew Missy was looking for Roger Cant. We found him pretty quick, cool-sagged up against the chain-link fence in his track letter jacket. Missy slipped behind him and knocked the back of his knee with the front of her own, and when Roger turned to grin at her, I looked past his shoulder and realized he wasn't alone.

I'd seen the other boy before. I knew who he was. James Makepeace Turrell. They called him Jimmy Make even back then, a name you didn't easily forget, and we kept track of those boys in neighboring counties, them with a luster the ones you've seen every day since first grade don't have, and as far as we were concerned, wasn't much to look at in our county anyway. So I knew who he was, but I hadn't known how fast he'd grown up over the summer. Jimmy Make was three years younger than me, but he'd grown into a hard rolling beauty made those three years go away.

He wore a fleece-lined denim jacket tight against his body, his bare hands shoved in the pockets of his close-riding jeans, and you could tell the new muscles making under there. Make you want to run your hands across. His hair thrust thick out of his cap, a bright duskiness to it, and I saw on his strong neck, his face, the brown of his skin despite summer being two months gone. Now Missy was facing Roger, their heads close, teasing at each other, while Jimmy and me hung back on either side of them. I made like I was watching the game, but really I was stealing looks at those earth-colored eyes. The thick of his mouth. Slipping my glance down his lean thighs there. And Jimmy Make would seem to notice, then would look away, and I wondered, was it lack of interest or was it shy? And that made me have to know more.

"I've got some weed out in the car," Roger was saying. Then Roger and Missy were ambling away, and me and Jimmy Make were following, him closer to my shoulder than he should be, and later I'd swear—I felt it off him for the first time right then. The hot wet. I learned it right there before I ever touched him. Us drifting towards the part of the field they used as overflow parking, star-pricked sky with a crackle to it, so dry and cold, new cold, and us drifting through those other October night dramas. Mothers beating cowbells in the stands, and little boys playing their own games of tackle in the shadows. The twelve- and thirteen-year-old girls huddled outside the bathrooms, whispering, and the older girls walking in twos and threes round and round the field, while the boys leaned on the chain-link fence where they could watch both the game and the girls. In the parking lot, the smell of pot. Low-laughing voices. By the time we reached the car, Roger'd forgotten about getting high. Him and Missy climbed straight in the backseat, and then it was me and Jimmy Make by ourselves in the dark.

I climbed up on the hood, braced my feet on the bumper. Jimmy Make did, too. I leaned back with my hands splayed behind me, and then Jimmy did like me, and we were side by side, not touching, and not facing each other, either. Then I could feel not only the hot wet, but also the nervous off him. I felt, too, his soberness, felt him there in a way all the drunk flirting and groping and messing around in Morgantown hadn't been there at all. And I felt also, although I only named it later, the familiar of him. Again, after all that Morgantown, how so simple and familiar Jimmy Make felt even though I'd never been near him before.

"Where you live at?" I finally asked him, when I realized he wasn't going to talk on his own.

Jimmy reached up his hand and rubbed the back of his hair under his cap so the bill tipped forward over his forehead. "Oh, out there on the other side of Watson," he said. Even from the side, I could see his teeth in the dark. I saw they were hard, straight, and white.

"You got any brothers and sisters?"

He did the thing with the back of his head again. "Two sisters and a brother way older than me," he said. "I guess I'm the baby." He laughed a little.

I kept asking him stuff, and he answered back, all serious sounding, but then the little laughs. Our hands still there behind us on the car hood, just far enough apart. I thought I could feel the want off him, but I wasn't sure, and him not trying to touch me was unfamiliar in a way that made me excited, and worried. And hungry like I hadn't been in some time.

Then the car started bouncing up and down, to where it bucked us right off onto the ground, and at first, both of us were embarrassed. Then Jimmy Make busted up laughing, and I did, too. And we took off running at the same time, through the cars and on out into the field, and then Jimmy Make fell and rolled over once, flopped out on the dew-damp grass like a dog. He grinned up at me with his white teeth. "Why don't you come on down here?" he said, patting the ground. When I did, he still didn't touch me, he never did touch me that night, but it didn't matter. Because by that time I knew for sure what was coming off him, and it wasn't lack of want.

I woke up the next morning with a Jimmy Make blaze. Stunned golden inside with the dream and the crave and the new of that boy. Daddy asked me did I want to walk with him up Cherryboy a ways, and I did, but I didn't see the mountain, didn't see that October I'd come back for, didn't hear Daddy talking and didn't hear his breathing, either. Too busy with that Jimmy Make and me movie in my head. The second I got a little privacy, which wasn't until early afternoon, I called Missy, and Missy said yeah. She'd already talked to Roger. Jimmy Make felt like me.

I cloudwalked the rest of that afternoon. Mom asked me to peel apples for apple butter, oh, I had no problem with that. Sheila asked if she could take down my posters in our room, I said go right ahead. Only worry I had in the world was when I'd see Jimmy Make next, and I held onto that golden until right before supper. When Mom started talking about church the next day.

"Well," I said, and I tried to make it sound as offhand as I could. "I'm not sure I'll make it to church in the morning."

Mom stood at the stove with her back to me, moving potatoes in a skillet. "Well," she said. "I reckon you will."

And then I felt things folding down to how they were before I left, and I drew a hard breath because I had to keep them braced. "Mom," and I tried to sound reasonable. "I'm eighteen years old. I don't even live here no more."

Mom didn't bother to turn around, and that she wouldn't fight me in a real way made me even madder. "Long as you're part of this family and visiting, you'll go with this family to church." She hit her taters with a shake of salt.

Then it fell, crashed down for real. I was fourteen again, the two months away hadn't happened at all. I snatched up my jacket and slammed out the house, managed to knock my elbow into a porch post, but I kept going, crossed the edge of the yard, and climbed on up into the trees, yelling at myself in my head, *why the hell did you work so hard to get back here? Haven't you yet learned any better than that?* Once I reached the big white oak where I could watch the house from high up but they couldn't see me, I pulled out a cigarette I had hidden in my pocket, and I smoked it for spite. And glaring down at the house, I saw it again how I'd seen it before I left. Grubby, grim, gritty, covered with that asphalt shingle stuff with fake brick shapes pressed in it. The bubbled greasy place where the coal-stove pipe came out of the wall. The old outhouse still tilted in the corner of the yard, we hadn't got an inside bathroom until I was two, and even now, Daddy sometimes used the outside one.

I dragged deep on my cigarette, wishing it was pot. I held it in my lungs and mouth as long as I could, still staring at the house, trying to shoot towards it the hate I had for Mom.

But then it seemed I could see Mom and Sheila behind the walls, day in and day out, moving like humped animals. I saw the slowness, the heaviness, that had come on Sheila in the three years since she graduated high school, a heavy that had only a little to do with extra weight. I felt the dread of church tomorrow, two hours of boredom and too-simple-to-any-longer-believe, and the old ladies gossiping about me in their heads. Then I saw myself heading back to Morgantown after church, and sharp, the homesickness came again.

And I asked myself, what is it about this place? What? I pressed my forehead against the oak. Because for a long time, I'd known the tightness of these hills, the way they penned. But now, I also felt their comfort, and worse, I'd learned the smallness of me in the away. I understood how when I left, I lost part of myself, but when I stayed, I couldn't stretch myself full. I twisted the cigarette out on the trunk. I reached for the sweet peach-pink. College, I almost said it out loud, was just something you had to get used to. Then I flinched. Because it was Mom's voice that had come in my head.

Once I was back in Morgantown, Jimmy Make took on in his absence an even greater glory than he'd had in the flesh. I'd dream his padded jean jacket up against me, I swear, for two weeks that's as far as I went. Lying on my back in my room when I should have been studying, I'd let down my chest and breathe the Jimmy memory in. Hunched over a library table, I'd read the same page three times straight because on top of the print would be a picture of me and Jimmy Make in damp October grass.

The beauty, beauty of that boy. Like what you feel off animals, big cats. Wet horses. It was a beauty could carry you a ways. I needed that right then. Against the grimy foreignness of Morgantown, the stale stink of dorm rooms and apartments, how hard it was to really get outside, the rain that started in November and never did stop. But it wasn't just his beauty, I wouldn't understand until later. It was also how, compared to college, Jimmy Make was simple. Straight. Something you could understand exactly where, how, why, he was.

I didn't see him at Thanksgiving because he'd gone deer hunting with his family up in the Eastern Panhandle, but we made plans through letters about Christmas break. I had to go get him because he was still fifteen, and at first, Mom nor Dad neither one wanted to let me take a vehicle all the way to Watson. But when my grades came and I got 2 B's and 4 A's, they both gave in. The grades surprised even me. Made me bolder. Later I'd wonder if my grades had been a little worse, would I have taken the risks I did that break.

Jimmy Make was waiting out on his porch when I pulled into his driveway. Boy moved down those porch steps like a bobcat, and like a bobcat, he had no idea how he moved, and that made me want him even worse. He wore the fleece-lined denim jacket. I could feel his blood running in him from clear across the seat. We hadn't made plans to get pizza, go to Beckley to see a movie, we both understood this wasn't what you'd call a date. Jimmy Make knew the Watson backroads as well as I knew the Prater ones, and he told me how to get there, he found a good spot. All these years later, I can still smell that good no-cologne scent of him. Soap and boy. His soft skin face, barely any bristle and only on his chin. The simple, the familiar, a beauty I could get my mind and arms around. I couldn't tell if he'd done it before. I guessed that meant he had.

I was home for three weeks. I'd never had it so bad. Daddy let me take the car one other time, and Mom didn't fight it, but I could tell she was getting suspicious. It had always been like that, a one-way mirror between us, the way Mom could see straight through me, but I couldn't see nothing back. What Mom did agree to, instead of me going to Watson a third time, was that Jimmy Make could spend an afternoon up Yellowroot, with us, and that didn't make me happy, but it beat nothing at all. His mother brought him and dropped him off two days before I had to leave.

You know Mom watched us close. Stayed polite long as Jimmy Make was there, but soon as he went home, asked, "How old is that boy?" When he first got to the house, Dad invited him into the living room to visit, Mom gave him a glass of ice tea, but Jimmy Make was too shy to talk much even to me. So eventually Dad stood up, turned on the TV, and said, "I guess I'll leave you two to yourselves."

There were no other rooms to go to but my bedroom. We stood outside in the cold bright yard. We sat on the woodpile, Jimmy grinning and snapping sticks in his hands while I talked to him about himself, tried to let slip a few things about me, and I could see Mom through the window at the kitchen sink, and I gave her a look, but if Mom even noticed, she sure didn't care. After a while, Jimmy Make reached out with a stick and traced down my leg. Once that happened, the other couldn't be helped.

I flicked my mind around, but everywhere was light, and I knew Mom wouldn't just let us wander off in the woods, not as far as we'd need to go with all the leaves off the trees. Finally, it was almost time for his mother to come back, and I told Mom I was going to walk him back to the turnaround. I'd figured it out. On the way, I ducked him off into the old chickenhouse just out of sight of our place.

My bare butt against raw splintery wall. His behind in my hands and the waistband of his jeans just below that. Stale bitter still stink of the long-gone chickens, and it was like gulping a meal without chewing, it was, big, hard, almost hurtful swallows. I can still remember the crunch of dry and very old shit under my shoes, the sun through one lost slat burning my shut eye. And always after, I hoped that wasn't the time. But always after, I knew it had to have been.

Bant

SO HE TOOK a blowtorch to it. He hacksawed it, and he blowtorched it, and I made sure to stay clear of that flame. But every once in a while he'd step back and motion at me take the hammer to the lock, try to spring it that way. I did what he wanted, but I did it leery, listening for a guard after every knock. Until Jimmy Make cocked his head, lifted half his lip, and kind of growled at me, "C'mon now, girl. Hit her harder."

Then, earlier than I'd expected, that lock fell right off in my hand. Fell off bigger than my hand. It was the biggest padlock I'd ever held, and I dropped it in the road, like it was something live I held, something I'd thought dead that turned out live. Jimmy Make picked it up and pitched it as far as he could up the side of the hill, where it fell with a swish and a thump in the very green brush. That year had been a wet spring and early summer, and it seemed the plants had grown to a green you could taste. Green like the plants were trying to make up for the other.

It was the May flood that finally made him go. Jimmy'd worked in the industry, he believed he'd be able to tell better than Lace what was going on, and for once, Lace thought so, too. Fuck their lock, he told her, I'm taking the truck. My father didn't walk when he could ride. That was two mornings before school was out, and all day, I'd thought about it, that feeling I was getting used to. Wanting to know and not. Then while I was helping him get supper, the phone rang, Lace on her break. "I think you should go up with him, Bant," she said. "I want you to see."

Jimmy Make hauled his tools back to his truck, leaving me to get the gate, and sometimes I'd wonder if that was why he hadn't left yet—needed us kids to hand him tools and open gates. The gate was iron bars welded in a longways triangle painted red and orange, and they'd bolted a sign across the bars that said NO TRESPASSING in blue letters. There was a long reason under it I'd stopped reading when I hit the part about my safety. I'd stooped under that gate a couple times since the coal company'd put it in earlier that year, but not often, and I never went much past it. Too exposed it was up in there, too easy to be spotted. Now I walked it open, and as I did, it squealed louder than the lock had rung. Loud enough for a guard to hear easy, so I stopped and listened. But it was near sunset, and the mine wasn't working twenty-four hours a day on weekends then, and Jimmy'd picked the time because it was the lightest hour with the least chance of us getting caught. Once I got the gate to where the pickup could pass, Jimmy Make gunned it through and waited on me. I let the gate clash back together and climbed in the cab. When I did, Jimmy Make muttered, "I will drive up in here whenever I want." He said the "will" with a weight to it.

For a couple hundred yards, it was just the same hollow it had always been, except for the flood mess in the creek. It had dammed itself head-high in the elbows and narrows, thrown itself up along the sides. Towers of treetops and logs and brush, spiked all through with tires and metal, then the little stuff gobbed in that, pop bottles, sticks and plastic, hung up and quivering. The creek water itself still colored like creamed coffee left for weeks on a counter. Then Jimmy Make said, "flyrock," and I realized the road was roughed up not just from flood damage, but from blast damage, too, and then I started seeing how big trees slid down the hollow side and water poured off the mountain in little runs where runs had never been before.

We got to these big dirt piles right in the middle of the road, and "company," Jimmy said, and I knew they'd dozed them up to keep out people like Jimmy Make and me. I slunk down in my seat, peered up high through the windowshield into what woods were left. Looking for guards. Now Jimmy Make wasn't driving the road so much as he was playing it, and when we hit the first dirt roadblock, he just plowed right up on it, the loose tools in the bed rolling and crashing down at the tailgate, and he rammed over, pow. "Hwoo," Jimmy said to himself.

Then the sediment ponds. I'd seen these before in other hollows, clear back to when me and Grandma were running the woods. They were put in by the company to catch the runoff, but I saw that Lace was right, Lyon Energy wasn't keeping them up. They were jammed with stuff, and you could see pretty quick how the sides of some were tore through by the flood. I knew Jimmy Make believed it was these busted ponds that had caused the flood, and I saw what he meant. He said the flood came because of the ponds and from the hollow sides being scraped, and I saw that, too. The sides of the hollow, as we got further in, more naked and scalped, more trees coming down, and up above, mostly just scraggly weeds, the ground deep-ribbed with erosion, and I told myself, yes, this is where the floods come from. From the busted ponds and the confused new shape of the land. From how the land has forgot where the water should go, so the water is just running off every which way. *That's all it is,* I told myself, *Lace is stretching things again.* But after what I'd seen three weeks ago in May, I wondered if it wasn't as bad as Lace thought.

I hadn't been home when the cloudburst hit. I'd been on the ridge above Left Fork, and I wasn't far from a good rock overhang Grandma'd always called the Push-in Place, and I holed up there until it stopped. The rain didn't last long, although the half hour it did, it came heavy, but pretty soon, I was skidding on down the mountain towards the Ricker Run, thinking nothing of it. The run was moving high and muddy, like it should be after a quick hard storm like that, but it hadn't left its banks. It had nothing to do with what happened to Yellowroot Creek because, I understood later, the mountaintop removal mine wasn't draining into the Ricker Run yet. But as I got closer to where the trees opened into the clearing before Yellowroot Creek and then our house, I started hearing something, and for a minute, I couldn't figure what it was. Then I started running.

Before I even got out of the woods, I saw the footbridge was gone, and how many years of cloudbursts like that one had the footbridge gone through and never washed out? my mind moving fast and blurry, but then I was out of the trees, into the open where I could see, and then I thought, *Tommy. Corey. Dane. Mom.* "Mom!" I shouted. By then the creek was blasting through our yard, torrenting against the house underpinning, terrible bright brown with white chops raging in it, and down its rapids torpedoed trash and metal and logs, logs, logs, them crashing into the upstream end of the house, careening off and spinning around, and as I watched, one tree batter-rammed the fiberglass skirting and just jammed itself stuck, the loose end whip-tailing in current. "Mom!" I screamed, and I was racing up and down my side of the bank like a penned dog, looking for a place to jump across, looking for her or my little brothers in the blank house windows, and how long would the house hold? until, at the downstream end, I slipped in the mud, slammed down on one knee, looked across the creek, and saw Lace.

The water boiled right above her knees, her sopped work uniform clinging to her, and I yelled, but she couldn't hear me, her plunging her arm under water to the shoulder, and I realized she was looking for something. Only later would I know it was the weedeater, she'd already got the lawnmower up on the porch before the current had gotten this bad, the weedeater and lawnmower were the only work Jimmy Make had now. And I saw a muddy log boring straight down on her, and I screamed, and she could not hear but ducked it anyway.

Then she gave up looking and started fighting current towards the front door, crouched over, her arms spread for balance, the debris barreling at her, tires, Styrofoam pieces, a pallet, I saw her twisting and swerving like in a dodgeball game. But she was hardly gaining ground, so she gave up on that, too, turned downstream now, looking over her shoulder always for what was coming behind, the flood force pushing her ahead of herself until she fell down, caught herself, stumbled back up, a clot of plastic jugs glancing off her back, then she dropped into water on purpose this time, I could tell she meant it, and started half-swimming, half-crawling, towards the stand of sumac and other little trees that marked the end of our yard. She fell forward into the thicket, pulled herself upright with each hand around a small trunk, and the trees stood close enough together to make like a cage around her, and although the water could breach the cage, the big pieces of debris and logs could not.

The water dropped quick after that. The roar sunk to where she could hear me hollering. She struggled out of the sumac, limping a little, her uniform muddy and torn. She waved at me. Then she pushed down on the air with that hand, like telling a kid to quiet, and I could read her lips: "It's okay. It's okay." But I knew better than that.

Another dike was looming ahead, and this time Jimmy went around it, jerked the truck onto the grassy outside bank of the pond, and made a road that way. Then we were riding smoother, but it felt like we were going to tip, and I locked the door with my elbow. I thought again of the guards, how they must leave a few nosing around even when the mine wasn't working, and surely they would hear the truck. The ponds stairstepped all the way up the hollow, and as the hollow rose, narrowed, those top ponds no longer even pretended at grass, nothing but flood trash and rock. And then it got to where not even Jimmy Make could drive a truck any farther.

He idled it there a second, no doubt considering just crashing on through, but then he switched off the ignition, stomped the brake, and swung out. I followed him. Hit ground, my bones still humming off the jar of the ride, and soon as I left the inside of the truck—sudden silence, clawed-up earth, sky shifting towards rain—even though I was fifteen years old, how small I felt. Like anything could get me. I craned my neck a little around the bend, and I saw for the first time the mine rim, just a piece of it was all I could see from that angle. A prickle moved under my hair. I recognized it from the others I'd seen from highways, sudden dead spots in what should be green, but then, in the car, you'd swing on by and not see it anymore. Jimmy Make didn't even notice. He was just swaggering on up towards the turn, and I knew why. Still preening in what he'd just done, the fuck-the-company pride of it. But when we got around that bend, even Jimmy Make's cockiness drained away.

The edge of the mine top towered several hundred feet right over our heads, a straight gray line that started at the east flank of Cherryboy, then ran as far to the right as my head could swivel. Lace had said they hadn't got Cherryboy yet, and she was right, but not even all those late-night listenings had got me ready for how the top of Yellowroot was just plain gone. Where ridgetop used to be, nothing but sky. Under that sky, what looked from this distance like raw colorless gravel but must have been piled-up rock. And beyond that, nothing at all.

Jimmy'd stopped too when we first caught sight of that full edge, but we had to walk a little farther around the turn to check what Lace had sent us for. When Jimmy started off again, I followed right behind, my head down, me closer to him than I'd been in some time. He wore a black T-shirt faded to a plum color, and I watched his back, not ready to see the fill, and telling myself, it couldn't be as high, as bad, as it already looked like it was going to be. But then Jimmy stopped, and I stopped, too, and there the fill was. And I couldn't pretend anymore.

The closest thing I'd ever seen to it was the Summersville Dam, but this was bigger, darker, and looser. I hauled back my head and looked up its whole height, and it seemed to me it must be as tall as the highest buildings in Charleston, but who knew for sure. There was just no way to gauge how tall the thing was because there was nothing natural about it, nothing you could compare it to, and then it dawned on me exactly what I was standing under—Yellowroot Mountain, dead. I knew from Lace and Uncle Mogey that after they blasted the top off the mountain to get the coal, they had no place to put the mountain's body except dump it in the head of the hollow. So there it loomed. Pure mountain guts. Hundreds of feet high, hundreds of feet wide. Yellowroot Mountain blasted into bits, turned inside out, then dumped into Yellowroot Creek.

We were standing at the edge of a big field of rocks that jumbled the space between the last pond and the bottom of the fill. Strange rocks that pushed me away when I looked, the rawness of them, no weather to them yet, despite all the rain. Jimmy had spread his legs and jammed his hands on his hips, and when he reared back to look up, the shirt jerked loose of his jeans. I watched him watching. He was all the time bragging about how he'd worked in the industry for years. He was supposed to be able to tell something about this. "Fuck," he said. The sky was making to rain again, pushing breeze ahead of it. Jimmy Make tightened one bootlace and started across.

I swallowed. He was picking his way, his arms winged out for balance, his chin tipped down. The breeze pimpled me along my arms and in the small of my back, even though there wasn't enough chill in the breeze to do that. Then I shut down my mind and plunged after him, taking the rocks like a bear would, bent all the way over so I was walking on my feet and my hands. I didn't want to touch those rocks with my hands, but I figured it would be worse to walk upright, then slip and skin an ankle, let it get in your blood. No. In the cracks between the rocks, gooey liquid stuff. Dark greens and blacks that turned blue when light hit them.

I reached the base of the fill on all fours before Jimmy did on his feet. I pushed my neck back to see to the top again, and now I noticed how it looked like it maybe had two tops, one in front, one behind. But I couldn't be sure. It was like I'd see two, but then my eyes would bend, and it would look like just one top again. And this close up to the fill, it was even harder to take it all as real. It was like my mind didn't want to make a place for this here.

By now, the sun had started dropping behind the blasted-off ridge, but we could still see easy the leaks in the bottom of the fill, water drooling out here and there even though it hadn't rained in a couple days. I watched Jimmy Make. He just stood there. All I could read on his face was mad.

"Maybe Lace is right," I said.

Jimmy spat into one of the leaks. Lifted his eyes off that and up-swept them the height of the valley fill. I asked him again, "Do you think she's right? There's water standing up behind it?"

Jimmy Make still didn't look at me. But he usually didn't. "That ain't no dam," he finally said.

"I know it's not no dam. Do you think there's an impoundment behind it?"

"Well," said Jimmy, "I doubt that."

I looked at him. His belly paunching out under the untucked shirt. His brown eyes narrowed under the camouflage cap. Then I understood that he wasn't exactly bullshitting me because he was bullshitting himself first. And right there I knew for sure what I'd suspected all along—Jimmy Make couldn't tell any more about what was going on than I could.

It was me was going to have to climb up that fill and see what was behind it.

Corey

IF I HAD me a four-wheeler. If I did, now. Seth has a four-wheeler, and Seth's only nine. And Seth hardly ever rides his four-wheeler, just goes to waste in the shed, why should Seth have a four-wheeler? If I had me a four-wheeler . . .

But Corey has to make do with his bike. Dad says they can't get an ATV because it's too dangerous, but Corey knows it's because it's too expensive. So he makes do with his bike. Which he can ride better and do more tricks on than anybody up and down Yellowroot, and probably better than anybody in town, too. If town would have some kind of bike contest, like Corey has seen on TV, but not their town. *Some town.*

Last day of school, early dismissal, and now Corey and Tommy sit under the house, each holding one foot turned up in one hand. Since the flood rammed loose some of the underpinning, they can get up in there easier, and with the flood-ripped insulation dangling around, it's like a spookhouse. The flood knocked loose the washer's drainpipe, too, and Dad won't fix it, says Lyon Energy can, so now when Mom runs the washer, the water gushes straight into a runnel it has worn under the house, so you can pretend it's an underground river. Gold in it. Corey and Tommy sit up under there, and also Chancey, the outside dog, flopped on his side in a dirt hollow he's dug. Corey has an old steak knife he keeps hidden in the tape that Dad wrapped around some of the pipe joints, and him and Tommy are testing how tough their feet are. Corey drills the dull point of the old steak knife, slow, into the calluses on their feet, and he counts until the person being stabbed yelps, cries, or winces. Tommy, who is six, tends to yelp or cry. Corey, ten, tends to wince or cuss. You can cuss and keep counting numbers. Then Corey writes the number of seconds with a ballpoint pen on the inside of his arm after each of their initials: C and T. There are four numbers total because they drill four times: ball of the left foot, ball of the right, heel of the left foot, heel of the right.

The front porch thuds, the screen door slams. Slippers scuff overhead. Quick, Corey wedges the knife back into the wad of tape. "That was Mrs. Kerwin on the phone," Mom calls. "She thinks our back steps might be in the creek behind McWain's." She stops. "Corey, you all get out here where I can see you."

He army-man crawls through the shallow dirt and broken cinderblocks, Tommy behind him, Chancey behind Tommy. "I want youall to go down make sure they're ours before I send Dad after them with the truck." She looks at their bare feet. "Get your shoes on, and stay out of the creek. And come right back after you're done. You head up past that gate—you know what's gonna happen." She fixes Corey in the eye.

She watches while Corey ties his tennis shoes, Tommy Velcros his, and then Tommy heads towards the road, Chancey already trotting ahead of him. After that, she disappears inside. Corey hacks his throat to spit. Tommy catches the signal and looks back. "This way, boy," Corey hisses. On the way to the creek, Corey stops behind the refrigerator that the flood dropped in their yard and takes off his shoes. Tommy does the same. Corey peeks towards the house, then opens the refrigerator door and puts his and Tommy's shoes inside on a rack.

Since the flood, Corey can stand in the creek and just about touch the wall of the house, and Bant, she can touch it. When the water rushed off the mountain, it blew out the backyard and washed a chunk of it downstream, the steps with it, leaving only two feet between the back corner of the house and the new sharp bank, cut straight up and down like a mattock was took to it. Tommy stands on the steep bank, patient, not asking, until Corey reaches up and swings him into the water. They have to go by the creek so as not to waste a chance to look for parts, and as soon as they're out of trailer eyeshot and can slow down, Corey feels his mouth water. He really does. Because before the flood, it is true, you could occasionally pick up an interesting thing or two in the creek if you looked careful and often. But since the flood, well . . . Corey won't even let himself think too hard on it out of fear he'll jinx it. Because with all the stuff people had dumped up the hollow above their house before the gate was put in, added to everything the company threw over the edge of the mine. Well, if you can unfocus your eyes right—and Corey can—wading the creek is like walking the aisle of a Wal-Mart made for Corey, with all the price tags saying free.

Water heaters and kerosene stoves and tires of all dimensions, lawnmowers and roofing, bike frames and car axles. Barrels and plastic toys, washing machine parts and oven racks, and on top of all that good stuff is the great stuff, the mysterious could-be-anything stuff dumped off the mine—rusted metal contraptions and cogs and wheels and iron bars and yellow steel sheets. On the way back, Corey will collect as many parts as he can carry, and he will bribe, blackmail, or flatter Tommy into carrying some, too, all these unmade, unbuilt parts, just waiting, and they will tote the parts back to Grandma's old house, where Corey stashes them and threatens Tommy with the monkey if Tommy ever tells Mom or Dad. Because Corey has a plan.

They slosh through pigshit-colored creek water that comes to right below Corey's knees, right above Tommy's. Used to be too deep to wade, but every year it gets more shallow, and the water with a bad odor to it, even though it was two years ago all the fish and crawdads died. A different thing to watch. The flood ripped and rearranged the neighborhood, and from here in the creek, behind the houses, you can see how people's property has changed. Some yards are smaller now, like theirs, while others have been stretched longer and higher with rock and trash and the dirt off the yards of the people who lost theirs. Corey likes the change. He watches Chancey wiggle into drift piles like the pick-up-sticks game they got once for Christmas and lost most the sticks down the heater vents. Chancey's blond-gray hind end twitching in the open air with his front end buried in the drift, until he gets bored, pulls out, sneezes, and trots to the next one. And Corey can't blame him. What a sorry-ass boring place this is.

Too narrow even to run a railroad track through, is Yellowroot Hollow, so narrow that if you drove a tractor trailer into it and tried to park with its cab against one side of the hollow and its back wheels in the other, well, it wouldn't even fit. That's how narrow this sorry hollow is, and the whole skinny mile of this sorry-ass hollow plugged with little houses and little trailers and their little chain-link fences. At times Corey torments himself by thinking what if Paul Franz and them from school came up this hollow and saw where Corey lives. He'll devil himself with this vision, although he can't really think of any reason Paul Franz and them would come up here. Unless it was to trick-or-treat. So what if they did, what if they came up to trick-or-treat? There are only two good things about Yellowroot Hollow, and one just happened this May. The stuff in the creek. The second and only other good thing about Yellowroot Hollow is the way the hardtop road breaks down before their house, leaving a big asphalt lip above the gravel and mud, a lip you can use to do bike tricks.

Like a readymade ramp, where you can fly into the air and jerk the handlebars and, your body gripping the bike body, you can pull it and spin a little in the air, then crash, POW, on two wheels and not tip. But besides that. What a nothing narrow hollow. Not even enough room to run a railroad track through.

Now, Slatybank Hollow. That's a hollow.

"Where's the monkey at?" Tommy asks.

"Oh, you wanna see that monkey again, do you?" Corey says.

"Nooo," says Tommy. "I'm just wondering where it's at."

"It's not til up there behind Chester's," Corey says. "You know that." He spots a metal bar, what may have been an axle, camouflaged in a pile of sticks. He writes in his head to pick it up coming back. He can't see to the bottom of the creek even though it's no more than five or eight inches deep in this part, but you never know what might be down there, too, so he feels careful in the silky muck with his toes.

"There it is!" Corey lies about the monkey. "In that pile right there!"

"Nooo," Tommy wails.

Corey starts to run away from Tommy, through the water, high-stepping his feet and plunging. But then there is Seth, watching them from his yard. Corey stops.

If I had me one . . .

Seth's fat body is draped in a new sports outfit he's put on just since they got off the bus. Potato legs sunk in Nike shoes with the tongues creeping up his ankles. Mesh shorts to below the knees, UNC basketball jersey to below the crotch. Seth watches them with his arms forked out from his body, which is too round for his arms to lie flat.

"Your dog stinks," Seth says.

"Rolled in something dead," says Corey. "Where's your four-wheeler at?" he asks, even though he knows exactly where it is.

Seth cocks his head, just an inch, back towards his house. "There in the shed." Seth always talks like he has too much spit in his mouth and can't swallow.

"You decide about what I said the other day?" Corey asks. *If I had . . .*

"My mom don't want me going up in them snake ditches," Seth says.

"How would she find out?" Corey says. It's hard to stay nice with him, but you have to be.

Seth turns suddenly and yells. "Hey, boy, you better not have your shoes on there!" Tommy has slipped past and got on Seth's trampoline.

"He didn't even leave the house with shoes on," Corey says. "C'mon, Tommy," he calls. "We got things to do."

Corey and Tommy turn their backs on Seth and walk on down the creek. Chancey must notice he's being left because Corey hears him thrash out of the pile he was into and splash to catch up. Corey beams Chancey a mind order to rub some dead stink on Seth's new outfit, but he won't lower himself to turn and look at Seth to see if Chancey does. He flexes his bicep under the chamois rag he's tied around it.

"Where's that monkey at?" Tommy is saying again.

"Up here behind Chester's, I told you." Corey spies what looks like a car battery trapped in the crotch of an uprooted tree. He's now carrying more parts in his head than he and Tommy can carry in their arms, even if they make three trips. He decides to be nice to Tommy in case he needs him for four or five. "I'll protect you," he says. "It won't get you."

Chancey has already found it again. He's scrambling into the spot where he always stands to bark at it, on top of a big gray metal box must have come off the mine, and once Chancey gets squared away up there with his special monkey view, the barks pour out of his mouth like big brass bubbles. Corey feels a little floaty in his head. The stinky gray water around his ankles, the way you can't see under it. He and Tommy plod their wide circle through the water, keeping a safe distance from the heap of wood and trash, but the heap sucks Corey's eyes to it, even though he knows you can't see the monkey but from one certain angle. Chancey barks like he's got something holed, his legs stretched out rigid in front of him and his hollering head tucked down between his shoulders, pointing at the monkey, and Corey and Tommy take smaller careful steps towards the spot where they can see it, Tommy sticking very close, his hand clutching the tail of Corey's T-shirt.

There it is. The blond curly knots of drowned hair on the twisted body and part of the creepy face. A face Corey can't put with any animal he has ever seen, but not all the face shows, mostly just an open eye too big for the body, and then a kind of what must be a snout, but most of that turned away and part buried in mud. Corey has no idea, really, what this thing is. He knows it can't be a monkey, yet that seems the best thing to call it. Corey stands, trapped by the sight of it, just like Tommy and Chancey are. He can't help it, can't help the staring. It's like you can't get your eyes to adjust, the thing won't come into focus, but, no, not like the focus of your eyes, but your mind, your mind can't focus it. Until Corey gets a little dizzy. And he backs away from it, Tommy still attached to his shirt, and when they get a safe distance, he turns his back and hurries a little on down the creek.

The big monkey drift is caught in a bend, and after the bend, the flood trash slackens, the monkey drift a kind of bottleneck. Then Chester's backyard, his garden, a few leftover seed packets impaled on stakes and crusted with dark flood muck—even dried up, it's dark, that kind of mud. A rusted swingset his kids used to play on, them grown and long gone and the swingset tipped over. Sorry-ass Chester's backyard, then the sorry-ass yard of Little Scotty Piles, and, *Slatybank*. Corey is thinking. Not like this hollow, this place. What if they lived in Slatybank Hollow?

Slatybank has trains moving through it, and not just any old trains. Dad went up in there to see a man about a truck part, and he took Dane and Corey with him, and Corey has seen many a train, but not a train like that train in Slatybank. Slatybank is a nice-sized hollow, wider than this one, and emptier, too, lots of people having left out from Slatybank Hollow, a leaving place, which is better than a stuck-in hollow like theirs. The houses and trailers and stands and churches up and down Slatybank Hollow in various years-along of abandonment, some just abandoned to where the grass is too high, and others abandoned to where the windows are busted out, and others abandoned right down to rubble. Of course, some people never left at all, like the man with the truck part, and Dad drove them up in there, tracing the train track, then crossing it, then tracing it on the other side, then crossing it again. The hollow way, way longer than Yellowroot. The train track drawing your eye to it, fresh rail and rock, so much newer, shinier, than the buckling paved road. Then they got to the man's house, and Dad told them to stay outside and be good. They filled their pockets with big pieces of gravel off the railroad bed and then whizzed the rocks at beer bottles they'd set up on the rails. Dane always missed. Corey always hit. Then they heard her coming.

The train came from up the hollow and three locomotives it took to pull her, the very first one blasting the beer bottles into the air to shatter on rock. And then the gondolas, so neat-heaped with even mounds of coal the coal looked clean, and the black gons, too, that was the thing, the gons new as fresh-baked bread, the gons hauling out their virgin load of coal, gons that had never felt dust nor rain nor cinder nor mud and *chock chock chock chock* them passing beautiful. So just-out-of-the-factory brilliant Corey wondered was there a train assembly line up the hollow *chock chock chock chock* them passing beautiful. Corey couldn't help but draw up closer *CHOCK CHOCK CHOCK CHOCK* heatful they feel, and the odors of metal and oil and creosote the train weight pumps from the ties *CHOCK CHOCK CHOCK CHOCK* Corey creeping up to where he could no longer hear Dane's yells, Corey washed in the breath of the just-made train, him gut-feeling the train breath in a place in his body he didn't know he had, a place deeper than he knew his body got, the train force humming the teeth in his head, and how the air breaks between cars staggered him back, the sudden miss of metal making more there the smash force of the gon following *CHOCK CHOCK CHOCK CHOCK* a no time dangle time train wash wafting up and over them time and then. Finished.

Corey, tottery, gutted. Dane behind him yelping does he want to get killed, and Corey grappling after it, the last coal car, no caboose, vanishing around a curve. The train in its beautiful passing past, leaving.

Leaving behind the brush-took-over stores and the overgrown drift holes into worked-out mines and the trembly wooden churches with their hand-painted signs, warning, and the floors with nothing over them and the concrete pillars with nothing around and Slatybank's steadfast hangers-on in their houses, which had looked just fine, just like houses, until the train. Diminished them to their shabby desperate left-behind selves against that marvelous train.

Now Corey and Tommy can see McWain's backyard. Four or five kids climb a set of stairs lodged in the middle of the creek. From the stoop, they jump off into a hole where the water's to their waists. As Corey and Tommy draw closer, Corey sees for sure the stairs are the ones they bought from a mobile home dealer in Beckley two years ago. And Corey starts to yell, "Hey, get off our property." But then he notices Tommy is already right there at the foot of the steps, ready to jump with them. So Corey sighs, and then he goes on and does it with them, too. Corey knows he can do it better than them.

Bant

IT WOULDN'T be an easy climb, scaling that slope beside the fill. But the fill, I knew from seeing it with Jimmy Make, I couldn't climb at all. I was going to climb the skinned-out slope on the side of it, and steep as that slope was, I figured I'd have to do most of it on my belly, like a snake. "Skin you alive." I had a grade school teacher used to threaten us that way. "I'm gonna skin you alive," she'd say, and every time the teacher did, I'd see a skinless kid, snagged on a barbed wire fence. Now when I thought of the slope, the teacher's voice would come to me again.

The last day of school was a half day, and I'd started sweating on the bus, and I was sweating heavier now. I tried to stick to shade, heaved my bookbag higher on my shoulder, my hair falling safe over my face. Now I turned up Yellowroot Road, and I could hear the machine noise overhead. I wondered if Uncle Mogey and Aunt Mary were home. I thought again of the busted-lock gate. Tomorrow I would talk to Hobart about the job, and after that, I was going to have a whole lot less time. But then I saw myself stoop under those bars, and the cold prickle came again in my scalp. I looked back up at Cherryboy. Mogey and Mary probably were.

When I got to where the blacktop broke down into dirt, to the thicket of sumac and other little trees that stood between our house and the rest of the houses in the hollow, I thought I heard Lace's voice. I stopped, pulled in on myself, listened. But I didn't hear anything more. I headed on, past all the trees, into full view of the house, and then I heard they were at it for sure. It wasn't constant loud, they were trying to keep it down, but every minute or so, something would break loose. I walked slower, squeezed tighter to the strap of my bag. Still standing in the yard was the side-by-side refrigerator that had washed down in the flood, and the ground still glittered, with glass, with coal, although we'd worked so hard to clean it up, and at the end of the yard, before the sumac trees, a big stack of logs and branches, waiting for Jimmy Make to borrow a chainsaw. Another voice, Jimmy's this time, came sailing out a window and cut the calm.

I stopped in the road at the edge of the patchy grass. I snuck real quick to the porch, dropped my bookbag on it, and shoved it across to the wall. For a second, I thought again of the gate. But then I took off around the side of the house, towards Cherryboy, and my short-cut to Mogey and Mary's.

"It's what's on the inside counts," my grandma used to say, and I didn't believe that about everything. But I did about my name. Bantella Ricker See. Bantella was a name Lace made up for me before I was born, and although she never told me, I figured she made it up for the speak-taste of it. For how when you said it—Bantella—it pressed every part of your tongue, and that they called me just Bant suited me fine. I liked the longer name a secret kept. Jimmy Make's real name was James Makepeace Turrell, but him and Lace didn't get married until I was almost four years old, and when they did, Lace still wouldn't change my name. She couldn't keep her own name after she got married, so she kept mine, Ricker See. My grandma had been a Ricker, my pap was a See, but now I was the only one in the family who carried either name. That was the other part of the secret, something else I held inside. And while See was better than Turrell, I also knew it was the Ricker meant the most because Rickers had been on this piece of ground at the foot of Cherryboy, west of Yellowroot, for more than two hundred years.

The flood had busted the footbridge all to pieces, so I jumped the creek and crawled up the other bank, the new loose dirt of it scaling down. Then I was on the old Ricker Run road and already I was reaching for the good I usually got in the woods, make the other go away. But I couldn't yet bring it to me, and I started worrying even though part of me knew it was too early for that. The road was soft for walking, the ruts nearly grassed over, and the sun was falling heavy and thick the way it does after passing through all those green leaves. Before long I was passing where Grandma's trailer had sat, and then I was moving on up the draw towards the Ricker Place where I'd lived the first four years of my life and Grandma'd lived all of hers until those last few years in the trailer. A couple hundred feet short of the old house, I reached the turnoff to the trail that would take me over the ridge to Uncle Mogey's house, so I cut through a patch of mayapple and angled up the first part of it.

It was narrow, not much more than a game path, hard to see if you weren't used to taking it, especially now, with all the green stuff trying to cover, but I'd been running this path since before I was born. I'd started running this mountain when I was still inside Lace—*Oh, that was a hard year,* Grandma'd say. *Hard times then. And your pap just a-smothering to death all along, you know*—and they carried me back up just weeks after I came out. If I said it out loud, Lace would say I couldn't remember, but I could, the ground moving below me, dead-leaf-colored, how many colors of brown. The smell of November rain on beginning to rot leaves. I helped my grandma from the time I could walk. *Good little helper, Bant. Such a good helper,* creasies,

Shawnee, poke, ramps, molly moochers in spring, blackberries in summer, mayapple and cohosh, then ginseng and nuts—hickory, black walnut, butternut, chinquapin, beech—in the fall. Yellowroot after the sap went down. Sumac and sassafras in November, come Christmas, holly and greenery. I knew these things before I could read. *You can live off these mountains,* Grandma'd say. *And in bad times,* she'd say, meaning layoffs, strikes, but also, I knew, the year I was born, *we did.*

Now that I'd got past the steepest part of the path to Uncle Mogey's, I was moving fast, watching always for the copperheads. The humid riding me like a damp shirt. This was full woods now, and I reached out one hand, touched the tree trunks that I passed, lichens, bark, moss. Up in here, you couldn't hear the machinery working. You couldn't see any sign of the flood.

After we came back to West Virginia from North Carolina two years ago, it was all different. It was different. But I still spent a lot of time up here. I didn't hunt stuff much anymore—some of it was gone, and even the plants that were left the dealers wouldn't buy like they used to—so I mostly just sat in my places. Those places where if you sat quiet, the space dropped away between you and the land. Some of them were places I'd discovered on my own, but others were ones where me and Grandma used to stop. She'd make me sit quiet, I learned that young, too, and when it was time to go, she'd say, *Now this is just between you and me, Bant. You and me's special place.*

Like the heart of the rhododendron thicket, the limbs bendy and matty and strong, it was like being inside some kind of body there. It felt animal live. The rock overhangs in the winter, how icicles would make off them, great scary masses, the rocks making faces, angry and beautiful. I'd feel closest in spring, before the leaves came all the way out, when the mountains show their hope with little color patches, redbud and dogwood, dogwood and redbud, the roll of the words in your mouth. And if you look real close, how all the leaves are tightly curled, bulging just a little beyond bud—leaf-wait, I'd call it. And inside them, right before they bust out, you see what looks like a feather.

But Grandma never said anything about how the places might make you feel. She wasn't a talker, especially not about things like that. When she did talk, it was to tell you how to do something, or to tell you something that had happened before you were born, or to remind you how to act right. She had strict ideas about acting right. She wouldn't touch you much either. What she liked to touch were woods things, things that came out of the ground. But even without the talking, she taught me to let into my insides the real of this place. From her I learned the deep of here.

Mogey knew, too. That was the main reason I went over there as much as I did. Since we'd got back from North Carolina it seemed to me Lace had forgotten everything but the bad, and, of course, Jimmy Make had never known. It seemed to me there was only one person left who knew, who remembered, and that was Uncle Mogey. He wasn't really my uncle, he was Grandma's nephew, a Ricker, too, and he was one of our few relatives who hadn't yet left. He used to run the woods with us a lot, clear back to when I was very small, and I remember how he'd carry me on his shoulders when I got tired, make me tall as branches. Gentle, Mogey was. Gentler than women. Gentler than dogs. The gentleness in him was the gentleness in trees. And it seemed to me only Uncle Mogey and his wife Mary tried to remember, I mean *really* remember. Quite a few people talked about what they thought was being lost, but already people weren't remembering.

Mogey and Mary always had a pot of coffee going, and they'd been giving me a cup since I was ten years old. They treated me like that. Usually there was a crockpot simmering, too, you'd smell it, venison with onions and garlic, or smothered round steak, or brown beans, and sweet tea, too. The inside of their house was always light, and that was so different from ours, dropped down in the narrow of the hollow like ours was. It was hard to get our house light. And sitting with them at their kitchen table, Mary's china cupboard that Mogey had made her gleaming and homey, poems about God they had hanging on their walls, I'd get a belonging feeling I didn't often have with people. It was like going back to when I was little, before everything started to change. When people would visit more, and me and all the other kids who used to live up and down Yellowroot would just be in and out of people's houses all day long. Like everybody's house was ours, and everywhere you were welcome, and if you ate lunch at Kerwins' house one day, they'd be up at the Ricker Place with Grandma feeding them the next. It still felt that way at Uncle Mogey's.

I could tell I was almost to the top of the ridge, the light changing a little. I was in truly deep now, all mountain and no sight of people, of things people-made, and down below me, this soft loft of heavy-leafed branches, and above me, the underside of the same. Finally, I was feeling the distance shutting. I stopped there to make sure, tugging after my breath, the gnats wavering in, and it was, the distance was shutting. A feeling closer to the trees all around. I took off again, really running this time, the curve and dip of the ground echo-shaping the curve and dip of my body the way a flat road never did, and the more the distance shut, the faster the badness dropped away.

It was only in the woods that Grandma ever whipped me. Lace would spank me a good bit down at the house, and Jimmy Make wasn't a spanker at all, you could tell it made him too nervous, he left that kind of thing for Lace to do. My grandma only whipped me a couple times, and all of them were on the mountain, and all of them were with switches she made me cut. She gave me her knife and made me pick one, and if I picked too little, she sent me back. Those are the whippings I remember. I can't even recall much of why Lace was spanking me, and hers never had real sting. Grandma's, hers hurt, they went deeper than skin, and after that, they stayed.

37

Once it was for throwing my trash. I'd carried some candy up with us, must have been Easter candy I was hoarding from my basket, we didn't get candy except on special occasions and I know it was spring when I did this. I was wearing pants without pockets, I carried the candy in my hand. Because I didn't want to carry the wrappers around after I ate, I threw them behind us and off in the weeds a ways, thinking Grandma wouldn't notice. Grandma did. "You can live off these mountains, Bant," she said. "You don't dirty up where you eat. You know bettern that."

Another time Uncle Mogey and Aunt Mary and their boy Kenneth were with us, and the four of them were digging ramps, and I felt left out, probably jealous of Kenneth. I liked being the only kid, getting all the attention that way. So I dug up my own patch of stuff where they weren't looking. Not ramps, just a whole bunch of different kinds of plants I pulled out of the ground. I remember Uncle Moge and Aunt Mary being polite, not looking at the whipping, acting like it wasn't happening. But I know Kenneth snuck a peek. Grandma didn't just whip me that time. She also made me plant everything back.

Then there was the killing of the snake. The worst whipping she ever gave me. That was spring, too, the snake still sluggish from the cold nights, that's the only reason I could kill him, him trying to sun on a rock, and I dropped another big rock on his head. I must have been about six, old enough to know how Grandma felt about snakes, but I knew how Jimmy Make felt, too. By that time, I'd been up to the snake ditches with him a good bit, I was acting out of the Jimmy Make part of me. It wasn't even a blacksnake, much less a copperhead. Nothing but a garter. And that time was the worst not because of how long and hard she whipped, but because it was the first time I saw she was honestly surprised, a bad sad surprise, at something I had done.

I'd rolled the rock back off his head, feeling a scratchy satisfaction, watching the juice seep out of his head while the body still thrashed.

Then there was Grandma. So surprised at first she said only, "Oh, Bant. What is wrong with you, girl? What is wrong with you?" And the way she said it sounded like there really must be something wrong with me, it sounded so much like that it scared me, and not because I was about to get beat.

After the whipping, me sniffling, that snake body still moving, Grandma said, "You know way bettern that. You don't kill what can't harm you. And you shouldn't kill what can harm you unless it's a threat to you right there. Snakes eat up other things that give us problems, like mice and rats." And even later, when we were heading home, the hurt gone from my behind but the shame still burning, she had to bring it up again. "Go around just killing stuff, it'll eventually come back on you. It throws things out of whack." She shook her head. "As much time as you've spent with me up on this mountain . . ." And there she stopped, like what I'd done was so bad she couldn't even think what else to say. She shook her head again, not looking at me. "You know way bettern that."

Since we'd got back from North Carolina, though, Mogey and Mary had changed, too. Although it scared me a little to say it, I had to admit that to tell the truth. While we were gone, a kettlebottom, one of those petrified tree trunks that sometimes drop out of mine roofs, fell and clipped Mogey's shoulders and neck. After that, he couldn't work anymore, and he was never the same in other ways, too. He started having real bad headaches, and this spring, they'd gotten worse than they'd ever been before. Also in just the past year, even Mogey and Mary'd started talking about the bad things, and it wasn't headaches they meant. I'd come over a lot that winter, more than I usually did, things getting louder and tighter at our place, tighter and louder. And although it would always be better at Uncle Mogey's house, sometimes we'd be leaning over the table, cupping our coffee mugs, me settled in, even close to happy, and then, when I least expected it, one of them would mention another thing lost. Honey-bees. A ginseng patch. A type of tree.

When they'd do that, I'd pull in on myself, I'd drop my head. The pretty sandy spot on the river we used to call the Beach, they'd say. Crawdads. Helgrammites. I'd stop sipping my coffee, I couldn't swallow anymore, because it was bad enough hearing it from Lace. But hearing from them was even scarier. They said it like somebody was dying and others had already died, quiet and prayerful and sad they spoke it. They didn't rant. And if even Mogey and Mary were so mournful, who still remembered, well, it was hard to tell yourself things weren't really getting as bad as Lace said.

But then, before they'd gone on very long at all, Mogey, like he'd just thought of something, would look at me and say, "Now Bant. You're too young to be so worried. You're too serious. You should be spending more time with kids your age, having more fun." Then he'd reach up with his fist and fake-cuff my cheekbone, so gentle he would just barely brush it there. And no matter how many times Uncle Mogey did that, it never once made me think of the look of my face.

But I was different from other kids my age. Uncle Mogey knew that. I didn't want to be different, but I was, either born or made that way or both. Take my friend Sharon, for instance. Sweet girl that she was, this place didn't matter so much to her. If you asked her, she'd say it was pretty, but it didn't reach her like it reached me, and near as I could tell, it was like that with most kids at school. Then Corey, he didn't care about anything he couldn't run a tire over. And Dane. Well. He couldn't help it.

My grandma would always say, "Now you young people. It's up to you." She knew where things were getting to. But then she started saying how it seemed the young people just didn't care anymore, "except for you, Bant," she'd say. Looking at me, but not in my eyes. Looking beyond the way she would. "I know you are different."

Finally I could see Mogey and Mary's house below me, and I stopped to try and make the bad feeling go away, at least a tiny bit. The tight square sides, the slate-blue siding, it was a real house, not a modular home, that Mogey had built with his hands. Everything in their yard was neat, toolshed and tarped woodshed and the empty dog kennel, old Brownie long dead. I scrawled down the shale bank into the backyard, shiny with sweat now, my tennis shoes muddy, but I'd take the shoes off at the door, and beyond that, I knew Mogey and Mary wouldn't care. I pushed my hair back out of my face. Their grass needed cutting some, thought I'd offer to do it for them, but a good thick it was, not like our yard, where nothing ever wanted to grow and now the flood trash doomed anything brave enough to try. I saw how they'd been working on their garden, saw how they'd put out tomato plants in the shade, probably planning to plant them this evening, tomatoes I knew they'd started in winter in Styrofoam cups from seed. But then I was standing at the foot of the porch steps, and the door opened before I knocked.

"Hi, honey. He's sleeping," Aunt Mary told me in a low voice. She shook her head. "So bad today he can't get out of bed."

"Oh," I said. Something dropped out of the base of my throat. "I'm sorry."

"Wait here on the porch," Mary said. "I'll bring out some ice tea and we can visit here."

"Oh," I waved no with my hand. "That's okay. I should be getting home." I took a step back. "They'll be wondering what's taking me so long getting back from school." With just the two of us, I knew, it wouldn't be the same. Even in the sadness, when it was the three of us, there was always a brightness, too. Uncle Mogey would always end us up there, in the brightness. Aunt Mary—like most people, I didn't blame her—could not.

"Are you sure, honey?" she said. "You just walked all the way over." Her face folded in tired on itself, the darkness a full circle around her eyes.

"Yeah," I said. "I just wanted to see how you all were doing. Starting day after tomorrow I'm probably going to be busy at work."

Mary shook her head again. "Well, drink some tea at least."

I drank it there on the porch, and I thanked her and told her the garden looked good. She talked a while about the tomato plants, what they were putting in next, but I had a hard time paying attention. One last time she tried to make me stay longer, and I told her I was sorry but I couldn't. Then I started back out the yard.

"Skin you alive," that teacher'd say, and sometimes it wasn't the kid on the barbed wire fence I'd see. Sometimes it was me. Sometimes it was my own arms and legs, skun naked, the blood beating through thick blue and red cords. And I knew—Lace having forgotten, Jimmy Make never having known, Mogey hurt bad as he was and never going to get better—my grandma would expect from me certain things.

The thing was, in the past year or so, I was starting to wonder if I was really that different from everybody else after all.

Dane

MRS. TAYLOR is the lady Dane takes care of. She watches TV with the sound turned down. Instead, they listen to Mrs. Taylor's voice, not nonstop, not rambly. Just now and again outing with what's on her mind. A TV screen glints in each of Mrs. Taylor's glass lenses so that Dane sees Mrs. Taylor's eyes as two little TVs, talking. And those two little TVs and the one big TV are the only places light comes into the room.

It is a dark place Dane enters every morning. Its two crouched windows, one blocked by a broken exhaust fan, and its dark plaid couch, the dark recliner, the dark paneled walls hung with dark pictures, daisies and praying children and pert terriers cut from magazines and somehow varnished onto dark slabs of wood. The other pictures, the dozen family photos under glass in plastic frames, Mrs. Taylor has already had Dane pack safely away after the blasts started knocking them down. The dark slabs of wood the blasts cannot shatter.

Mrs. Taylor doesn't expect Dane to answer her. She seems to like it better when he just listens. Most people prefer it this way, Dane has learned, and he's good at listening. It's the only way he knows how to be liked. Sometimes when Mrs. Taylor's friends visit, they'll talk about Dane as though he's not there, the privilege or curse of those who talk very little, an assumption on the part of the talkers that the nontalkers can't hear either, or at least only hear what you want them to. Which means Dane hears a lot. Mrs. Taylor's friends find it unusual that Mrs. Taylor has a boy instead of a girl to help take care of her, and once in a while, they'll mention this out loud. They'll ask, "How's the boy working out?" Then Mrs. Taylor will say, "Oh, he's just a pleasure to have around," and Dane will feel a warm goodness, "and more thorough than any girl I've ever had," then a hotter shame. Dane even more girl than girl.

As Dane sits there listening in the dark room, he feels his own self get darker and darker. Dane fading, receding, without even glasses to light his face with reflection, Dane a dark barrel for the voices to fill. All those months before May, while he and Mrs. Taylor sat in the living room between chores, Mrs. Taylor talked of any number of things. But since the May flood, she speaks of only three: her kids' wanting her to move to Cleveland. What happened at Buffalo Creek. And, less often, more hushed, the upcoming End of the World.

Mrs. Taylor begins to rock her body up out of her recliner and onto her walker, and Dane moves to help her. She wears a garment, part smock part dress, that falls straight down off the shelf of her breasts so that Mrs. Taylor looks like a wide piece of culvert pipe standing on its end. The smock dress is not white anymore, even though it is clean. The garment has darkened somehow in the dark close house, the house like a den, like a clean hole where a very clean animal might hide, darkening all that comes in it. Mrs. Taylor begins walkering towards the kitchen, and although the distance between recliner and kitchen table is maybe twelve feet, about halfway there she rests on her walker to catch her breath. The emphysema, and Dane listens to her lungs working, the lung sponges squeezing, he can hear them as clearly as if she's inside out. Then she recovers, and she takes a fresh breath. But she doesn't move after it, so Dane knows she's going to speak.

He tightens inside. If it's the disaster at Buffalo Creek, he knows she'll start in one of two ways. "Should've known better, but Dooley had work over there . . . But, we should've known better." Or "Here I've moved right back into it. That was Pittston, this is Lyon, but one company or another's bound to drown me before I die a natural death." Dane waits, and in those four or five seconds, Dane prays. And to his surprise, he is answered.

"Well," Mrs. Taylor says. "I got company coming in three weeks. Avery called last night. We got to Lysol that bathroom good."

Dane has never met Avery, Mrs. Taylor's youngest son, but it's from Avery his check comes. Mrs. Taylor keeps detailed records of Dane's time on a chart magneted to her refrigerator, then she sends the chart to Avery, and Avery does the math. Avery is also "a history buff. Oh, he loves to read." And a "vagabond." "He's just been all over the place. Itchy feet. I'm so glad he finally settled down." Now Mrs. Taylor shuffles forward. Her feet foreshortened bread loaves stabbed into slippers, blue terrycloth folded over the instep. The toenails, flakes of brown mica. She fumbles with a kitchen chair—she won't often ask for help, Dane has to see it and step in—and Dane does, pulls out the chair and guides her down. "Let's do them dishes first," she says. "I always say do the kitchen first before you get bathroom all over your hands."

When the May flood hit, Dane'd been finishing his most important job for Mrs. Taylor, the main reason her kids have hired somebody at all: her toilet arrangement. Because Mrs. Taylor has running water in the kitchen and a bathtub that works, but she doesn't have a flush commode. Instead she has a metal chair fitted with a plastic toilet seat, and under the seat is fastened a big metal pot like the black kettles with white flecks Grandma used for sterilizing canning jars. Mrs. Taylor's kids can afford to install an indoor toilet. Mrs. Taylor has told Dane they have not as another way to get her to Cleveland. The special chair with the pot has its own room, a sizable room with its window propped open with a brick even in winter, the room empty of everything else but a dish towel wall-hanging of white kittens. Dane feels sorry for the kittens. Every day but Sunday, no matter what else Mrs. Taylor might ask him to do—wash dishes, vacuum falling plaster, help check her sugar, dust, follow her directions on cooking supper—Dane has to carry the slop pot to the outhouse and empty it there.

That Saturday in May, the sky cracked open right about the time Dane was ready to carry out the pot. "Coming down that hard, won't last long," Mrs. Taylor told him. "You just wait a while, honey." And he did, the two of them watching the silent TV while rain clamored the house roof, until Mrs. Taylor started fretting about leaks in the bedroom, but Dane checked, and there weren't any. Then finally they heard the roof ring a lighter pitch, and Mrs. Taylor said, "Okay, darlin, why don't you take it on out. I don't think it's coming down hard enough to splash any up on you." And Dane let himself out the back door and headed for the outhouse in the far corner of the yard.

He had his head ducked, his face turned down from the rain still falling, so he heard it first. And when he recalls it now, he also hears it before he sees it. An unfamiliar alto "*aaaaaahhhhh*." Not a rumble, no, there was no bass to it. All he could think was a new kind of machine must be coming, and he turned to look into the rain up the hollow to see. Mrs. Taylor's house wasn't on the creek side of the hollow, between Yellowroot Creek and her backyard stood the row of houses across the road, and those house's yards and fences, and the road itself. Which is why when Dane picked up his head and saw the creek coming at him, he couldn't make sense of it. A thigh-high water wall the color of chocolate milk driving ahead of itself logs and tires and other stuff

Dane didn't have time to tell what they were, more things surging and bouncing behind the wall's foaming face. And the wall itself not solid across but split, the water having found every place the hollow lay a little lower and then hurtled through the low places in channels, and because the road rose a few inches above the house, one of those channels bore down directly on Mrs. Taylor's house and yard.

When Dane thinks back now, what scares him most is not the water wall, although the wall scares him bad. It's how he didn't move. He just seized up halfway between back door and outhouse, prickled sharp in his scalp, the slop pot held away from him, both hands gripping the handle and his eyes swelling and bulging out his head. Like if only those eyes could get closer to the water, they might understand, Dane trying to make sense—creek on the wrong side of the road, water on its end—while Mrs. Taylor screamed at him from the back door, "Move, boy! Move!" But he did not. Dane frozen, rapt with his slop pot, while the water wall came crashing through the backyard above Mrs. Taylor's, sucking into itself lawn ornaments, a doghouse, a blue plastic wading pool, spinning, until all of a sudden, the thought struck Dane that the water would have hit his own house first.

By this time, Mrs. Taylor was hammering her walker against the inside of the aluminum door, trying to wake him that way. But only the idea of his own house finally moved Dane. He wheeled and sprang towards the back porch, pot still in his hands, he didn't think to drop it, liquid sloshing up its sides, the pot itself awkward, heavy, slowing him, but still Dane without the sense to drop it, until it did leap up and splatter his arms and stomach and hands, and that's what finally told him let go. And he did, and vaulted onto the back porch just ahead of the water wall and its battering logs, flattened himself against the side of the house while the current and all the debris it carried in it smashed against the upstream house wall and broke and split and spun around it, never reaching as high as the porch. Behind him, inside the screen, he could hear Mrs. Taylor wheezing even over top the water rush, and he could smell the odor of urine and shit on his arms, and he thought of Mom and Corey and Tommy up at the head of the hollow where the waters had to have hit first, and a big chunk of something rose in Dane's stomach and slammed into the bottom of his chest. But Dane didn't cry.

Ever since then, day after day in the darkened house, while Dane cleans or between chores, Mrs. Taylor tells the horrors of Buffalo Creek, February 26, 1972. And she doesn't tell them as history or legend. She tells them as prophecy, as threat. The twin lights in her twin lenses flash, a signal, a flare, and Dane, trapped, listens, Dane gulps what she tells him. The stories filling his already crowded guts, them full of nerves, and of logs and fish, and now of stories, scrawled all over his insides, but Dane listens. She doesn't do it to scare him, it's not mean like the kids on the bus, it's simply what Mrs. Taylor has to do, and it's what Dane does, too. Dane is the listener. So he listens, wondering when he'll finally get so full he'll bust, have to bust, and day after day after day he strains, braces, he prays, just to keep from busting. Flood inside.

Dane is the darkest of his family. He has fine black hair and skin that darkens fastest of the four kids even though this summer he is the least out in the sun. He's the darkest, and, at twelve, the shortest for his age, and, he knows, the weakest. Sometimes, when Lace is at the Dairy Queen and the five of them are eating supper, Dane will study everybody's arms. His arms are shorter than the others, pudgy and stumped, puffing down along their bones to end in even puffier hands. When Dane looks at his arms, he shrinks another ounce in his chest. Beside his own arms lie Tommy's. Who is made to wash his hands before the meal, so Tommy is clean to his wrists, while above, the arms are grimed in rings and the elbows chuffy, but even at six years old, Tommy's arms are stronger, more solid, than Dane's arms are. Then Bant. Nothing but a girl. Her arms peppered with blue paint and odored, mildly, of gasoline, board-shaped and hard-boned, sharp-angled in the elbows and wrists, steady and broad. Those are Bant's arms. Next there is Jimmy Make, at the table head, his arms dark-skinned like Dane's, but with none of Dane's fragility. Jimmy's arms are blocky and tooled with scars, cut scars, burn scars, the muscles having collapsed under the skin like they grew too big too fast and fell, yet still visible. Sleeping lumps, lazy flesh that can flash into hard-ness when Jimmy wills it. And last, Dane studies the arms of Corey. Two years younger than Dane's. They are blunt and thick and already swept with hairs, already making muscle, bulges that Corey gloats over, flexes, draws attention to in any way he can. Steel-made Corey. Little man. And all those arms, and the bodies and heads they are attached to, are sounder and stronger and better matched than Dane's, Dane knows this. Yet it is Dane who must take and carry the stories.

Somehow that makes a scary kind of sense.

Mrs. Taylor is saying, "And Avery's going to pester me the whole time he's here. And what can I say back? I'd rather sit in this hollow and drown than live in Cleveland?" Her emphysema rises, Dane can hear it over top the spigot running in his dishwater. "But you see, Dane. That's exactly what Lyon wants." The wheezing. "Scare us to death and make everybody miserable to where we all just move out, then they can go on and do whatever they want. And you know what I say to that?" Dane knows. "This is my house!" She slams her palms on the kitchen table, jumping the salt shaker, her canisters of pills. "There have always been Ratliffs in this hollow! My father bought these two lots in 1928, and we *worked* for what *we* have!" She pauses, her throat straining after breath. "I won't be run out," she murmurs now.

Dane wipes his dishes. Cleveland. Just to taste the word, the for-eign citiness of it, makes a homesickness thicken in the back of his throat. But at the same time, he sees the map of America in his room

49

at school. The way the paper is drawn in rumples, lines, and swells to show where the mountains are. West Virginia nothing but a slant of rippled lines, dense, relentless, the lines marked thick and deep. While Cleveland at the top of Ohio is blank. Where the land lies flat. Which means the water has no way to rush down on top of you because it has no place to start.

The tapwater foams out of the spigot, boils into the sink, and Mrs. Taylor says, "Honey, make sure you get them glass rims."

Bant

I STOOD in front of the office door, an old metal screen with a curly metal pattern, and behind that, a heavy door shut. Looked like a kick dent in it halfway up. When there weren't any cars passing in the road, I could hear the window air conditioner, a flapping wheeze with a rattle underneath. The place was a flaking green the same color as the high school bathroom walls, and with all the fresh money Hobart was making, he'd decided to get his motel repainted. Jimmy'd heard it from a friend who was Hobart's nephew. Nobody called it a motel but Hobart, it was the boardinghouse to everyone else, although nowadays I'd heard some calling it "Scab Resort." And I knew Hobart's was the only place in Prater doing decent business besides the Dollar General and Scott's Funeral Home because Hobart rented to the miners the companies imported from out-of-state to work the mountaintop mines. "Miners, shit," Jimmy Make would say. "Nothing but ditch diggers, what they are." Jimmy wasn't crazy about his daughter painting scab walls, and Lace was even less happy, she'd fought him for a while. But eventually, both gave in. There wasn't anyplace else around where I could get work.

My chest felt like two hands pressing on it, but Jimmy Make was watching me from out in the truck. He called it an interview and had given me pointers. I stepped up on the stoop. I opened the screen, nervous about doing even that without permission and half afraid it would make the inside door open and there I'd stand. I tapped near the kick dent with my knuckles. I waited, but no one came, so I figured he couldn't hear me with that air conditioner running. But when I knocked harder, somebody right away called out, "Now just hold on. Hold on," and I stepped back quick. I brushed off my pants in case I'd sat on something riding in and checked to make sure all my buttons were done. *Shake hands*, Jimmy'd said. *Speak up. And keep that hair back outta your eyes.*

When Hobart opened the door, I stuck out my hand, but he turned around before he could see it. Jimmy'd told me to wear a pair of pants not jeans and a fake-silky blouse that belonged to Lace. Hobart was in mud-colored sweatpants and plaid bedroom slippers cut open across the toes, and I followed him, that air conditioner gasping, the office still warmer than it was outside. "Sit down," Hobart said, pointing behind himself because he still had his back to me. It was a lawn chair he pointed to.

He was lowering himself onto the front edge of the recliner, straddling his legs around the footrest still in the air, the recliner must have stayed stuck reclined all the time. I was already noticing his breathing, and I thought it was because it reminded me of the air conditioner. He was staring at me, but I couldn't tell how, this blank to it that hid something behind. I could feel the places on my face. Red spots with a heat behind. At the start of each breath, his throat rattled, but the exhale sounded like speaking, only you couldn't catch the word.

"You're Jimmy Make Turrell's girl?" he asked.

"Yessir," I said.

"And I hear you've done some painting before?"

"Yessir," I said.

I waited for him to ask me more, but he just kept looking at me, so I looked off to the side. Wanted to drop my hair in my face, but I did what Jimmy Make'd said. The recliner was patched with duct tape (*WD-40 makes it go, duct tape makes it stop*, Jimmy again in my head), and the room smelled like air closed up for a very long time, and in it, an old man with no woman. Him not talking made my face glow hotter in its spots, but all he did was that huff-breathing, the wordless speaking at the end. Then the TV audience suddenly clapped, and I just took a breath and told him. "I painted the bleachers at the Little League field with my church group summer before last. And I painted Mrs. Glenella Taylor's fence, lives up Yellowroot near us." I had Mrs. Taylor's phone number in my pocket.

Right then, somebody else knocked at the door, and first thing I thought was Jimmy Make had gotten impatient and was coming after me. "C'mon in," Hobart hollered. We waited. "C'mon in!" Hobart bellowed, then the door swung in.

"Your pop machine's jammed up again."

Hobart kind of snuffled. "I got somebody coming from Beckley take a look at it."

It was a man a little older than Jimmy Make. A man who had to be staying here. Which meant he was a scab. That was one of the few things Lace and Jimmy agreed on anymore, even if some of them were union, didn't matter, scab, and I looked at him there, he was the first one I'd ever seen for sure. Olive-green T-shirt, greasy creased jeans, just like any man around here wore. Cap like a cap any man would wear pulled over a face could've been on any man's head. But then I saw the difference. His boots. The dirt on them a different color than Jimmy's used to be. The scab would know what was behind that fill. I looked away from him. Saw Hobart was back to staring at me.

"I lost sixty cents in there."

Hobart hacked his throat, paused a second. Swallowed. "I'll settle up with you later. I'm talking to this girl now."

The door shut. Hobart shifted on the end of his recliner and reached for a dirty cup in the mess of motel check-in cards and what looked like shredded newspaper covering his coffee table. His breathing kept itching my memory. Somehow it carried both a pleasure and a sad, and neither one made any sense in that office with Hobart. "How old are you?" he said.

My throat hardened. Jimmy Make had told me not to lie about my age, but not to bring it up either. "Fifteen," I said.

It was the first time he nodded. "Can you start tomorrow morning, nine o'clock?"

"Yessir," I said. "I'll be here then."

"Good job, Cissy!" Jimmy Make clapped one fist on the steering wheel, then reached down for the ignition and gave the gas a good loud stomp. *Don't call me Cissy*, I said to myself. "When do you start?"

"Tomorrow." We were pulling past Hobart's sign. SPECIAL WEEKLY RATES. I could still hear the breathing. Hear that air conditioner run. The look of the dirt on that man's boots.

"How much is he gonna pay you?"

My face flinched, but Jimmy Make was busy driving. I hadn't thought to ask. "Minimum, I guess."

Jimmy Make grunted. "Minimum. Should pay you more than that, a painting job."

I looked out the window.

"Well," Jimmy Make decided. "That's all right. Your first job and all." Then suddenly he braked, pulled off on the shoulder, and U-turned back up the road. "Know what I'm gonna do?" he said. "Gonna buy you an ice cream cone."

I knew it was in part an excuse to check up on Lace, or maybe he actually missed her, who knew. They were both crazy that way, couldn't stand the sight of each other, but then when one or the other was out of sight, they'd want that sight back. So they couldn't stand each other again, I guess. Hobart's was on our side of Prater and the Dairy Queen on the far side, so we drove back through town past the sunfaded FOR RENT and FOR SALE signs in the storefronts, and then the storefronts with nothing in their windows at all, had just given up, and you could see clear through to their empty backs. *Poor old Prater. I can remember when there was . . .* A movie theater. Three clothing stores. A Ben Franklin, a real hotel, and that was Grandma talking years before where it had got to now. Two of the three stoplights were either broken or just turned off, but the video store/tanning parlor was still going, and Maria Lake's beauty shop, and the post office. In the old IGA lot, weeds pushed high and thrashy out the pavement cracks, and people came in from out in the country and sold stuff out of their pickup trucks there. Old bikes, greasy tools, ceramic figurines, sometimes strange things like a load of brand-new paper towels I'd seen one time. Permanent portable yard sales, you never knew what you might find there, Corey was all the time begging to stop. And we'd bought a VCR there to replace our broken one, but then that second one didn't work either, and we never did see that man in the IGA lot again.

We pulled into the Dairy Queen, and Jimmy Make slammed out the truck and headed for the door without waiting for me, like he always did. His walk had a kind of curve to it, he'd been hurt at work when he was real young, and although the doctor said it was his back, it showed itself in the leg. Either way, it didn't matter. Jimmy had made the limp a swagger. It'd cooled down since yesterday and clouds'd moved in, unusual cool for June at two o'clock in the afternoon, and inside the air-conditioned Dairy Queen, it was downright cold. I caught up with Jimmy Make right at the door, which he slammed through like he owned the place, calling out to Lace, "Bant got her job! I'm gonna buy her an ice cream cone." Lace, standing at the milkshake machine with her back to us, didn't turn around.

"Heeey, Jimmy." A voice crooning from somewhere back in a booth. "Heeey, there, Jimmy Make," kind of lazy and jokey, and I couldn't see who it was, but Jimmy spotted him, grinned all big, and forgot about me and Lace. Lace had turned back to the counter where she was taking the milkshake buyer's money, but she was looking both at the customer and past him at me. Her face told me she wasn't as excited about my new job as Jimmy Make was, but once the customer left, she said, "That's real good, honey. Your first interview. You must've made a good impression." She turned to make the cone, and I watched her, in the blue DQ polo shirt and the visor cramping down her blonde hair. Kind of things she would never wear except for the job, it still surprised me a little to see her like that, even though I saw it every day. And her face sometimes looked to me like a fox and sometimes like a prism. But it never looked like mine. She handed me the cone. "Tell Jimmy Make I'll be over in a minute. And tell him he owes me a dollar fifteen."

I looked back into the eating area and saw Jimmy sitting across from some guy I didn't think I knew, but sometimes they all looked alike, especially in their caps and their beards. Washed down to all the same, like the scab had looked. I walked on back, my places going warm again, my hair shawling down around my face, even though there was nobody there besides Jimmy's friend and a pack of big women and little kids working silent and serious on hot dogs and sundaes. I slipped into the booth behind Jimmy and his buddy, them teasing each other over something that meant nothing, then laughing like it was the funniest joke ever heard. Licking my cone careful to catch every drop, I looked past Jimmy and back to Lace, idle behind the counter now.

She was talking to somebody who didn't seem to be ordering, a woman standing off to the side, out of the way of the cash register, and I wondered why I hadn't noticed her while I was getting my cone. Then the woman turned to where I could see the side of her face, and I thought I recognized her. I was pretty sure it was Loretta Hughes. Whoever it was did all the talking, but I started studying Lace's face, and what was traveling across it made me know it was Loretta for sure.

I swabbed my tongue around my cone. It was beginning to taste like nothing but cold. Jimmy Make and the crooner had moved on to the glories of Jeff Gordon, and I cut in. "Lace says you owe her a dollar fifteen." Without looking at me or breaking the Jeff Gordon sentence, Jimmy reached in his wallet and pulled out two bills. I reached over and took them. I held them still for a second, the pressing on my chest again. But the need to know got stronger.

When I handed the money to Lace, she didn't look at me or speak either, just rung up the price while listening hard to Loretta, shaking her head and making the growly sound she used when she was somewhere it wasn't good to cuss. I listened to Loretta, too, pretending that I wasn't, but Loretta was talking mostly letters that I knew stood for government agencies, but I didn't know which ones. Then, when I reached down to take the eighty-five cents from the counter, I saw that what I'd thought was some kind of menu or tray liner wasn't that at all.

I knew because it was black and white. I squinted at it, wanting to lean down, but not wanting to draw Lace's attention. It was pictures that had been printed off a website, I could tell that, and they hadn't come out so good, smeary and dotty. Lace was still concentrating on Loretta, so I ducked my head, did lean over a little, and squinted hard. They were upside down, facing Lace, and I'd never seen pictures of it before. But I understood right away what it was.

Like most people, I'd never really seen a mountaintop removal mine, only seen their edges, down the turnpike and along Route 60 towards Charleston when the leaves were off. Up Yellowroot with Jimmy Make two days before. But although I'd never really seen one, and these pictures weren't color and weren't clear, and although I only looked for seconds, I knew.

A dead terraced the whole width of the frame. Hacked gray stumps where mountain peaks had been, and flung all over, skinless white snakes. Roads. A gigantic funnel, sloppy and dark, running down off it, funnel big as the mountain itself, *is the mountain itself*, then *fill*, it made a dry place in my mouth.

I wanted to look longer, and didn't want to look longer, and I for sure didn't want Lace to see me looking, although I also knew that didn't make sense. But it was like dirty pictures I was seeing, and I peered from the corner of my eye to make sure Lace hadn't caught me—she hadn't—and I shoved off away from the counter. Then I was back in the booth against the window, Jimmy Make laughing like there wasn't a thing wrong in the world, my ice cream cone melting onto my fingers, and I leaned out and pitched it in the trash. I pushed my forehead against the streaked window, the pull in me to go back to the counter, look harder, get it clear in me for sure, like looking at pictures of naked people. Like looking at pictures of dead bodies. My breath making a greasy steam on the dirty window, and then I was hearing Hobart's breathing again, pricking at my mind, *just a-smothering to death all along,* and all of a sudden it came to me. Pap. One of the only pictures of him I carried in my mind, Pap wheelchair-bound and drawing breath through straws in his nose. And how when I was little I never even questioned it, I'd just thought that's how old men got their air, worked for it, sucked it through straws, until I grew up and found out most old men didn't and Pap wasn't that old anyway. The huffing, Pap, the printout pictures scalded and bald, the look of the dirt on his boots. The gate behind the house. I swiped the back of my hand across my eyes and forced the wet back down.

Then Jimmy Make's buddy was getting ready to leave, and Jimmy slid out the booth to let him. "Don't do nothing I wouldn't do," the buddy said, and Jimmy Make laughed again, then turned. And saw Lace and who she was talking to.

I didn't know how he knew. Lace had told me Loretta Hughes was one of the people getting involved against the destruction with a bunch over in Boone County and that Loretta felt strong Lace should join the group, too, but that was not something she'd tell Jimmy Make. Still, he knew. Went rigid as a crowbar from his ankles to his shoulders, I could feel that cold hard off him. Then he swagger-stomped past Lace, his bad leg swinging out like a bolt had got loose, him louder in not saying good-bye than he would have been if he had. Lace, though, just glanced at him go, then turned back to Loretta. Her mouth looking always on the verge of breaking in, but then Loretta would start on something else, and Lace'd hold back a little longer to hear that too.

Standing there by the empty booth, I realized Jimmy Make might just take off without me if I didn't get out there right away. I don't really remember leaving the Dairy Queen, don't remember crossing the lot, but I can recall passing the counter. The pull of the pictures again. I was climbing in the cab when Jimmy was putting it in gear, and for a few seconds I felt pure rage at the both of them, but quick, the scared came back. Then I just wanted the whole thing to not have happened, and the first way to start erasing it was to calm Jimmy Make down. So I said, "Thank you for the ice cream cone."

Jimmy Make spun out of the lot, throwing a little gravel as he did, then he braked right away. Pinky McCutcheon was slumped in his sheriff's car by the pumps of the shutdown BP. Pinky lifted one finger, a point or a wave. "That was a loan," Jimmy Make said.

Corey

THAT TRUCK is his dad's "pride n joy." When Dad calls it that out loud, says, "pride n joy," he always slaps the fender, and the truck grunts back. Yeah, that truck can talk a little, even when it isn't running. And when it is running? The *WHOOOM whoom whoom whoom whoom WHOOOOM whoom whoom whoom,* muffler clearing its throat like before you let fly a big hawker. But better than a hawker, more muscle to it than that, who knew what that truck might let fly. Six-speed suspension lift limited slip rear axle one-ton F350 custom pickup. Vampire black, eight cylinders under the hood, rippled panels over it like a weight-lifter's chest, *pecs,* Corey thinks, and the roll bar. *Could you put a roll bar on a bike?* He's pretty sure you could put one on a four-wheeler.

Dad's pride n joy. Corey would like to find Dad one of those air-brushed license plates people put on front, but instead of something like "Angel n Butch" or "Lace n Jimmy," the license plate would say "Pride n Joy." Just gazing at that truck can fill Corey so hard-happy inside he can't keep his grin pinned back, even though he tries—bite your lip, look like a man—no, can't help it. And then. Then there's the way his dad can drive. Can that man handle a truck, you better just get in and hang on. Dad could power that truck over any terrain, using nothing but two-wheel ninety percent of the time, Dad could drive it over anywhere, shit, Dad could drive it over nowhere, that's how good Dad could drive, and the time Little Scotty bet he couldn't take the rise to the above-the-hollow road in two-wheel, and Dad did, spin-clutching, all four kids in the bed, then hauled ass to the Dairy Queen with the bet money, them hollering all the way like in a parade. And the only reason Corey would ever want Paul Franz and them to come up the hollow was if Dad would load them all in the back of the truck and take them for a ride. They'd have to just get in and hang on, they'd be dodging low-hanging branches and bloody their faces some, they might get bounced out and muddied up, they might get muddied up even if they didn't bounce out, but, buddy, that'd be one ride they'd never forget. *Wouldn't it now.*

But nowadays. Well, anymore . . . the truck concerns Corey. Just a little. It is starting to rust around the wheel wells, just a little, Corey has noticed. Corey thinks to take some black hobby paint to the rust spots, but then he wonders if hobby paint would be an insult. And some motherfucker in a parking lot opened his little prissy white car door on the truck door and left marks. And sometimes when you run it nowadays, something smells funny. Not every time, but sometimes, and Dad can't for the life of him figure out what's causing that smell. And other times, instead of the smell, there's the sound.

"Hear that?" Dad asks, his head cocked forward and his eyebrows scrunched down. The four of them, Dad, Corey, Bant, and Tommy, are driving into Prater, taking Bant to work. Dane's already gone to Mrs. Taylor's.

"Huh-uh," Bant says, staring out the window like it's not important. Bant is a girl. Corey listens keen as he can.

Dad leans forward to where he's not watching the road. He dips his ear here and there around the dash, slapping it in different places. Tommy begins, "I'd—"

"Shut up, Tommy!" snaps Dad. "Shit. Shit. Almost had it."

Corey crawls down onto the floor and sticks his head partway up behind the glove compartment. Bant kicks at him a little to get out of her way. He tunes his ears into the truck motor as best he can, but he can't hear anything out of the ordinary. Then Dad busts out laughing. Corey scrambles back into the seat to see what's going on, cracking his head on the glove as he does.

Somebody is driving a riding lawnmower up Route 9. The right pair of lawnmower tires on the shoulder. The left pair in the road. The lawnmower is yellow, probably a Cub Cadet, and its owner has rigged up a little cart to pull. As they get closer, Corey sees the driver is Rabbit. Rabbit rarely wears hats, and you can tell who he is from far away by his hair. Wet-looking copper coils, like short springs. Dad drives right up on the cart, then blows his horn and rips around it. Rabbit doesn't seem to care. He just raises one hand without bothering to look at them.

"What's he driving that on the road for?" Tommy asks.

"Oh, probably got him another DUI," says Dad. Corey has turned around on his knees in the seat to watch Rabbit out the rear window. Pretty quick Rabbit disappears from Corey's sight around a bend, but Corey is wondering where Rabbit found the little wagon—Corey could use something like that. He wonders if the wagon came down the creek in the flood, and he wonders how he missed it and Rabbit did not. *Rabbit,* Corey is thinking. *Now that Rabbit . . .*

Rabbit lives way down at the mouth of the hollow, and he has back behind his house something between a gully and a ditch just full of stuff, but Corey doesn't know if it's trash or parts because you can't tell from the road. All you can see from the road is a bunch of different colors that aren't the color of the ground, but *Rabbit's always working on something. He is.* Corey has never visited Rabbit, never got close to the gully, not because they've been told to stay away from Rabbit, but because most people up Yellowroot just do. It's not only the drinking and the contraptions, but Rabbit is thought a little crazy, and, further, nobody can tell what color he is and he himself won't let on. If he was definitely white, nobody'd care, and if he was definitely black, most wouldn't care, but you just couldn't tell by looking at him, and you couldn't tell by his last name, either. He hadn't come from around here. But the color of Rabbit doesn't worry Corey. The sight of his little cart has got him to thinking.

"How come they call Rabbit Rabbit?" Tommy is asking.

"I heard it's because he used to drive those Volkswagen Rabbits," says Bant.

"Oh, it's just what they call him," says Dad.

The parts in the old house are piling up. They sneak them in through a hole in the kitchen that he and Tommy'd had to make a little bigger. At first they'd just put the parts in the kitchen, but now they were filling the living room, too. Corey has the parts. He has the parts. He just doesn't know how to put them together. *Like a little low-to-the-ground speedwagon.* That is his plan. It'll make a noise like a lawnmower starting up, with more of a grumble and grunt to it than a four-wheeler, lower-pitched than your average four-wheeler, but it'll go over any kind of ground like a four-wheeler can. It makes his heart tick louder to think of it. It makes his body bulk big. *Just like a little low-to-the-ground speedwagon,* he likes that idea, skimming and bouncing at radical speeds right down low to the ground. Corey has the parts, if he only knew how to put them together. If he had tools. He doesn't know how, he has no tools, Dad says he'll help, but it's always "next week." But Rabbit, *he's always working on something . . .*

*

The next morning, Corey waits until Tommy goes in the bathroom. Tommy usually takes so short in the bathroom he doesn't even close the door, so Corey slips out the front screen, careful the catch doesn't click, grabs his bike, and pumps down the road as fast as the bike will go. He hunches his shoulders, bullets his head for the aerodynamics, and he's going so fast he keeps his eyes closed, in part so he won't have to look at that sorry-ass hollow, in part to keep out the bugs, in part because he doesn't have to look. Corey has that hollow memorized.

Rabbit's lawnmower is parked in his driveway behind the fake-wood-paneled station wagon, and Corey finds Rabbit where he thought he would. In his backyard fooling in a freezer. One of those enormous old-timey freezers that swing open from the top like a coffin, and Rabbit has crawled into its motor through a panel he's removed from one end while at the other end, he's hooked up a washing machine with cords and hoses. Rabbit lives on the side of the road opposite the creek, and his backyard is bigger than most because it's near the mouth of the hollow where the land opens and spreads a little. At the foot of the yard before the hill starts, there's the big ditch full of stuff. Corey hesitates to walk past Rabbit and right up to the gully, but from where he stands in the yard, he can already tell it's garbage and parts both. Corey knows Rabbit knows he's there, but Rabbit doesn't say anything. That's another reason people don't visit. Rabbit is buried in the freezer past his waist, only his calves and his rotten tennis shoes sticking out in the air, and around the yellowed tennis shoes, tools are fanned out, some Corey can name, most he can't. *Next week, now stop buggin me about it.* Corey can smell the tennis shoes from where he stands. Finally Corey asks, gesturing with his thumb towards the lawnmower in the driveway, "Do you have to be sixteen to drive that thing into town?"

Inside the freezer, Rabbit's tool sounds still. Then Rabbit backs out. He stands up and squints towards where Corey's thumb points. When he squints, his lips pull open, and Corey sees the car wreck of teeth on his bottom gum. Rabbit wears a grease-smeared T-shirt with something about Jesus on the front and something about a well-drilling operation on the back. "Nah, I don't think so," Rabbit says. Then he crawls back into the freezer.

Corey waits a minute or two. Then he takes a few steps towards the driveway, the mower and the cart, the twenty-five-year-old station wagon. He looks over his shoulder at Rabbit, still safely stuck in the freezer, then Corey saunters over to the station wagon and peers inside.

A year or so ago, the authorities attached to Rabbit's steering column a contraption he had to breathe into before the car would start. At first, nobody believed this, but *now that's the truth*. Lace heard it was the truth at the Dairy Queen, then somebody saw Rabbit in the Big Bear parking lot in Charleston pushing carts around and around to where he would sober up enough to start his car. Then somebody else said her husband's cousin in Welch had to do the same thing. So Dad finally went down to Rabbit's to see, and, sure enough, here was this anti-drunk-driving device the state police or Pinky McCutcheon or somebody had installed in Rabbit's car. But Dad had not taken Corey that day, and Corey couldn't for the life of him figure out how such a thing might work. Today he sees nothing unusual in the car. They must have taken it back.

Corey returns to the freezer. Rabbit's shirt is hiked up so Corey can see his bare back, and like the rest of Rabbit, the back is not reddish or yellow or tan like other part-black people Corey has seen. It's gray. And even this close, Corey can't tell if the gray is a skin color, or if it's a layer of strange tiny hairs, or if it's just dirt. Corey wonders what Rabbit's making from the freezer, but he knows better than to ask. Instead, he says, "You reckon that Cub Cadet could drive up them cement ditches on the side of the mountain?"

Rabbit doesn't bother to pull out to answer that one. "Honey, that there couldn't pull a ramp into a truck."

Corey thinks. "You could fix it so it could."

"I ain't fooling no more with that thing." Rabbit's voice rings tinny from inside the motor.

"What are you working on?" Corey asks. Rabbit does not answer.

Corey sidles away, nonchalantly in case Rabbit might look, towards the gully. Closer he gets, more jealous he is. *Where'd he find all this stuff?* worrying how many parts from the flood Rabbit had found before Corey. If Corey had only been quicker, if only school'd been out, *and probably, Rabbit, with the cart, he could carry . . .* Corey with nothing but Tommy. It is not fair. He stands on the edge of the not-quite-gully, not-quite-ditch, grass above his knees. Up on the mountain, way out of sight, he can hear the big machines working. Some of the stuff is just garbage in olive-drab bags, and some of it's just garbage in the raw—you can smell it ripening as the day heats up—but Rabbit also has appliances—a dishwasher, another washing machine, a small refrigerator, a couple push mowers, naked car engines, and—*what's that?* Some big kind of motor Corey can't recognize at first. Until into his mind comes a picture from the time they went fishing at Summersville Lake. The men pulling the big motorboats out of the water up ramps on special trailers made just for boats, the water shedding glorious as the boat surfaced back to earth, and last and magnificent, the tail end. That big raw motor pulled loose of the water, shaking and free, dripping water like a mighty dog, and the way the motor was bared out there. You couldn't exactly see all of it, couldn't see the little parts inside, but you could see enough of it to get your blood up and Corey has almost driven a boat.

It was like driving a boat, it was, there towards the end . . . The day of the May flood, Dad had gone to Madison, and before he left, he took the lawnmower and weedeater out of the truck and set them in the yard. As soon as he left, Corey pulled the lawnmower and the weedeater into the place behind the house you couldn't see from any windows because he wasn't supposed to fool with them—it was not just a lawnmower and weedeater now, it was Dad's job—but Dad was also not supposed to go to Madison without Corey, because he'd said earlier in the week Corey could maybe go. So Corey snuck the lawnmower and weedeater behind the house, and him and Tommy started working on them. Or he started working on them, and Tommy fetched Corey's tools—the steak knife, coat hanger wires, tomato stakes, bottle opener. Dad wasn't dumb enough to leave his tools behind, too.

It had rained for a couple days, so the creek was already up some and the ground still soppy, but that morning it looked like it was going to clear off. But not long after Dad left, while Corey was working on the mower, the clouds started to make, quick. The mugginess and the haze, unusual thick for May, the clouds boiled and built, and Corey nodded, *yes, you go right ahead,* the clouds like how Corey felt inside, *it was not fair,* him not able to get the cap off the oil pan, and, *you know,* pretending just wasn't enough anymore. He sat back on his heels, looked up over the ridge, *good,* all that empty violence, thunder and lightning, motor noise in the sky.

By the time the lightning started, they were inside watching TV and Mom made them shut it off so it wouldn't get hit and blow up. Which Corey wouldn't mind seeing. Very soon after the lightning, the clouds busted so wide open it was like somebody'd reached up with a knife and slashed them end to end. Mom and Tommy didn't want to watch the rain, but Corey did, so he climbed into the deep sill of the big threeway sticking-out window in the dining room at the front end of the house, the end that faced up the hollow. He knelt in the sill and watched the force of the rain.

Until he started to notice the creek. The rain actually slacked some so he could see the creek better, and he realized the creek was coming up so quick you could watch it rise. It wasn't like you could only tell if you looked away a while, then looked back. No, you could see it rise. It thrashed right up and over its banks, and there it slowed some, the

ANN PANCAKE

extra room to spread, and at that point, it was still carrying in it just the regular flood stuff, sticks and pop cans and leaf wads and such. Then the downpour eased off even more so Corey could see up the creek farther, and he looked up to the big drainage pipe above the house, and, all of a sudden, the creek took a leap. Either the pipe was jammed or there was simply too much creek for it, and the creek jumped off its belly and stood on its knees on top the drainage pipe, then took a tremendous dive right over it. Corey hollered, "Mom! There's a flood coming!"

Then Mom was beside him, said, "Oh, God," and then she was gone. By that time, the wall of creek had rushed the yard, had smacked up against the house and split around it with a hammering and a roar, this second part of the flood carrying big stuff—car parts, a mattress, but mostly what Corey could see were logs, and plenty of them, and the logs were spearing at the house, the house itself cracking and ripping, and the thuds. For the first time, Corey felt scared, but not a soft scared, it was a bright hard scared, riding the salt n pepper shaker or watching *Friday the 13th* scared, not scared like Tommy sitting on the kitchen floor, sobbing, "Where's Chancey at? Where's Chancey at?" He could hear something on the outside walls flap and zing—a piece of siding split loose—while Baron, the inside dog, perched like a rooster on the back of the couch where he could look out at it and yip. Corey stood in the sill on his knees and watched the wild water split around the house, and that was when he saw how it was like driving a boat. Like piloting a big old boat, not some little open boat, no, but like a captain in a pilothouse with a wheel. Corey put his hands on his wheel and steered.

He looks at the big motor in Rabbit's ditch. He feels the go of it buzzing in his arms. *It was like driving a boat, it was, there towards the end,* Corey told Tommy later. Bant overheard. She smacked Corey right over his ear with the hard bone in the heel of her hand.

Dane

"CLEVELAND," Mrs. Taylor is saying. "Now flat places like that, they make me feel lonely."

Dane kneels in the commode room with a bucket of Pine-Sol water and a can of Lysol, scrubbing the stains and knocking out the odor. Mrs. Taylor sags over him in her walker, directing. He sprays Lysol in circles around the bottom of the seat like she's told him to, holding his breath as long as he can, and Mrs. Taylor is saying, "Yeah, they wanna drive every last soul out of southern West Virginia, then the governor and them can just sit in Charleston and count their money." Dane stares into the empty pot.

Somebody knocks on the back door. Mrs. Taylor inhales and throttles herself into motion, heaving the walker towards the kitchen, and Dane knows it's Lucy Hill from down the road, whose well has been ruined by the blasting. Mrs. Taylor's well has held up so far, so she gives the Hills water, and they cut her grass. Dane wonders why she thinks he can't cut grass. He can hear the rumble of empty milk jug bundles as Lucy and her daughters maneuver them through the door. They will have their wagon in the backyard, and as they fill jugs at the sink, they'll bucket brigade them out the door, Lucy herself at the sink, handing off jugs to the oldest, special ed Casey Ann, then Courtney, the youngest, on the porch, passing them to Paula, the middle girl, Dane's age, who arranges them in the wagon. Dane usually helps the Hills. But he knows Mrs. Taylor won't want him moving directly from the commode room to the drinking water.

He scrubs at the floor around the metal chair, the stains from the gap between seat and pot. She's trained him. Before she cut herself down to three conversation topics, Mrs. Taylor told him how she has fought coal dust and road dust off coal trucks, has kept a clean house without garbage collection, without sewer system or city water, sometimes without septic, has suffered the stench of straight-pipe plumbing. Mopped up the black slime of Buffalo Creek. *And here in my final years, when it's my time to rest, blasting dust and flood trash and my house falling down all around me in little pieces.* She has trained him. Dane rinses and wrings out his rag, and now Mrs. Taylor is thumping back towards him. Even though water still runs in the kitchen, she feels more urgency to supervise the cleaning than the bucket brigade. Again, she hovers over him, her large failing body lodged in the walker, even the body, despite its emphysema and fatness and diabetes, antiseptically clean, smelling always of perfumed powder, the powder in smudges on her exposed skin, speckled on her blue slippers. Mrs. Taylor continues the subject of Cleveland. "And people don't speak. You may have noticed that when you-all were down there in Durham."

Dane nods, although he doesn't remember, and although they'd lived in Raleigh.

"Change rags, honey, and wipe the windowsill, and I believe we're done."

The Hills have left, and he's making them tuna salad for lunch, which he likes to do because she calls his tuna sandwiches the best. Mrs.

Taylor is chattering on about Avery, she drops the Cleveland and is just looking forward to the day he will come, when a blast goes off.

Mrs. Taylor cries out and grabs the sides of the kitchen table. A big stump whams into the bottom of Dane's chest and splashes back down in his stomach. For a terrible minute, both of them wait. But it's not as big or as close as a blast can get, soon the shaking settles, and nothing else happens. Dane breathes again. Then Mrs. Taylor, tilting her head towards the other room, gasps, "Run in there see if any more plaster come down in that bedroom."

The stump whams back up into Dane's ribs. His breath thins. He stirs his tuna.

"Did you hear me, honey?" Mrs. Taylor asks.

Dane stirs his tuna.

"Dane?"

Dane's heard. He lays down his spoon, turns, and makes himself do what she says.

This bedroom was where she slept before the ceiling started falling. Then Dane and Bant moved her things into the smaller bedroom off the kitchen, the ceiling there for some reason more stable. He remembers Bant helping him, how it made him feel both shamed and loved. Shamed at how little he could lift, at how strong Bant was, a girl; loved by Bant's patience with him, by how she clearly saw the helping as just something she would do, not something she should do. That was clear back in March or April, the bedroom didn't bother him then. Now he can hardly pass its door, and not because he's scared the roof will fall on him. Still, at least once a week, he has to haul in a can of Pledge and a vacuum cleaner with attachments and sweep fresh plaster off the floor and the furniture, the cold fish cutting in him, Dane finishing as rapidly as he can and never touching the old cabinet-style stereo, even though it is coated with dust. Now he stands rigid in the door, getting ready to tell Mrs. Taylor everything's fine and then escape into the bathroom, when Mrs. Taylor calls, "Go on in and check close, darlin. I can't bear to sit here and worry about that, too."

Dane looks down at his feet. Obedience tells his foot to move, his heart says no. Obedience wins. Dane steps in.

Besides the stereo, the room holds the smaller guest bed they swapped for Mrs. Taylor's double, covered with a dark blue chenille bedspread Dane's always having to shake out, and a chest of drawers with strange burn marks on top, and a pile of wilted cardboard boxes. Mrs. Taylor has her car packed with more boxes, Dane helped her, all the family photos, and the family Bible, and her important papers, and a pile of quilts passed down. *The young people can run for the hills when they hear the rumble,* Mrs. Taylor always says. Apparently forgetting what happened to Dane in May when he heard the rumble. But for sure Mrs. Taylor cannot run. She'll have to shuffle to her Taurus and try to drive away.

He edges on into the middle of the bedroom, keeping his body well distant from the broken stereo. But no matter how hard he tries to look away, his eyes won't leave it. His eyes are pasted to the papers scattered over the stereo's top, mostly junk mail and old magazines, and he watches like he would watch a copperhead, a black widow, he was somehow forced to pass. On top of the junk mail, full out open, not an inch of it covered, is the pamphlet. He can see.

He wants to throw the pamphlet in the creek downstream from the house. He wants to take a match to it and burn it to ash. He wants to plant it on Route 9 for a coal truck to run forty-eight tires over it and crush it to dust. But he can't do any of that. He's afraid to even close it. Even to turn it facedown. The pamphlet has a liveness in it, its paper, its ink, its staples, throb, every pamphlet part throbs with this power. The pamphlet, he knows just by standing nearby, can, in its own pamphlet way, feel and think, and worse. Do to you.

The cover of the pamphlet, which Dane can't see because the

pamphlet is open to a particular page, announces "The New Millennium: What Does the Future Hold For You?" Exactly two weeks ago, Dane had come in and there sat Mrs. Taylor, poring over the pamphlet. She waved Dane over to show him a special page that listed a bunch of categories, like a list of school subjects—"Economics," "Health," "Human Relations"—but then Dane looked more closely and realized it was a way to organize the End of the World. Even without reading very well, he saw that each category had written under it Bible verses about that subject and what would happen around the subject during the End Times, and then, under the verses, were some sentences that explained in plain English just how near the End was. The world is teetering-tottering right on the brink, the pamphlet says, get out your Bibles, please, and read: 2 Timothy for the personality traits people will exhibit during these "critical times." Matthew and Luke for the "last days." Jeremiah for "To earthling man his way does not belong," earthling man, Dane said that again in his mind. Open your Bibles, please. Mrs. Taylor, though, was tapping with her clean horny nail the category titled "Environment." "God will 'bring ruin to those ruining the earth.' Revelation 11:18." She shook her head. "Now will you just look at that."

Dane sidles through the bedroom, his eyes darting from pamphlet to floor, pamphlet to bedspread, pamphlet to boxes, checking for bits of fallen plaster. Before Mrs. Taylor had shown him the pamphlet, she had mentioned the End Times, which Dane had heard about at church, too, and he thought both Mrs. Taylor's talk and the church talk scary. But he knows now, after seeing the pamphlet, that before, he hadn't truly believed. He hadn't truly believed that it could possibly happen before he was well dead and gone until Mrs. Taylor showed it to him in writing. And it's not just some old funny-sounding verse in a beat-up Bible, it's all recently written, like a magazine or newspaper, new, and after he saw it there, everything changed. After the pamphlet, the thought started coming all the time in Dane's head: "I'm only twelve years old. And I'm going to see the End of the World."

Finally Dane backs out of the bedroom, keeping close watch on the pamphlet, then he's clear, he breathes, and he calls to the kitchen, "Nothing fell." His voice like a piece of ripped plastic caught on a branch and waving in wind. He goes in to use the bathroom but can't make anything happen, and he's all the way back to his tuna bowl when it comes to him: since he told her about the plaster, Mrs. Taylor hasn't spoken a word back.

Dane freezes. Her silence means she's thinking about something. Given the blast, he has a good idea about what.

"You know last fall two of em drownded over at Arnette? A woman and a teenage boy in a car?"

Dane swallows. He shakes his head.

"Yeah, they put the families on our prayer list. They were driving to church, downstream of one of these things we have in here."

Even though it doesn't need any more stirring, Dane whips his tuna and mayonnaise hard, the spoon ringing loud in the metal bowl. Mrs. Taylor sucks her spongy lungs full of air and lets loose a three-second sigh, the end with a tremor in it. He's held off until now because he knows if God listens to prayers at all anymore, He listens only to a certain number of them. You better be careful, ration them out. But, finally, he can't help it. He balls up a place behind his eyes.

God says nothing back.

"Here I've moved right back into it." Mrs. Taylor sighs again, squeezing a crumpled napkin in her hand. "Thirty years later, and I'm right back in it. That was Pittston, this is Lyon. But one company or another's bound to drown me before I die a natural death." Then Mrs. Taylor reaches out her hands and grips each corner of the table, the skin purpling where the wedding ring sinks in.

"Dooley never wanted to talk about it, you know. He'd get up and walk right out of the room." She always says this, and when she does, Dane always feels close to Dooley, since walk right out of the room is what Dane wants to do. But Dane is the help, not the husband. "A lot of em," she goes on, "just heard the roar and looked outside and seen that black wall of water a-coming straight at their houses. But we was further down the hollow. It had room to spread a little, you see, by the time it got to us. It was a Saturday morning, around eight o'clock, and me and the kids was sleeping in a little. Dooley wasn't home.

"He was coming off hoot owl so he was one of the ones saw it happen. Actually watched the dam break. Now can you imagine, standing up there and seeing that dam go with your family sleeping in your house down below it? Just imagine that," and Dane imagines. Not standing at the drift of Buffalo Creek Mining Company in a cold February rain twenty-eight years ago, but standing in Mrs. Taylor's backyard in a warmish one last month. "He tried to call us—all the men coming off that shift tried to call their families—but the lines was already down. It happened that fast. A lot of people just heard the noise and saw that black wall, but we was staying at Braeholm, further down the creek. What woke me was those folks who'd been driving up the hollow and seen the water coming at them, then threw their cars around and tried to outrun it, you know, with their hands blamming their horns to warn the others of us. Those crazy car horns, at a little after eight in the morning, and, at first, half asleep like I was, it made me kind of mad. I thought it was kids. But then I thought, not at eight in the morning. And I got worried and got up.

"Now you know them pictures of the clouds in Japan when they dropped the bomb?" Dane has never seen these pictures, but by now, he carries his own version in his head. "That's the kind of cloud that dam made when it caved in, Dooley said. They all said that. When the dam broke, the water behind it shot out onto the gob pile. And when the water hit that smoking gob, it exploded up in the air like a volcano and threw this steaming mud all over their windshields.

"Well, I got up and got my robe on and went out on the front porch. I could hear car horns above and below, but wasn't any cars passing right then. But once I got outside, I heard it. I did. Thought at first it was a thunderstorm, but that was February, and then I saw our next-door-neighbor's, Clarey Mason's kids, running out their side door to turn loose these goats they was keeping, and Clarey's one boy screamed at me, 'Mrs. Taylor, the dam's broke.' And I understood everything right then.

"I turned to run inside. I whammed my hip into the door frame and almost fell down, but the whole time I was screaming at the kids to get up. It wasn't until then I remembered Avery wasn't home. Avery—we called him Bucky then—was spending the night up the hollow in Lorado with a friend of his, Tad Compton. It wasn't until my other three come down out of the upstairs that I remembered Bucky, my baby, was up the hollow in Lorado."

Mrs. Taylor stops. Dane waits, his back to her. Mrs. Taylor wheezes a bubbly sigh.

"I thank the Lord to this day that my kids was big enough to get theirselves out of the house and up the hill. Deed, I don't know what I'd done if I'd had any little ones then. A lot of little ones died, you know."

This means she's going to spare him the middle because this is what she says before she gets to the very end. Dane slowly lifts his hands from the counter, swabs the tuna onto bread, and turns and sets the sandwich in front of her. He lowers himself into a chair, staring at the sparkles in the tabletop. It is sunny outside, but Dane can feel the weight. The water hovering overhead. Mrs. Taylor finally gives her ending, her benediction, which never alters, just like the prologue never does.

"Oh, we didn't lose nothing. We didn't lose nothing. Not compared to what other people lost."

She falls silent again. Then she seems to wake up and notice her food. "Honey, ain't you gonna eat something?"

"I ain't too hungry," Dane says.

Mrs. Taylor nods. She picks up her own sandwich. When she lays it back down without tasting it, she misses her plate.

Bant

BY THE TIME Lace's ride dropped her off from the Dairy Queen, the rest of us had long been in bed, but I'd hear her. Lace never knew when her shift would end because they stayed open until the manager decided there wasn't another soul in the county wanted a bite of ice cream, "worse'n working in a bar," Lace would say. "At least in a bar, you know last call's before two." But I'd hear her, even when I didn't want to. I slept light, and my room was on the road. She'd wake me with the car door slamming. And back in the spring, when I heard her, I could make myself not care, force myself to lie there, will myself to sleep. But after me and Jimmy drove up to the fill, I couldn't help it. I'd get up. I started having to listen.

Nights that summer I slept light. Penned in my little room, like sleeping in a stall it was. A blast from the mine had messed up my window so it wouldn't open right, and the gas smell built. Me float-ing always in a gasoline hover. Hobart was too cheap to buy tur-pentine, so it was gas I used to wash off the paint, a bad blue that lodged in your eye after looking too long. I found out why Hobart'd nodded when I'd told him fifteen, turned out he was paying me under minimum because, he said, I wasn't yet sixteen. "That cheap bastard," Jimmy Make would say. "I'm gonna report him." But he wouldn't. We needed even that little bit of money too bad. The gas took off most of the paint on my skin, but then I couldn't get rid of the gas, and how much would it take on you to catch fire? Hard to tell. I painted every day in the same cutoff white jeans, in one of two paint-ruint T-shirts I handwashed every night to get out the sweat. I wore those paper caps that came with the paint, but my hair was so used to falling forward to cover my face it was always dragging in the cans and matting up blue. And then, more gasoline. The miners drove nice trucks with out-of-state tags—Illinois, Wyoming, Indiana, Kentucky—and I learned they worked twelve-hour shifts running heavy equipment unless the company wanted them to work longer, and then they did. Few were union, so they had no choice. Besides working, they couldn't do much but eat, shower, and sleep, but still, to get from work to bed, bed to work, they had to climb the wooden stairs, walk the porches that ran around the place. They had to pass me.

Squatting in my paint clothes, a cloud of gasoline and sweat, drawing my brush or roller back and forth, back and forth, I'd feel the steps shake as they came my way. I'd feel the floor tremble. I'd turn away on my knees, draw up closer to the wall, and stare at my brush, it flicking. Hump my shoulders, toss my hair forward to screen my face. But there was no way to keep their eyes off me. Just them passing at my back put a bad heat in my skin, and then it was not just the paint, the gas, and Hobart I had to suffer, it was being looked at by strange men, too. Although, it is true, they said little to me. Except the one who asked, "You got a sister?" The fat one who teased me for hiding my face. And the youngest one, a skinny boy, who drove a big Ford pickup with Ohio plates.

Then my best friend Sharon started going away from me. We'd been friends since second grade, two of the few girls from then still around. I had helped her through the grades, let her copy off me. She lived not far from Hobart's in one of the made-over company houses as you headed out of town, and although she never ate lunch because she was trying to lose weight, she'd sit with me when I did. While I was made of boards, Sharon, she was made of bubbles. She wasn't fat yet, no, she was what they liked to look at, thigh-squeezing shorts, her chest lunging against last summer's tops, but she'd be fat soon, Sharon knew. Despite the copying, Sharon was what you'd call a good person, always worried about hurting someone's feelings, went twice a week to church, struggled over the right thing to do. For the last six months, she'd been going with Donnie, five years older than us, and since Donnie, she'd closed shut to me in places. It was already familiar to me, how a girl'd get with a boy like that. Places you could no longer go with her even when she'd talk about the boy nine-tenths of the time. But Sharon had never gone away on me like that, and now that she did, it made me wonder more than it made me mad. I had been a lot of places, but these closed places were one place I hadn't yet seen. And at times, I'd think on it. Donnie. He didn't look like much to me. Then I'd think about Lace and Jimmy.

For a long time, I never saw that Ohio boy clean. I only saw him in the mornings when he was coming off night shift, so pale-blown with dust I couldn't even tell the color of his hair. By the time he went back in the evenings, I was gone. In the mornings, I'd feel his eyes on me, like I did the others' eyes, but one time, with him, I turned and looked back. Pale-blown, he was, no black on him. A different kind of miner. Different kind of mine.

With the part of the money Lace let me keep, I bought every skin treatment the Dollar General sold. I slipped in there during lunch, my hair dangling forward, shoulders hunched, hopeful the cashiers would forget who I was. They did not. There was no privacy in this county, "no secrets in this town," everybody said. At least not about people, I'd think. At best, I learned, the skin stuff would dry up the spots so you could see them even whiter, and along the way, dry up what good skin was left. But it wasn't just my skin, I knew, that was the problem. It was the high jag of the cheekbones, the hollows under them. It was the long bony nose, my eyes too small, my chin too thin. And you couldn't buy nothing for those.

Scraping the old paint was the worst. Those nettling paint chips stuck to my slick skin, the fingernail on blackboard sound, and the sweat bees drawn to my stickiness. Knocking wasp nests out of eaves—how many times was I stung that summer? Grandma'd known something in the woods would pull out the hurt, but I couldn't remember what it was, and busy as I'd been, I never saw Mogey and Mary. Now and again I'd rock back on my haunches, away from the bad blue walls, and I'd look up onto the hills around me. Rumpled over with the heavy trees, those green, those holding hills, them holding you, and looking was like touching moss to the lid of your eye.

The Ohio boy took to coming out of his room more often. His dust washed away (dust from where exactly?), him passing me, and I found myself watching him, just a little and despite myself. Even if some of them were union, didn't matter, "a scab for your new millennium," Jimmy would say. Scab. A thing that makes you want to pick.

One of those afternoons, the Ohio boy told me his name was R.L. He didn't bother to ask mine. Just tossed the name over his shoulder as he climbed the stairs to his room.

I'd taken to walking up the road behind the house when I got home in the evenings. Up to the new gate with a brand-new lock. After I got done with the supper dishes would be my first free time since I'd woke up, and I'd walk in the cool coming on, the hollow narrow there, long early twilight, and I'd stop at the gate. I'd stand there without touching it. The bugs starting to chant. I'd stay there for a while, staring past it towards the head of Yellowroot Hollow. Then I'd turn around and walk back home.

Those nights when I couldn't help it, when I had to listen, I'd find Lace in the living room with just the one lamp lit. She'd have her shoes already off. She'd be drawn up on the couch with her knees bent, her back against an armrest, and she'd have a window open. Blowing cigarette smoke out the screen. Straining her neck a little, and when I'd walk in, she'd push out the smoke, a sucking sob, and "Hi, honey" was what she'd say.

I wouldn't say much back. I wouldn't sit. I'd lie on my back in the middle of the floor, far from her cigarette glow. She'd be running her little radio low, that hillbilly music, twangy and urgent. Carried high in the head. I'd spread my arms and legs to catch any air that might be moving down there, and when Lace started talking, I couldn't help it. My stomach would draw up under my heart. She'd start with the easy things, funny stories, what happened at work, or people who'd got on her nerves, or who all'd come in that night, stuff I didn't have time to hear. Then, after not too long, she'd start complaining about Jimmy Make. That was worst of all, me lying there, needing to hear what mattered, but scared to hear, desperate for her to get to it and over with, and she'd have to run through her Jimmy routine. Because, yeah, Jimmy Make irritated and disappointed and confused me, too, but still, once in a while, I'd go on and say it, I'd say, "Mom, that's just how he is." Wanting to add, "You're the one married him, how could you not see how he is?"

Then the hillbilly music would turn Jesusy, although it stayed twangy, it stayed high in the head. And the talk of Jimmy Make, his lack of spine, would finally carry Lace to what I needed to know. The Dairy Queen was one of the few places in town where people could gather anymore, and while Lace was working, she was told an awful lot, and on top of that, she eavesdropped, she overheard. Lace's brain worked fast ("My wife's smarter'n me, I'm not ashamed to admit it," Jimmy Make would snicker. "Smart enough to marry me, wasn't she?"), and wound taut like it was with so little to catch on, sometimes it would skip cog teeth and spin, crazy and quick.

She'd tell me where the newest permits were going—"Lyon's put in for another one there on the far side of Carney, so the water'll be coming down on Burginville next"—and she'd tell me who was getting laid off and where. She'd been telling me this stuff for a year, but now I had to listen. She'd tell me about the latest blackwater, the latest fish kills—"Maureen said up there at Rock Branch she can't even walk into her back bedroom, stink's so bad"—tell me who was selling out now. At first, I'd roll towards her as she told me, I'd raise up a little so I could see her, while she told of overloaded coal truck wrecks—"they couldn't even tell them three kids apart, mangled up bad as they were"—fly rock crashing into people's houses, chemical leaks in sediment ponds. Drownings in flash floods, people breathing cancer-causing dust. But it was still hard to believe her, even if I had to listen, how hard it was to believe things could get that bad. The government or the companies or God or whoever was in charge, it seemed to me they just wouldn't let it get like that. Seemed to me like they couldn't.

Then she'd go too far. Even though I'd come out to the living room all on my own, even though I had to hear—there'd come a point where I couldn't take no more, where I'd suddenly think: I'm just a kid. I'd look at her ranting from the couch over top of me, and then I'd slide far away from her, without really moving at all. There she'd be, across a wide river from me, waving a cigarette and ranting away, and I'd think, *Why do you tell me everything? This is not how moms do on TV, not how my friends' moms do, not even what you do with the boys. Go on. Keep away that flame.* "And Nathan Brill said he's heard too Deer Lick was piping slurry up above Yellowroot." And there it'd be.

Because no matter what else she told, she always got back to piping slurry up on Yellowroot. The rumor she'd been hearing that the coal processing plant at Deer Lick had filled the old impoundments where it stored its liquid waste and was now pumping slurry into a new impoundment behind the Yellowroot valley fill.

Then even the Jesus music would sign off, the station would go static until the obits at five AM, and Lace would drag off to her and Jimmy's bed and sleep. But I would not. Burrowed back in my little room, I'd breathe through the sheet to strain out the gas, but then I'd feel about to smother. All summer, that double pressure. Something about to give, to bust. Flood or flame.

When they'd first get started, they'd fight in code. No privacy in that house, so while they were still to themselves, they'd fight on the slant, until they got to where they didn't care, and then they'd fight wide open. Lace would be too tired to fight when she got home at night and Jimmy Make'd be in bed, so mostly they'd fight in the late mornings and early afternoons. Baron, the little dog, he loved it when they fought. It got his little dander up and set him into a prance. Dane would be at Mrs. Taylor's, that was good. It upset him most, even though he said nothing. Corey, of course, took Jimmy Make's side, such as he could, Jimmy Make not wanting any help, and Tommy trying to interrupt with stupid questions, like why's cheese yellow when milk's white? And the fight going—

If you're so goddamned certain that fill's coming down, then why the hell don't you let us leave out of here?

Because a coal company's not going to run me out of my house and off my land. If you had any spine, you'd fight em with me.

It ain't a matter of spine, it's a matter of common sense. I've worked for em. I know you can't fight em. You won't never win.

At least I'll die trying.

Yeah, you and the kids, too, not to mention me.

Thought you believed we wouldn't ever get washed out?

I'm talking about starving to death. I'm talking about how there ain't no work around here and you know it.

Oh, you could get a job around here. You're just too good for em.

Well, I will starve to death before I make pizzas. Not when there's jobs going begging in North Carolina.

You're just like the rest of em. Too chickenshit to fight anything but their wives.

And what the hell are you doing to fight? Making phone calls nobody answers? Running your mouth down at the Dairy Queen? Why don't you go on up there and lie down in front of one of them dozers, you're so keen?

Then it would unravel into name-calling—*lazy, crazy, chickenshit, dumb*—and then it would drill back into the past, old bad things jerked from the closets of their minds, and occasionally it would bank down, you'd think they were finished. Yet about the time you let out your breath, here it would flare back up, house-fire high. But the bottom line never changed: Lace wanted to stay, even though she was convinced we'd be washed out. Jimmy Make wanted to leave, even though he didn't think it would ever get as bad as Lace thought.

Of course, we'd left before. Four years ago, when Jimmy Make got laid off at Witcher Run, we went to North Carolina, left Grandma behind. We lasted almost two years, and by the time we came back, the company had reopened Witcher Run under a different name and made sure not to rehire any former union men. And Grandma was gone.

Lace

I TOLD Jimmy Make two weeks after I saw the doctor, us parked again in my dad's car under a shutdown coal silo about six miles from Jimmy's house. February, just above freezing, and a rain coming down with a hardness to it, crackling a little when it hit the windshield and roof. I'd thought it'd be Mom who'd be hardest to tell, but now I sat with a balloon in my chest, and every time I started to say, the balloon'd press up and shut my throat down. We'd been there long enough for the car to get cold, I was sitting on top of my hands, and I glanced sideways at Jimmy Make, but he was just sipping, content, from his can. By this time, we should have been all over each other, surely Jimmy Make must sense something was wrong, and why wouldn't he say something, help me out? I swallowed, hard, opened my mouth. Swallowed again. And, at last, Jimmy Make asked me why I wasn't drinking the beer I'd bought him. Apparently the waste of beer was most on his mind.

I said it looking straight into the dark hillside out the window. There was no way I could have said it while looking at him. After I did, he asked, "Are you sure?"

"Yeah," I said. "I did the store-bought test. Then I went to the doctor, too."

Then I did turn towards him, just the corner of my right eye, because I had to know what he thought. He'd put his beer can between his legs and was staring at it. Rubbing his thumb around its rim.

"Does this—," he started. He stopped and rubbed another circle around the can. "Does it mean you want to marry me?"

"No," I said, and then I looked out the side window away from him, into the icy rain, and I wondered how bad the roads would be getting home. I remember plain thinking no more than relief that at last he knew, and wanting to get away from him and home.

He nodded. Picked up his can and swallowed the rest. When I dropped him off at his house, he kissed me good-bye, but I didn't meet his tongue. Not until the next day, replaying it all in my head, did I notice how the "are you sure" hadn't been followed by "it's mine." I'd had enough pregnant friends to know how often that got asked. Then I realized Jimmy Make hadn't asked it because he wasn't unsimple enough even to wonder. And then I didn't know whether to laugh or cry.

I was the first Ricker, the first See, to go to college, and now I disappointed my family three ways: first, by getting pregnant; second, by dropping out; and third, by refusing to marry Jimmy Make. It was the third one hurt them the most because that one they understood least. But I could not marry Jimmy Make. The marriage would fall too short too soon of the life I'd always seen for myself. It was just as simple as that. The baby I had no choice about—you don't around here, especially not back then—but the marriage, that I could decide. Since I couldn't get rid of the baby, the only other choice it seemed I could make was get rid of myself.

I thought about that second choice for nearly two months. Late February, all of March, into April, rain and darkness and everything used-up looking. I burrowed back into my room, turned off the lights, and pulled my knees to my chest.

It's funny, how I remember that time and don't. A forgetting with vivid holes. I remember in bright spots, everything else dim or gone. The little knobs on my bedspread fielding out eye-level. The cracks and stains on the ceiling and walls, pools of blood, I'd see them, ghosts, animals deformed. Hurling my radio against the wall because it would bring in nothing but country except at night, and how I didn't know it when my birthday came, and Mom left an untouched piece of cake on my dresser for four solid days. I remember being doubled over on the linoleum at the foot of the commode, if only I could throw it up, I didn't think of it as a baby inside, but as a deadly illness I had to cure. And I remember Daddy's breathing in the living room when both Mom and Sheila left and we were alone. The doctor'd finally put him on oxygen, tubes through his nose, and now every rasp breath came a *shick. Shick. Shick.* A spider in his web, I couldn't help but hear him, trapping one breath. One breath. One breath more.

I learned what it is to grieve your life lost while you're still living, and I learned that there are few losses harsher than that. It was grief beyond anything I'd imagined. I can still feel sometimes that dry raw socket. The slash, then the body-burning pain. For so many years, I'd only seen myself at all, I realized then, because I could see myself as different, as more than ordinary. The sweet peach-pink. But now I saw that was a make-believe choice I'd only pretended I'd had.

Daddy got over his disappointment pretty fast, why cry? milk's spilled. Mom reacted exactly like I knew she would. Because when you did something really bad, Mom never did get angry at you, that would have been too easy, would have given you too much credit, too much respect. Instead, she'd let you know, without saying much of anything, that you'd disappointed her so deep you didn't even deserve her anger. Weren't even worth the energy of that. Mom kept me fed, tried to keep me clean, made me get out of bed and on top of it even if she couldn't force me out of the room, all the while throwing off that disgusted disappointment. And I knew it was supposed to make me want to prove myself back into her favor, but all I felt, once I got to the point where I could feel anything at all, was fuck your disappointment. Fuck it.

Once in a while during those dark months, Jimmy Make would call. Sometimes I'd talk to him, sometimes I'd say I was too sick. Once I knew about the baby for sure, the Jimmy Make spell had cracked wide open and blown far away. Jimmy Make was a stranger to me again. When I did talk to him, he had even less to say than he'd had before. "How are you feelin?" was about as far as he could get. And at times, I'd feel a blunted anger at him, for what he'd done to me, and for his childishness. But I was in all kinds of other pain then, and truth was, Jimmy Make didn't any longer matter enough to make me feel much.

By April, I still had spells of tiredness felt like stones packed in my bones, but my nausea was fading. And because of that, and I guess because I was simply getting used to the loss—what a person can get used to, if I've learned nothing else in my life, I've learned that—once in a while, and just for a little bit, I might take a peek out of that tunnel I'd dug for myself. But I was denned up good that April afternoon, pouring rain and cold, not much above forty, when the scrape of muddy boots on the porch steps brought me full awake. In the living room, Daddy cleared his throat and hollered, louder than he needed to, "Well, c'mon in there, Mogey!"

I curled up tighter on myself, my knees nearly to my chin. I'd woke up needing to go to the bathroom, but now I'd have to wait, I'd made sure not a soul had seen me aside from Mom, Dad, and Sheila since I'd come back from Morgantown, and I wasn't walking through the living room now. "Does make it easier to draw breath, I'll tell ya,"

Daddy was saying in his loud company voice, and the cheerful in it made me even madder. "Can't complain." Then I heard Mogey, quieter, only a rumble to his voice, couldn't tell what he said, and Daddy, "Cold, ain't it? Gonna get a late start on fishin this spring."

I jammed my pillow over my head, and when that didn't work, I punched my fingers in my ears. My drawn-up legs holding my bladder. I lay there like that for many minutes, willing Mogey the hell out of here and on home, until my ears finally hurt so bad, I had to pull my fingers out. When I did, I heard a tapping on my door.

I knew it wasn't Mom. Mom would bang and yap "Lace!" at the same time, so I pretended I didn't hear it. I rolled over and faced the wall. The tapping didn't stop. He'd tap a while, then rest a while, I could feel him on the other side of the door, then he'd start again. Mogey was a hard one to give a no to, even a no you weren't actually having to say, but I told myself, just hold out. Still, he kept on, and finally I slammed my fist in my pillow, jerked upright, and dropped my feet to the floor. I wasn't wearing a bra, just a T-shirt and an old pair of sweats, and when I moved, the cloth of the shirt stung my nipples. I stepped over to the mirror above Sheila's dresser, reached up to smooth my hair, and then, a hand on each side of my head, I stopped. Because what I saw there scared me. I'd been glancing in that mirror for months, but now I actually looked, and it scared me. I backed quick away, hit the end of the bed with the back of my legs so fast I half fell on it. Then I pushed myself up, crossed to the door, and set my hand on the knob. I opened it the width of my face.

"Hi, Lace," Mogey said.

He looked me straight on, then dropped his eyes down and to the side. I knew it was out of politeness, had nothing to do with shy. I wanted to be mad when I opened the door, tell him leave me alone, but both the sight in the mirror and the gentleness of Mogey stopped me. Gentleness of Mogey always had. He had his dark green khaki hat folded in his hand, his thinning blond hair crushed uneven, like a kid who just got up from sleeping, and I could smell off him woodsmoke and coffee. He didn't ask me how I was. I appreciated that.

"Mary's got a real bad cold," he was saying. "I was counting on her to help me dig ramps tomorrow. Don't got another day off for a week and I promised the fire department I'd get some for their feed. You wanna go with me?"

I knew it wasn't just because Mary'd caught a cold, and I figured Mom could go just as easy as me, Mom'd already been getting in the woods every day. I wondered had she put him up to it. I started feeling for words to say no, but then Mogey's voice, the soft flannel, dropped to a whisper. "Your mom don't know I'm asking you. It's just you and me, Lace."

I looked over my shoulder then, buying time more than anything else. I saw the wrinkle of my body on the bedspread. The mirror, now without me in it. I turned back to Mogey, although I didn't look at him. I sighed. "Okay," I said.

He picked me up in his truck the next morning between rains. The sky a fresh-washed watery blue and the clouds on the move, and as I stood out there under it, waiting for him, my insides felt like that sky. Thin clouds blowing through me. Once I was in the truck, Mogey talked light at me, to keep me comfortable, I understand now, because I was too sucked in on myself to recognize it then. He drove us down Route 9 a ways, then turned up the dirt road to Carney Mountain, and I realized I hadn't been back in there since I was twelve or thirteen, although I'd probably gone every spring before that.

Higher we pulled the road, quieter Mogey got. I didn't say anything either. I hadn't been out in three months, and I tell you, it was like light in your eyes after a long darkness, only it was not just my eyes, but my self felt that way. A squint with my whole body, and I pulled my jacket closer. No leaves on the trees yet, no redbud or dogwood either, but nubbly little coltsfoot nudging up out of the ditches, and you could see sarvis here and there. Like fairy's breath, I remembered that's how I'd thought about it when I was little, but I hadn't thought about it at all in such a long time. Finally Mogey pulled over as far as he could get on the narrow road and shut off the engine. He pointed up the hill. "Should be up that little draw there."

Then he was out and throwing his leg over a small stream, carrying his shovel and hoe, and I was following with a big empty white detergent bucket in each hand, the trowels rattling inside them. I had a hard time pulling just that short draw, a rise I would have leapt in no time just six months before, that worried me a little, and then I saw it. The wide patch of fresh new green spearing up out of the dead leaves. *First thing out of the ground you can eat,* it was Mom talking in my head, and Mogey was already loosening the dirt with his shovel while I just stood there. The body-long squint. Then Mogey said, "Get you a trowel."

I got down on the dead damp leaves. Then my knees were pushing deeper into the black loam under that, and I could smell the ramps from where Mogey was already pulling them up. I shoved my trowel in the ground and starting working around the bulbs, easing them out, careful not to nick or chop. Then I was just digging, and after a while, I realized I'd dropped the trowel altogether and was working them out with my hands, my fingers mud-crusted, the black pushing up under my nails. I worked steady with my hands only, not thinking, dropping them into the buckets by their hair, first the clump sounds as they hit the plastic bottom, then no sound at all as the bucket filled up. And then, suddenly it seemed to me, Mogey surprised me with his laughing.

"That's enough there, Lace." I looked up. "No reason to dig em all. Other folks'll be up here, too."

We hauled the buckets back to the truck, and then we washed our hands clean as we could get them in the run. Afterwards, Mogey swung back on his haunches and pulled out his knife to pry the last of the mud from under his nails. "You know," he said. "I'm giving my half to the Fire Department, but they're buying, too. What if I sell your half to em?"

I shook my head. "Half ain't mine, Mogey. All of em's yours."

"Like heck they ain't yours." He snapped his knife shut. "Hard as you were going at it." He pulled my bucket to him and looked down in. I'd dug as much as he had with his shovel. "They are yours, or I'll throw em out on the ground right here."

I lifted a hand to push my hair back out of my face, smelled in my fingers the dirt still ground in my skin. "Okay," I said to him. "Okay." I nodded. "Go on ahead."

The next morning, while Sheila dressed, ate, and left for the turn-around to catch her ride to work, I stayed in bed like I always did. "Lace, get up out of there and make that bed," Mom called in at me, and then I listened until the house door shut behind her and the shed door slapped open. I peeked out my window to see which way she'd go so I could go the opposite, and after she disappeared up the Ricker Run, I got some jeans on and slunk into the kitchen. Daddy sat in the living room listening to the nine AM obits and sucking after breath. He didn't hear me slip a few paper bags under my arm. Mom hadn't left anything in the shed to dig with besides this heavy old thing closer to a mattock than a shovel, but I took that. Then I headed straight up on Cherryboy.

That was the mid-'80s, people leaving the coalfields in droves, unemployment in the double digits across most of the state and over twenty around here. We had Dad's check, miner's pension, we didn't have much else. After those first couple months when it became clear me and the baby were going to be around for a long time, I had money to worry about on top of everything else, and my guilt about it was almost bigger than my worry. Jimmy Make was only a sophomore in high school, not even old enough to drop out and work. Sheila'd got on at a little sewing factory down at Labee making one dollar over minimum, but they had a long waiting list for a few spots, they'd never take me. Far as I could figure out, there wasn't a place within fifty miles might give me work, and although I had no choice but to get a medical card, I knew Mom would throw a fit over food stamps or welfare. But now, whether he'd meant to or not, Mogey had shown me a way I should have seen from the beginning. Hadn't because of how stuck I still was pretending I was different.

Truth was, I'd had plenty of practice. Mom had always kept those old-time ways, she'd step them up or ease them down depending on how tight things got. A tight we'd got in then. *You can live off these hills,* she loved to say, *everything was put in them for a reason,* but I'd stopped listening by the time I hit age twelve. Old people talking. Before I got hazed over with the peach-pink, though, I'd helped—the gathering, the digging, the gardening, the canning—and as I climbed Cherryboy that April morning, for the first time since December I felt my spirit stand up inside of me and push.

I tried for a week. By the third morning, Mom and Dad both realized what I was up to, but Mom said nothing and Daddy just said good luck. But what I knew by the second day was how much I'd forgotten, or maybe just never really known. I knew ramps and molly moochers must be in season, but I wasn't sure where to look for either one. The few morels I did find I just stumbled onto, and there weren't enough of them to try to sell. I wondered how much I must have just followed along as a kid and done what I was told. I wondered how much might have been washed out of me by those years of looking hard away. I kept at it. I was frustrated, but I was hardheaded, I spent all day every day out there, tired, tired, I tried. I got angry at myself, I even broke down and cried that last day when I didn't find a single thing. But I couldn't give up.

After a week, I saw something had to change. That morning when

Mom headed out to the shed, I followed. I didn't say a word. She didn't, either. Once we were standing in the dank dim, my face hot with embarrassment and anger, she just handed me a hoe and sack. She picked up her own stuff and turned to go, but halfway out the door, she stopped and looked down at my hands. "Anybody works with me," she said, "has to wear gloves." She leaned her things against the wall and rooted in a crate. After a minute or two, she pulled out a pair, cobwebby, but nearly new, and she slapped them against her thigh to shed the spider dirt.

I wore those gloves for the next four years. I wore them until they were more hole than glove.

Mom had married and raised her children late, she was in her fifties those years we ran the woods together. A round muscly woman who never wore pants, glasses she hadn't changed since I was born, lord, how they used to embarrass me, and brown hair with steel rimming through it that she set each night with curlers, her only vanity, I guess, if it was that. When we walked the hills, she wore a zip-up sweatshirt over her dress, those see-through plastic boots over top her oxfords, and I never saw her slip. That first desperate year we hunted anything we had the least chance of selling, stuff I hadn't even known you could use, could eat. Yeah, ramps and molly moochers, but also Shawnee lettuce and woolly britches and poke. Yellowroot before the sap.

If I close my eyes and look back on that spring, the first thing I see is Mom moving ahead of me, her burr-shaped body there. Me dragging behind, hauling sack, bucket, trowel, clippers, whatever we'd need that day. I see everything as heavy and on a steep slant, I see it in grays and browns, no green, and once in a while, I remember, I'd slip all the way back into the tunnel again.

For the most part, though, I stubborned on. I still carried that river-rock weight in my bones, I was tired every day, but I'd just harden my head to a numb, and if nothing else, the grief would hang off to the side, like it had that first day digging ramps. Most of the time, I felt like some dumb scolded little kid, Mom the know-it-all boss, but occasionally, just occasionally, after the first few weeks, Mom would shift. And we'd be grownups together for a while. Then, once in a while, I could again see the beauty of the place. I'd see the beauty quick and sharp, and as we moved into summer, despite the haze, the heat, I started seeing it more often.

It was also in the woods where the baby first moved. May, and I'll always remember the spot, I've shown it many times to Bant since. Mom and me were hauling ourselves up a steep hollowside way back in the Upper Cove, the leaves a mucky slipperiness, we had to walk careful using the sides of our feet to keep ourselves from falling. We'd both stopped near the top to catch breath, me braced against the hoe and Mom leaning on a pignut tree, when I felt something like a gas pain, sudden and sharp. I heard myself make a whimper. Mom looked back at me, saw my hand on my belly, and right away she knew. She smiled at me. And if I didn't feel myself smile back. There Bant made herself for the first time real.

By then it was garden time, we laid rows and rows. Got Mack Kile with his tractor to plow and disk, then we furrowed by push plow, sowed and weeded by hoe and by hand. We worked her close. When I look back on that summer, I see first the pie plates for spooking the crows, rattling and flashing in breeze and in sun. I smell the tang of tomato vine, the scent of corn tassel, of where the green bean snaps loose. I remember Daddy in a lawn chair, his tank alongside him, shucking ears into a bucket, doing what he could. I feel the wet heat, the damp dammed down between the ridges, and everything with a weight to it, even the blank of the sky. Mom and me sweated over the rows, weeding, then picking, and with Bant moving inside, it seemed like she already struggled right along with us. By that August, the grief was no longer a constant slash. It didn't lose its fierceness, and it never left me altogether, but it tore at me less often. But I also know, when I look back now, that already that summer, the peach-pink was gone.

Jimmy Make came over exactly twice. He'd finally turned sixteen and got his license in May. Both times we sat out on the porch, me in the swing, pushing off a little with one foot, him hunkered over in a lawn chair, elbows on his legs, his cap half-hiding his eyes, and his jaw jutted out. He was shorter than ever on things to say, and I didn't have the energy or the desire to hold up the conversation for us both, so we just sat there with the swing creaking. Neither of us made a move towards touching, much less sex, god knows that was the last thing I wanted then, and Jimmy Make, I figured out later, was afraid he'd hurt the baby. Without the want of him, I realized I didn't know how to feel. I didn't know what else was left. I looked at him, picking at where the knee of his jeans was wearing out, and although my mind knew he'd fathered this baby, it still wasn't real for me in any way but bare mental. Through those terrible hard months since January, it seemed to me now, me and the baby'd got bound inside this tight tough circle: the woods work, the garden work, Mom, Dad, Sheila, house, mountain, hollow. Jimmy Make was a thousand miles outside all that.

The second time was August, and I really wished he hadn't come. I was already embarrassed about how big I'd got, and then I caught the surprise on Jimmy's face when he saw my belly after six weeks away. That made me outright mad. We sat there on the porch for a while, saying nothing after a few sentences at the start, me thinking how much work I had to do, why wouldn't he just go on and leave, when he said, "Can I touch it?"

I was so surprised he'd spoke up without me asking a question first that I didn't know what he meant. "Touch what?"

"Your stomach."

I looked down at it. I wanted to say no, then I thought how that might not be fair, so I shrugged. Jimmy Make waited a few seconds, then he rose out of his chair, but not all the way. In this bent-over crouch, not a stand, but not a real squat—as though if necessary, he could make a quick getaway—he crept over to me on the swing with his hand sticking out.

Once he got close enough, he waited again, several seconds. My body drew away. I could feel the heat off him, he was that close. I could smell his breath. Then he laughed, ducked back, and shook his head. But in the seconds he was close, I sensed for the first time the excitement he had for this child.

I went hard against it. Up to the moments he'd bent there in front of my body, up to where I could feel his heat, his breath, I'd thought of that baby as mine alone. And why shouldn't I? What I'd gone through, what I'd lost to have it. While Jimmy Make, far as I could see, had suffered nothing at all. I pushed back on the swing, stood up, and told Jimmy Make I'd suddenly got sick. I told him he better go home.

That night was so hot I couldn't even get cooled on the porch, so I left it and walked to the back of the house, to where the dark yard blotted into woods. I stood at the edge, but then I felt the trees drawing me on up, and even though I knew it'd be a hard risky climb, big as I was, I pulled the steep anyway, one hand cupping my belly like that would cushion it from harm. I reached the big white oak, and I leaned my side against it, and when my breath started coming normal, I looked up at Cherryboy. And although I could see only the very bottom of it before it ran out of light, I could feel it rising solid above me.

It had been almost exactly a year since I'd left for Morgantown. I realized it was that, too, had been tearing at me all day. I turned my forehead against the trunk, and I ground it in until it hurt. I needed that little pain there. But then I remembered how up in Morgantown nothing had touched me. That great swallowing lonesomeness I'd felt for known place.

I recalled that late afternoon last October when I'd climbed up here, in a rage at Mom and, yes, at myself. And I recalled the question I'd tried to ask myself then but couldn't get to, all racing like I was in my head. Now I had words for that question. *What is it? What makes us feel for our hills like we do?* I waited. The chunging of cicadas around me, the under-burr of the other insects. Something small twisting through the always dead leaves. And although I didn't get an answer, I did know you'd have to come up in these hills to understand what I meant. Grow up shouldered in them, them forever around your ribs, your hips, how they hold you, sit astraddle, giving you always, for good or for bad, the sense of being held. It had something to do with that hold.

That year, we canned tomatoes, green beans, pickles, peppers, corn, blackberries. We'd always canned before, but never like that. Daddy snapped beans, sliced cucumbers, he'd help until he got tired, and even Mogey and Mary pitched in for a few days when I knew they had theirs to do, too. Their youngest boy Kenneth sat cross-legged on the floor, moving his plastic horses around. To watch him brought a tenderness in me, then a panic strong enough to gut my breath. With those jars boiling, window panes streaming down, the kitchen felt like the inside of a blister, a body heat and body wet like that. It was during one of those last canning days that Bant decided to come.

Bant

I WOKE UP and saw the sky clear as a shout. No haze, deep blue, kind of sky we didn't often get around here in July, and the temperature unseasonable cool. Yesterday I'd run out of paint, and Hobart hadn't yet got into Beckley to get more. He'd been mad because I hadn't told him earlier that I was getting to the end of the bucket, but he couldn't do much but tell me not to come in today. And it was like this day knew about me—no threat of rain, fewer gnats, less sweat, and maybe the slope would be drier, simpler to handle. Climbing weather.

I laid low until the boys and Chancey went off somewhere, then I snuck up the road and stopped at the gate. Took a quick look for guards and slipped on under. Then I just stood there in the unruined part of the hollow, the way I had with Jimmy Make that evening, smelling that green around me. So many flavors of plant. Sometimes I'd wonder. I had a pretty good idea how Corey and Dane felt about it, but sometimes I'd wonder on Tommy, if Corey had already spoiled it for him. Because when I was real little, moving over this land, I never saw myself, never felt myself, as separate from it. I didn't even know to think about it at that age. It wasn't until I got older that something started rising up between it and me, and I started feeling a distance, almost a distance more in time than in space, like the land is in a different time from you, a stiller one, and you're always just past it. And every year since I was about nine it had gotten harder and harder to get back to how I was in it as a little kid, but this year was worse by far. For a while I'd wondered if growing up would mean I just couldn't open to it anymore. Now I was thinking something else was going on. As it was being taken, seemed I was drawing away.

I started on up, keeping my head low like that would hide me from the guards, then I realized how stupid that was. The sky so blue it had a hardness to it, like you might reach up and hit the underside of a blue-domed skull. Usually in July, this time of morning, the sky'd be taking on a haze, and by noon, the whole thing would be milky. Come August, the sky would whiten up by nine AM, sometimes with a tinge of poison yellow, but this year it seemed the seasons were running backwards. The summer strangely cool and wet following a warm snowless winter, that winter following the worst drought summer in sixty years. Anymore, seemed there was either too much water or too little, the temperature too high or too low. "Strange as this weather has been," people would say, or, "With this crazy weather we've been having." And I knew Lace believed the weather was linked to the rest of this mess, but I wasn't sure how.

Then I was in the part where the trees were sliding down the hollow sides, I was passing those sediment ponds, simmering in themselves, so green with God-didn't-even-know-what I couldn't see a quarter inch under their surface. I had my ears pricked for guards even though I realized I had no idea how a coming guard might sound, we never saw Lyon's nosers drive up in here, so they must have slunk around on foot, and what would you hear? Dirt hiss as they took the long slide off the rim? A crunkle of rocks? I heard nothing but the machines destructing overhead. It sounded different up in here, you could hear it more clear, the noises separated out—revving motors and backup beepers and crashes and bangs. Scrape of that humongous shovel against rock.

I tried to squint through the tore-up trees to the used-to-be ridge, thinking of guards perched up there with binoculars, pistols. Most of the ponds were jammed with logs and junk, I could see it even better now on foot than I had in the truck, and that meant next time it flooded, the ponds would hold back even less water than they had last time. *Evil,* Lace called it. *All of it. Calculated evil.* Jimmy Make'd roll his eyes. *It's not evil,* he'd say. *How can a woman bright as you are be so goddamned backwards? It's just greed and they-don't-give-a-damn. It's money.*

Greed and money and they-don't-give-a-damn are *evil,* Lace would say.

I was finally coming up on that last bend before you swung around and took it full in your face. I ducked my head, hair falling over my eyes. I watched the shattered rocks under my tennis shoes, breathed with my mouth to lighten the gas smell, but the destruction kept calling me to see it. Like the pictures in the Dairy Queen had, like the sex chapter in the ninth-grade science book we never read.

So I stopped and looked up.

The first hurt I felt wasn't for myself. It was for Grandma. Many times I'd been in a car with her and seen a highwall from a strip mine, even a small one on a mountain we didn't know, and how my grandma would flinch. I was scared to think what it would do to her to see this kind of violence on a piece of ground she loved. But after I felt for Grandma, it was like I no longer knew where I was. I all of a sudden got dizzy, so many times in my life I'd walked up this hollow, followed the creek, and back then, you couldn't see the top of anything. You were just in it, in the hollow, in the mountains, in the woods, up above you trees and vines and rock overhangs, and higher than that, a change in the light that let you know where the top should be. But then, finally, I did feel the hurt for myself. I understood. It was like they were knocking down whatever it is inside of you that holds you up. Kicking down the blocks that hold up your insides, kicking, until what the blocks kept up falls and leaves you empty inside.

I gazed away from the fill to a couple left-behind trees on the ridge, raggedy. I'd seen at church a picture of Calvary. Thorn trees set in a bleached earth and sky. Then I turned my head to the far left, to Cherryboy and beyond, still wooded, I tried to take comfort from that, and for a little while, the comfort came. But almost right away, the separateness set in.

I didn't stop moving again until I hit that field of eerie boulders at the foot of the fill, sharp-angled and unweathered. *Shut up and grow up.* Jimmy's voice. I looked around for guards, then I dropped on all fours and started bearwalking it again. I'd noticed last time a narrow strip of ground on one side of the fill, rusty-colored and bald, not a lot of rock on it. Solid. Then I was at the base, and I straightened up, checked over my shoulder. Scanned the mine rim, saw nothing live up there but those sorry left-behind trees. Once I got right against the bank, I smelled the ground odor in it, and that made me feel safer, and I started climbing again, this time more like a spider than a bear, and along the bottom there, it wasn't as steep as I'd thought. Maybe it wouldn't be so hard after all.

I'd clawed up maybe two body-lengths when the voice came from so close it didn't even yell.

"Hey. You. What're you doing up in here?"

I waited for a minute with my face to the wall. Then, without lifting my hands or feet, I looked back.

He wore a goatee and black sunglasses like skiers have. Carried a little Igloo lunch cooler. *And where in the world did he come from,* I thought for a second, but right after that, I knew—of course that was how he would come.

"Thought you were a girl," the guard said. "That hair."

I let loose and slid down. My tennis shoes slipped when they hit the rocks, and I felt the burn of a scrape on my ankle. He'd fixed on me those wrap-around black lenses, his eyes so gone it seemed it was his mouth was staring at me. And my first fear, that he'd arrest me, sunk back a little, because him looking at me there called my outsides back. I went bony and ugly again. I dipped my head, and my hair fell forward and screened my face, and I stood there hating every little gut in his body. And scared to the core over what he'd do next.

"C'mon over here," he said. He'd found a flat place on one of the sharp rocks to set his butt. I did what he wanted, balanced my own behind on the rock he pointed out for me. I kept an eye on the holstered pistol jutting off his hip. I held myself as far away from him as I could without leaving the rock, my hair over my face, I could smell the gas in it, while he opened his cooler. Held out to me a Little Debbie fudge brownie. "Have a bite to eat," he said.

I couldn't tell if he was teasing or serious. The brownie made my stomach roll, but I figured I better do whatever he said. I went on and took it, then he pulled a sandwich from a baggie for himself. I could smell the salami in it, and he started grinding away on that sandwich, a slow eater he was, sounded like a dog in something wet. I sat there, sweating now under that shout sky, the cellophaned Little Debbie slippery in my sweaty hand, thinking, *Could he arrest me himself, or did he have a cell phone he'd use to call Pinky McCutcheon come do it?* I didn't see cuffs, but I didn't see a phone, either. I thought about that story Jimmy Make liked to tell, about when he was a kid and him and his friends were messing around a strip job after hours, and a guard they never even saw fired a bullet right over their heads. *Gave ole Ronnie a new part in his hair.* Jimmy would laugh about it. The sweat sliming my skin fired the gas odor higher, and I wondered could he smell it, too, and finally he finished the sandwich. Cleaned his goatee with a pull of his palm. Turned to me and took off the glasses, and I saw his eyes, blue, with pale stubby lashes. "Where you live at?" he said.

"Down there at the head of the hollow." It rolled right out of my mouth.

"So what're you doing up in here?"

Again, the question too fast, me too scared, to lie. "Looking to see if there's a slurry impoundment behind that fill."

When I said that, the guard looked away. Put his sunglasses back on. The goatee looked coarse as pig bristle. Then he laughed, just a little, not a nasty laugh, not like he was mocking me, but he laughed.

He wadded the baggie back into the cooler and pulled out a banana he laid across his knee. He eased over heavy onto one haunch, his belly following in a wave, and he wrestled from his front jeans' pocket a little pearl-handled knife. He ate the banana off the knife in slices, the knife teasing up against his tongue, and each time the blade touched it, I both cringed and wished for it to cut.

"Now honey," he finally said. "We wouldn't put nothing up there to hurt you-all." He held out to me a banana slice on his knife, and I didn't bother to shake my head. "How you're gonna get hurt is roaming around up here where you're not supposed to be. That gate was locked for a reason." He finished the banana and slung the peel off into the rocks where the yellow showed up foreign and bright. "You don't got no hazard training," he said. "What happens if you're up in here and a blast goes off and you don't got no hazard training?" *What happens if we're down at our house and this fill fails and we don't got no hazard training?* the backtalk surged quick to my tongue, but I didn't say it. I didn't say it. Now my blood so hot in my face I wondered for a second would that gas catch flame, but I didn't say it, and the noser just rattling on, "No, it ain't a pretty sight. Nobody's crazy about this here, you know. But men got to feed their families." He kept nodding to himself like I was supposed to nod with him, like I'd never heard that before, and I thought, *go on and say what comes next, say Coal's all*—"Coal's all we got around here," he said. "And when we're done, we'll clean er up. Pile it back on and smooth and grass it up. It'll look nicer than before we started."

My hands had made fists. They were squeezing through the brownie I still held, I realized the brownie was oozing out of its wrapper and onto my fingers. I looked away from him, I raised my face to the mine. Before, when I'd looked up at that dead mountain, I just wasn't able to see it as real. It wasn't like the separateness I felt these days from live mountains. It was just that my mind didn't have any way to hold the dead ones. But right then, the guard still rambling—"and rabbits'll come on it. Your daddy and brothers can hunt. It'll be good for rabbits"—I stared my eyes into Yellowroot, I opened my eyes so wide they burned, and, *show me,* I thought. Pushing my hardest towards the real. *Show me.*

And sudden, like waking up, my mind did let it in. My mind opened and let it past my eyes. The recognition hit my scalp and collared my throat, and my mouth swelled thick—but I couldn't hold the realness for more than a few seconds. I had to drop my face away from what I saw. But all I had to drop it to were those rocks, those rocks fresh from the center of the earth and what those rocks carried, some warning from the world, and always the end of something, it just always was, something in this place had been at its end since I was born, me forever butting my head against it, the end, and him saying, "Wish you'd go on and eat that. I don't like eating in front of people."

By the time he cracked open a Dr Pepper and started sipping slow as whiskey, I knew for sure. He wasn't going to arrest me. I didn't matter enough for him to bother. My punishment was this—the waiting. Then once I knew he wasn't going to arrest me, I realized that ever since the fear had drained away, I'd been wanting him to arrest me. I had. And I knew something else, way underneath. Something even worse.

I knew I'd wanted him to arrest me because if he did, I could have felt okay about not doing nothing more.

After he drained the Dr Pepper, his voice went back to how it really was. Nasty, poisoned, and low.

"Okay, let's see how fast you can get your butt back across them rocks and down that hollow. You done pretty good getting in."

Dane

DANE LIES in the extra-dark of the bottom bunk, his insides full of flipping. A nausea of fish swimming. All day it has looked like rain. The underside mesh of the top bunk, where Tommy sleeps, is ripped, and it clouds down to darken Dane's bunk a third time. The first dark the regular dark of the darkened room. The second dark the dark the top bunk makes. Despite the three darks, Dane can see his feet, enormous, under the covers at the foot of the bed. Tommy finally shut up about ten minutes ago, and Dane can hear Tommy's breath, wide-spaced flutters. Dane is full of fish, Tommy of moths. Corey is full of metal, a little steel-made man.

Dane had the fish swimming in him, the slosh of dirty water, long before they went to bed. Then they went to bed and Tommy riled the fish even harder by telling Dane about the monkey. For weeks, Tommy has gone on and on about the monkey in the drift pile behind Chester's house, a monkey that returns to Tommy every night when the lights go off. A monkey Dane has not seen, will not see, because Dane does not need to see the monkey. Some things Dane understands sudden and sharp, a slap of understand. The monkey Dane understands. Tommy and Dane have to go to bed earlier than Corey and Bant because Tommy and Dane are the youngest. Even though Dane is twelve and Corey is ten, Jimmy Make explains that Dane is younger in his mind than Corey is, so Dane needs more rest. In truth, Jimmy says this because Tommy won't go to bed by himself, and Corey will fight Jimmy Make about going to bed, while Dane will just sulk. Still, Dane has to go to bed.

All day it looked like rain. It did rain for twenty minutes or so mid-afternoon, then the rain slunk back up in the sky to hang there and taunt. And again after supper, it started, steady, but soft, raining right on into the dark to where you can't see what it was doing, you can't tell. Rain too soft to hear on the roof. Sneaking. *All we can do is listen for a big rumble,* Mrs. Taylor talking. And Tommy, *But, but, but, when Chancey chomps down on it, the baby monkeys might come out and run. They'll run under people's houses, and then what'll we do?* The fish flip and butt through pinkish stomach waters. *Set traps for em . . .* Dane leans out of his bunk and reaches under the bed.

Tomorrow, Sunday, is Dane's only day off because Mrs. Taylor doesn't believe in working on Sundays, like his grandma didn't, so Dane doesn't work. The Dairy Queen does believe in working on Sundays, so Mom does. When his grandma was alive, they went to church every Sunday. Then they moved to North Carolina and lost the habit, then Grandma died, then they moved back home and Mom went to work. Dane was a little boy when they went to church, a true little boy, not just little in his mind, but little all over. Dane matched himself and God matched Dane, back then God was big enough to cover him all over, a cape. *God's trying to tell us something,* Mrs. Taylor will murmur, shaking a finger towards her roof, and beyond that, the valley fill, the mine. *God's telling us something.* And Dane believes her. But God tells Dane nothing anymore.

He tries to remember. Those hours and hours spent in church

beside his grandma, never speaking, never sleeping, not even permitted to sag. Dane understanding not the content of what the preacher said, not the words, but absorbing the atmosphere like a tight mesh net, the reward and punish, the protect and threat. And along with that, the patience and restraint they learned from those hours of sitting still in church, from the age of three or four, the endurance. To take it, they learnt. Dane learnt well, better than many, and he will always carry that in him. But now he knows what can get past God. *An act of God, they called it. Tried to blame it on him.* Mrs. Taylor says, *I say God must be getting awful tired of being blamed for what man does.* But. Still. Dane sees. God may not have done it, but God let it be done. His will be . . . God smaller and farther away and no longer big enough to cover him, even little in his mind like he is.

He lies in the extra-dark, listening for rain. A rumble. He hears only the television noise. Dane sleeps in the bottom bunk because he used to have a problem. The problem had to do with wetting the bed. He's done it outside of bed, too, although he hasn't done it for a long time. Dane has learned to hold back, hold in, but then there was the day at the bus stop with Corey and B-bo and David from down the road when they saw the AEP truck run over a cat. Truck clipped the cat into the air, cat coming back down under it and the wet sound of the tire. And the pee just let go, B-bo screaming, *Him pissed himself, him did, him did! Him pissed himself, him did!* Dane's stomach clenches down on the fish swimming in him. He strains to hear rain, his eyes wide open, staring at the lumps in the foot of his bunk. *Still young in your mind, your mind needs rest,* Jimmy Make says.

His mind is not growing right, and Dane knows this by looking at his body. In the last nine months or so, Dane has grown strangely shaped. Hips, waist, thighs, swelling to a bigness without any length, and his body not bothering to grow at all above his waist. The bottom of his body out of proportion to the top, leaving him . . . Dane fears it so bad it'll barely bubble into words. Leaving Dane. Strangely woman-shaped. And Dane looks at his body, this peculiar taper, and he imagines his head there at the top. Although on the outside, it looks more or less like a normal head—thin dark hair, large dark eyes, the dark half-pennies under them—Dane figures Jimmy knows that the taper continues to his brain. The brain as out-of-proportion to his upper body as his upper body is to his lower body. A little handful of shy stubborn slow-to-grow brain.

Last year in school Mrs. Baker had Dane sitting on the side of the room beside the map, and a lot of the times he was supposed to be doing something else, he would sit and study North Carolina. Part of North Carolina is lined and humped like West Virginia is. As a matter of fact, Mrs. Baker tells them, the humped part is their own mountains, just stretched farther south. But the other part of North Carolina has no black lines, bald but for town names and dots, red roads and blue rivers. Jimmy Make took them to that unlined part of North Carolina. Jimmy Make wants to take them back. Mrs. Taylor has heard about a school they built on a mountaintop removal site after the company was gone. One day all the kids were eating in the lunchroom when the school dropped six inches into the ground, and when they ran to the doors to escape, the doors wouldn't open. The six inches of ground held them shut, so the kids had to crawl out the windows.

The middle school is not built on a mine site. Dane asked Mom, and she said no.

He hears Corey shut the bathroom door and start the shower. Hears him clear his throat and spit in the bathtub the way Corey's heard Jimmy Make do. It's the spitting that hits a nerve in Dane, and he stares at the ripped bottom of Tommy's bed, but at the same time, inside his eyes, he's seeing Corey. He sees Corey in the shower and the fish kick up faster in him, turning in tight circles, tearing at his stomach lining with the jags in their fins. Dane looks across the narrow room to where Corey sleeps, an old couch made up with sheets. He imagines himself getting up, slipping silent into the bathroom, Corey hearing nothing over the sound of the nozzle spray, the hack and spit of his own throat. Dane grasps the shower curtain, takes a breath. Rips it open, snatches Corey's leg, and flips Corey, the slap-thud of wet Corey hitting the wet plastic tub. Slap-thud.

Then Dane is back in his bed, staring into the dark mesh cloud. The imagined hurt he did Corey doesn't quiet him because Dane couldn't help but see, before he flipped Corey, Corey naked. How Corey's put together. How all Corey's parts match. And then, after that, Dane sees Corey when he was little. Corey in his Pampers, the always grimy circle smudged around his mouth. *There's your charge,* Mom would say, and Dane would take Corey's hand. The fish keep ripping. Dane's insides bleed.

Things are gettin awful, Mrs. Taylor will say. *Things are gettin awful.*

His grandma called him Minnow. Minner, she called him, his grandma tendered him, didn't mind his soft. Didn't hate his softness like Corey does, didn't deny it like Jimmy Make does, didn't ignore it like Lace and Bant do. He still keeps up there in her trailer spot his pieces of God. He went up there just this afternoon, after Mrs. Taylor finally made him dust off the stereo top. He finished and snuck up the hollow, couldn't think of what else to do. The sky sagging over his head, sneaky with unfallen rain, and Dane's fingers, scrubbed, but still tainted. "I am only twelve years old. And I'm going to see the End of the World."

He hadn't asked Mrs. Taylor for help with the dusting, of course not, it didn't even occur to him, and if it had, he wouldn't have asked anyway, because then he would have had to explain why he was asking. At first he kind of bunched up the junk mail, thinking maybe he could scoop up the pamphlet with the other papers then throw the whole heap on the bed. But then he understood to toss the pamphlet like that would be a deep disrespect, and the pamphlet most likely wouldn't let that go unnoticed. So he tried to figure out how to move the pamphlet without touching it. Him standing there staring at it, his insides waiting, not moving because they had no place they could move to, his insides completely jammed full. Until he realized there was no way around it. The pamphlet would have to be touched.

He put one hand in the bottom of his T-shirt and reached for the pamphlet with the shirt covering his fingers like a glove. He picked up the paper between his two fingers, twisted at his waist, and laid it gently on the bed. He dropped the shirt. Then he stood quivering, the fish loosened now, risen almost into his throat. And in the distance, he could hear the whispers of the End. A mutter. Soft-chutter. Moany, moany in their mouths.

After the dusting, he returned the pamphlet the same way he'd picked it up, wanting to put it back facedown but fearful of its retribution. So he didn't. Then he went to the kitchen and scrubbed his hands, again, afraid of insulting the pamphlet, but it couldn't be helped, he had to take this chance. He told Mrs. Taylor he was sick to his stomach, and Mrs. Taylor looked worried and told him go home early. He wasn't lying. On his way to the trailer spot he stopped at the house to change shirts, and the shirt contaminated by the pamphlet he shoved deep under the couch Corey slept on.

The mountains shall be thrown down, and the steep places shall fall, and every wall shall fall to the ground, Mrs. Taylor would say. *Ezekiel 38:20.* Open your Bible, please, and read.

Although his grandma's trailer been gone two years now, you can see clear the rectangle it left behind like a shadow on the ground. The trailer spot grows a different kind of weeds than the old yard does, kind of weeds crave such poorish rubbly soil, rabbit ear and mullein and pepper grass. The multiflora rose creeping in. It is Dane's place now, and the rosebox he calls it, not just for the multiflora rose, but because it's shaped like a rosebox, which he saw once, on Jimmy Make and Mom's anniversary in North Carolina. Usually not much is made of the anniversary, but that one, Jimmy Make sent Lace a box of roses, and the trailer shadow is shaped like that. The rosebox is the first box.

It used to be all Dane had to do was walk across the line marking the rosebox and a heat of God would come in him. That hasn't happened since April, but this afternoon Dane had stayed hopeful. He'd had to. When he stepped over, he did pause, he had opened for it. But his heart felt nothing but a light dry wheeze. He'd moved on to the TV a little more quickly than usual, moving fast so as not to think. Getting the TV into the rosebox hadn't been easy, but Dane had done it, over a year ago, walking it corner to corner like the corners were legs. Before they'd sold Grandma's trailer, they'd taken all the furniture out, sold what they could, put some in their own house, and stored most of what was left in the Ricker place. Somehow, though, the TV got forgotten and left behind outside. So there the TV sat, its finish dissolving in the rain, until Dane found the picture at Tudor's Biscuit World. Then he knew where the TV went. The TV is the second box. When he'd knelt by the TV this afternoon, he'd prayed a real prayer. He balled up behind his eyes the reach for God. He'd pushed. But still nothing came, and even if it had, he knew it wouldn't have counted, he'd had to try too hard.

Then he reached out and unthreaded the screws, the dryness in his heart now moving up into his mouth. He lifted off the back and set it aside, his mind moving ahead of his body, and every fish stood still. Everybody waited. He reached in and took hold of the third box (three's a charm), a lunchbox Lace had carried to Prater Elementary School. Each side was painted with a scene from an old show

Lace calls Gentle Ben. Dane studied the lunchbox pictures, the boy leading his faithful bear, the boy playing with friendly cubs while his smiling parents watch, the boy's father bandaging the leg of a deer. Dane stroked his hand across the raised metal surface of the pictures. He saw how that hand trembled. *Cut the mountains all to pieces.* Mrs. Taylor again. *Nothing left to hold the water back. Just listen for a rumble, now, that's all we can do.*

He unclasped the lunchbox lid. The faint odor of overripe bananas, somehow twenty-five years still present. The "Safety Instructions" on the inside of the lid about how to be careful on the playground. He paused a second, then pulled out, one at a time, his pieces of God.

There was an order to it (three's a charm. Father, Son, and Holy Ghost, three crosses on a hill, on the third day he rose. Rosebox). First, an acorn he'd taken from the white oak beside the Freewill Baptist Church, the acorn three years old now and shriveled up in an unusual way acorns never got when left alone outside. He placed the acorn on the ground in front of him. He took out the second piece, the broken-off leg of a plastic horse, its foot with a black shoe painted on its bottom. He lay the tiny horseshoe beside the acorn.

The third piece was by far the most powerful, so powerful he kept the paper folded in fourths so he wouldn't accidentally see it. He had to open it, take some time. He'd gotten it a year ago at the Tudor's Biscuit World in Nitro. It had been in a pile of old magazines left for customers' entertainment in the condiment area. He, Jimmy Make, and Corey were headed home after visiting Jimmy's father in his retirement apartment in Poca, and Dane was leafing through a magazine in his lap under the tabletop while Jimmy and Corey argued over something Corey had done.

When he hit it, at first he hadn't understood. A page-load of black and gray billows and blurs. Clouds or smoke, yes, he knew that, but why were they pictured in a magazine? He could read well enough to understand all of the caption except the name of the town and the state, and the state he figured out later. "Face of God in clouds over T—, Oklahoma."

Dane'd slapped the magazine shut, his finger in the page. He was terrified to look twice, but, at the same time, not only did he have to look again; he had to have the picture. He peeled the page open. Ducked his head and squinted. Now the God face came into focus, in the upper-right-hand corner of the page. He closed the magazine once more, this time more casually, wondering if Corey or Jimmy had noticed. They had not. They were too angry at each other to notice Dane. He knew he had to act quickly, and he wanted the whole page, even though he was afraid a whole page would be missed by the Tudor's Biscuit World workers. He would take the risk. But it would be hard to smuggle a whole page home without Corey and Jimmy Make noticing because Dane was wearing sweatpants without pockets.

Now Corey and Jimmy Make had shut up, each glaring at his food. Dane could hear the raw onions crunch in Jimmy's jaws, the metal on plastic stab of Corey's fork trying to work a very gnarled piece of fried chicken. Dane waited, his left hand holding the page in his lap, his other hand feeding himself his pepperoni and cheese biscuit. Finally, Jimmy cracked. Busted into another tirade at Corey, hissing, not loud enough to attract everybody's attention, but loud enough to cover at least partly the sound of Dane's rip, and Dane tore out the page, folded it roughly, and tucked it in his sock under the sweatpants' elastic, pretending like he had an itch.

The picture warmed his calf the whole way home.

It has to be done right, it must be done in order, but Dane kept moving a little faster than usual, the need to get there desperate. The feel of the pamphlet, End Times, still prickling his hands, and he closed his eyes again and prayed. He prayed good, a proper beginning, middle, and end, and he didn't only ask, he tried to praise God, too, he tried to thank, give something himself, a trade. But the words dried up soon as they left his mouth. Dropped in the wasteweeds and blew away.

He was shaking so much now it was hard to pick up the picture. He wiped his hands on his pants to smear away the pamphlet, didn't want that to touch the face. Then he took a breath and reached back in.

Seems like there are two laws. One for the rich people, and one for the poor.

Gentle as cupping a butterfly, Dane lifted the paper out. The page in fourths resting on one hand, he passed his other hand over it without touching it. Then he unfolded the first crease. Now the paper overlapped his palm, he balanced it there, a driving inside him to open it, fast, but he pressed that driving down. He touched the page and started the final unfold, but, suddenly, the desperation took him, and he snatched the page by its corner and shook it, just a little. The page unfurled to its full self. Dane heard in his mouth an animal *uhh* that shot out his soul, and he leapt back on his knees and dropped the page in the weeds. Where it fell upright and open.

The page was held in one piece by a little bit of paper at its top, a little bit at its bottom. In its middle, a tear ran through the face of God.

The paper in the weeds, Dane's breath quick-ripping, the fish fast dull blades in his belly. Horse hoof, heat fear, his eyes little color dots swirling, and he saw he was smashing under his knee the hand that had shaken the page, but he couldn't feel it hurt. He knelt even harder on the hand, until he had to wince, and then it all started slowing. It slowed down, much more quickly than you would have thought, his heart, his breathing. The fish relaxed into a meandering slash. And Dane was still afraid, but now it was a calming of-course kind of afraid because he realized he wasn't surprised. After the initial shock, he wasn't at all surprised. Because, truth be told, Dane had known for over a month that God wasn't working around here anymore. God had been leaving ahead of time to get safe from this mess. Save Himself.

The rain finally started, just a little, sloppy careless plops. Dane hurried his pieces back into the lunchbox and clicked it shut, shoved the lunchbox into the TV and rescrewed the back. The picture would be ruined by rain, and despite the rip, Dane couldn't let that happen. Couldn't take that chance, because that much stayed with him, the punishment stayed, even if the reward did not. Although there was no longer any comfort, there was still plenty of threat.

Dane lies in his bottom bunk, his ears straining for rain. He knows it's still falling, sneaky and gentle, and Dane listens, the fish a restless hateful school that ram and slash each other. Corey has gone to bed, Bant has gone to bed, Jimmy Make has gone to bed, Dane has heard the tooth-brushing, the toilet-flushing. He listens. The murmur of Tommy's mouth as he dreams of killing monkeys. Jimmy Make's uneven snores, like cloth tearing. Barking dogs down the hollow, answering each other. The rain gathers itself at the head of the hollow, and Dane listens.

He hears the car crunch over the broken asphalt and into the gravel. Mom's ride. Several minutes later, he smells her Dairy Queen odor, french fry oil and the pink-orange cones. The shape of Mom enters the room, a shape formed of smells, the smell-shape floating to the bunks, Dane can't hear her feet on the floor. First she checks on Tommy, Dane able to see only her body, her head gone, and he smells Dairy Queen strong. Now she bends down to Dane. That's when she notices the lumps in the bed.

"What you got under those covers, Dane?" she says.

"Nothing," Dane says. "Me."

Mom reaches down and pulls loose the sheet and the spread from the bottom. She lifts them up. Then, despite Corey and Tommy sleeping, she switches on the lamp to make sure.

Dane wears an old pair of Jimmy Make's steel-buckled black rubber boots. Lace doesn't ask why.

Bant

IN THE DEAD afternoons, when the days got a sag, I'd be the only thing moving in the world. Hobart hiding in his air-conditioned office. Sharon home chewing ice cubes and writing Donnie's name on her arm. The night miners snoring behind the walls I painted. Snuffling. Coughing. Sometimes pissing. Yeah, I heard them. But the only thing moving would be me. The mornings went easier, the mornings had a hope to them, in the mornings, I stayed careful. But by two o'clock, the paint would be dribbling down my arms, I'd be turning all over that bad blue, and my thoughts would start following my brush, covering the same spaces, again and again. And always, the hover of gasoline.

Twice in two nights in early July, somebody spraypainted a wall I'd finished that day. First they graffitied "Scab Resort" in black, and the night after I repainted that, they did "Local Jobs for Local Miners" in red. Each morning after it happened, Hobart waddled out the second Jimmy Make dropped me off and ordered me to take care of it right then. Before too many people saw, I knew, but I didn't want to paint over what they wrote. I thought about sloppying up my repainting so at least people passing could see something had been there, but

Hobart would never let me get away with that, so the most I dared was not blend the fresh blue with the old very well. Scab. I dragged the blue over the black letters. I said them to myself, *S-C-A-B*. I said each letter again and again until finally, the blue smudged them out.

Right when I got done that second time, R.L. came out with a can of orange Fanta and a plastic hotel cup. Poured half the can in the cup and handed it to me. Then he asked my name, and moved right into telling a story about a bar in Anida.

I couldn't follow the story, my brush twitching. I was too heaved inside with him asking my name. I was too heaved with him telling me a story at all.

"Guess what I heard last night?" Lace asked while we were sitting in the living room Sunday after lunch.

"What?" Jimmy Make didn't take his eyes off the TV.

"Your ole buddy Bill Bozer's got on up at Yellowroot."

I looked around quick at Jimmy Make. Bill Bozer was his friend back to grade school. I saw on Jimmy Make's face that he already knew about the job.

"I can't believe it," Lace went on. "Where things have got to. Even Bill Bozer's sold out now."

Jimmy said nothing. The cars on the TV roared round and round.

"Scabbing." Rock-dust blown, most of the men at Hobart's were, this R.L., too. Where was it he worked? I couldn't help but wonder. I found myself wondering quite a bit of the time. Yellowroot? I wondered. Seemed most of them at Hobart's did.

Jimmy said nothing.

"You knew." I could hear in her voice that she'd just figured that out. "Why didn't you say something?"

Jimmy said nothing.

"One of your oldest friends. A scab."

Jimmy whipped his head around. "Well, what the hell else was he supposed to do?"

I looked at Lace, and I saw she was honestly surprised, she honestly was, that Jimmy would defend him, and she said, "What? What? Two days ago, you were calling em scabs right along with me."

"At least he's local."

"He's still a scab."

Then Jimmy lunged up off the couch, favoring the bad leg, but he was up, hissing, "What the hell was he gonna do? What the hell was he gonna do? He's gotta wife with a kidney problem. He's gotta have the hospital card."

Then it was Lace who said nothing, and I kept my eyes on the TV, waiting, and when she finally spoke, I heard she was worried, genuinely worried, more than she was mad. "You're gonna try to get on there now."

"No, I'm not."

"That's what you're thinking. I know you, now that Bill Bozer's up there . . ."

Now Jimmy Make was right on her, she was messing around acting like she was making a sandwich, and he was right behind her, but not touching, like a shadow he was, and he spoke right in her ear, he did not yell. "No. I am not. I am not gonna work up there." He stepped back, his whole body stiff, his fists clenched. But Jimmy Make never hit her. "I'm gonna get me a job away from here," he said.

The mess on my face came and went. Would clear up for a day, then bubble back like boiled soup, and Sharon gave me some kind of tannish makeup to cover the spots. Sharon was big on such stuff, but then Tommy asked me if I had peanut butter on my face, like he wanted some for himself. After that, I left the tube in my drawer.

For a while, I knew R.L. was just playing with me, but still, I found myself keeping notes in my head, my brush moving. Even before the orange pop and Anida, I noticed—what he did different, what he did more. Me dipping my brush in the can, wiping the tip on the side, stroking, I tracked the mildest change. The day he started passing by more than once. The day he wore cologne when he did it. The day he held my eyes a few seconds longer. Then he started talking to me—*I hope that old bastard's payin you decent. Hard as you work every day*—and after he went back in his room, I couldn't help but replay his words in my head. *Bant's a name I ain't never heard before. Pretty though, ain't it?* First I'd hold them still, hold the words up so I could look. *Once I finally get a day off, maybe me and you'll take a ride to Beckley, get us a bite to eat.* Then I'd thrust into them, pull them into pieces, roll them around in my hands. My brush moving. Then, once I got home, I'd listen to those words all over again.

I'd noticed him from the first, he was younger than the others. But gradually he had changed somehow, he came into focus, he snapped big and sharp. It was like he started under murky water, then he rose up, dripped clear and brand-new. And yeah, for a while, I figured he was playing with me (how could he want this ruin of a face?). And a deep part of me knew it was because he had nothing better to do. But yet another part of me wanted to believe. And after not long, the believing part won.

I felt him stop behind me, could feel his body in what had been empty space. I kept my brush moving. I was on my knees, working on a low spot, my legs tucked under me. I felt a boot toe pry under one bare leg. I kept painting. The toe lifted. Wiggled as best it could in a steel toe, the end wagging. I finally turned. R.L. play-frowned at me, then he kicked my leg, gentle. Then he went on.

Corey

SETH AND them are inside people. They stay in their house with their air-conditioning on. Most people along Yellowroot don't lock up. Seth and them do. But even Seth and them, if they open their shed in the day, don't lock it again until night. Corey counts on their having got in the shed already once this morning.

He doesn't want Tommy going with him, and he waits until Tommy is watching cartoons, but Tommy catches him. Tommy's like a dog that way. Knows it whenever you come or go, even if he doesn't see you. He catches Corey before he's out the yard.

"I'm going to check on that monkey," Corey tells him, even though the monkey is beyond Seth's house and Corey hadn't planned on going near it.

Tommy hesitates a few seconds. Then, "I don't care." *Doankeer*, he says it. Mumbling mad with his mouth balled up. Corey gives him the meanest look he can scowl up, but Tommy just keeps right on following.

They go by the road, not the creek. Chancey pads along with them, dipping his head and hunching his shoulders when they pass yards where dogs come at them. *Chickenshit Chancey.*

"Chancey's chickenshit," Corey tells Tommy.

Tommy doesn't say anything. He pats Chancey on the spine, then hugs his head. Chancey sticks close.

"Now that Baron," Corey says. "He's a feisty sonofabitch." Corey has three sticks of Juicy Fruit wadded between his cheek and gum, like snuff, and he spits at a squashed toad in the road. "If he just hadn't had that accident."

Tommy stares straight ahead. He's trying not to ask, but finally he can't help it. "What accident?" says Tommy.

"You know," Corey says.

"Nuh-uh," says Tommy.

"Oh," Corey says. "Thought you did." Corey squats and busies himself retying his shoe. Build the suspense. "Baron used to be a Rottweiler. But somebody stuck him in a air compressor and shrunk him to what he is now. Dad found him and rescued him."

Tommy is quiet for a while. "No, he wasn't."

"Look at how he's colored, his markings. At how he acts."

Tommy is silent. His hand rests on Chancey's back as they walk down the road.

Corey shrugs. "I don't care if you believe me or not. I'm just telling you what happened."

"A air compressor couldn't shrink a dog," Tommy says.

"They put chemicals in there with him," Corey says.

"Oh," says Tommy.

They're passing Mrs. Taylor's neat blue house. Corey sees Dane carrying the slop bucket through the backyard to the outhouse, Dane struggling with it, leaning to one side. Dane feels Corey looking at him, and he looks back at Corey, and then they just look at each other. *Chickenshit, too. Dane and Chancey.* Corey rubs the Juicy Fruit between his teeth and cheek.

"Where'd Dad find him at?" Tommy asks.

"Oh, it was somebody he worked with in North Carolina. Kept Baron in his glove compartment all day. Wife couldn't handle him by herself at home. Dad saw him when they come off work and the man opened the glove to show Dad a gun."

"Oh," says Tommy.

Now they're passing Seth's. Like most of the other houses up Yellowroot, Seth and them's house has a fence around the front yard. But while most of the other houses have waist-high chain-link fences, Seth's fence is made of tall redwood-painted boards laid hip-to-hip so you can't see through them. Still, Seth's house is two stories tall, plus a little tower at one end which Corey thinks is probably fake, and tall as the house is, you can tell what it looks like from the road. While most houses in the hollow are trailers or modular homes or former company houses, sold long ago to locals who've changed them from look-alike to different—added plumbing, porches, carports, awnings, siding—Seth and them's house is none of the above. It is younger than Corey and built of a scab-colored brick, and the house perches on a little dozed-up mound, "like they knew when they built it we were gonna get washed out," Mom says. "That was eight, nine years ago," says Dad. "How in the world would they know?" Despite the size of the house, the yard is no bigger than anybody else's, so the house is all cramped up inside the fence, looking ready to flop out. Seth's dad cuts the yard with a ride mower. And when the front gate is open, you can see they have in their front yard not regular lawn ornaments, not geese or kissing Dutch children or wooden bears or ceramic deer, but two white statues of robed women carrying jugs on their shoulders. Dad calls them the waitresses.

Just the three of them—Seth, his mom, his dad—live in that big house. Not even any dogs. *If I had me one . . .* Corey wonders if this is the kind of place where Paul Franz lives. He would know if he'd been invited to the birthday party last year, but he wasn't. *Didn't know him that well then.* Corey spits his gum on the ground near Seth's gate.

Things with Rabbit aren't moving too quick. Rabbit doesn't tell Corey to leave or anything, but he doesn't pay any attention to him, either. It's only a matter of time until Mom or somebody figures out what Corey's got in the old house, and Mom isn't going to like it. The way him and Tommy whacked that hole. But Dad won't show him how, makes sure Corey gets nowhere near his tools, either, *patience,* Corey tells himself about Rabbit. *Be patient.* Like the time they found the baby possum, and it didn't want much to do with them at first, either. Then finally it let them pet it. Then, true. It died. *Well, just be patient.*

Chester's fence is made of a rusted loopy wire that looks like things have been butting their heads against it to get out for many decades. Chester has a single lawn ornament, a ceramic buck about four feet high with antlers that Chester keeps covered with a Wal-Mart bag so nobody will take a shot at it from the road. Tommy and Corey know where there's a fair-sized gap in the fence, and they hold the wire apart for each other to crawl through. Finally understanding where they're going, Chancey snaps into an ears-up head-high I'm-headed-for-something-dead-and-juicy prance.

As they get closer to the creek, Corey's legs get weighty. He glances up the creek, back towards Seth's. The problem is, at the same time that you don't really want to see the monkey, the monkey sucks you to it. You don't want to see it, you don't want to see it in a bad way, but, then, you do want to see it. In a bad way. Chancey has already scrambled up into his monkey-barking spot, the gray metal box, he has his head lowered and the chops pouring out his mouth like he's puking copper bells. Dad says he must have a thimble of coondog in his blood, but you can't tell it any place but his voice. Now they're near enough the creek to smell the water, and Corey wants just to turn upstream towards Seth's. Skip the monkey today. But, if he does,

Tommy will think he's chickenshit, and *goddamn that Tommy, why can't I go anyplace by myself?* Corey plunges into the water running and splashing as fast as he can go, his brain turned off, to where they look at the monkey. Tommy squeals and rushes to catch up, not wanting to see the monkey alone, and when he reaches Corey, he snatches Corey's bare arm with a pinch that has nail in it.

"Quit that!" Corey snarls, and he snaps Tommy's hand off him.

Under the mild current the crinkly fur ripples. The monkey hangs close enough to the surface that you can see it easy through the murky water. Parts you can't tell what they are lift a little, sink, lift a little, sink. You would think something would have eaten by now on that big open eye, but something has not. And what does that tell you. *What.*

Corey rips his head away. He turns and runs up the creek, hooting and splashing like he's having fun. Smashing his legs into the water, windmilling his arms. Fun. Tommy tears howling after him, until they get close to Seth's backyard. Where Corey halts, puts his hand on Tommy's mouth, and whispers, "Shut up now."

Seth's fence along the creek has been washed away, so Corey and Tommy stand in the water, looking up into the yard. They keep the ride mower in the two-car garage. The four-wheeler stays by itself in the shed. A corrugated metal shed, beige, with double doors that swing open in the front and a regular door on the side that doesn't face the house. Corey shoots Tommy a glare that means *do whatever I do.* Tommy understands. They sprint at top speed through the yard with their heads ducked, dart to the hidden side of the shed, and flop down, gulping air, looking at each other without smiling.

But then Corey feels something else coming up in him. He doesn't want it to come up in him, but it does. He's going to have to see what Seth's doing. He's about half scared Tommy will try to get on the trampoline when he leaves, so he pushes Tommy against the side of the shed with his palm on Tommy's chest until Tommy slumps down.

"You wait here," Corey tells him. "Hold Chancey. Don't move. If they catch us, they'll arrest us." Corey stares Tommy in the eyes. "You know that, don't you?"

Tommy nods, his lips sucked into his mouth like that might hide the rest of him.

Corey ducks from his waist, keeping his legs straight, and darts towards Seth's window like a DEA agent. Once he's squashed under the sill, his back to the brick wall, he catches his breath. Then, cautious, he turns around and rises to his toes.

He crawls to underneath the next window, then stands, leery, half expecting to pop up and be staring Seth's mom in the face. But he's gotten it right this time. He's looking over Seth's shoulder at Seth's computer screen.

Seth is shooting people-looking shapes that rush around his screen. The carpet is littered with toys and videogames, more videos and videogames jammed in bookshelves. A Washington Redskins trashcan stands in the corner filled with every kind of ball, and the TV plays a video, looks like *Aladdin*, maybe, Corey thinks. Seth has just got his hair cut again, gets it cut every other week, seems like. An arrested three-quarter inch of brick-colored bristle across the crown of his head. Corey watches the fat wrinkle at the base of Seth's haircut while Seth continues to blow people away on the screen. He drops back to the grass, this time in a football HUT! position. Then he duckwalks to the far side of the shed, where Tommy crouches, clinging to Chancey's collar, his lips still sucked in his mouth. Corey reaches for the side door. Before he touches it, he crosses eight of his fingers.

When the knob turns in his hand, he clenches both fists in silent victory. *Had me a feeling on this one. I did.*

He steps in, quick, Tommy attached to his waistband, Chancey's collar hooked in Tommy's other hand. Corey shuts the door behind them. The shed is dark and unventilated, ten degrees hotter than outside, and livid with the odor of gasoline. Corey pushes his eyes to adjust, tugs at the little daylight cracking through the unstoppered eaves, but he can feel the machine, feel its every detail, before he actually sees a thing.

Three times he has looked at it up close. A thousand more he has dreamed it. A 2000 Suzuki Quadrunner 250 4 × 4, four-stroke engine, advanced drivetrain design. Front differential lock, massive suspension, three-speed subtransmission with thirty-five forward gear combinations, and finally, here it comes, out of the dark, and oh, it is beefy, and rugged, and tough tough tough. Green with camouflage fender covers, cargo racks front and rear, those blocky bad-ass tires, and now Corey is circling it. He circles, studying it from every angle, and when his sight's full up, he starts to touch. The speedometer, the key in its ignition, the choke, and then he strokes the fenders and the vent, he grasps the handlebars, he thumbs the throttle. Finally he kneels, all the time inhaling the shimmer of gasoline, and he lies on his back on the dirt floor to look up under it in awe. There is not much to see down there in the dark, it is really simply that he needs to be under it, needs to have it over top his body. But then. Something occurs to Corey. The dirt floor. Most of these prebuilt sheds come with floors. This shed just sits on the yard.

Corey lies there a minute longer before he rolls out and gets to his feet. Then, slowly, savoring, Corey climbs on. He straddles the seat and stretches his legs to reach the pedals. He spreads his arms to grip the handles. And now Corey extends in four directions. Corey's a big man now. Corey is not just as big as Corey spread out, no, Corey can feel how Corey keeps on, how Corey courses right into the four-wheeler parts. The handlebars a lengthening of Corey's arms, the clutch and gears and brake an amplification of his legs, the engine under him a swelling of Corey's guts and crotch. Corey. Corey. Corey Turrell and his kick-ass four-wheeler.

Bant

"IF PEOPLE would just stand up . . ." Lace was talking towards me, but I knew it was Jimmy Make she wanted to hear. She'd been going on with the usual for some time, us eating supper, fried baloney sandwiches and fried potatoes, it was a supper we were eating quite a bit, and when Jimmy Make had come to the table, he'd snarled his lip and said, "See we're eating steak again." Us eating, and nobody but Lace talking, and nobody at all listening, until she said something a little off the routine. "I heard that over in Malwell, too, people are starting to organize against it."

"Huh?" It caught Jimmy's attention. "What are you talking about? The union?" I knew why he was confused. The union hated Lyon. But it supported mountaintop removal because some outfits had a few union jobs.

"No. Not the union." Lace took another bite of her sandwich. "Another environmental group." It came out in a muffle, but Jimmy heard fine.

"Environmentalists!" He threw his fork down on his plate. "I'm telling you again, Lace." He was glaring at her. "I've told you a hunderd times. You stay clear of the shit-stirrers. You get too close to the shit-stirrers and we really will get killed."

"Oh, Jesus," Lace said. "You don't even know what you're talking about."

"Like hell I don't." He had each hand on a table corner now, and the muscles leapt up in his arms. "You know, there is a reason people don't speak out. A damned good reason they don't stand up. I've worked for these outfits. I know what they're capable of."

"Do you think you can tell me anything I don't already know?"

"What do you think they did to them environmentalists over in Hernshaw last summer? That slip your mind? They hit an eighty-year-old man in the head. An eighty-year-old man who is also a politician, if they beat up old-man politicians, what do you think they'll do to people like you?" He was raised halfway up from his chair now. "I hear stuff, too, you know. That woman had her house burned down. Environmentalist. And that crazy Caspar Seeber, he got joined up with them, put bumper stickers all over his truck, and next thing he knew, he was run off the road and totaled the thing—"

"And what about burning up them dummies in Logan?" Corey chipped in.

"Shut up, Corey," I said. If it had been my fight, I would have pointed out how nobody'd got killed yet. But Lace, like Jimmy, always went for the drama.

"Well, I'd rather die showing some spine and get shot in my front than sit and watch them kill everything matters to me."

"You are crazy, woman." Jimmy Make skidded his chair back from the table. "I'm getting the hell out of here." He reeled through the kitchen and slammed out the front door.

"You just do that," Lace said, quiet.

*

It was all in the wrist. I thought in time to my hand. How many flicks in eight hours can you do? But at least with the painting you could see what you'd covered, at least you'd see you were moving ahead. Sometimes, those long humid afternoons, after R.L.'d already come out twice and talked to me, when I knew I probably wouldn't see him again until the next day, I'd try to push my thoughts past high school. Where my mind wouldn't go. Graduation my mind could get to, two years from now. The gowns and picture-taking, the caps, I could see. But all I could think past that was a little unlit space smelling like a cave. And not a real cave, but the rockledge cave up on Cherryboy, where you could get your body in, but then you crawled about ten feet and hit where the wall closed down in a V. That kind of cave.

Eventually, he told me. It turned out he was a big talker, he told me plenty after a while. He didn't ask much back, but that was okay, around him I found it hard to put my words in a line. "Jesus, I hate those fuckers," he'd say, "makin us work ten, twelve hours, hell, you never know when you're gonna get off. And fifteen minutes to eat somethin, and breathin that dust." Him leaning against a dry scraped wall I hadn't reached yet, my brush moving towards it. "But I gotta have me a job, and it's good money. It is that. But once I save up enough, I'm quittin. Goin home and open a gunsmith shop. Work for my own self."

Good money. Twenty-year-old R.L. with his badass truck, bigger'n Jimmy Make's truck. Newer, too.

"What mine is it you work at?" I finally asked. Bitex 4, he told me. And that was the one. What the industry called Yellowroot now.

I'd pray against it, I would, I didn't know where else to turn. I'd pray not to feel for him like I did. I'd start out praying to God, but somehow it always slipped into praying to Grandma, that's how my prayers anymore tended to do, and I didn't want Grandma even knowing about this here. But no matter who I prayed to, didn't nobody help me. He put the pull on me. I could feel this pull from his skin, it made me need to touch it, and I had never felt such a pull before. And it wasn't only that, it wasn't only the skin pull. It was also like he made me small, or cut me up into only a few parts, so I was only parts of myself, but those parts controlled me. On my days off, I'd force myself not to think about him. Practice at it. But next day, there I'd be back at the motel. He started getting up earlier, sleeping less. He'd bring me stuff to eat and drink, he'd tease, tell me stories. He'd watch like I was something worth watching.

They never have to grow up, Lace would say, *stay babified. Never have to because the women always take care of them, first their mothers, then their wives, and then they die. The women always wait and die later,* Lace blowing smoke through the screen. *Everybody around here is raised to take it and take it,* Lace would say, *to put up with it and take it, that's what makes us tough, but especially the girls, the women, are tougher than the men, because the men just take it from the industry and the government, and then they take that out on the women. So the women are tougher, because they take it from the industry, the government, and the men, which means the women are stronger and for sure older, because the men never have to grow up because . . .*

Didn't keep you from wanting them anyway. You go on and do.

Then it wasn't just Sharon closed to me in places, but me closed to Sharon, too. I finally knew where Sharon'd gone. Each of us in our separate places now. Together in that separate sense, talking of it sideways, Sharon and Donnie way, way ahead of me, who hadn't even touched R.L. yet. And Sharon not bright enough to know how much she was letting on. *What do you think, Bant?* Her face lowered, Sharon picking grass. *If you love him, is it still a sin? I mean, I'm not going to, but what do you think? If the girl loves the guy, is it?* I told her they said it was a sin if you weren't married, the love didn't matter. But it was not sin I worried about (this I didn't tell her), it was the punishment you got for the sin. It was the baby. But on the other hand, I was starting to think, what did it matter? Stay here and lose myself like Lace had, like Sharon would. Leave out and lose myself a different way (and what do you remember of North Carolina?).

But I wasn't going to touch him. All I needed was the sight of him, or, no, it was even less than that. All I needed, all I was taking, was just knowing that he was and that he saw me. My brush blending. Skinny-strong boy, his boots bigger than his legs, the sweet lift of his butt in his Levi's. Freckles under the dust-blown, and his hair colored like white corn, and the eyes dark brown where you didn't expect such dark to be. Arms like snakes. Them big snakes in Africa, in India. Skin calling me to touch it.

We celebrated the Fourth of July that year on the fifth because Lace had to work on the holiday. Hobart went on and gave me the fifth off, too, maybe because he liked seeing me work on the Fourth. And it was another of those coolish blue-domed days we had that summer, strange weather, beautiful skies, and for some reason, from the time we got up, Jimmy Make and Lace were working with each other instead of against.

We put picnic stuff in the truck and drove all the way to Holly Creek Park, which was empty, just a bunch of overloaded trash cans. Corey found some fireworks, fountains and Roman candles and even black snakes, that somebody had overlooked when they were leaving the night before in the dark, and we set them off, Tommy so excited he ran around in circles making motorcycle sounds until he dizzied himself and fell down. Me and Corey built a fire and all of us cooked hot dogs on coat hangers, and Jimmy Make was sipping a beer, then I saw him sharing a can with Lace, they never did that anymore, and I saw that Dane was smiling. There was Dane smiling. Tommy was running in circles again, hollering, "I'm drunk! I'm drunk!" and

Jimmy Make and Lace were laughing and teasing at each other, Lace pretending like she was going to squirt mustard on him, and Jimmy grabbed her from behind and held her around the waist. He was shorter than she was, he kind of rocked her there. Then Tommy nudged up under Jimmy's arm to get in on it, and Jimmy Make's face went even softer, and he said something into Lace's ear.

I couldn't hear it, but when Lace ripped away and wheeled on him, I knew it was about North Carolina. I knew it was soft because of the hurt in his face. Maybe "C'mon, baby, please. Let's just try it down there one more time." Then, quick, he hardened that face and stagger-stomped off to his truck where he stood with his back to us, hands clutching the bed and elbows cocked out. Shoulders heaved up and his head hung, his toes kicking at a tire. Tommy made more motorcycle noises, louder now, and he ran around Dane in little circles, pinching Dane's fat when he went, Dane trying to push him off, but Tommy dodgy as a fly, and I said, "You quit that, Tommy, or I'll pinch you so hard you'll have places for two weeks."

After the picnic, it was the silent treatment until we hit home, and then it was the fight. The worst one yet, unless it just seemed that way to me because of the sweetness earlier. Or maybe all that sweetness had made the vicious build up in them. It got so bad I left the house, took my pillow, and locked myself in the truck. I couldn't really sleep there, lying in the dark with my eyes open, breathing that gasoline in my hair, wondering how close to a flame you'd need to be for it to catch. Hard to tell. After an hour or so, I rolled down the window, and I couldn't hear anything else from inside. I figured they'd gone to bed. So I slipped back into the living room, quiet, and there they sat on the couch. Limp. Like they'd finally popped each other, taken all of each other's air. Lace was doubled over so you couldn't see her face, her arms in her lap and her head in her arms. Jimmy Make had one elbow on a knee, he held his forehead in that hand. And I thought I heard somebody sniffing. I don't know which one it was, didn't neither of them ever cry, no matter what, they didn't. So maybe I imagined it altogether. What I noticed for sure was that even though they were sitting side by side, their legs weren't touching.

We could hear it getting closer. I knew they were going to take Cherryboy next, I didn't need to learn that from Dairy Queen gossip. And I wondered, my roller gliding, how could I feel so mixed up about it? Know that what my parents had together wasn't good for anyone, yet still feel such terror watching it finish?

And what did I remember of North Carolina? Get my body killed here, kill my insides if I left. I knew you never take all of you with you. I knew, it came to me with the brush moving, how if you left out, your ghost stayed behind. What I called the live ghost, the ghost you carry in you before you die. It stayed behind and hovered the hills, waiting on you. And what did I remember? (How the pavement would bloodbeat the wet stinking heat and how nobody came to visit. How the land opened wide to where anything could get you. How you walk only the skin of the world, nothing in you reaching any deeper. So that you know how you're blowing away, feel always the airy empty insides of you.) That's what I remembered of North Carolina.

R.L., clomping across the porch, carrying a can of Pringles to share. With every less inch of space between him and me, the hum heightening in my skin. I felt him. And how could I. What he did for the money just to buy the chips. *You know bettern that.*

He squatted down beside me. His boot tops had little give, and he was perched awkward, balanced on his toes. He dragged a finger through the wet blue paint on my arm. He lifted the finger and painted a line on my face, the spoiled cheek. He touched that cheek anyway.

I want to stay, I want to have, I want to be, without leaving. All the little ghosts, hovering.

Lace

So THERE were the five months in Morgantown, the nine pregnant, and then Bant. I did almost all my growing up right then. All that growing up pressed together so that each month held several years, and you can see it in my face, and in my body, too, if you look at pictures of me before and after. All along I told everybody I had no idea what I'd name the baby, but truth was, I'd chosen the girl name not two weeks after I felt Bant move. I made up Bant's name not just for the pretty in it, but because it made her more singular mine. And I called her Ricker See because it made her more of this place.

When Jimmy Make got to the clinic and found out her name was on her birth certificate and it wasn't Turrell, he left without seeing me or the baby and told Sheila he'd never be back. Sheila looked scared when she told me, and I have to admit, at first it scared me a little myself. Hurt a little more than that, despite that I'd thought I was beyond hurt from him. Then I asked myself—what had Jimmy Make done for this baby so far? Not a thing, I answered. Not one thing beyond come in a cold chickenhouse.

Three weeks later I was finishing up nursing Bant when Daddy said from where he was getting a glass of water at the kitchen sink, "Well. Lookee here who's a-coming." I knew right away who he meant. I pulled my shirt back down, laid Bant against my shoulder, and I stooped so I could see out the window and on out past the porch. Jimmy Make pouting under his camouflage hat and carrying a package, I saw when he walked up the steps, wrapped in "Happy Birthday" paper.

Daddy was inviting him in before I had time to decide what to do or how to act. Jimmy Make was trying to be all polite and friendly to Mom and Dad while at the same time cold-shouldering me, not an easy balancing act for anyone, least of all for some kid hardly knew how to talk. When I took the package from him and said "thank you," he looked away from my face and bit his bottom lip. But I saw him sneaking a peek at Bant. I reached up and turned her face gentle into my neck. But then Mom had to take her from me so I could open the present—a new dress could of fit a four-year-old—and before I could grab her back, Mom was handing my baby towards Jimmy Make.

"Ummm . . . ummm." Jimmy Make backed away, his hands thrown up and facing out like it was something hot that Mom had. "Oh, no."

Mom laughed. "Ain't no snake, buddy. This here's your daughter."

Now he'd backed his way into the couch, his hands still thrown out, and his giggle had genuine panic in it. "Oh, no. Oh, no. I don't know how to hold no babies."

Mom took his arm with her free hand and drew him sit down on the couch, him plunging down hard and surprised. I stood stiff across the room, torn between not wanting to watch and not wanting to leave my baby alone with this boy. Now Mom was getting him set up like an older toddler brother, pillow in the crook of his arm, arm propped on the end of the couch, and now she was settling Bant there. Jimmy Make sat paralyzed, his knees drawn together like a girl in a short skirt, his hat bill tipped over his face so you couldn't see how he was looking. He sat there for a long time, not moving anything more than his eyes, if he even moved those. Then he stretched out one knuckle-chapped finger and pulled it along her pink arm.

After that, he was back up every other week. He didn't let on I might be alive, but he came to see Bant. He did his talking with Mom, while I'd sit sentry across the room, and he'd hold Bant like glass and whisper. This father who wasn't yet shaving.

Then it was full fall, the season you could make the most money, and I was following Mom again, only now with Bant on my back and even deeper debts than last spring. Cohosh, seng, sassafras, black walnuts, hickory nuts, butternuts, pawpaw. It was the ginseng you'd make the real money on, two to three hundred dollars a pound, but the dealer would take other roots, too, sometimes nuts, and the rest we'd sell to neighbors or out along the road. Eat what was left. Fall meant wild meat as well, and Daddy tried to hunt some squirrel, even got a few, and Mogey and his older boy brought over more than that, turkey, and later deer, and that was the only time in my life I ate groundhog.

When I first got started, it was just plants I'd expected Mom to reteach me, things I could sell, but she knew she couldn't teach that without the other, and when I look back now, I see how much else I relearned. The names of all the little streams off Cherryboy. How the game paths went. Where you could find you a safe drink of water, where you could duck under overhangs to shelter out of storms. It was shortcuts across ridges from hollow to hollow, it was how easiest—footholds, handholds—to scale a particular draw. And although before that year I'd never been the type of person listens any closer than to what comes out of a mouth, all those quiet hours in the woods, I couldn't help paying other kinds of attention. I started listening in other ways.

Every few hours I'd have to stop and find a good log to get my back against so I could feed Bant. Unbutton whatever old shirt I was wearing, the fall cool tightening the skin on my breast, pull the blanket up around Bant to protect her warm. Mom would look away, that deep modesty of hers, while I couldn't do anything but look at Bant. Bant's sweet face working for the milk, that concentration, pull and let go, and I'd love out of a part of my heart I hadn't known I'd had. Like Bant herself had made that part while she was inside me, her tiny hands reaching up into my chest, secretly shaping, then left the new part behind to wake up when she was born. But then, sometimes, I'd get worried. Her face worried me clear back to then. She was a silent, solemn, watchful child, even as a little baby you could see all that in her. It was like, I feared, she was born with the age in her. It was like all the grief and disappointment and growing up I'd done while I was carrying her had seeped into her before she was born. I worried a lot about that.

We kept following the seasons. Walking the ridges. Working the hills. Sometimes Mary and Mogey'd come with us, sometimes Sheila when she was off, but it was mostly just the three of us. First Bant on my back, and then Bant waddling, stumbling, picking herself up, and finally Bant working with us. Bant buckle-legged, chubby-armed, all serious to help, squatted over hickory nuts, pulling berries off canes, by three she knew how to keep clear of the briar. By four, how to climb a leaf-thick hollowside using the edges of her feet. And although I kept worrying about what she carried in her—my age, my grief—I also realized the ways I was changing for the better—what had trickled into me to fill that loss—I realized Bant got some of that, too.

Strange thing was, those turned out to be the best years for me and Jimmy Make, too, although I'd never have believed you if you'd told me that back then. Because of course Jimmy Make was still in high school, still living at home. Still his mom's baby, while I was busy with a baby of my own, and the fact that things went best that way, well, it tells you something. By the Christmas after Bant was born in

September, he'd gotten over the naming enough to talk to me again. At first I hardly answered back, told myself I didn't need him or care, but I mostly just wanted to punish him a while. Only wants sex anyway, I justified it to myself, even though deep down I knew he could get sex in easier places. But by February, when he'd call to say he was on his way over, I found myself, despite myself, watching out the window for him to come bobcatting around that bend. And by two weeks after that, we ended up in the backseat of Jimmy's daddy's Blazer.

The summer before Bant turned one, between Jimmy Make's junior and senior years, that summer was the best. Despite all the heaviness in me, that summer I also found a fragile happiness I'd never had before. It was partly the love that Bant had shaped in me; partly the relief, the contrast, between this summer and the spring and summer before. Partly though, I have to admit, it was what grew in me for Jimmy.

He was supposed to be working for his uncle remodeling houses, but not many people were having work done that year, Jimmy Make was free a lot. I'd wake up early, get as much of my work finished as I could in the cool, and then afternoons, a couple times a week, Jimmy Make'd come up.

Mom would take Bant for a few hours. Me and Jimmy Make were going swimming. We'd walk back out to his car in the turnaround, pull the old bedspread out of the hatch, and head up Yellowroot Creek. Back then, there were two swimming holes up Yellowroot, and the first one was everyone's favorite because it was deep, and bottomed with the smooth little stones, and it had diving rocks. But if you pushed past that one, and we did, you eventually hit the Hemlock Hole, only chest-high, muckier than the first hole, but almost always, on weekdays, nobody around.

Usually he'd pull off his shirt as we climbed. The way his back browned, then went white where it slid into his pants, I tell you, it brought water to my mouth. Sometimes one of us would grab the other soon as we got there, crash up into that flat place under the hemlocks where nobody could stumble on us and see. That holey stained bedspread, the little needles gluing onto your skin, where all you'd find those needles later, and the tiny cones crunching under you when you'd wiggle and roll.

Other times we'd tease ourselves with wait. Pretend all this interest in swimming first, Jimmy Make's pale tight butt moving under and over water, the muscled leanness of his legs, those muscles still new enough that even Jimmy Make was surprised by them, pleased by them, we learned his new body together. We'd paddle away from each other, splashing from a distance, until maybe he'd go to floating on his back, eyes closed. I'd ripple up beside him, stand and hold him underneath with one hand, while my other'd find his nipples, finger their hardness, play the grooves of his ribs.

Or all of a sudden Jimmy Make might plummet down deep, snake between my legs, then heave up fast, water spraying, with me on his shoulders, him stumbling forward finding balance under my weight, and the inside of me beating against his neck. The liveness, I could feel it. My liveness, our liveness, his, liveness of the land around us, oh you felt it quicker when you were opened up like that. And the hemlock needles on my back, the low dense branches just past that.

Afterwards we always crawled back into the long afternoon light, and we stretched out on the flat rocks up where the creek took the plunge into the hole. Jimmy Make would drop straight asleep while I lay awake, watching. I watched the water dry off our bodies, you could see the sun take it, go. Watch the flesh sleep-jump under Jimmy's tight skin. Watch his face move, like Bant's, when he rubbed away an insect with the back of his sleeping fist, that like Bant, too. I could smell the sun in Jimmy Make's skin, his back, his shoulders, cinnamon brown and freckles both. I'd lie on my side, I'd reach out my tongue. In Jimmy Make's shoulder, I'd taste the sun.

Once in a while after those afternoons, he wouldn't leave. He'd spend the night. On the living room couch, Mom wouldn't let us share a bed unmarried despite that we had a baby and she had to have an awful good idea what we were up to those long afternoons. After everyone was good and asleep, though, he'd usually slip on in with me. Sheila not waking in her bed, Bant curled up in her crib, I'd feel him slide under my sheets, push me over on the narrow mattress, and then all of us in there together. The sound of Jimmy Make's breath in the middle of the night. I remember the comfort of him there. Because somehow only in sleep, only in my childhood bed, did Jimmy Make ever feel older than me.

Through those first few years, despite the constant hurt for money, despite how I sometimes still resented him, despite we weren't even allowed to share the same bed—me and Jimmy Make got tied together tight. When I look back now, I see the tie as a light spring green. I see it as a new slim vine. It wasn't just sex. That would have run down in no time. Of course, part of it was Bant, I couldn't see a lot of him in her, but I saw enough it didn't let you forget. And part of it was isolation, eventually I was separated not only from my high school friends, but with jobs getting tighter and tighter, many people I'd known my whole life were leaving the hollow desperate for work somewhere else. But I can tell myself it was lust, the baby, loneliness, that it was nothing else to look forward to, when, in truth, I know it went beyond all that. I loved him. I'd look back later and want to believe I had not, because that I did love him and couldn't keep on loving him is harder to face than to think I just never did. What else, though, could you call how it felt? The singing in the air around us when things were good. The way I'd want to cover him when he was cold. And even more amazing, I understood later because I couldn't afford to then, Jimmy Make loved me. Even if I hadn't wanted Jimmy Make, not much of anybody'd fool with a girl with a baby and no money. Jimmy Make, though, was seventeen, eighteen years old, and one good-looking boy. But he stayed. He loved. At least how Jimmy Make could.

Those years Jimmy Make was getting deeper in me, Daddy was going further away. We'd always known that someday the black lung would take him, but then we waited quietly so long for him to die that eventually he really would die started to seem less and less real. By a year after Bant was born, though, his coughing took a terrible turn. Mornings were the worst, when I'd be in my bedroom dressing Bant, and right on the other side of the wall, I'd hear his struggling gooey hacks, like his lungs were coming up, and coming up, pulling the rest of his guts right behind. His eyes got glassier, like they were letting in less light and reflecting more back, and his eyes moved less often. Mom kept him in constant clean rags, old bedsheets that she tore into neat squares, and I was so occupied with Bant that it took me a while to realize how quickly she was gathering up the dirty ones and washing them. One morning when she'd left for Prater and Daddy was dozing by the radio and I was doing breakfast dishes, Bant came toddling towards me offering one of those hanky rags crumpled in her fist. When I pulled it away, it dropped open, and I saw it wasn't any longer yellow. I saw it was black.

By Bant's second birthday, he was in a wheelchair, and then it wasn't the smothering that tortured him most. It was how he was no longer able to get up into the woods. He was all the time wanting to be pushed up into the trees, even though he hadn't seemed that interested in the woods those last few years while he could still walk. "When you have a little time," he'd say now. Say it polite, and patient, and unselfish. "When you have a little time."

So I'd muscle the chair over root and rock up into the trees at the foot of Cherryboy, then somehow I'd wrestle him even higher than that. Terrified the whole time I'd hurt him some way, knock him clear out of the chair with a log hidden under leaves, or jiggle that tank loose and that'd be it. "How you doing, Daddy?" I'd ask as we went, and how strange it was, to be standing with your daddy's blue-flanneled shoulders only at your waist, and Daddy saying, "Oh, I'm" breath "just fine" breath "honey." Breath. "I thank ye so much."

I'd finally get the chair to a flattish place, level it as best I could and block it with rocks. Then I'd drop down on the ground nearby and try not to listen. Concentrate on Bant wobbling around, squatting and picking up stuff, turning it over in her hands like she liked to do, then carrying it all somber to show Dad. I'd try not to listen, do numbers in my head, how much Pete was paying us, how much I needed, how much more I still owed. Watch Bant again, cross-legged in the leaves now, stacking twigs like Lincoln Logs, and when neither Bant nor numbers could keep me from listening, I'd move on to Jimmy Make, relive in my head the latest time, but often not even that could drown the listening, could drown the one breath. One breath. One breath more.

Jimmy Make graduated in May of '86. I went with him to his senior prom, me twenty-one years old, and Jimmy Make carries the picture still. His arms circling my waist, him behind me and even shorter than usual because of my heels so it looks like he's trying to see over my shoulder, and a backdrop of electric blue drapes. That summer, the one Bant wasn't quite two, he couldn't find a job at all, and we spent it like we had the summer before, or even happier than the summer before, at least for me, because him finally being out of school made us more legitimate, made me less ashamed. He's going to grow up now, I thought. Now he's going to grow up.

For the first time, the three of us did things together. We took Bant to the Firemen's Carnival in Watson. We even drove all the way to the New River Gorge one day, like a vacation, and I can still remember Jimmy Make picking her up out of her stroller, putting her on his back, telling her, "I'm your motorcycle, girl," as he jogged her to the lookout. The love settled down a little, but as it did, it vined into me deeper and wider. I felt the vine itself thicken.

Then the Sunday of Labor Day weekend he showed up all full of himself, and at first he wouldn't tell me why, him leaning cocky against a porch post with his ankles crossed, his big beautiful teeth grinning across his face. Finally he said, "I got me a job working in the pulpwood," then he swooped down and grabbed Bant up. "I'm takin you-all out to dinner tonight."

The work his outfit got that year was two counties north and east of here, which meant he rode two hours each way every day to get there and back. Which meant I started going two or three weeks at a time without seeing him at all. He did start giving me a little check, and god knows that helped, but then when he did come over, he was too tired to stay long, and more than once he fell asleep on me with us sitting straight up. I'd have been more understanding if it had just been the work that kept him away, but he spent a lot of his free days and nights partying with his high school friends, just like he'd always done, only before, without work, he'd had time for them and us both. "Well, he's only eighteen," Mom said one afternoon when we were stacking wood, and I knew what she was getting at. "I wasn't a parent yet when I was eighteen," I hurled right back. "And single," said Mom without missing a beat. That made me so mad I grabbed Bant and took off.

Since that sleety February night, marriage hadn't come up once, at least not between me and him. Each of us had our reasons, I guess, and mine was that by staying single I could still hold onto a little bit of myself. I loved him, but I didn't want to marry him, and I'd made sure we were much, much more careful after Bant. I loved Bant more dearly than I'd thought a person could love, but no way did I want a second one.

That year passed rough. Yeah, we had more money, but me and Mom still worked hard in the woods, Daddy just got worse, and I only saw Jimmy Make about every other week. I tried hard not to let it get to me, I reminded myself that of course he had to work, and a part of me knew Mom was right about the not getting married. But to get through the absences, through his distance even when he did come around, I had to pull back.

In July and August of that summer, he went over a month without even calling. The longest he had ever gone. Then one Saturday afternoon, right about the time I started resigning myself to being abandoned for good, he left a message with Mom that he'd be up at two o'clock.

He was late. I started waiting in the living room, then I moved on out to the porch. A full hour went by past the time he'd said. I was madder than I could remember being at him, but even so, I found myself clear out in the yard where I could spot him at a farther distance. And then I was mad not only at him, but at myself, and running under all that anger, a bruised vein of fear and hurt, making the anger even more desperate. Thirty minutes more and I couldn't any longer hold still. I was raging down the Ricker Run towards the turnaround place, and I got to the bridge just as Jimmy Make was pulling in.

He unfolded himself out of that car he had then, runty little orange Ford Fiesta, and I swear, I could smell the beer on him clear from the bridge. I waited for what strategy he'd use on me, he only had two, act all cheerful like hadn't nothing happened, or act all hangdog like he'd already beat himself up so no need for me to. He sauntered over towards me, rolling on his feet, hands sunk in his jeans pockets and head cocked to one side like he knew that was cute, and I saw it was cheerful he'd picked. He got within a couple feet, spread his arms out to catch a bridge cable on either side, and then I saw the tiredness pressing behind the cheerful, a kind of thinness to the skin under his eyes, but I knew the tiredness could be a hangover as easy as it could be work. He swung forward from his waist to give me a kiss, his chest swelling out in his white muscle shirt, and I shotsurged so full of hate, and love, and hurt, and want, I felt tears loosen under my eyes. But I hardened them back, and ducked his mouth.

"What the hell are you doing, drinking early in the day and then coming up in here late?" I hissed. "When your daughter hasn't seen you in over a month and asking for you every other day?"

He stumbled back then, restuck his hands in his pockets, pretended he hadn't been after a kiss at all. "Aw, Lace, now. I ain't been drinking." He was still grinning, but I could see he was sidling towards mad. "I just had me one beer on the way over," and he threw his thumb towards the car like there were full cans on the floor would prove him honest.

A hundred comebacks flitted through my head, and my fist balled up to smack him, but all I did, quieter than I expected, was say, "When the hell are you gonna grow up? When the hell?"

Then the grin was gone and away, and he thrust his hand in his hip pocket and pulled out a check. "Here's grown up for you." I could feel him just this side of furious, I could feel him holding it back. "Calm down, now, baby, why you always gotta ruin what little time we got?"

"You spend more time with us and less getting drunk, and we'd have more than a little. You pathetic babified fuck."

Then I pushed past him and into the turnaround and then I was charging up Yellowroot Creek. I could not resist it, I hated myself for it, but I had to go, and at the least, I didn't want to be following him. I could hear him, feel him, scuffling along after me, we were both moving fast and not talking, our twin breaths, rushing, and the terrible rip in the middle of me, wanting to slap him, then wanting him, period. I fell once, he didn't move forward to help me, I picked myself up and plunged on. And there we went, fighting each other without words while at the same time searching for a place to have sex, yeah, that was that year in a nutshell. Of course the first swimming hole was just foaming with a whole slew of little kids, Mr. Williams's grandchildren visiting, and him and Sam Kerwin and some other parents watching them, and I knew me and Jimmy Make passing would give them one more juicy thing to talk about, but I didn't care. Then when we were still a good five minutes from the Hemlock Hole, I could already hear people hollering, and once the path passed out of the trees, there they were, kids about Jimmy's age, and beer cans all around. Me and Jimmy Make didn't even look at each other. We veered off and shortcutted the half mile through the woods to the above-the-hollow-road, me feeling the heat of him behind me all the way, his heat horse cat, sweat and brush and briars and sun, the anger and the hunger. The hate and the want. Finally we stumbled into the backup place we'd used a few times before, under the snake ditches, and then I did turn to face him. I saw the two red thorn scratches down his shoulder, how the sweat drenched his hairline, how his eyes seemed to be moving forward out of his face. I pushed him down behind this big honeysuckle thicket, then he was on top of me, the sharp stones and rotty branches in my back, he struggled with his pants, I shoved him back until he got himself ready, his fingers trembling, him cussing the foil. Then Jimmy Make driving hard and me coming right back up to meet him, then me turning him over and driving just as hard back, and then he rolled me, it was wrestling, I was under him again and I took a piece of his arm in my mouth. And then I felt it. Sudden spurt of warm wet that wasn't me. I understood immediately. Rubber'd broke.

That time, when I missed my period, I knew right away. No. I knew before I missed. I said nothing to no one for several weeks. Partly out of embarrassment—fool me once, fool me twice—partly, I think, because I was once again trying to pretend I had some kind of choice to make.

It was fall again, right after Bant's third birthday. Mom was going out that morning to scout for ginseng, and I'd planned to go, too, but anybody says you don't get as sick the second time . . . I'd been over the commode off and on for two hours, trying to muffle what I was doing by flushing the toilet while I heaved. After about the third time, when I opened the door, Mom was standing right there in her sweatshirt and boots. Looking hard at me.

I wiped my mouth with my hand. "I'm too sick to go, Mom."

She nodded. She didn't turn away. She kept looking at me. I swung my eyes down, wishing she'd move so I could just go on, then I looked back in her face. And I saw she didn't look mad. She didn't look disappointed. She just looked sad. And that sadness scared me to death.

"All right," she finally said. "I'll take Bant with me."

I went back to bed. Daddy, who I knew wouldn't have any idea until I told him, sat in the living room with the radio. I was thankful for that. Twice more I had to lock myself in the bathroom, and Daddy's gospel music covered everything up. Around eleven, I finally got some clothes on, and I was standing in the kitchen trying to eat crackers when Daddy called in, "You feelin better, honey?"

I swallowed. "A little," I said. Not because I was, but because I knew what he wanted to say next.

If you'd asked me later, I couldn't have told you if that day had been cloudy or clear. I remember it was cooler than it looked because I had to go back in the house to get a padded flannel for Daddy. I remember I went bare-armed, I remember how I craved that cold. Give me some pain from the outside for a change. I seized the chair handles, I shoved the wheels into the leaves, I forced it hard up the hill, trying desperate to drown out the *what you gonna do? What you gonna do, Lace, now?* I jammed it over rocks, I split dead branches in two, it felt good to have something solid to push against, and I did stop once and ask Daddy, I heard my voice at a distance, "You okay?" and him, "Don't bother me none. I'm fine." When we reached the place we usually stopped, I just tilted the chair and pushed harder, higher, until I came up against a long thick log I was finally too winded to get around.

I'd almost forgotten Daddy until I was stooped over and hunting for rocks, and "Thank you, honey," I heard him say. Then I looked at my daddy. Bundle of chicken bones in flannel and jeans. A hand gripping each knee, the gap where the two fingers were missing, him glassy-eyed as a mounted buck, not speaking, not knowing, not even enough lung to talk, and *what are we going to do? What? Why us?* I chocked his wheels, my mind moving so fast it tripped over its own legs and somersaulted wild, me grabbing at it to get hold of it long enough to think clear, when all of a sudden, I heard, outside and on top of all that racket in my head. The one breath. One breath. One breath more. Then my mind was screaming, I squeezed my ears between my hands, and *Shut up,* I yelled at him and me both without a sound leaving my mouth, then my mind jumped a track, and it came to me—he's being buried by it. He's being buried by it.

His lungs are being buried by it, by coal, which is earth, which is this place, and, still, he wants nothing but to be out in it. On the land, like me, like us, despite the burying it does, and what the hell, what the hell is it? Why do we have to love it like we do? The Bible says we are made of dust, but after that making, everybody else leaves the dirt and lives in air, except us, oh no. We eat off it, dig in it, doctor from it, work under it. Us, we grow up swaddled in it, ground around our shoulders, over top our heads, we work both the top and the underside the earth, we are surrounded. And still, Daddy wanting nothing at the end but to sit and look at land. Even though inside it drowns him.

Within a month, Daddy died. And if I'd thought my life was over when I got Bant, I realized how little about over I understood until I got Dane and Daddy died. If I'd thought my choices were narrow before, well. And although I'd spent a lot of my life laughing at those old-time stories, it is hard to ignore them completely, especially around birth and death. Because while Bant was inside me when I grew up and lost the self I thought I was, Dane was inside me when I lost Daddy and what little independence I'd hung onto with Bant. So while Bant was born aged, old people in her, Dane was born peculiar, mournful, and sad. Sad Dane. The way Dane never did get quite right seemed a mark of the marriage.

Because that time we did marry. Shortly after I missed my period, before I'd even told Jimmy Make, Jimmy's cousin helped him get on at a union underground mine, making real good money. Me with two kids, no job, the loss of Daddy—it all forced my hand. The union job gave Jimmy Make courage, the second baby must have amped up his guilt. He asked me for real. I told him yes.

Bant

I STEPPED out and let the screen snock shut behind me. But even when I walked to the very edge of the porch, I couldn't shed the sound of them, despite that they weren't fighting loud. They'd started in the bedroom, and Jimmy acted like he was going to walk out, but then he stopped in the hall. Now he stood there with his back to the outside wall of the bedroom where Lace sat up in bed, him clenching and unclenching his fists, taking a step or two towards the front door, then a step or two back, and they fought each other without looking at each other, through the bedroom wall. I reopened the screen, reached in for the regular door, shut that. Then it was just Lace I heard, through the window. Her and the machines working up overhead.

My face surged full. I pushed back on it. Corey and Tommy sat in the road with their bike and trike upside down, resting on handlebars and seats. They called it working on their cars. I'd thought I'd been right, about the phone yesterday, what I'd overheard. Now that Jimmy Make had said what he did to start the fight, I knew I was right for sure. My nose tickled way back in, my hands started to tingle. I made my face hard. And then I felt the need to go.

I hadn't felt that in a while. It was that need I used to get when I was younger, twelve or thirteen, back when my body was coming on me rapid-quick, and it brought with it this thrusty urge to go. My guts standing up and pushing forward, thrusting against the front of me go, it was like if I pushed fast enough, I'd bust through something and be free, and I hadn't felt it in some time, but I did feel it now, and *go*, I thought. *Just go.*

Corey and Tommy pumped their pedals with one hand and felt the spin of the tire through the other. Then Corey stood up on his knees, put his hands on his hipbones, swiveled his head, and spat. Just like Jimmy Make would. I looked at Corey there, that stupid rag tied to his arm. And all of a sudden, the go thrusting in me, I wanted to smack Corey. I wanted to shake Corey (*there at the end it was like driving a boat*), I wanted to rub his face in it, show him (*you can live off these mountains*) because Corey did not understand. Jimmy Make copycat did not understand, and now the go was behind my teeth, a mad with a whipping pleasure in it, and I knew another way, a most likely unguarded way, not to the top of the fill, but to the very edge of the mine.

I jumped off the porch and ducked under it, jerked out my old bike, too small for me now and coated in flood crust. I was in my paint clothes, I'd been waiting for Jimmy to quit fighting and take me to work, but I didn't care anymore. I pushed my bike over to the boys, clamping back the go in me so they wouldn't see. "C'mon, Corey," was all I said.

Corey squinted up from under the heavy bangs, that oil-colored hair. "Where we going?" he said, still pedaling with one hand.

"Up on the mountain. I want to show you something." I straddled the bike now, but the go I tamped down. I wanted Corey to think I was doing him a favor, not him doing me one.

He kept pedaling with his one hand, looking at his spokes instead of me. I looked away from him, too.

"I'm going up through the snake ditches."

Then I saw the pedal hand slow, just a little. I started to walk my own bike away. The pedal hand stopped. Corey stood up, tossed back the bangs, wiped both palms on his just-too-short jeans, and as he flipped his bike upright, he eyed his piddly bicep under the chamois rag. Tommy hurried and turned his trike, too.

"Tommy, you can't go," I told him, keeping my voice even again. Hiding the urgent in it.

"You think that rusted-up sorry-ass tricycle could make it up them snake ditches, boy?" Corey said.

Tommy whimpered and scrambled onto his trike, but me and Corey were already moving. Tommy left the trike and ran after us with a chunk of coal in his hand that he let fly with a shout, and it thumped me in the small of my back. But we were gone.

And then me and Corey were moving. We were shooting, tearing, flying, we were leaving behind. We went. Gravel spitting off our tread and ringing the bike fenders, and then there came the hardtop ledge, but I still knew what to do, wheelie up and twist a little, crash down on the hardtop flat and steady (like we used to do), and then we could really travel. The houses and trailers and sheds little run-together color lumps in the edges of my eyes, and the wind we made cooling us against the already humid day, and it was like it used to be, me flooded with them punchy gusts of got-to-go, part joy, part rage, part hope, part put-behind-despair, my body thrusting to get ahead of itself, no mind to it, and I'd forgotten how good this here felt, body grunting: Move, girl. Move.

I was always in the lead, despite the bike being at least three years too small, midgeted up under me, my knees splayed. I was back to twelve, eleven, ten, pistoning my pedals in too-short-for-my-legs strokes, and we took a turn and pumped through the Williamses' backyard, cranking as hard as we could in the grass to get a good run on the rutty diagonal path that would shoot us up onto the above-the-hollow road. The old dirt road that had been dozed before I was born for a strip job long over, and trees and brush had pushed in on the road, like a tunnel it was, and water had worn it, rutted and puddled it. This was the way to the snake ditches. When I was real little, Jimmy Make used to bring us up here all the time, me and Dane, on the dirt bike he had back then. Now me and Corey balanced our bike tires on the ridges of the ruts, the road bombed with puddles as long and as wide as cars and deep to above your knees (wet spring, wetter summer, this crazy weather), then, pushing as fast as I could go on that rut edge, I saw a monster puddle looming. I kept balanced, I hung on, and it came to me, as the water sprayed and I won, I remembered again, what I had known when I was younger and tended anymore to forget. I knew again what the truck meant to Jimmy, what the speedwagon did to Corey, why Tommy and B-bo and David ran around with motorcycles in their mouths, I remembered, the glory of forgetting and that stun of blind power that came with that gut-urgent go.

Then I realized we'd passed the turnoff to the snake ditches, and I slowed down and hollered at Corey to come back. I knew exactly where the turnoff was, I could spot it even in the jungle of July, Jimmy Make had taught it to me good. Dane was wee little, he would ride in front between Jimmy's legs, and I'd hold onto his back, so much older Jimmy Make seemed then. "It's in here," Corey was shouting from way down the road, and I knew he was wrong, little pissant know-it-all, but I didn't care. I just thrashed on into a big web of honeysuckle towards where I knew the snake ditches were, and I noticed for the first time since I'd left our yard the machines working overhead.

Then I heard Corey burrowing behind me, but he didn't say nothing, he'd never admit out loud to being wrong, he was like Jimmy Make that way too. Our wheels and pedals hung up in the vines, we had to rip and tear, it was not just honeysuckle and kudzu, but tougher woodier stuff, and greenbrier, too. The mud on me was beginning to itch, and I could smell the gasoline mixed in the mud, and R.L. came up in the odor of gasoline, but I pushed him away by gritting my teeth and throwing hate at myself (*you know better than that*). Finally we got into decent-sized trees you could walk normal under, but we still weren't finding the ditches, and Corey started whining about how I didn't know what I was doing. Then there they were.

That was how you'd always hit those snake ditches, with a startle. Even if you were looking for them, they were a startle when you hit them. You moving along, feeling woods, hills, wild—then, sudden-smack, that crazy concrete zigzagging all over the mountain.

Because that was the other part of it, the other way it was in these hills. You had your quiet places, Grandma places, your places where peace would settle in your chest—then you had these places, places with a sharpness, a hardness, so utterly opposite all the rumpled deep green, you'd have to slow down and refocus your eyes. Like the Big Drain, and the crumbling-down coke ovens at the far side of Yellow-root, and old driftmouths covered with rusty steel bars, and tilting-over tipples, and the mine cracks like earthquake scars in the ground, all my life I'd stumbled onto these used-up left-behind places, and sometimes I saw ahead—only these places would be left. And then there was the newer places, places they were getting ready to use up, bulldozers and front-end loaders, surveying tape, raw muddy road gashes, yellow and copper with black flecks in them, like a nasty kind of shit. And then there was the way these places made you feel, the way they could draw you to them, draw you with something I didn't believe in but that I knew. I remembered. *We're going snake hunting,* Jimmy Make would say, and before we left the house, he'd put on me my toy pistol, metal and plastic, in a holster around my waist. I'd hang tight to his back while we rode, his smell in my face, the laundry soap and gentle sweat. Sleepy smell. I lifted my bike into a ditch. *Go girl,* I said in my mind. *Go.*

Those snake ditches were a smooth ride, but they were steep. There was a trick to riding those ditches. The ditches themselves were scummy white veins, but here and there they drained into each other over broad flat tall spillways, algae-slick, and then the ponds branched out into yet more ditches. Grandma'd told me they'd been poured in the early '70s for the same strip mine that went with the above-the-hollow road, and that cement had held up good. By the time Corey was old enough to go along, Jimmy Make had gotten rid of the dirt bike and lost interest in the snake ditches. We weren't allowed up here by ourselves, it was too dangerous for all kinds of reasons, but Corey couldn't keep his want off them and I knew why. I knew why because of the way Jimmy Make used to be contagious to me, but Jimmy was contagious to me no more, and I'd break Corey of it, too. Learn him.

We stood on our pedals, leaned forward into the switchbacked drains, fought for enough momentum to keep the bikes from tipping. I could hear Corey huffing. The ditches ran with water only right after it rained, and the belly-warmth of the concrete drew lizards and snakes. Mostly we'd just throw rocks at them, make them coil up or wiggle away, and Jimmy'd tell us what they were, garters and blacksnakes and watersnakes and copperheads. Once or twice he said *rattler,* but he may have made that up. I called him Daddy back then. He got younger the older I got. Sweat started melting the dried mud on my face and dripping gray drops onto my handlebars, my hands, but that kind of moving, that kind of grunting along, there was no good go in it to drown your thoughts. I thought of what Jimmy Make had said that morning—a deep mine was opening in Mingo County and he was going to apply. If they didn't hire him on, he was going down to North Carolina and find him a job there—and I thought about how he had said it. *Go girl,* I thought. *Just go.*

I had on my shoes, but Corey didn't, and although I was still mad at Corey, I flinched at how the pedal must feel in the tender caved-in part of his foot, but I also knew Corey thrived on that kind of thing, stupid rag fluttering on his arm. We hit a nearly vertical spillway, and Corey acted like he was going to ride it, but I made him get off the bike and walk up along its side, on the ground. I realized we'd have to walk our bikes all the way off from the top, and before we did, I'd have to talk Corey into it, else he would coast down and kill himself. Then we were back in the ditch, huffing, pumping, and I studied the concrete, passing slow under my front wheel, and I saw no snakes except one dead garter. I took care not to run over it. Jimmy only used his pistol on the big ones and never on lizards. *I'm gonna make you a snakeskin belt, Cissy,* he'd say. He never did. But now even all the snakes'd been run off, and as we got higher, the machines got heavier, thicker, the sound like grinding your molars while you have your fingers in your ears, only you don't have the say-so to stop it.

Now we were passing more and more thrown-over trees, so we were getting closer. To the coal company, trees were nothing but in the way, they just bulldozed them over the side, and there they dangled, their roots spooky, hairy and dirt-clotted. Waiting to wash down on top of somebody, and Corey, nodding at the trees, called at me, "You could make you a good fort out of them there" (*learn him*). When Dane would get scared of the snakes, Jimmy Make would hold him. He'd stroke his back. But he'd also say, *Look at Bant, Dane. She's not scared. Ole Cissy, she's a tough one,* he'd tell Dane. Every time, whether he really shot his pistol or not, we'd all three lie flat on the ground, playing at escaping ricochet bullets. I'd aim with my pistol, pretend, and Jimmy would pretend right along with me, Jimmy Make was always better than Lace at playing that way. Jimmy Make could mean it.

The culverts had given up switchbacking and now they ran nearly vertical, our bikes nearly up and down under us, it was like riding ladders, and we leaned every ounce of our bodies over the handlebars just to keep the bikes from bucking over and backwards. The air burnt my lungs, and the muddy sweat, odored with gasoline, still dripping on my hands and arms, and even in all that, the thought came to me: *better lie low up there, what if he's working close enough to see,* and then I cussed myself. *Girl, You know bettern that.* At this point the contest was not who was in the lead, but who had to get off their bike first, and although I didn't care, Corey lost anyway, not by giving up and getting off, but by forcing on until he wrecked. He skinned his knee in the ditch, stopped a few seconds to lick and suck the blood. I got off, too, and we pushed the bikes awhile, and then we reached where the ditches ended. Soon after that, we got to where the live trees ended, and we had to drop our bikes altogether and crawl. And then the go was really gone, there was nothing left but push, but try, and I knew Jimmy Make wasn't bluffing this time. And I knew that meant I would have to choose.

The dead trees dangled all around us. We chinned ourselves up by the roots of the vines and scrub still left in the ground. Then everything live stopped, and the ground under the tree trunks was shale, loose dirt, and rock, and it was easier to climb the trees than climb the ground. We climbed the trees backwards, from their tops into their roots. The machine noise had turned from the teeth-grinding sound to rumbles and clashes. Up here out of the woods, the sky was easy to see, hurtling overhead, heavy with clouds, making to rain. I was using the side of my shoe to cut little steps in the loose dirt, I tested each step ginger, shifted my weight onto that one while I made a new one, the first one already collapsing under my sole. Corey gripped with his bare toes.

At last we reached the final boost to the very lip of what was left of the mountaintop. A vertical loose-earth wall. Then we were fingernailing it, and Corey toenailing it, then I got my arms up over the lip, and

I tried to drag my body after, but there was too much give. The bank caved in and scrawled out from under me, until finally I just swam at it with all fours, swallowing a little shale as I swam, and eventually the bank fell enough and I rose enough that we were the same level, and I had enough of my body lying flat on some kind of shelf that I could pivot the rest of me onto it. I looked back at Corey under me. He was still scrabbling, his face bunched hard with effort, the light dirt showing bright in his hair. I got up on my knees, reached down for Corey, and throwing everything I had left into my shoulders and arms, I clawed Corey up by the straps of his tank top.

Corey

COREY staggers to his feet, still a little off-balance from Bant's grab. He shakes his arms and legs to shed the dirt, tosses back his bangs. And then he sees.

As soon as he sees, he can't see enough. His eyeballs aren't big enough to hold what he can almost see, he wants to stretch his eyes wide like you can do your lips, for a big ole burger, for three-layer cake. Corey's stomach hardens, his chest, his arms clench.

It's too far to walk to. It is across a long long way of dirt and rocks and raw roads and terraced earth and black mounds. But it is there, *if I had me one* . . . It is a great grand giant thing, here in this place of puny things, you can see big things on TV, but this place full of sorry-ass piddly things, only things around here big enough to stretch your eyes are the coal preparation plant at Deer Lick (to look on it, a glory it was, gasp in his chest, they passed it at night, lit all over like a carnival ride and roller-coaster-shaped, but a real roller-coaster, not a game one, the livening violence to it) and that one silo at Performance Coal. And now this here.

Corey has seen this machine in *Gazette* pictures, but in real life, he's seen it just once, and that was in the dark. Them driving up

Slatybank, trying to take the shortcut because Dad had stayed too long at the man with the parts' house, and Dad pointed out the giant on the ridge overhead. Corey looked back, and he saw it on the night horizon. They were mining twenty-four hours a day, so it was all lit up along its neck, and instead of seeing it in metal, Corey saw it in lights, a cluster of stars, Corey saw a swinging constellation come down. When Corey'd seen it in the paper, Dad had told him its real name was dragline, but its nickname was Big John. *Like something out of* Star Wars, *Dad said*, *maybe the biggest piece of machinery ever built, twenty stories tall, for sure the biggest shovel in the world, and we have it right here in West Virginia. And they call us backwards,* Dad said.

Now Corey sees it in its metal, in daylight. It's big enough to dry up the spit in your mouth when you look on it, Corey can tell how big by the D-9 dozers and haul trucks antcrawling under Big John. Big John's neck looks like one of those huge power transmitters that straddle the mountains to carry off the electricity the coal makes, and the neck is planted in a pivoting base the size and even the shape of sixty army tanks welded together. Swinging off the neck, the shovel itself, roomy enough to hold twenty or so of those monster rock trucks and throw them over the ridge, the rock trucks themselves so big Dad's truck, Dad said, would only come halfway up one tire.

If I had me a four-wheeler, if I did, Seth, Seth has one, and he is only nine, Corey's brain, soaked in the size of this thing, *if I had . . .* He could sneak up in here when they weren't working. Sometimes they do stop working, you know by the surprised stillness in the hollow, and Corey could sneak up in here and ride across the site for an up-close look. Blare that four-wheeler through craters and traps, tear around and skid and wheelie, jump ditches, and when he hit one of the roads, he'd really cut loose, ride like hell to the very edge, brake, burn rubber, slam stop at the last minute before hurtling over the fill. And if there was a blast when he was at it . . . Whoa.

Then, no, matter of fact, he wouldn't just look at the machinery. He'd go on and climb right in. He'd start with those big rock trucks, monkey right up and swing into a cab, grip the big wheel, that plastic hard as steel in his hands. Try the D-9 dozers next, he'd take his time, saving the best for last, he'd handle the controls, pump the pedals, them big treads rumbling under him, they can go over anything on earth.

And, finally, he'd scale Big John. That vast mountain-handling piece of gorgeous machinery. And as Corey climbs it, the smell of its fluids, the good grease he'd get on his clothes. And maybe he'd cut himself a little on something. Maybe he'd bleed a little there. He'd crawl in, settle in the seat, take a look at how it ran, push his legs to the pedals, grip sticks and handles. That giant, his body in that gigantic body, his body running that body, and the size, the power of that machine: inside Big John, Corey can change the shape of the world. Corey can.

Bant

WHAT I SAW punched my chest. Knocked me back on my heels. At first I saw it only as shades of dead and gray, but I pushed my eyes harder, I let come in the hurt, and then it focused into a cratered-out plain. Whole top of Yellowroot amputated by blast, and that dragline hacking into the flat part left. Monster shovel clawed the dirt and you felt it in your arm, your leg, your belly, and how lucky Grandma died, I thought. I thought that then. And past where Yellowroot had been, miles of mountain stumps, limping all the way over to what used to be horizon, and what would you call it now? The ass-end of the world. *Moonscape,* that's what many said after they'd seen it, but I saw right away this was something different. Airiness emptying me. Because a moonscape was still something made by God and this was not, this was the moon upside down. A flake of the moon's surface fallen to earth, and in that fall, it had kept its color, nickel and beige, kept its craters, its cracks. But then it landed not up, but moonside down.

My tongue moved in my mouth. It had lost all water, tasting what I saw. Then I realized I had my knee and one hand in that weird brittle grass, and I jerked my hand to my stomach and got myself up quick.

Deer won't even eat that grass. Now you know if deer won't eat it . . . We'd come out on this raised embankment at the very edge of the mine, and I got back my balance, but the wind across that dead flat stirred the gas in my hair. Then I noticed Corey standing a few feet below me like he'd been freezetagged, his fists on his hips Jimmy Make–style, that stupid rag fluttering. There you go, Corey. There you go. *You kids won't have nothing but to clean up their mess.* I hardened my face again and scanned the killed ground until I got to where I thought the Yellowroot Creek valley fill should be. Thing was, you couldn't tell anything about size or distance up here, because, I realized right then, this was nothing. And you cannot measure nothing. What I could tell, because Cherryboy was not nothing yet, was how close they were getting to it, creeping viselike around the head of Yellowroot Hollow.

I tightened my chest and turned away. Walked down the spine of the bank a piece. A haul truck passed under us, machinery jarring in my teeth, and more blocks inside me, tumbling down. Tumbling. Now I had my back to Cherryboy. I was just staring at where Yellowroot wasn't anymore. Then I was remembering what Yellowroot had been. Yellowroot, shaped like a rabbit with its ears laid back, Grandma showed me that. It took its name from goldenseal, she said, that was the real name of yellowroot. *Yellowroot's the country name,* Grandma said. *Now yellowroot's what you use for a sore throat, gargle that, nothing better for it. Turn your mouth yellow, your throat yellow, too. Everything in these woods was put here for a reason.* Then I was hearing something else. Corey. I'd nearly forgotten about him, but it was Corey making a noise. Making a motor noise in his mouth, soft, I don't think he even knew he was doing it out loud. And then I knew Corey had learned nothing at all.

My arms flooded with wanting to knock him down, fling him off the bank, and rub his face in dead dirt. I wanted to hear him yelp and cry. But truth was, deep down I'd known all along Corey couldn't understand. I'd just had to try, but, no, that was a lie, too, why I'd really brought him . . . The real reason I'd brought him was I was scared to see it first time by myself. And I knew I had to see it before I could decide. Of course Corey did not understand, and Dane understood only in a way before word, before memory, and what did Jimmy Make understand?

Understood that move-the-mountain draw, the power, the suck, the tempt. Understood anyway the wrongness of it all. Understood he could not stop it. Understood he had to go. Did he understand how Lace would choose? How I would? Would he understand why? That's just how he is, I wanted to say to her. Why can't you see that's just how he is? Go on and love him anyway. And I remembered the sleepy smell. The ginger in how he held me little, him my father and just a little older than I was now. I remembered how he'd never left, not through all those years, not even when she wouldn't marry him, not even afterwards when she did and things got worse. He never left.

The memory picture of Yellowroot faded fast. And the feeling it left behind scared me worse than the mine site did. Because what I was feeling again was nothing. The distance between me and the land had set in, complete, but this time, I didn't even have any want in me to cross it. Nothing. Just like you couldn't measure the site because it was nothing, you couldn't feel for it either, because there was nothing to feel for. Nothing stirs nothing. And it came to me for the first time: was it worse to lose the mountain or to lose the feeling that you had for it?

I still stood with Cherryboy at my back. I couldn't see Cherryboy, but I could feel it behind me the way you can feel an animal hiding close by in the woods. How Uncle Mogey always said that an animal throws off itself a hum felt not by your five senses, but by something else you carry around you. Cherryboy I could still feel like that.

Mogey

ALTHOUGH I have been a Christian all my life, I have never felt in church a feeling anyplace near where I get in the woods. This worried me for a very long time. Even when I prayed in a church, I couldn't make much come, where woods, I had only to walk in them. To walk in woods was a prayer. But I knew it was wrong. Some kind of paganism or idolatry, I didn't know what you'd call it, but I knew it must be sin. I used to feel so guilty about it I finally talked to the pastor one time. This was years back, me maybe in my late twenties. Pastor Dick, that one was, and I respected him. I respected all of them, I figured they had something I did not, why else would God have called them to be pastors? So I told Pastor Dick my concern, and he said, "Mogey, God gave man the earth and its natural resources for our own use. We are its caretakers, and we have dominion over it . . ." And he went on like that, saying stuff I'd heard since I was little.

But part of me knew, even back then, that's not what it is. I knew we wasn't separate from it like that. I started to say something, to explain to him—I think I wanted to get him around to where he'd say what I knew was okay—but he looked at me like Mary'd look at our younger boy Kenny when he talked about his pretend friend. So I cut it off and shut up.

The first time I felt it was the Wednesday before Thanksgiving, 1958. I'm sure on the year because I know I was ten, and that'd make my cousin Robby thirteen. We was standing right under the ridge on the backside of a mountain in Pocahontas County, a place they called the Ribs.

That buck come out after the last drive. I don't mean he was driven to us. He was not, he come out on his own. Out to the side of Robby and me, and a little below us, and I felt him before I seen him. The way a big animal throws something off himself, something he carries around himself that you can feel without seeing. It's like a higher hum than the still things, trees and ground and rock, although I only call it hum because I don't got no other word for it. It's not something caught by ear. As I got older, I'd catch it off small creatures, too, and after I got to be a man, I mean really a man, got past the early man and come to know myself and settled down, I could catch it, just quieter, even off trees and dirt and stone. But in the beginning, I only got it off big animals. That morning when I felt the buck and turned and saw, I thought at first he was a doe, his antlers blurred in the branches like they were. Then he moved ahead, stepping, and the antlers focused, come clear, and he was nodding a little, I remember. Like his rack was dragging his head a little with the weight.

I pushed my elbow into Robby. The buck held himself still, like he should not have, an animal that old knows better, and I stared at him, wondering at that stillness. The color their coats get in the fall, grayish, a kind of grizzled to them that comes on after the tender red-brown they wear in summer, as though they age by seasons instead of years. I watched him. Robby lifted his gun.

When he fired on him, that buck didn't show in any way he moved that he'd been hit by a gun. The shot knocked him off the ledge more like a punch than a bullet. And after he fell, he didn't just crash and come to rest on the next outcrop like he was supposed to. No. He went to rolling. It was the third strange thing he done that day, after showing himself to boys with a gun and then standing still, practically posing for the shot. I've seen nothing like it since, big buck hooping down that mountain end over end, antlers over backside, whiteside, the antlers, then the white rump, coming up over and over again. Me and Robby leaned out, each of us hanging off a tree, and we watched him roll what had to have been well over five hundred feet, and that buck never hung up on a thing. Not a bush, not a ledge, not a rock. He just never hung up, like he should have. After a while, he disappeared out of our sight, although we could still hear the thumping and even the rattle of dirt and rock, and then, after a little bit, we lost the sound of him, too.

I'd never been to the very bottom of the Ribs. There was a fair-sized creek down in there, and running pretty full like it was, it took up most of what flat lay between the mountains, and there wasn't much flat to begin with. We'd tried to come straight down as best we could so we'd end up about where the buck should have, but we didn't see no sign of him. Not only no body, but no blood, and no tore-up leaves or brush, and no knocked-loose rocks. I looked at Robby, waiting for what we should do. Robby squinted and shook his head. He said, "You walk up the creek and I'll walk down. Holler when you find him."

I nodded and took off quick up the bank. I've always loved looking for stuff in the woods. That feel you get when you sudden-spy, as you're moving, the deep green leaf of a ramp. The crinkle of a morel. Presents the woods give you just for paying attention, that's how I saw it. And here I was, a little boy hunting a big buck, maybe a ten-pointer, wasn't much you could look for more exciting than that. I slogged along through them rain-blacked trees, it was steep down there even at the very bottom, most of the time I had to kind of stagger along with one leg higher than the other, and many a time I near slid in the creek. But I didn't feel the cold or the wet, didn't feel the mud soaking through the seat of my pants. It was sweet in that gorge, I'll tell you. Rhododendron and fern, lichen and moss, big rocks, pretty even in such weather. I had my eyes sharped good. I'd been hunting game with my dad since I started school, hunting greens and stuff with Mom even before that. But, hard as I looked, I still couldn't find no sign of the buck. Not even tracks or some mark of struggle in the brush. My excitement started running down on me some, and eventually I got to a point where I knew the buck could not have come off this far from where he was shot even if we had got way off course during our slide down. I figured he must have come off in Robby's direction, even if Robby hadn't hollered yet. I started heading back.

I run into Robby about where we'd parted ways. He had dropped down on a soaked rotty log, his hands between his legs for the warmth there. "Well," he said to me. "He didn't come off that way."

"Didn't come off my way neither," I said back.

He cocked his head up at me. "Had to've," he said.

I shook my head. "Ain't no sign of him up through there. I looked real close."

Robby blew his breath out, loud, to show how ticked off he was, then pushed up off the log. "Guess I'll have to go look myself." He picked up his gun and left.

I watched him go. Just stood there for a while, my nose running hot and heavy and fast, me wiping it over and over again with the cuff of my coat until that cuff was about glistening. Then I started shivering myself, and I couldn't just stand there freezing to death in the rain. So I decided to double-check Robby's direction, too.

Now this next little part I don't remember as good. This time the hunt for the buck didn't have the look-forward-to it had had before—I trusted Robby, I figured the buck wasn't up his way. I really just needed to move. I was starting to feel hungry under the cold, and also some worry over whether Dad would whip me when I got back for not telling him where I was going. I was feeling bad for the buck, too. I knew he had to be wounded, and it is a very bad thing for a hunter to clip a deer and never find him again. Him dying a slow death someplace, or being killed brutal by some other animal. To cripple a deer was a terrible thing. I was blundering along, thinking this, when I come up on it.

It was a spot where the shelf between the Ribs and the creek broadened a little. Turned out, although I couldn't see that yet, that it made enough space for a little sunk-down place like a room, and it seemed even more like a room because there was rocks all around it. Somehow a rock fall had come and made like this room. And I come up on the rock border and the widened place, and, sudden, I knew that beyond it, the buck would be there. Somehow I knew that, I remember exactly how it felt in me. Then I climbed up the little rise and dropped down.

The buck was not there in body. But something else was.

I stepped into that little room, I stopped and looked around me. And something layered down over my self. At first it seemed to wrap me. But then it was somehow in the center of me, starting there, and then it washed on out through all of my parts. It was the feel of a warm bath with current in it, a mild electric, it prickled my skin, every inch of my skin it touched. And the thing was, once it had currented all the way through me and reached my very ends, it kept on going.

It melted my edges. It blended me, I don't know how else to say it, right on out into the woods. It took me beyond myself and kept going, so I wasn't no longer holed up in my body, hidden, I saw then how before I'd been hidden, how I'd believed myself smaller than I really was. It made me feel bigger in myself, and it made me feel more here even though you might have expected such a thing to make me

feel gone. And with it came total sureness. And with the total sureness came peace.

I had to leave out of here for a while. I got drafted, Robby did, too,
they loved us hillbilly boys for how good we could shoot. All those
fall days hunting deer and squirrel, it'd be funny if it wasn't so sad.
But it meant I left out of here and saw other mountains, and now I
know people not from here probably don't understand our feeling
for these hills. Our love for land not spectacular. Our mountains are
not like Western ones, those jagged awesome ones, your eyes always
pulled to their tops. But that is the difference, I decided. In the West,
the mountains are mostly horizon. We *live* in our mountains. It's not
just the tops, but the sides that hold us.

I tried for a long time to pull the two together, what I knew from
church and what I knew from mountains. Of course, it would only be
right if I could keep the church part ruling the woods part. So when
I'd first walk into the woods, I'd say to myself, "Look here what God's
give us." But just about as fast as I could have that thought, this second
one would come from deeper: "This is God." And then, from under
that thought, from deeper yet, another thought would come, saying, "I
go here. This is where I go." And last of all, the most certain thought,
but also the most dangerous: "This is me. This, all this, is me."

I used to dream a good bit about that buck. It was mostly the same two
dreams I had, but I'd have them fairly often. I'd dream we'd come up
on the sunken place, me and Robby together, and the buck would be
there, but the feeling would not. The buck has a broke back, but he's
still alive, trying hard to get up, him hoofing in the sloppy wet leaves for
a grip. His big rack is dragging at him, pulling on his head, and there
comes in me a tear in my chest, like cloth tearing, such pity do I feel.
The rocks lie in a circle, making the room where the buck struggles,

173

and Robby is afraid to shoot him for fear a bullet might ricochet off a rock and hit one of us. But I crouch down behind a big beech, I press my cheek to it, those trees that look like they're wearing human skin, and Robby takes aim from behind another one. I hear the explosion and then the echo off the mountain across the creek. But when I peek around to see the body, there ain't nothing there.

Or I'd dream it different. I'd dream the buck was dead. Me and Robby come up on him not fresh dead, but a day or two dead, his body twisted unnatural and his coat matted with rain. His coat matted in a way it would never get live. He's shrunk up, how much littler he looks dead, and collapsed around his ribs like somebody has gutted him already. I look at the rack. The rack looks huge. It looks aliver than him. And something has already ate on his eyes, even though you would have thought the cold rain would have kept them back in their holes. There comes again in my chest the pity-feel of cloth tearing. And then, after the pity feeling, once more he is just not there.

Nights, I lay in bed in this house I built, Mary sleeping beside me. Since the little strokes, I don't sleep so good. I usually go to bed early, have to, and fall asleep right off, but after a few hours I wake up with a headache, or with worry, or both, and can't get back to sleep. So I lay here feeling around me this house I built with my own hands, falling apart. Blasting's cracked my Sheetrock, cracked the walls in my bathroom, cracked the cinderblocks under my house. Just a few weeks ago, it split my concrete porch in two. In this valley now we are completely surrounded by the mining. Soon it'll be directly over top the house. And it's across Route 9, too, across the river, those mountains being taken not only by Lyon, but by Arch, then you go south—more Lyon, some Peabody—and you go north, it's there, too. You work all your life to have you a home. And you want your home to be quiet and peaceable. I built this house, I know how well-made it is, and it's the only thing I got to leave my boys. And here they can take it from me without even walking on my land.

I lay awake, sometimes pressing my fingers to the hurting places in my skull, and I say to myself, *What are they doing up over your head? What are they doing above you?* Funny, seems to me, how they keep it hid not inside someplace, and not under someplace, like things are usually hid. Funny how they hide it up over your head. There's some kind of meaning in that there, in how they hide it. But given how my mind fails me anymore, I cannot puzzle together what that meaning is.

After that kettle bottom dropped on me, my deer dreams turned different. My brain worked different in a lot of ways, them dreams was one of the worst. I dreamed deer not quite deer, deer like something got in their blood and turned them in funny ways, and I'd have a terrible time leaving behind me the feel of the dreams after I'd wake. I dreamed I come up on the mouth of a cave, it surprised me, and there flushed out of it a whole herd of these deer-elk creatures with antlers longer than they was. Rising off their heads in pairs, then fusing to make a single knife blade running longer than their backs, and after they got out of the cave, the whole mountain collapsed behind them. Then it got to where I was dreaming deer coming after me with bared teeth like mad dogs. I'd be in a nice yard someplace, and there'd be all kinds of deer gone wrong, and some of them lying in the grass you couldn't tell was they dead or alive. And the mean deer leaping over the lying-down ones, coming at me, swinging them wolf-teethed heads. It was like I done something to them. It was like both me and them known what it was.

Me and Mary look for greens where we can still find them, and nuts and stuff. These days it's more for the sake of getting out and looking, the pleasure of that, than what we actually find. They've tore up our ramp and ginseng patches, they've run off all the game. And you can't fish. Even if you found you a live fish to catch, I'd be scared to eat it, you know. For a long time, it was the trees dying scared me worst. I don't mean how they clear-cut the mountains before they blow them up, although of course that's an awful thing. But that is a thing you can see and understand. What scared me was the trees that are slow-dying. You don't really notice, that's why it's scariest, until one day it just dawns on you—how long's it been since I seen a mulberry tree? A butternut? Ain't there more logs down than there used to be, or am I just nervous? What happened to that sugar tree used to be at the head of Nell's Hollow just five years ago? The scariest is when things are lost before you know you're losing.

Then one morning last fall I found something that spooked me worse. It was real early, just after dawn, I hadn't been able to sleep the night before. I was climbing up the road to Bleak Knob to look for a ginseng patch used to be up there. Bleak Knob is a good ten miles from here, I hadn't been up there in some time. It's been all mined out underneath, I knew that, but I didn't know how far they'd got with the stripping. I decided to go up and see.

I got over there, and of course they had a pipe gate across where you used to be able to drive up, so I parked my truck and started climbing the dirt road. Wasn't too long before I heard some kind of vehicle coming down, which surprised me a little. Then here it come around the turn, and it's a tanker truck of some sort, and I stood off to the side, half-expecting it to stop and say something to me about trespassing. But the two men in it didn't so much as look at me. Then I realized the truck didn't have a trace of lettering on it, and I noticed, too, that they had a gun rack in the cab, some kind of rifle in it, I couldn't tell what. They went on down the road, and last thing I seen was that truck didn't have no license plates neither. Now that scared me.

It got worse. I hadn't gone but a hundred feet when I saw something on the ground shouldn't have been there. You get used to seeing all kinds of weird stuff up these hollows below valley fills and mines, especially around sediment ponds, but this hollow, near as I could tell, was more or less untouched. And here in the road was this goopy gray junk. Like in clots, dribbled along the road.

Right there a bad feeling socked in my gut. It hadn't even got to my mind yet, but I knew to back away and not touch that stuff, not even with my boot.

I watched it for a while, the feeling in my belly making me a little sick. Then I tried to track it. It didn't go too far, kind of dribbled along in a line maybe twenty feet long, a fair-sized gap between each gray glob. Then it just petered out. I knew it had come out of the truck when they was driving up full, and when I seen them, they was no doubt driving out empty. So I followed the tire tracks. The tire tracks was heavy and easy to follow, and I got up top in under an hour to where I could see clear where the truck had turned around. But it was strange. I couldn't find no more of the gray stuff, and I couldn't see where they might have been dumping it. Nothing. It was like the truck just went up there to have a look, turned around and went on home.

I hadn't yet heard any rumors about them dumping what they call hazardous waste, not yet. But I can't say I was surprised. Once I got home, I called the Department of Environmental Protection about it. I'd called them quite a few times over the years, and they were always polite on the phone, then, near as I could tell, didn't do a durned thing. But what else could I do? There ain't nothing else but throw a lawsuit at them, and lord knows I don't have the money for that.

My church has never spoke out against the destruction. Some churches have spoke against it, but mine has not. I still go every Sunday.

I can guarantee you I've never talked before about any of this out loud. The buck, the dreams, the feel in the woods. Before, I didn't even want God to hear, I especially didn't want God to hear, but, of course, they say he hears everything. I was ashamed at how I couldn't match up what they teach at church and what I know from the woods. But as I get older and, it is true, sicker, I understand more and feel less guilt about it. I understand that church mostly touches just the part of me that knows right from wrong. The part that says, "You better not." As I get bold enough to think it, I understand church don't seep into me no deeper or fuller than that, and it is very sad, to feel no more than that from church. Still, I can't know no different: any sacred I have ever got close to has come straight out of these hills.

My headaches have got worse instead of better. I kept telling myself they wasn't, and I didn't say nothing to Mary, but then this spring, they took a leap. Seems they've near doubled in what they was hurting before, and I thought what they was hurting before was just shy of unbearable.

As the headaches get worse, the dreams do, too. Looking back now, I believe it started, these new ones, with me dreaming animals with metal for teeth. A couple times I dreamed just that, normal deer with metal pressed in their gums. Then I dreamed I shot a buck and went to gut him, and I found he had a plastic bag for a belly. After that, I dreamed I was out walking and found glass scat. I dreamed leaves falling as ash. Then those dreams passed, too, and I stopped dreaming animals, I stopped dreaming woods at all. Instead, I dream that the world tilts, and I see crowds of good people can't keep their footing, and they all fall and slide into a corner. Or I dream I'm out in my yard, and everything just stops. It's like a clock running down, one where you don't notice the ticking until it stops, but then it does stop, and I feel the universe dead quiet in its halt. And now, finally, I've got to where I dream without pictures at all. It's just a dream of sound. There is nothing to the dream but an alarm going off, a horn with a beat to it: *Mwaaa. Mwaaa. Mwaaa. Mwaaa.* I don't need no Daniel to interpret that dream.

There is what my reason tells me. There is what my church tells me. There is what my dreams tell me. There is what this land tells me. I'm coming to accept that I'll never bring all those things together before I die. But on my strongest days, I can tell myself without guilt or fear, it is not paganism or idolatry or sacrilege or sin. It's just what I know. And what they tell me, these things I finally let myself trust, is what we're doing to this land is not only murder. It is suicide.

The day before Thanksgiving, 1958, was the first time I felt it. It wouldn't be until a very long time afterwards I could put words to it, like I have now. For a good many years after it happened, when I talked to myself about it—because I sure didn't talk to nobody else about it—I just named it by the buck me and Robby never did find. I needed to call the feeling by something solid, I didn't know how to do it better, and looking back now, I think the way I called it was just fine. Even though the buck hadn't really been there. Him being gone, seems to me, made calling it by him even righter.

As I got older, like I said, I started feeling the hum off all live things, even dirt and rock. And I could make myself feel how I was part of the land just by letting down something inside me, I got practiced that way. A letting-down at will. But the warm current and the loss of me in order to become me huge, me all, only happened three times after that Thanksgiving, and only once as strong. And I've never been able to make the feeling come. Only a word comes that until now I've never felt safe using for it because I know that word as a Christian thing.

It's hard to tell stories about hunting for things that never get found. I try not to be downcast. I try to keep hold of my heart. I have Mary, and I have my boys. Some of the woods are left, and I still have the strength in my legs to walk up into them. Even with the problems in my head, I can get back in the mountain, and many people, like Robby, sick now with diabetes and the cancer both, can't even do that. And despite my recent terrible dreams, something different happened in my sleep, just a week ago.

I went to bed real early, before it was dark, with a headache so bad it was upsetting my stomach. I fell asleep pretty quick, and then I dreamed I was in a little grassy clearing. It felt good to me in that clearing, how I do love being down in a place, the good safe feeling of land all around. Then, while I was standing there quiet and glad, an old doe walked up to me. She stepped right up to me, and I looked back into her brown eyes, and she said, "This is what it's like inside my head."

Then she shelled her head open. It just fell open in easy halves. And as she did it, there spilled out of it and over me this light a color of green I'd never seen before.

The light from her head carried in it the feeling I'd had in the little room where the buck wasn't. That feeling I'd only had twice since. That feeling I had never been able to make come on my own. Only this time, when I blended beyond myself with the sureness, the peace, the sureness and peace kept growing. Bigger beyond anything I'd ever felt, it swelled and spread, I swelled and spread, until there was not anything else. No woods and no doe and no light and no me. Until there was all. It was all. Not nothing. Not something. Just all.

I guess you'd call it the peace that passeth understanding. I guess you'd say it come by grace.

Lace

DANE CAME looking more like Jimmy Make than any baby I ever had. That was good. Make sure Jimmy Make knew. The next eight years passed blurrier than any other part of my life, my life became my kids then, and I have not one regret over that, but when I look back on the thirty-five years I have lived, those are the eight I remember least. After Dane was born, Mom gave us a piece of ground out by the turnaround and we put a modular home on it. Jimmy Make always was the type had to live on a hard road. Two years after Dane, here comes Corey, and around that time, Sheila finally got married to the Parker boy down at Labee, and she moved out. We got the used trailer for Mom because that was easier, Jimmy Make argued at me, than keeping up the "old house," even though what he called the "old house" was, of course, the homeplace to us. I fought him hard on that. We went three generations back in that one house, three more in an even older place now ruint down to foundation stones further up the cove. But Mom wouldn't fight him along with me. I was up there on the porch one afternoon fetching Bant—Mom still kept Bant a good bit, and a huge help to me that was—outright begging Mom not to give up and go, and finally she said to me, in her case-closed voice, "Don't look a gift horse in the mouth." I see now what she did then and I would soon. Whoever's bringing in the most money—that's the way things finally tilt.

After Jimmy got Mom set up in her trailer, he bought his first truck. He did take care of Mom first. He'd been starving for that truck all his life, and I didn't begrudge him. How men are, him especially. With Jimmy Make pulling down more money than my family had ever had, and me with two, then three, eventually four kids to watch, I ran the woods with Mom less and less often. Most of the time I was so drowned in other work I didn't even think about it, but Mom would take Bant, and, oh, then I'd remember. Then I'd remember. Bant coming in all quiet like she always was unless you asked her something, like a woods thing herself she was in her quiet. I could see and smell and feel the woods fresh in her, her cheeks a good red from out there, and her eyes shiny and still away. The scent of mast, of duff, of air soaked in trees, all through her jacket and deep in her hair. How damned jealous, that's the word for it, I would get. Jealous of a six-year-old I loved more than my life. Then I would try to go again, as far as I could with the kids when I had any time, up the creek where they could wade, along the bottom of Cherryboy to pick up nuts, Yellowroot for berries. But I couldn't just let myself be there in it, the way I could when I had only Bant and Mom was with us, too. It was always the kids, not the woods, I had to be with first.

Things between me and Jimmy Make were different, too, and while the fact of that didn't surprise me one bit, the ways it was different did. After the wedding, it was hard to want him anymore. I learned that for me it was either have sex or have a home; sex in houses, in beds, meant something else and not enough. But sex was the least of what changed. In less than a year of us living together, things that I'd kind of half-known about him before but had got muffled, now those things came clear. Like how simple he was, no distance or depth in how he could see. While in the confusion of Morgantown, I'd craved that simpleness, now it irked me deep. Like how inside the bobcat walk crouched a confused little kid, and him not even unsimple enough to see that when I did. Like how he started spending all his free time either watching or working on things that ran, because, I couldn't help but think, that engine noise blotted out anything else might turn up in his head.

"At least he's not a drinker," Mom would say when I'd complain. "You got lucky like me that way." And she was right. The older he got, the less he drank, and I knew I was lucky, I knew where the kind of work he did could push you. Liquor, painkillers, illegal drugs. Take the edge off. A little of the uncertainty. Some of the hurt. But I'd never thought that was the kind of lucky I'd need, and I could tell from the way Mom said it, she'd expected more for me, too. I have to give her that. And I thanked her in my head for not saying what some others did—"and at least he don't beat on you or the kids." I still couldn't be grateful for a bar low as that.

During those early years, though, sometimes I did truly love him, my mind still remembers that, even if my heart cannot. It was like the love and the unlove moved in cycles: I'd unlove for a week or so, then love for a month. Unlove two weeks, love for three. And part of me hated him for going away from us without leaving. But another part could see he wasn't going so much as being taken away.

Back at the very beginning, before Corey was born, Jimmy Make was working a swing shift, and if I wasn't completely wrung out, I'd nap on the couch after Bant and Dane went down and wait for him to get home. Wake to the sclop of him dropping his dirty boots on the porch, then his sock feet passing the door, he'd swagger in all gruffy and rough—"That motherfucker Grady, if he . . ." or "Gonna work us dead into the ground this week"—boy wearing a tough man mask.

Him in his loose jeans, faded grease stains down the front, his big black-and-white-checked flannel, sweatshirt hood hanging out of that. They had showers at the mine, but black as they'd get and tired as they were, Jimmy'd always miss some places, and although he wouldn't say anything, he'd want me to find them. He'd walk into the kitchen and strip to his shorts while I fetched from the bathroom a soft washcloth, then I'd pull up a chair to the kitchen sink, get the water running to just the right hot, and Jimmy Make'd settle cross-legged between my knees. I'd hunt the secret places still smeared black, the nape of his neck, the hollow between his shoulder blades, the jut where his jaw-bone met cheek. I'd pull the washrag across his chest, and once in a while, if I went slow enough, he'd let down and tell me where he hurt. "There in the small of my back," he'd mumble. "See if you can rub it out." "Around my kneecaps, just pull up and down."

Usually I'd do the rubbing in bed, Jimmy Make asleep before I finished, and in the damped light off the bedstand lamp, in the gold-flecked mirror on the closet doors, his body still looked like it had at fifteen. I'd watch it there. Even though Jimmy could feel the work in his body, where it showed first was only in his face, and there, only around his eyes. I could get the black anyplace else, but not under and around those eyes.

But that was early on. By the time Corey was born, Jimmy Make had stopped touching me unless he wanted sex and stopped touch-ing the kids unless I reminded him to. And it wasn't only us he lost interest in. He stopped visiting his mom and dad, too, said he didn't have time or energy to make the drive. Then his mom died of cancer, quick—Jimmy Make would never talk about that, like he wouldn't talk about anything—and after the funeral, he seemed to go away from that family altogether and even farther away from us.

Interesting thing was, during those years, me and Jimmy Make hardly fought at all. Way less than we did before we got married. Yeah,

I was frustrated, I was disappointed, but mostly I was numb. I figured that's just what marriage was. I saw Mom and Dad as the exception, because I'd seen it in other grown-ups all my life, and now I learned how you got there by watching the girls my age who'd gotten married even younger than me. Watched their early excitement erode into disappointment, the disappointment fester into anger, and then the anger rub, chafe, grind, until it finally broke them into numb. By then he is your kids' father, you and him own a house together, you've slept in the same bed for thousands of nights, shared thousands of meals, and he is bringing home that union paycheck. I tell you, that is important, no matter how when you're younger you swear it won't never be. Kids change that quick. But even without romance, without touching, without even much talking, me and Jimmy Make kept getting tied together tighter and tighter, only it no longer had anything to do with that slim green vine. This was rope. Knotted rope, scratchy and binding, and if you didn't feel it always, you sure did if you turned.

As the years went by, even Mom went into the woods less often, partly because her arthritis was slowing her down, but mostly because the companies were shutting us out from more and more land. "If they don't got a gate across the road," Mogey'd say, "they'll hoove up dirt in it so you can't get over, and I've seen where they've deliberately cut trees across the hollow to keep you out." "Getting everything posted," Mom told me, "so even if you're on foot, you got to worry the whole time are they coming after you." Maxie Maxwell from down the hollow came up for a cup of coffee and to check in, see if it was happening to us, too. "These are roads and paths into places I been going all my life. They was everybody's places before."

One day Mogey came back and told us he'd blown a tire up on Carney Mountain. "Got out of my truck to see what happened, and here it was a roof bolt they'd sharpened and laid bolt-end-up in the road. I found a few more scattered around." Then where we still could get in, it seemed everything was getting scarcer, harder to find, but the ginseng especially, then the government put more regulations on how much we could take. "Companies can destroy every blade of grass," Mom said. "But us with our little trowels and hoes, we got to follow the regulations." And Mom'd always been one who I thought stuck way too tight to rules.

We'd lived with the stripping since the '50s, but we'd always hated it. I remember vivid how hurt and mad Mom and Dad were over what the company did to the one side of Yellowroot back in the '70s. But now we heard rumors that the operations were getting bigger than anyone'd imagined, and although I never saw those mines myself, by the last few years before we left for North Carolina, I knew it was true because I saw the coal, running hard and fast and high right out of here. I saw it heaped in endless cars while I waited for ten minutes at railroad crossings with cranky kids, heard it at my back, the rails whining and clicking and groaning, while I loaded groceries in the car at the IGA. I felt it every time I got stuck behind an overloaded coal truck going up a mountain, every time I nearly got creamed by one coming down. But the telling thing was, as those tons and tons of coal went out of here, laid-off miners and their families went right along with them. I look back on it now and feel the fool for not putting two and two together, but with the nose-wiping, bump-kissing, diaper-changing, toddler-chasing, breast-feeding exhaustion, even though I heard the rumors and saw the coal, it didn't yet mean that much to me.

Six years into the marriage, me pregnant with Tommy, Jimmy Make hurt his back at work. They operated on it, and I still partly blame that. "Whatever you do, don't ever let em cut on you," Daddy always said, but Jimmy Make was the kind of person trusted doctors more than himself. He was a good patient, hardly a word of complaint those three months he laid abed at home. Tommy was born in the middle of it all, and Mom, thank god, moved right in for a time. We set up the hospital bed in the living room where he could watch TV, and while Mom would look after the oldest three, I'd nurse Tommy and hold Jimmy's hand while I did.

I hadn't held that hand in years, and I realized it by the way the hand had changed. Hardened on both sides now, calluses underneath, chapped skin and jutty bones on top. When the doctor said he'd probably never lose the limp, it cut right through me, I swear it felt like I'd crippled a leg of my own. But Jimmy Make wouldn't talk about it, and if you tried yourself, he'd turn it into one of his boring borrowed jokes. "Mean as I am, don't even need two legs."

Then he went back to work, too early, far as I was concerned, and after that, he ignored us even worse than before he got hurt. I asked him what was going on, if he was in pain all the time or what, but he just shook his head and shrugged. I tell you, I wanted to keep some kind of love fanned up in me, but I couldn't sustain it with getting nothing back, and by that time, the cycle was moving in reverse. I'd love for just one week, then unlove for a month or more.

We went without sex for some time, his back not mended enough, me recovering from the baby. I won't never forget that first time back. Me on my back, ears pitched for whether the kids could hear, Jimmy Make on his hands over top of me. His elbows bent, him lurching back and forth, and I felt nothing at all except an irritated patience until I felt the new fat of his belly slapping down against mine. I opened my eyes, and I saw his were closed, I saw him gritting his teeth. Those teeth that had drawn me moonwhite that first October night, darkening now to a walnut stain. I looked, and I not only saw no love in his face, I saw no pleasure, either. What I saw was urgency. Pressure. Strain.

By the end of that year, the extra weight had clobbed up into his cheeks, his skin, and changed the look of his face. It was like his body had been holding on as hard as it could those first eight years in the pulpwood and underground, but then that one big knock had triggered a chain reaction, and even the smell of him changed. What grieved me worst, though, was that live hot wet. That hot wetness in him, what had first pulled me to him, what had kept me coming back—not exactly for the sex, or at least not for the pleasure of the sex, but because of the life, the liveness in him—that hot wetness had been dripping away for some years, but with the injury, it drained clear gone. Jimmy Make was twenty-five years old.

I'd hate myself for feeling that way, I would. *Who do you think you are*, I'd ask, *you're getting old, too, who are you to look down on him like this?* But the truth was, even after four babies, I'd done most of my aging those months carrying Bant, and after that quick-up, I kind of just stayed still. And while most of my age happened on the inside, Jimmy aged only on the outside of him, when it was inside I needed him to grow. Still, I felt guilty about it. Huge guilty, and guilty's never been a place I often go. I'd get to feeling so guilty that I think I could have overlooked everything else if it hadn't been for this one thing: I knew he wouldn't ever see the all of me.

I was pulling in with a load of groceries that February of '96, Tommy almost two years old in the car seat behind me and the other kids at school. It was early afternoon, we'd had a short high thaw, everything in mud. Jimmy Make was supposed to be on day shift, but with the leaves off the trees, I could see all the way from Mrs. Taylor's house his truck parked in front of ours. My heart punched hard once against my ribs until I remembered he wouldn't have driven himself home if he was hurt. And then there tingled from my every pore a colder kind of fear.

I got Tommy in one arm and two bags of groceries in my other, and in that short walk from car to porch, my body went to shivering. I couldn't help it, it did. Jimmy Make sat on the couch in his work clothes, clean, him leaning forward with his elbows on his thighs, his head lowered, and an orange juice glass of whiskey on the coffee table. The TV was off. He raised his head so little he had to roll his eyes way up to look at me.

"They shut er down," he said. "Laid ever last one of us off." Then he dropped his face back down.

I didn't go to him. I looked away. I walked the few steps to the kitchen, my knees locking on me strange. I didn't even think to cry, I guess I knew it was too bad for that. But something must have leached over into Tommy because the second I set the groceries down, I felt his whole body stiffen and his chest hollow into wail.

If it had been up to me, I would have stayed in West Virginia at least the six months until the unemployment ran out, but two months into the layoff, Jimmy heard about the construction work in Raleigh, and he said it was smarter to grab that while we could than wait six months and most likely end up with nothing at all. I argued him back, but not really that hard. I knew what he said made sense. And like the back injury had, the layoff thrust us closer together again. At least for a while. Fear can work like that. Or so I thought then.

A week before we left, I carried up to Mom's trailer a couple garbage bags of stuff she'd said she'd store. We weren't selling the house, I'd put my foot down on that, Bill Bozer was going to rent from us, but to make room for him and his girlfriend, I had to clear out more than we could take with us south. As I came up on the trailer, I saw Mom out back stacking stovewood that Mogey's boys had dropped off.

I stopped at the end of the trailer where I could watch her, but she couldn't very well see me. I set my garbage bags quiet on the ground. She wore a dress that used to be the bright small flower kind but had now drained to beiges and grays. It was part of her dress system, I knew, the way she ordered them by age and stains and tears, this must be one of the oldest, to use for wood-stacking work, and still, over top of it, she wore a sweatshirt, despite that the air was barely cool, and I knew it was to keep the old dress at least a little clean. She bent to the stovewood with a jerkiness, her arthritis, I couldn't help but flinch, hooked chunks into her left elbow, straightened up, then wobbled the few steps to the neat stack against her back wall. The wood clapping into place, she was making ready, the way she always had, even though it was May and she wouldn't be burning this until late September.

Then suddenly she stopped, one hand on the pile, the other on her hip, and she looked at me like she'd known all along I was there. I could hear her soft panting. I tried to read her face, but right then, she turned away. "Good for you-all to get a fresh start," she'd said when we told her we'd decided to go. "Pretty soon won't be nothing at all left for young people here." But that's not what I'd seen in her face before she turned it.

I walked over to the dumped wood and piled a load in my own arm. Hickory, red oak, good long hot-burning wood Mogey'd sent her. Then I started ricking with her. The bark raspy on my bare hands, scraping up my wrists, but I just piled heavier, moved faster, and I felt Mom alongside me, but I never lifted my eyes to see her straight on. We worked side by side for a full hour with no sound but the chunks falling and knocking. Worked until we had two pickup loads ricked, and then it started to rain.

That North Carolina, I tell you. Down there, you just can't get any grip on the land. No traction. No hold. If the eight years between Dane being born and us moving to North Carolina were the fastest of my life, the two years we spent in North Carolina were the emptiest and the least real.

I won't ever forget driving down there, maneuvering six lanes and more of traffic with a panic perched in my chest. Me in that old

Cavalier with all four kids, the three not in car seats with their faces jammed against the windows, and Corey saying, "How come there's so many cars, Mom? Is there a football game or something?" I was following Jimmy Make with his truck loaded scary high with our stuff, tarp flapping over top of it, I could see that flapping all the way around the U-Haul he was dragging. Then I lost sight of him, had to risk our lives in the fast lane to find him, and *goddamn you, Jimmy Make,* I said in my head because how like him that was. Then I saw the exit he'd written on a McDonald's napkin for me, and his rig ahead, already down below us at a light, and right past that, there "Foxwood" was.

He'd gone down a couple weeks before and rented this tall skinny half-apartment, half-house crammed between a bunch of other houses looked exactly like ours. A "townhouse," they called it, and I lived there a year and never did figure out why. When I pulled into a parking spot beside him and stepped out of the car, first thing I noticed was a nonstop *aaahhhh* like a broken refrigerator running hard into an amplifier, but not until that night did I realize it was the interstate and it wasn't ever going away. Jimmy Make was already unbolting the U-Haul, the kids clustering anxious and close. "How do you-all like it?" he said.

I really looked at it for the first time. "It's nice," Bant said softly, and I saw what she meant. The outside looked newer and nicer than anyplace we'd ever thought of living, but of course that was before we learned how shoddily it was built. "Yeah, it does look nice," I told Jimmy Make, and he grinned.

Jimmy Make and me carried in the couch, the beds, the dressers, balancing each piece between us, and Jimmy took the harder backing-up way even though I could see the back pain in his face, and I tried to get him to trade or stop, but he'd just bite his lip and shake his head. Bant and Corey toted boxes and smaller things—I had Dane watching Tommy—and we spent hours moving in. And right there, I should have known, I should have seen how it was going to be. We'd gotten there mid-afternoon, and many people passed us, on foot, in their cars, and there had to be people all over those cramped-up buildings looking out. But most people didn't even act like they saw us, much less volunteer to offer a hand. That never would have happened back home.

By the time we finally got everything inside, we were too tired to put the beds together, so we slept on mattresses on the floor. At first, me and Jimmy and the boys in the room that would be ours, Bant saying she'd stay by herself, but within five minutes she was there with us, too. Once everybody got settled, Jimmy Make rolled over to face me, grunting like he always did when he shifted his back. "Don't worry, Lace," he whispered. "We're gonna make er here." Then he rolled over on his other side, and within a minute, fell asleep.

I wasn't even tired. I lay stiff on my back, not touching Jimmy Make, my eyes squeezed shut. I heard the kids quiet into sleep—they went almost as quick as Jimmy—and then, the silence they left behind—I listened as it filled full of noise. At first, just the constant interstate *aaahhhh* I noticed, but then, my ear tuning, doors slamming in the parking lot, cars starting, an alarm, the gun and brake of vehicles on the access road, them layering into the room. Then, closer, the layers drawing in, to the left of me, a TV pressing, a *wah wah* of muffled conversation under that, I shut my eyes even tighter like that would keep it out, then a second TV, behind the wall on my right. I finally opened my eyes, try to figure out where everything was coming from, and that's when I saw the outside lights surging in, staining that room nearly the color of day, and it wasn't so much the noise or the light, I didn't understand then, but I would later, it wasn't the interruption of sleep. It was the foreign place pressing in on us. I flipped onto my side, pulling my pillow over my head, and as I did that, I noticed beside the mattress where Dane and Corey slept, the old chest of drawers. Daddy's chest of drawers, that had been in his and Mom's room until Mom moved out and gave it to me. And a loneliness came into me like a wind blowing through, and for two straight years, that wind never stopped.

Down there, I learned fast, you couldn't ever really get outside. Couldn't even get in trees, in brush, much less get into hills, you weren't ever out of sight or sound of a road, a building, a parking lot, and sometimes I'd miss backhome woods so bad I'd feel land in my throat. The townhouses had around them skinny strips of grass, then a whole bunch of parking lot like a hard hot lake. There was no other place for the kids to get out and play, and the first summer, I'd drag out a kitchen chair in the morning before the heat got past bearing and watch Tommy and Corey ride their Big Wheels, until the apartment manager told me kids couldn't do that. We'd been there two months by then, and as the manager walked away, I realized she was the first person in all that time who'd said more than three sentences to me, aside from people who worked in stores, where they were paid to be friendly. People there lay as flat as the land, no up and down to them, and it was like everybody walked around with a door in front of their faces, no, two doors, this thick screen door, and behind that, a heavy storm one. And occasionally they'd open the storm door and speak through the screen. But then they'd close the storm door behind them again.

"People around here won't speak to me." I finally brought it up with Jimmy Make one night.

"Oh, hell," he said. "People around here don't speak to nobody."

"I thought the South was supposed to be friendly."

He broke another piece of cornbread into his chili and shook his head. "This ain't the South," he said. "That's what the guys at work from the real South say. 'This ain't the South.'"

Jimmy Make did try a little harder down there. One of the things he did was find us a park, oh, he was proud when he came home with that news—"I found us some woods to get into!" We drove up there the first weekend we got, and he really had found woods, and yeah, they were flat and tameish, you couldn't feel the land as easily around you, but at least you had real ground under your feet, real trees over your head, and if we could just get out here, I thought. If we could just get out here every other week.

But then the first airplane passed overhead, low to where it looked like it was moving no faster than a car in a parking lot and loud enough to make Tommy whimper. Within five minutes of that one, a second came, then a third, a fourth, Corey leaping up in the air with a stick pretending to hit it. Finally we gave up and went back to our car, where we saw on the map what we'd decided not to see before. This big pink square of airport right above the small green of park.

A lot of that first year was just a floating, it makes it hard for me to even tell about it, nothing to touch. Bant was nearly as unhappy as me, quietly surly about it she was, and Dane just lived in a daze. Jimmy Make was earning less working construction than he had with the union job back home, and in Raleigh, everything except food cost more. But it wasn't just the lack of money that made us poorer in North Carolina. It was what you saw around you, what you had to compare yourself to, and I'd never understood about that before. And if that didn't keep us in our place, then there was the way people looked at us, regardless of how much money they had. Somehow people knew we were different from them, even before we opened our mouths, although I couldn't for the life of me see how we looked much different from anybody else. It took me back to Morgantown again, the way the out-of-state students saw us, the way some professors did. And I know now that if we hadn't moved to Raleigh, me and Jimmy Make would have frayed loose even faster than we did, and it wasn't really the roses on our anniversary, the extra time he spent at home, the way he looked for parks, that kept us together. It was that smallness North Carolina made me. I was nothing in North Carolina, nothing or nobody I knew counted for anything in North Carolina, while Jimmy Make, he could pass in and out of that North Carolina world. He didn't love it, but he could move in it. Jimmy Make got a little bigger in North Carolina, while I got a whole lot littler.

When the lease was up on the townhouse, we had to leave for a cheaper place. Almost didn't find one, and never did find one big enough, but Jimmy Make finally heard of something through a guy at work. This huddle of two-story brick buildings behind a shut-down textile mill, them squatty and dribbly-stained, the Cat Piss apartments I still call them to myself. I'd taken back up smoking by then, I'd quit clear back when I got pregnant the first time, but in North Carolina cigarettes were cheap, and god knows I needed something to put inside of me. And often, that second summer, late at night, the only time I had to myself, I'd sit out on the stoop of the building and have a cigarette. I'd sit there, and naturally I'd be thinking of home, of Mom, of mountain dark, and I'd try to keep my eyes down low, to the concrete, the ratty grass, because Raleigh had no sky at night. Over Raleigh at night, at best a fuzzy film, at worst, if it was cloudy, a strange orange dome. And sometimes the churchy part of me would whisper, is this punishment? Another part of me whispered, is this a joke? All those self-important teenage years, how I'd wanted nothing but to get out. And here I sat, my sweet peach-pink—an orange glare stinking of exhaust.

It was in those apartments, our second March away, that we got the call. I was on my knees under the dining room table, trying to rub peas out of the filthy carpet, and I could hear Bant beating on Corey in the living room and I was yelling at her to quit, and then the phone rang. Jimmy Make answered it. To this day, I thank God for that.

"Lace?" There was a crack in his voice. My scrubbing hand stopped.

195

He walked up behind me and swallowed so hard I could hear his throat. "That was Mogey." I looked up. His face had gone white with red stripes through it. Right there I knew somebody'd died, and then I knew if it'd been Mogey on the phone, it was Mom who was gone. "Mom?"

Jimmy Make nodded like a sleepwalker.

A heart attack, and that was it. I hadn't even known she'd had heart problems, and if she'd known it herself, she never let on.

What do I remember of the trip home? That my mind let very little in. I remember standing in that leafless dead-grass cemetery on the far side of Prater and seeing how every one of my kids had outgrown their Sunday clothes, and I hadn't known it because since North Carolina, we'd stopped going to church. I remember at the reception afterwards spying on the table a jar of blackberry jam that I knew was one of Mom's, and you'd think it would have made me cry, but instead I nearly threw up. I remember on the way back to Raleigh rolling down my car window in the last little town before the interstate because I all of a sudden wanted woodsmoke smell. I remember Jimmy Make saying roll it up, the kids are cold. I don't remember much else.

It took me ten days back in Raleigh to thaw. And then there I was in North Carolina with Mom dead and nobody to talk to but the kids. I mean nobody even to speak to, and it wasn't like when Daddy died, when I'd had all kinds of time to get used to it, and then afterwards, I still had Mom at home. I crawled into bed, turned off the lights, and I drew my knees to my chest. I couldn't help it. I fell in the tunnel again.

Usually it was the black ball I'd carry. Black ball, like all the grief and guilt were gobbed together, the grief huge, dark, and round, the guilt moving in the grief with sharp points, and the whole ball of it would grow heavy black big enough that finally it was outside instead of in, and right there I'd know I couldn't any longer bear it. But right after I'd know that, it would ease off just enough to let me rest and get strong enough to hurt again. *Not gonna kill you.* That was Mom, too. Most of the time, I slept, the seduction of that—although the horror of coming awake—and if Tommy hadn't still been at home, it's hard to tell. It's hard to tell. I thought on it again.

But Tommy was at home. I'd make him play on the floor beside my bed, and I know now I must have scared him bad, as well as he behaved those weeks. Him whispering and hissing as his superheroes schemed and fought, *let Mommy sleep,* I'd told him. *Now Mommy has to sleep.* Then one afternoon, I woke up suddenly, not even remembering having fallen asleep, and as soon as I did, I felt the empty of the room. I rolled to the edge of the bed, saw the Power Rangers scattered on the carpet, and Tommy, he was gone.

"Tommy?" I called out, and I heard the groggy in my voice, I must have slept longer and deeper than I'd thought. I swung up to sitting, pushing my hair back out of my eyes. "Tommy?"

I got up and started checking from room to room, "Tommy?" my voice rising now, the "Tommys" coming faster and higher, "Tommy?" The boys' bedroom empty, the kitchen, the living room, the bathroom, and "Tommy!" now I screamed. Then I was pouring into the parking lot in my bare feet, whipping my head around, "Tommy!" and the few people there looking at me, but not a one asking what was wrong, when here comes Tommy around the end of the apartment building, a woman older than me leading him by the hand.

"Is this who you're looking for?"

I dropped to my knees and grabbed him to me, I felt him stiffen away, and I looked up at the woman, and "Thank you," I said. "Thank you so much."

Then I saw the look she was giving back. Self-righteous. Smug. Redneck woman with so many kids she can't even keep track of them all. And there crashed back onto me, straight through my grief, through the Tommy terror and the relief, the nothingness that North Carolina made me. Not Morgantown, not getting pregnant, not having to get married, not losing forever that sweet peach-pink, none of those had made me feel the nothingness the way North Carolina did. Because people outside of back home always thought they knew exactly who I was, when they had not the slightest idea. When they'd never see me because they didn't know how to look, knew only to look for what they already thought they knew, so they always saw somebody else.

Memorial Day weekend we went back to help Sheila do the final cleanup on Mom's trailer. Mogey'd found a buyer who would haul it off, and it seemed too early for me, but we needed the money to pay the funeral home. We were staying in our house, with Bill Bozer and his girlfriend, and when we woke up Monday morning, the day we were supposed to drive back to Raleigh, I told Jimmy Make I wouldn't leave. I told him I could not. You might call that a decision, I'm sure Jimmy saw it as one, but in a way, it was not a decision at all. I didn't any longer have a choice. And yeah, he was mad, but that wasn't all he was. Always afterwards, Jimmy would blame the moving back entirely on me, but the truth was, Jimmy Make, too, had been upended by the loss of Mom. He, too, felt how much harder it was to be away without knowing Mom was holding you down back here.

I did go back to Raleigh to pack, for Jimmy to work his two weeks' notice, and for the kids to finish the last of school. Then we hauled everything back up here. I was driving the Cavalier with all four kids—that was the last trip that Cavalier made—and when we left the interstate for 52 just past the West Virginia line, it was mostly relief and even hope I felt, but I'd be lying if I said I didn't feel scared, too. Threading those little choked-to-death towns, so humid you could see the vapor in the air, and what is it? I asked myself again. Makes us have to return? My parents were dead, my cousins and aunts and uncles besides Mogey had all left out to find work, so many neighbors and friends had, too, and me and Jimmy Make with no jobs and up to our eyes in debt, why do you have to come back?

But I'd already figured out it wasn't just me. How could only me and my thirty-three years on that land make me feel for it what I did? No, I had to be drawing it down out of blood and from memories that belonged to more than me. I had to. It must have come from those that bore me, and from those that bore them. From those who looked on it, ate off it, gathered, hunted, dug, planted, loved, and bled on it, who finally died on it and are now buried in it. Somehow a body knows.

Dane

MRS. TAYLOR'S boy Avery looks like city, but he talks like home. In Avery's shoes is where Dane sees city most. Shiny across the tops, thin in their depth and width, slick on the bottom. No laces. The kind of shoes walk on pavement and cement, tile floor and carpet. His broth-colored hair sheds back from his face, and the shape of his head Dane can't help but see as a figure eight—how it's dented over each ear—and when he wears his glasses, which he only does occasionally, they make a figure eight the other way. He has been to college, and he is not a smiler. He is not a talker, either, and Dane can feel off him how he doesn't want to fool with anyone much. Avery looks like Cleveland, but he talks like home, at least until Dane heard him call his wife, who is not from here. On the phone, Avery talks like he's away from here, too. Avery can talk both ways, and Dane has never met anyone who can do that. Around Avery, Dane keeps his distance.

It's late afternoon, and all four of them are crowded in the kitchen while Dane cuts up potatoes and carrots for Mrs. Taylor's stew. Avery slouches in a chair, his long legs spider-sprawled. His face laced tight. At the table head sits Mrs. Taylor, her back to Dane at the counter, her walker by her side. Lucy Hill's across from Avery, but she's too shy to look at him directly. She hadn't known him before, but yesterday, when she came for water again, Mrs. Taylor asked her to drop by tomorrow, meet her baby. Lucy sits with her tight-jeaned legs pulled close together, and except when she sips her coffee, she hides her hands in her Myrtle Beach long-sleeved T-shirt pockets. Her gray hair she has pulled back tight in a fresh-made ponytail, the skin at the edges of her face pulled back with it.

"Well, what exactly *is* up there?" Avery is asking.

"No telling what exactly it is, it's up there so high, and they tell us one thing, but there's no telling. And with these floods and all—" Mrs. Taylor tries to explain, but Avery interrupts her.

"What's the company say it is?"

"Company says it's just a valley fill," says Lucy. Dane hears the shyness in her voice. "But we're scared there's a big ole slurry impoundment up behind that thing."

"There ain't no way to tell," Mrs. Taylor says.

"Can you see a prep plant up there? Belts? A silo?"

"Not where you can see any of it," says Lucy. "But they could be piping the slurry up from Deer Lick. They got that huge one up over the plant, but people are saying that one may be full." She looks over at Mrs. Taylor, looks back down. "I don't know. That's the thing. Don't nobody know." She sips at her coffee. "And they got nosers and gates all over the place, so you can't get up in there to see, and even if you got to the foot and tried to climb, it's steep, buddy. And slick. Especially with all the rain we've been getting." Shakes her head. "This crazy weather. And even if there ain't one right above us, we're still in the path of others. That one up behind Deer Lick, they say it's nine hundred feet from bottom to top, that's higher than the New River Gorge. Then there's another one up at Mayton, and who knows where all else."

"And they throw just anything in them ponds," Mrs. Taylor goes on. "Broke-down equipment and logs and chemicals, just anything they're too lazy to carry off the mountain, just push it in the ponds. So who knows what all's in that water when it comes through here. Even when it's not that deep, you know, it's still poison. You want that in your garden?"

Lucy nods. "Lots of people just not putting in any garden this year."

"And seeping in your well water, and kids walking in it barefoot—"

"Well, Mom, how come I been trying to get you up to Cleveland for the past three years?"

Mrs. Taylor says nothing back, but her bottom lip butts out a little. Lucy is looking down at the hand lumps in her shirt pockets. The only sound for a while is Dane's knife ringing the chopping board and the labor of Mrs. Taylor's lungs. Then Lucy says, "And there's not a thing you can do about it. Not one thing. His mom," she tips her head towards Dane, "has called every agency she can think of, and won't a one of them do nothing. Won't even come in here and look. Why, their house is nearly in the creek, how bad it tore through there, you know. It's just pitiful." Lucy shakes her head. Then she looks at Avery for the first time since she met him half an hour earlier. She looks towards him even if she doesn't meet his eyes. "I tell you, Mr. Taylor, it's gonna take another Buffalo Creek. Gonna take all of us warshed out of here and killed before the first thing's done about it."

Now they fall quiet for even longer, but a different silence it is. Dane can feel the ripple in it. He brings the knife down on the cutting board, shoves the potato chunks he's finished off to the side. He pushes his stomach against the counter to calm the fish down. Finally, Avery speaks.

"Well, Buffalo Creek was a different situation than it sounds like this here is."

"Big ole dam, wasn't it?" Lucy asks.

"Well," Avery says. "Dam was what they called it. But it wasn't nothing but three big slag piles dozed up into walls. Dumped the wastewater from the coal-cleaning plant behind them. You could see they weren't nothing but slag piles."

Mrs. Taylor lets loose a sobby kind of sigh. "And that's why I won't never forgive myself. Won't never."

Avery grimaces. "Oh, Mom. You didn't know. Come on now."

"No, no, we all knew, it was just a matter of when." She wags her head, stares down at her hands. "And there you were, wanting to spend the night up at Lorado, and I said yes, after three solid days of rain, and I won't never forgive myself, not long as I live."

"Mom, there was no more rain those three days than was usual, I know that for a fact. And they rumored that dam to bust every spring. If we listened every time that dam was supposed to break, we would of had to live in tents on the hill."

"Still." Mrs. Taylor is slumped over now, her back bowed. She's taken off her glasses. "But Dooley had work in there . . ."

"Well, now, honey," Lucy comforts her. "You didn't know. Hindsight's twenty-twenty."

"Mom, you didn't know. I haven't blamed you for a second. Besides, here I am." Avery opens wide his arms and grins, trying to make a joke. Mrs. Taylor doesn't smile back. Dane pounds his cutting board with his dull paring knife, the chopping louder and louder.

"How old were you, Mr. Taylor, when it hit?" Lucy asks.

"Twelve years old," Avery says. Dane's knife slips, clips the finger holding the potato, but it's not sharp enough to break skin.

"He don't remember nothing about the water itself," Mrs. Taylor says. "He don't remember nothing until he woke up on the side of the hollow after the water passed. God took care of him that way."

"Yes," Lucy nods. "He sure did."

"And the happiest moment of my life was when I finally saw Bucky—we called him Bucky then—Bucky trudging along that hillside in them big ole clothes and all covered black, but I knew it was Bucky by how he walked."

"Mmm-mmm." Lucy shakes her head, imagining.

"I had to believe he was alive all along or I would've lost my mind, Lucy. I would've lost my mind right there. Dooley I wasn't worried about. I knew he would have been up above. Patty told me she knew Bucky was alive, too, we held hands and prayed on it. And a hard prayer would hold me for ten minutes or so, then it would start to fade, I'd start to break down again, you know, and then Patty'd grab hold my hand and we'd pray again. Some people come through and said it wasn't over, said a second dam was gonna blow, and that's the hardest I've prayed in my life. And that second dam didn't break."

"Wasn't no second dam," Avery mumbles.

"Lord, lord," says Lucy. Mrs. Taylor has found a tissue in her sleeve, and she shreds at it, her glasses still off. "Mmm," says Lucy. She continues to shake her head. No one speaks for a while. Then Avery clears his throat.

"Well, Mom," he says. "You sit here and tell us that, but you won't leave."

Mrs. Taylor sighs thickly. "Well. You know." She places the wadded tissue on the table beside her coffee. "Anymore, I wonder if maybe I ain't just bound to die in a flood." She pauses. Lowers her voice a little. "Didn't get me the first time, so it's coming for me now."

"Oh, Mom. That's ridiculous," Avery says.

Mrs. Taylor shrugs, slow and weary. "Gotta die some way."

"Mom, you're not yet seventy. Most people live past seventy."

"Not around here, they don't," Mrs. Taylor says. She looks back at Lucy. "They asked me later how come I didn't send Ronald up to look for Bucky, or why didn't I go myself even. But you see, I just couldn't let the four of us break apart. Still, every person I saw heading back up that hollow after the waters passed, I told them, I said, 'You look for my boy, Bucky.'"

"I don't blame you a bit," says Lucy. "For not wanting to separate apart."

"Oh, Lucy." Mrs. Taylor shakes her head. "After that flood. I can't begin to tell you. There never was a time like it. The world just went inside-out. People climbing out of that black mud near naked, your friends and neighbors climbing naked out of mud. People just squatting and going to the bathroom right there in the open. Wasn't nothing else they could do, you know. And you just stood there and watched like it happened every day." Again, she lowers her voice. "Truth was, you didn't have nothing left to feel with. It was kind of like the water washed out your insides."

"Hard to imagine," Lucy murmurs. "Hard to imagine." Dane rinses his knife to get ready for the carrots, and there comes to him a sudden memory of one time in church when a man told an end-time dream he had. He turned on the spigot in his kitchen and the water came out in his glass as blood.

"And some people, when the water was going past, they got sick to their stomachs and threw up while they watched." Mrs. Taylor places one hand on her own stomach. "And afterwards, they told how lots of people up the hollow above us heard other people, kids, too, screaming for help, and they couldn't do nothing to help them."

"Oh, lord," Lucy murmurs.

"Now you know that would stay with you. For a long, long time. At least we didn't have none of that. We saw people in it, but we didn't hear no screams for help. At least we don't have to carry that guilt, too."

"Oh, lord," Lucy repeats. "We're all gonna get warshed out." She huddles down into her shirt collar, like tucking in from a hard wind. "I just know it," she says, and Dane, cutting carrots now, draws shallow breath, the fish pitching sharp in his gut.

"Cold," Mrs. Taylor goes on. "You know it was. Us in our nightclothes. People drifting past, hollering, 'You seen so-and-so? You seen my mother? You seen Tommy Hatfield?' Like that. I was scared to let anybody go back in our house, even though it hadn't moved. Now Ronald, he kept wanting to go see, but I wouldn't let him. Something just told me not to. Then Chip Mullens come up there, said he'd just talked to Kenny Smith's son, told how he went back in his house—now his had moved a ways—and stepped right on a body in his kitchen door. Then come to find a car half in, half out his living room wall with two drownded people in it. They was all kind of stories like that, and ever one of them true. You don't make up that kind of stuff."

"We're all gonna get warshed out." Now Lucy can't stop wagging her head. "That's what's gonna happen here. We are, too. That's what it'll take. Another disaster."

"When I did get back in the house, Lucy, we had two foot of that greazy black mud in there. I mean, it got everywhere. It was in your bedclothes, it was in your refrigerator, your stove, it was in every dish you owned. Why, I had stuff wrapped in plastic, fabric I'd got to make Patty and Kelly dresses, and that mud got right through that plastic. We scrubbed, and we sprayed, and we wiped, and we mopped, and for as long as we stayed in that house, you could still smell that ole coal dirt in the walls." Mrs. Taylor wrinkles her nose. "But here I am, complaining about mud, when we didn't lose nothing." She nods, mechanical, slow. "We didn't lose nothing at all, not compared to what other people lost."

She pauses there. Lowers her voice. "Buffalo Creek was never the same afterwards. I don't just mean how it looked, but how people acted. I was glad when Dooley found something else and we moved. That was about eight months after. And we were fortunate we hadn't lived up there longer than we did. We'd only been there about four years. Now the ones who'd lived there their whole lives, that flood kilt em, in a way. Even the ones not kilt in their bodies."

Avery shifts in his seat. "That's right," he says, softly. "You're right there."

"Remember that Clancy boy?" Mrs. Taylor asks him.

"Sure. Steve," says Avery.

"Rode out the whole thing in a bathtub—can you imagine?—lived through that, then went and got himself killed in a car wreck a year later. Crazy stuff like that." She looks away from both Avery and Lucy, towards the window. "That's what I mean by it's like something's trying to get you."

Lucy nods. "Same thing happened down at Oceana. This boy lived through a house fire, then a car wreck, and then right after that, the cancer got him."

"Well," Avery says, "I heard that Steve Clancy figured if he lived through the flood, he could live through anything. That's how come he was driving like he was. Wasn't something out to get him."

"Well," Mrs. Taylor says. "I never heard that."

"I heard it at school," says Avery.

"Well."

"Does make sense," Lucy says.

Avery studies the linoleum. "To tell the truth," he says after a while, "I don't believe that was the reason."

Lucy shakes her head, takes to murmuring again. "It's gonna happen. It's gonna happen here."

"That's why I've been trying to convince her—"

"Avery!" Mrs. Taylor says it so sharply Dane jumps. "This is my home!" She lifts the walker and punches it on the floor. "Every penny of my savings is in this house. Every last cent." Dane has turned around now, he's never heard Mrs. Taylor this mad at anybody besides Lyon, and he shrinks from her, but watches as she lifts her arm and points up the mountain. "You want me to let em take everything away from me? Everything? Just let em have it all?"

Avery doesn't meet her eyes. He stares into his coffee cup, biting his lip. Mrs. Taylor's breathing huffs heavy as machinery, her arm still raised, trembling. Lucy glances nervously into corners. Gradually, Mrs. Taylor drops her arm. Her breathing quiets, at least as much as Mrs. Taylor's breath can. Then, gently, without turning to look at him, she asks, "Dane, honey? You through with them vegetables?"

"Yeah," he says, and he winces at the weak in his voice.

"Well, get that tube of biscuits out of the refrigerator and put em on the cookie sheet." Mrs. Taylor looks back at Lucy. Both of them pretend the outburst never happened. Mrs. Taylor smoothes her skirt. "Now one thing I won't never forget," she says, "was when Shirl Benson come up with that pot of soup. She lived on down the creek towards Man, maybe a mile from us, and here she comes with a pot of soup in hot mitts. She'd got it hot on her gas stove. Now she didn't have bowls or nothing, but she had spoons, and we passed it. She'd made it the night before, had it in her refrigerator like she knew something was going to happen. Vegetable soup with a little stew meat in it, chunks of fat, you know. Oh, it was good. Bucky was with us by then, you remember, don't you, Bucky?"

She's trying to make up with Avery now. Avery nods.

"Well," Mrs. Taylor says. "That was Shirl Benson for you."

From behind her, for some minutes, Dane has been thumping the biscuit tube. No matter how hard he hits it, or what part of the label he strikes, the tube won't bust. This surprises Dane so little he's not even frustrated by it.

"Oh, lord," Mrs. Taylor says. "I've got down to making store-bought refrigerator biscuits for my baby."

"I can't get it open," Dane says.

"Wham it there on the edge of the counter like you see on TV."

"What can I do to get her out of here?" Avery asks Lucy, loud enough for his mother to hear.

"Won't bust," says Dane.

"Wham it real good. There on the sharp edge," Mrs. Taylor says back.

"I'd get out if I could," Lucy says. "But we can't get enough for our place to buy nothing else. Won't nobody buy a house with a bad well under a mountaintop mine."

"Can't get it to split." Dane again, his voice even weaker now.

"Oh, lord have mercy. I'll help you after I use the restroom. Just hold on." Mrs. Taylor hauls herself up onto her walker with great huffing, finds her balance, then lunges towards the door.

"Won't listen to a word I say." Avery shakes his head.

Mrs. Taylor halts. She lifts the walker, turns a quarter way around. Plants the walker there. Dane turns, too, braced for another outburst. But this time she just looks at Avery. Then she looks away. "Well, Bucky," she says softly. "You know. I been thinking on it." She turns back, and stumps out of the room.

Left together in the kitchen without Mrs. Taylor between them, Lucy and Avery sit for some minutes in an itchy silence. Finally, Lucy tries to make conversation again.

"So, you don't remember nothing about the water itself?"

The fish flip and slice in Dane.

Avery sits there for a minute. Then he shakes his head. "Nope. Don't remember a thing between the time I went to bed and when I came to on the hillside with that dog up against me."

Avery

HE WAKES in the middle of the night in a dark cramped room, low-ceilinged, burrow-like, and beyond the window screen, the shriek and chung of the plants crowding around. Avery hears the insects as plant voices, and the humidity, which cramps too, he feels as plant breath. Although it's not "plant," "plant" isn't word enough for this, not dense enough, not slick enough, not heavy enough, not green enough, for this here, no. This is vegetation. He is always smaller in this place than he is outside, the close updraws of the hills, the hemming hollows, the vegetation, they diminish him, no matter how long and far he's gone, the land here is always heavier than he is, than any person, and how late the sunrise, how quick the sunset, how small the sky—those wither him, too. And although where he wakes is not his childhood home, it could, at the same time, be any of those homes, the dark cramp of a humid July, interchangeable, and when he wakes, he does not feel the momentary confusion, the disorientation, the loss of place he many times feels when waking in his own bed, beside his own wife, in his own house in Cleveland. No, when he wakes here, even though he has never lived here, even though he has never actually slept in this room because it's only recently become the guest room, still, he knows exactly where he is: he is home. And when he fades back, into sleep, there is to it a comfort, a peace, it should not have. But does.

In the morning he decides to walk up to the head of the hollow and see for himself. He decides he'll do this even though he hasn't brought the shoes for it. He has only the leather-soled loafers he wears to work because he'd planned to spend just two nights, get back for work on Monday, but it is worse than he'd expected, and he'd been down here for a week as recently as December. Not that it surprises him. He's seen it coming over the past few years—how the coal trucks got bigger as the towns got smaller, how you could glimpse from the highways huge raw patches of earth way back between ridgetops where it wasn't easy to get. Eventually the dimwit governor condemned the Methodist Church for condemning the mining practice—that even made the Cleveland papers—and the article carried the first clear description Avery had read of what his mother had been calling "some new kind of crazy strip mining." But none of it surprises him.

He came down this trip to find the hollow freshly wrecked, a wreck that begins with the plugged-up creek and the flood-trashed yards before you even get near the devastation on company land, and then there is the damage that you can't see from outside: the ruined wells and dropped foundations and cracks in walls and ceilings falling. As he walks up the road, a retarded man who lists to the side like a tree about to topple staggers off his porch and trails Avery a while. He twists one fist in the palm of his other hand, a polishing motion, and Avery asks him, "How you doing, buddy?" but he does not talk back, and when Avery steps off the hardtop into the dirt road, the man stops altogether. He'd seen Bell Kerwin on her front porch, hanging out rugs, and he called to her, and she spoke back, but instead of coming on out to her fence, she vanished inside her door. The final house before the locked gate, where the boy, Dane, lives has been especially flood-hit, the yard now neatly piled with junk they've gathered up, a big side-by-side refrigerator standing all by itself like a monument. The base of the modular home is a kind of plastic or fiberboard molded and painted to look like cartoon rocks, and on the upstream side, the current has battered and ripped the fake rocks clear away. As Avery passes, out of the hole jogs a homely wire-haired dog, barking like a maniac with its tail wagging, then a chicken-skinny kid in gym shorts, cowboy boots, and a pistolless holster. "Hi," Avery says to him. The kid stares back.

Once Avery stoops under the gate—newish gate, he notices, padlock newer yet—and gets to where the trees have been slaughtered, the liquid July sun splashes down unstopped from every direction, and it dizzies him. He hasn't worn a hat, doesn't usually wear a hat, despite growing up in a place where a man wears a hat almost as often as he does pants. He has a white handkerchief his mother insisted he bring to protect his lungs from dust in case of a blast, and he drapes it over his head and hopes nobody sees him. At first he thinks the loafers will be okay, but as soon as he begins pulling a little elevation, his heels start to blister, and after the road buckles up into flyrock and shale, he slips and twists an ankle. Bangs his shin.

He senses his mother about to give in. It is mostly the stories makes him think it. Of course, for three or four years after Buffalo Creek, she told the stories because she had to tell them. He understands that now, how her stories put shape and control and a kind of finality on a thing that was obscenely shapeless and uncontrollable and forever unfinished. She found new audiences wherever they moved—she had lived through Buffalo Creek, and it gave her, gave the whole family, both a luster and a taint, so there were always plenty of people to listen. And she told the details like a ritual—the car horns, Patty's prayers, people half-naked climbing out of mud, Shirl Benson's soup—so when Dooley always left the room and Avery followed, Avery told himself it was out of boredom. Eventually, though, his mother either spent herself or cured herself, and she quieted. She did tell the stories on special occasions, like February 26, the anniversary, and she liked to tell them on the anniversary of Dooley's death, too, but in general, for a long, long time, she quieted. Then a couple years ago, when they began the mountaintop removal, the Buffalo Creek stories started seeping back out of her. She'd need to tell them at least once whenever he came down, and now that he was grown up, he stayed, he listened. But after the floods this year, she began telling the stories even over the phone, and long distance in his mother's world was only for reporting who'd died and who'd got born. When she began telling the stories long-distance where she had to pay to tell the stories, Avery knew he better come on down, and once he got here, he realized she was talking about almost nothing else. And although that scared him some, he sensed he might be about to win. That's the main reason he decided to stay a little longer.

He climbs past the first series of terraced ponds, the water as opaque as mustard and colored like the inside of a sick baby's diaper. The only growing thing left up here in the head of the hollow is the grass covering the pond banks, no doubt the same stuff they've genetically engineered for reclamation. Grass that can grow on asphalt. Besides the grass, everything is dead, the hollow an amphitheater of kill, and the grass itself isn't even green. His mother grew up here in Yellowroot. She ran right back the second Dooley was forced to retire and she could, and Avery has thought on it, how that promise of return is yet another reason people from here put up with what they do. If you work hard enough, you can retire back home, not unlike the promise of heaven, Avery thinks, yeah, "Almost Heaven," and he snorts to himself. But Yellowroot was never really Avery's home. It was the place where his mamaw lived. Dooley had kept them moving from the time Avery was born until he left for college, and after that, his parents kept right on going, Dooley laid-off here, mad at a foreman there, mine worked out in this place. But despite all the moving, they not only never left the state, they never even moved farther north than Nicholas County. They'd just circle and wander their range, like nomads or bears, so that Avery's home, finally, is not a particular hollow, town, farm, coal camp, not even a particular county, but the whole foot-shaped swath of ground that holds the southern West Virginia coalfields. Until he turned eighteen, and left out, and learned.

He has an eye open for guards, not because their authority worries him—boys playing cops and trespassers—but because of the stupid hanky on his head. As the hollow narrows and draws in on itself, the ponds seem to widen, taking up more of the hollow floor, and all the debris in the rock channels is stained the same flat gray so he can't tell what is live and what is garbage. The dull gray is not a real color, not a color water around here would ever run. It is a fake color, every-thing up here is fake—fake color, fake grass, fake ponds, fake stream. Avery ducks his head so he won't have to look around him, and he smells his sweat, fruity.

Back when they'd visit his mamaw up here, he wasn't Avery. They called him "Bucky" then. Bucky, their baby, everybody was proud of him, it was not only Mom who doted on him, but Patsy and even Kelly, too, and his parents decided Bucky had promise and would go to college, the first in the family and all that. And Bucky, too, be-lieved he had "promise." Until a lot later, when he learned, among other things, that it had more to do with the times than any prom-ise he held. He graduated from high school later than Patty, Ronald, and Kelly, in 1978, when more kids were directed towards college. And it had more to do with the high school where Dooley's work-rovings landed Avery his junior and senior years, a high school with more middle-class kids than many schools in their territory. No, not promise. Happenstance, timing, and luck.

As he climbs, he grows mildly nauseated, his thoughts floating in his head like waves off hot pavement. For some time, he has felt the meat of his feet grinding up in his shoes, and finally he stops, takes off his glasses and sags over, his hands on his knees, and he pants. After his breath quiets, he hears no bugs, no birds, and the water in the ponds, that is silent, too, stagnant—no sound but the machinery overhead. A guttural amping up and down, it is not even white noise, doesn't even provide the false peace of that, no, it is gun and grind and brake and back-up beepers in the distance. He sits himself on one of the rocks freshly blasted from the hill, and its sharp edges cut into his behind. He pulls off his loafers and his socks and wobbles a blister with his finger, tempted to bust it. Then, for some reason, he pulls back and really stares at his feet, and he is washed in a hot wave of shame. Shame at their pinkness, their baby look. At the thin lines impressed by the dress socks. Quickly, he squeezes the loafers back on, and he limps off his raw-edged rock and pushes up the hollow.

Although he pretends that he doesn't, Avery understands what you lose to leave. What his mother learned she'd lose was different from what Avery learned he'd lost, but both of them learned it firsthand. She and his siblings closed up in the swelter of Baltimore for the two years Dooley tried to get out of the mines. Avery not yet born, and his mother trying to keep all five of them clean in the rundown row-house, Avery imagining, the gritty stoop and no yard, trash sweeping up and down the street, catching in their railing, and the stink of rotting things. But that wasn't it. In Baltimore or Detroit or Cincinnati or Cleveland or whatever city, it's not just a matter of keeping down the dirt, Avery knows his mother knows. It is a matter of you yourself being perceived as dirt. To leave home is not just to leave a piece of land and family and friends, it is to leave your reputation, the respect you've earned from others, your dignity, your place. That's the dilemma of his mother, how much more you lose than you'd ever imagine unless you'd already left and lost it before. Avery knows.

The leaving out, the education, how he paid. His mind forever after speaking to itself in two Englishes, there were many ways he split, but for him, they were all embodied by that double language. The hard sharp language spoken by the educated, clever language, language you pull out of your head . . . all the time shouting down his first language, an English smooth and wet, soft and loamy. Language you can wrap around, language that will work for you, play for you, easy in your mouth, welling up from a deep-knowing place under your tongue. His first language never bound him, it didn't pen him in, while the other language's words—"standard," "proper," "correct"—you must use like coins, shiny and rigid. The value of each one already fixed before you get hold of it, you can use each word in only one way. Although eventually, it wasn't a split at all, couldn't really call it a split, because a split would have meant he became both, and he didn't. He fell in between both. He became neither.

He got the business degree at Marshall although it was the history classes that spellbound him, because even at nineteen, he knew he would eventually need job security a history major wouldn't give him. Neither of his parents had enough schooling to know to warn him off the humanities, Avery somehow already knew that, so he worked on his business degree while taking as many history, philosophy, and sociology classes as he could, staying on a ninth semester because of it. Mom still liked to believe Bucky went to college because he was smart, but Avery learned why it was people went to college. And just how much or how little it had to do with brains.

Now he is rounding the final crook in the hollow, and then Avery finds himself face-to-face with the inside-out mountain. The perversion towers directly over his head. A wall of dead world the height of a small skyscraper, it is the biggest valley fill he's ever seen, as sterile as a recently erupted volcano. Behind the top of the fill, there are some kind of heaps, might be a second wall, but it's hard to tell, and behind those, the edge of the nearly level butt of the used-to-be mountain. But although he's never seen anything quite like this, and although he is already dizzy from the climb, the sight does not make Avery stumble or gasp. It doesn't surprise him. To the contrary. Avery feels calm. He stands with his neck craned, sweat weeping down his temples, dribbling the small of his back, and he knows this is the best view of the hollow head he's ever going to get. He cannot tell, of course. It could be just a valley fill, but it could also be a dam, could have a sediment pond behind it or even a slurry impoundment. But he cannot tell, and you never know what they might be up to now, what new system or "technology." That's part of the reason what he sees doesn't surprise him, even though he's never seen land destroyed in quite this way, on this scale—and quite a few man-made disasters Avery has seen.

He drops his head, casts his eyes over the plain of bleak rocks filling what used to be a creek where he and his cousins fished, caught crawdads, built their own little dams. He can see between the rocks in some places, even from this far away, glossy colors of deep turquoise and brass orange. No, it not only doesn't surprise him, it also, if Avery is honest, doesn't horrify him either. And if he is more honest, the way he responds to it is even more revolting than feeling no horror and no surprise, because what Avery feels deepest—tell the truth, go on and say it—is a kind of satisfaction. Yes, the sight satisfies him in the way it confirms all he knows and all he suspects, and it brings with it too a perverse relief. Because if the entire truth be told, the slaughter also fulfills a secret unspoken urge Avery carries always. This itchy voice, this desperate chant, that begs: Okay. Let's just get it over with. Let's go on and get it over with, and at least then we won't have to worry about what's going to happen next. If we just go on and get it all over with.

Because there was one thing his mother was right about: nobody who went through Buffalo Creek was ever the same. Even though in the years immediately following it—the years his mother told her stories—Avery didn't give it much thought, at least not when he was awake. Then, during a sociology class his sophomore year at Marshall, everything changed.

It was an upper-division class, fairly small, maybe twenty students. Avery kind of got into it by accident. The professor, a youngish man, took an interest in them all, and through that interest, he somehow discovered Avery had lived through Buffalo Creek. As soon as he learned this, he asked Avery for his story—actually, he pleaded for it, pleaded even before he knew whether Avery would resist or not, which Avery didn't. He didn't think he cared. He told Dr. Livey he didn't remember anything before he woke up on the hillside after the water passed, which was what he'd told everybody all along (which was, almost always, what he told himself), but Dr. Livey wasn't disappointed. He'd take anything he could get. He asked Avery to speak about it into a tape recorder, told him he'd pay him as a research subject. Avery hadn't understood his enthusiasm, but it flattered him, and he didn't speculate too much about the professor's fascination with his story. He just considered, first, the money, which he needed badly, and, second, pulling hard against his desire for the money, nearly overriding it, his fear of being alone in a room with a man so different from anyone he'd ever met before coming to Marshall. That worried him. Dr. Livey was not a West Virginia name, and he definitely didn't have a West Virginia voice. He didn't look local, either, and not just his clothes, but the long nose with its rounded lobes, the coarse longish black hair, the dark droopy moustache, and dark droopy eyes. In the weeks before he recorded his story, Avery mostly worried about what he would say in the office with this Dr. Livey before the tape recorder started. Telling the story itself seemed no big deal.

So one afternoon late in the semester, he found himself perched stiff on an orange-cushioned metal chair at a little round table, clutching a Coke Dr. Livey had bought him and talking into the purr of the black recorder. After a year and a half in college, he was acutely conscious of his accent and how it would replay through the machine, but he hadn't yet learned how to tame it. He went on anyway, speaking as close to how he imagined a research subject should sound, while Dr. Livey nodded and made silent encouraging *yes, yes, and?* expressions, mute so as not to mar Avery's precious story. The office had a single tall window that took up most of the only wall not gorged from floor to ceiling with more books than Avery had ever seen in a room so small, and through the window, the tepid November sun fell mild and full over every surface: the flat of the table, the tape recorder, Avery's arms. Avery, the Coke can sweating in his hand, told his story as straightforwardly as he could, beginning with waking up on the side of the hollow and continuing into a few weeks after, while Dr. Livey scooted in closer and closer, as though the sharing of the story created a familiarity between them, when Avery felt exactly the opposite. And he tried not to look at Dr. Livey, the watery lemon light exposing every blemish on his face, the black pores, the errant hairs, but he could smell him, a smell like clothes closed up for a long time in an airless closet. Avery concentrated so hard on his accent, on his story, on keeping as much distance as he could from Dr. Livey without drawing attention to it, that it wasn't until the next day it dawned on him he'd never told the story straight through like that to anyone. And he didn't think he'd told it even to himself in the light. It had always been for him a wake-up-in-the-middle-of-the-night story when, half asleep, he was too unprotected to stop it.

When he got done, he looked up at Dr. Livey, waiting for him to pay him so he could get out. But Dr. Livey was in no hurry. First he praised Avery for how well he told the story, then he puffed up with righteous anger—this didn't surprise Avery, he'd seen it in class before—and he paced around and lectured at Avery a little about how Avery and all the rest of them had been exploited and abused, the companies, capitalism, and Avery nodded obediently, the urgency of his need to escape crushing any attention he could give this speech. Then Dr. Livey selected for him a book from his shelves, told Avery something about it that Avery didn't listen to and stuck the check between its pages, and finally Avery was hurtling out the door, down the stairwell, and into the day.

It was mid-afternoon the Tuesday of the week before Thanksgiving. The sun thin and steady without heat in it. Avery, the book still in his hand and his backpack over one shoulder, found himself seeking dark. He ended up in Boney's Hole-in-the-Wall on Sixth Avenue, the bar completely windowless and the lighting inside so weak you could hardly see the bartender. That afternoon, he was the only customer. He tucked himself into a back booth and waited. No one came over to see what he wanted. He placed his hands palms down on the sticky table, steadying himself, and he tried to think, but all that came to him were odors: the sour beer soaked into the table, the faint urine and sharp disinfectant from the bathroom behind him, the smell of Dr. Livey's sweater. He felt that something had happened that he needed to figure out, but he couldn't think. It was like he'd left part of his mind behind in the office and it hadn't caught up with him yet. Something brushed his leg, and he leaned down and squinted and saw a dog under the table. The dog collapsed on its side and closed its eyes. Avery waited a little longer, burrowed there in the cave of his booth, the booth, in turn, buried in the bar, the bar also a close dark cave, and finally, without buying anything, he stuffed the book in his backpack and left.

As he reflects on it now, sitting on a gray-mucked log at the foot of the fill, the badness in the land looming over him, he decides he understood as early as Boney's that he'd made a tremendous mistake. He decides he understood what speaking the whole story in the daylight had done. Because that afternoon in Dr. Livey's office introduced into Avery two irreversible changes: it made him start thinking about it in the daytime, and it made him want to learn.

He never asked for a copy of the tape. After that semester, he avoided Dr. Livey altogether. Avery never heard the tape, so he isn't sure what all he told on it, but he does know what he didn't tell, because his mother was also right about how nobody would ever forget. He remembers, for instance, that old steel bedframe where he slept that night, and the chill of Tad's room more real to him right now than the July sweat tickling down his front. He remembers the cube steak they had for supper, how it made Bucky feel grown-up, a special guest, he remembers its flavor sharper than he remembers the stew he ate at his mom's last night. Remembers Tad's little sister, something bad wrong, her head droopy like a tomato when it's time to pick it (and Avery found out later that even though the parents and the little girl survived, she died when she was eight or nine anyway). He even remembers the smell of Tad's breath.

He hadn't known Tad before that year, and it was his first time to spend the night at Tad's house. Tad's family had moved into Buffalo Creek just that past summer, so Tad was new at school. It was a Friday night. They'd watched the Brady Bunch, and, on top of the cube steak, Tad's mother made Jiffy Pop, something Bucky's mom never bought. *Spend the money on that when you can buy regular cheap and pop it in a pan?* Even at twelve—they were young at twelve back then—Bucky was impressed with that Jiffy Pop, but Tad was more taken with the Brady Bunch. Not so much the charismatic California kids, but their house, Avery remembers. *Look, Bucky, how their living room's sunk down. And how their steps are kinda like a ladder. When I grow up, I'm gonna get me a house like that.*

Tad slept on the bedroom floor, bundled in blankets on a woven rug. He gave Bucky the bed because Bucky was the guest. They talked for a while, covers drawn up around their chins in the chill room and the rain pelting the tin roof. Then Tad went quiet, and Bucky lay there awake a good while longer. Avery can't recall what they talked about. He's pretty sure the rain didn't bother him because he can't remember that it did. He does recall what Tad wore: a pair of too-small pajama bottoms, pants legs halting halfway between his knees and ankles, the fabric splotched all over with cabooses, those and a long-john shirt. Bucky can recall the dried spit in the corner of Tad's mouth the next morning.

Avery didn't say anything to Dr. Livey about how Tad was a good half foot shorter than he was. Nothing about how Tad sat with one leg tucked under him and bounced up and down when you played board games with him. Nothing about Tad's breath. He's not real sure what he did tell Dr. Livey, but he knows he didn't tell him any of that, and he knows what he tried to tell him happens over and over in his own head like this:

He comes to on the hollowside with a dog curved against his body. He's lost his own pajama bottoms in the water, he's barefoot and wearing only his T-shirt and underwear. He wakes there on the ice-crusty dead leaves, that cold rain still drizzling down, but what he feels first, more than cold, fear, or panic, is shame over his near-nakedness. Then he realizes he is coal-dirt all over. His hair is crunchy with it, coal-dirt is greasy in his ears, and he digs in to clear them only to discover his fingertips are greasy, too. He raises himself up on his elbows—only his arms will work for him, his mind tells his legs to move, but they can't hear him yet—and he turns to study the dog, pushed against him for the warmth he carries in him. The dog is colored and slicked like Bucky is, and when Bucky shifts, the dog sits up on its haunches and whines in Bucky's face, and Bucky studies the dog. At first, he thinks the dog is a black dog, like the dog, if it was thinking about Bucky, probably saw him as a black boy, then he realizes the dog's really beaglish-marked, and Bucky studies the beagle dog for some time.

After a good while, Bucky sneaks a peek down past his feet. No further. He sees he's hauled himself way far up the hill, much higher than he needed to go, this he can tell by the oily black watermark all those yards under him. He has no idea how long he's been knocked out, or asleep, or whatever he was, that stretch of time is no different from the stretch of time during which he studied the dog, it seems time left with the dark when the dark dissolved that morning, and Bucky hasn't touched time since. And he feels nothing. Not for Tad, not for his family, not for the little figures making motion in the bottom of the hollow that soon he won't be able to ignore.

The dog pushes up against Bucky, but Bucky doesn't touch him back because of how dirty he is. The smell of the dog is not a dog smell, just like the smell of himself is not a boy smell. Both smells are coal smells, coal as familiar to Bucky as dog smell, almost as familiar to him as boy, and also familiar to Bucky is how this gluey taste-smell lies at the base of your tongue, on the back of the roof of your mouth, like it wants to speak itself. Bucky spits. Then at some point in that unraveled time which lies limp and unspooled around Bucky, he's sitting up and hugging his bare legs against his chest. The legs can't yet stand, but he gets them bent like that. They're bad scraped in the nastiest ways, Bucky traces the raw places and gashes with his black fingers, but the legs aren't paralyzed. Bucky knows that the way the legs won't move is the way they won't move in bad dreams. Although he continues to study the dog like it's a new species, occasionally he's now stealing glances through the narrow trunks of the second- and third-growth trees down into the valley. Another glance. Another. Until the glances start running together.

The water wall's gone, he knew that as soon as he woke by the quiet. The water that's left is what followed in the wall's wake, shallow cranky wastewater, black and trash-glutted, butting its way through the lowest-lying places. Part of the bottom's scoured bare. Other areas are jumbled in a crazy misarrangement, houses stacked up against each other like they're pushing in line, others tipped at odd angles, and then all kinds of splintered piles might have been houses but now no telling what they were before. Power poles toppled, wires tangled spaghetti, and he tries to gauge where he is, how far downstream from Lorado he's washed, but he can't tell, wouldn't be able to tell if he'd lived in Lorado his whole life. His mind tries to spread and wrap around what he sees, but his mind won't stretch that far, and it snaps back, dizzying. What holds his eyes tightest is the railroad. The waters have peeled the railroad right off the ground, scattered ties everywhere, then coiled up the rails into lassoes. Water did that, Bucky thinks. Then, without really noticing it himself, his legs stand up. And he knows to go home.

He's not sure exactly how far home is. He's always ridden from Lorado to Braeholm in a car. He knows it's longer than you can walk easy, but he knows, too, that it is walkable. Now his body's coming back to itself, an ache all over, and he feels the more concentrated particular stings in the cuts and scrapes, and finally the cold, the goose pimples, him unnumbing, but still he feels only the outside of his body, his insides are yet empty. He does not wonder if his family is dead, his house washed away; he doesn't wonder about Tad. He feels nothing inside but the call to get home.

His body, working by itself, drops into a crouch and part-creeps, part-slides, down the steep side of the hollow. The dog's right with him. His naked feet skid the icy leaves, them soppy underneath and that cold rain still fizzling down, and Bucky is jarring against root and rock, scraping over rotten half-buried logs, the thorn brush, the saplings. Bucky's skin is bared to all of it, his feet bared to it, his pimpled legs and arms. Then he knows he has to get some shoes. The get-the-shoes crowds the get-on-home out of his head, and he grabs hold a root to lower himself down the last steep slide, the root jerking free and dropping him, skittering, scratching, onto level ground, hurting him all over again. But he picks himself up, and he heads for the nearest house.

To reach it, although it's not far, he leapfrogs from debris pile to debris pile, over the black water braids between them, and Bucky is careful about where he steps, the glass, metal, wire. From the back of the house, he can't see how to get in except through a busted-out window that's bound to cut him even worse than he's cut now. He picks his way to the front, again, careful of his feet, and the dog sticks close, never acting doglike, never pausing to sniff or piss or dig. It's as though the dog has given up his dogness just to keep alive, and Avery realizes a long time after that the same thing happened to Bucky. They find the front door blocked by trash and by most of a twisted car, so Bucky eyes the next house, downwater from this one, a house that looks like its side is bashed in.

He's scrabbling across piles of wreckage again. He pulls at his nose over and over to stob its running, the nose raw, his fingers greasy. Twice, when he walks upright, his weight's too much for the trash and he crashes through to his hip, then the right leg is torn and rawed all over again, but the leg does not break. At times his body shivers so hard it's difficult to keep his balance. The dog follows close, and down here, Bucky can't see any figures moving, sees nothing alive but the dog. He thinks nothing besides getting the shoes. Finally, they reach the bashed house and stoop in where the green aluminum siding has parted.

The moment Bucky sets foot on the floor, he's lit by a bolt of fear, in his shoulders and head, that the house is about to shift. He thinks he does feel it lift a little, throws out his arms for balance, digs in the mud with his bare toes. He waits. It's not a fear he recognizes. He's standing in a living room, all its furniture toppled and pushed towards the upstream wall, and waves of black muck lie terraced across the floor, the terraces rising on the upstream end to two feet deep against that wall. The house seems to hold steady, so Bucky wades the mud to the closet and forces the door open partway against the weight of the muck outside it. He sees only coats, no shoes, and he chooses one, a heavy plaid wool, and pulls it on. Its lining is nearly dry, the wool having shed the floodwater for the brief time it surged through the house. Bucky pauses, tensed for the shifting of the house like listening for a noise. But the house stays put. He slops on through the muck, it sucking his ankles and feet, him scanning everywhere for shoes poking out, and then the dog gets himself bogged down nearly to his belly, and he cries like he has a whistle in his nose. Bucky considers looking upstairs, but the fear of the house moving stops him.

The kitchen appliances have rocked out of their places, the refrigerator overturned, the stove tethered at the end of its cord still plugged in its socket. Bucky studies the room from the door, and spies, against an upended table, among sopped cereal boxes and plastic bowls, red rubber. He jerks them free, red rubber woman's boots, red laces and a matted fake fur cuff. They are full of mud, and he turns them over and works on squeezing out the mud, then he loses patience and carries the boots to the sink where he opens a tap and stands bewildered for some seconds when no water comes out. In the other room, the dog, still stuck, has given up whistling for panicked yelps. Bucky claws the mud out of the boots as best he can with his hands and forces his feet into them. They are squishy, but too big by only a little bit. He pauses once again, feeling for the house to move. Then he struggles back into the living room, where the dog has unstuck himself from the mud, and Bucky hauls him back through the wall and into the rain.

The plaid coat covers him to five or six inches below his underpants. The sleeves mitten his hands.

While still on the hill, he'd assumed he'd follow the road home, but he never does find any road. It's either buried or washed away. He picks a path through wherever the debris lies most open or most shallow, Bucky mazing it with his eyes to the ground, the dog right behind him, Bucky thinking nothing but where it's safest to step. Step. Step. He steps over railroad ties and asphalt chunks, sticks, furniture, and trees, aluminum siding and aluminum cans, Insulite and trailer underpinnings, plastic, barrels, cars, roof slabs, cats, tires, washing machines, and, most often, splintered lumber. He's passed a motorcycle and is approaching a pallet with something under it, he can't tell what it is (he doesn't pay any attention, really, to what it is; it's only Avery, later, who slows it down, isolates out of the rest of the memory Bucky's first sight of the pallet), and Bucky draws closer to the pallet, not because he's curious about what's under it, but because the channel he's following, his path, goes that way. Then it occurs to Bucky it's a kid's doll there, and then he doesn't consider it again. He's just watching where to step. And now he's right up on the pallet. And Bucky sees a woman's rings on the doll's hand.

Bucky stands still. He stands poised in a time hole, time pools around the hole's outside, but Bucky's inside the hole, timeless. Looking. There is no how-long to this stare, no matter how often Avery reconjures it later, Bucky stares, and the dog stares, too, undogly, never smelling the body or using his paws. And there is really no sight to the stare, either, no sight that Avery can remember, until finally, Bucky is leaving the bottom.

Bucky is leaving the bottom. Bucky is running when he can, Bucky is crawling when he has to, he is scrambling, he is falling, he is picking himself up without stopping, he is scratched, pulled, tripped, bumped, scraped, he no longer worries about finding the most open way, no,

Bucky heads for the hills in a crow-flies line. And all the way, he is murmuring, he is soft-talking himself down, the voice like a mouth over sponge cake, like the kindest mother ever to the scaredest ever child: *this is how you go, honey; yes, this is the way*. At one point, the only point he remembers vividly, he sprints around a toppled garage and finds himself vaulting headlong into a triple line of electric wires, and he manages, some brilliant instinct, to leap all three, boom boom boom, like hopscotching tires in an obstacle course, the voice sweet-talking, *this is how you go, honey, up there will be safe*. And he's at the base of the hill, *go on now, almost,* and he's mounting straight up, easier than it was coming down, *almost, up there now, you'll travel safe,* and he is passing the watermark, the brush turns from black to a rain-wet deep brown, and, *see, honey, here,* he skids to a stop, doubled over, his breath spearing in his chest and his ribs.

Avery remembers how sometimes walking the hollowside was fairly easy, him traveling a bench or, if not, it wasn't all that steep anyway, and he was used to walking hillsides like that. At times he'd hit a cliff or a rock overhang where he'd have to climb up above it to get around. The red rubber boots are slippery in two ways, their soles sliding on the ground and his feet slippery inside the boots, and the skin rubs and blisters up, he can feel it. The legs aren't cold anymore, now that the main part of his body is covered, and the dog sticks close, he hasn't lost him yet, and Bucky stays up high. Down in the bottom, where he tries not to look, but can't help not, he sees live people moving. They mill around, sifting through wreckage, as far as he can tell, and their very liveness down there makes it all look more ruined. On the hollowside below Bucky, other people have already cobbled together makeshift shelters from the cold rain, and on the far side of the hollow, a few campfires, he sees, smoke smudges and tiny bursty flames. He feels the torn skin up and down his legs, and bruises in his hands. The black taste still clogs his throat. The pressure to spit. His nose is running nonstop, and his sleeve reaches up, again and again, and wipes it on its own.

He's moving fast and easy along an unreclaimed bench under a highwall strip when he meets his first live person. The man pulls himself up on the level some fifty feet distant from Bucky, and then he's coming at him. Bucky panics. It's like he's been gone from people for twenty years, and the man comes on. They pull closer to each other, the collapse of in-between, and then Bucky stops, his legs tensed, and he almost steals off the edge of the bench, flees, but the man comes. As soon as he gets near enough, the man calls, "Hey, buddy, you seen Martha Adkins?" His voice is thinned, tattery, and high, and Bucky can hear that it is already an old, old question. The man is only rain-wet—no black on him—and he wears all his clothes. The rain has twisted his long brown hair into little tails, and when he gets even closer, Bucky sees that under the patchy beard the man is pretty young. The man doesn't show a second of surprise or even curiosity over Bucky's blackness, or his lost pants, or the woman's boots. Bucky is already, like the question, an old old sight. When the man speaks, Bucky shakes his head.

"It's my mommy," the man keeps on. "Fifty years old. Dark-brown hair. Stays up there at Lundale. She's missing these teeth." The man drops his jaw and grabs a couple bottom teeth on one side.

"Sorry, I don't know her," Bucky says. He hasn't spoken, not even to the dog, since he was on the chickenhouse roof, and now his voice crossing his teeth makes his teeth feel funny.

"How bout a little boy, round six, blond-headed?"

Bucky shakes his head.

"Latricia, she's sixteen, blonde-headed, too. Heavyset girl."

"I ain't seen nobody at all," Bucky says.

The man pauses. Not like he's taking the time to feel disappointment. He just seems to rest. Then he nods. "Thank you," he says, and then he hurries past, on up the hollow.

Not too long after that, Bucky passes a bunch of people holed up in a lean-to not far under him, close enough that they could spot him if they wanted to. But if they look anyplace, they look into the valley floor, not behind them. He can hear a little kid crying, sees two men trying to shelter each other to light a cigarette. Bucky keeps moving, and the men don't hear his boots in the leaves. It begins to snow, big wet flat flakes, kind of snow you get on just that other side of rain, and below the watermark, when Bucky has to walk near it, he can watch them fall stark white on the black. For an instant, you can see them, then the black sops them under. Twice more, he runs into men looking for somebody. Bucky just shakes his head and goes on. One of the men has an arm so broken Bucky can tell it from yards away even though he's never seen an unset broken arm in his life. And now and again, he stops, sits, and pulls off the boots, feels at his feet, but there's nothing he can do for them. The first blisters have already busted and coal dirt got in the sores, and already, a second layer, a third, of fresh blisters coming on. As he walks, he watches the bottom more deliberately, tries to reckon where he is. Downstream here, the valley is still wrecked, but it is less scraped bare. More stuff stands where it should. He even sees a couple people trying to drive pickups in it.

Then, not paying enough attention, he comes over the top of a gully too quick and finds himself at the edge of a crowd of people around a big fire. He starts to angle back above them and slip away, but they spot him and holler for him to c'mere. *Hey! C'mon down in here, honey,* they call. *C'mon now. We gotta tell you something.* Despite himself, Bucky drags a little—it's not just the urgent in their tone, it's how he's been raised to obey grown-ups—and *listen, sugar,* one insists, *it's dangerous. Get on down here, you hear?* When he finally does give in, though, it is mostly because the dog goes first.

As soon as he's within the heat ring thrown by the foul-smelling fire, a voice warns, *Second dam's gonna blow. They say this one'll be worse than the first. You better stick close here.* He's in a commotion of more than a dozen panicked or numb people, most of them staring at him, and he heats with self-consciousness over his naked legs, the barely covered underwear, all the new voices, the new faces, like confetti in his head. The fire gushes a greasy black smoke, nasty-odored, and what are they burning? Tires? Ties? Plastic? big ash flakes funneling up off it, clashing with the snowflakes funneling down. The woman who'd been hollering at him loudest, the most persistent, is saying, "Lord have mercy. You went through it, didn't you? And here we are without even any water to wash you off with." She's in a big puffy coat, her body under that puffy, too, like angel food cake. In Bucky's head, the glob of people starts to divide into individuals, him seeing now that some are fully clothed, others stripped and blackened and huddled in blankets somebody's fetched up, and Bucky notices most a man wrapped in a pink quilt on the far side of the fire, Bucky drawn to something funny about him, but Bucky can't place what the funny is. "Oh," the puffy woman is saying, "wish we could get down in the house and find you a pair of pants," and somewhere past her, he hears a man: *I couldn't even tell how many bodies I seen hung up in that bridge abutment.* The people continue to divide out like cells, and Bucky recognizes two kids from the school bus whose names he knew yesterday, but not today, and he notices a stringy-headed woman, wattled in her throat, who's counting everybody, over and over again. One to seventeen, she does a round every three or four minutes, and when she hits seventeen, she crows, her voice nearly cheerful, "Well, we're all here. We're all still here." Bucky watches the man in the pink quilt, studying on what's funny. "Believe I'll just go on down, get you them pants," the angel food lady is saying. "Mommy!" this a teenage girl. "What if it breaks while you're in there?" "Well, now, I'd hear it. I'd hear it, and it wouldn't come so fast I couldn't get back up here." The gray flakes, the snow ash. A woman lies curled under a blanket, not pink, a second woman sitting beside her, holding her hands. Bucky turns back to the pink quilt man, studying on it. "Seventeen!" the stringy-headed woman crows. "Well, we're all still here!" "Why, that's Dooley Taylor's boy," a man's voice now. "What are you doing up here above Braeholm, buddy? Why ain't you home? That's Dooley Taylor's boy." He's speaking to the angel food lady. "I work with his daddy." There's a little girl won't come out of her mother's coat. You can see nothing but her legs under the hem. Screams if the coat falls open. "Mr. Roberts's gone down, get you them pants," the angel food lady is saying. "He works with your daddy." "Well, we're all still here!" Bucky studies the pink quilt man, the something funny worrying him like a brier in his thumb. "It had to have been the number three went, that much water, and can't be more water left up there than what just come down." "Well, Grady, I don't know. Who knows what all they got up there. I wouldn't take no chances." The pillowy snowflakes falling on Bucky's face, an open-mouthed cold kiss. "Seventeen! Well, we're all still here!" One of the school bus kids, who Bucky remembers now is Angie, comes up to him with a two-week-old box of Valentine chocolates hived in a soiled heart box, the box now mostly empty. Bucky's stomach surges sour into his craw, the coal dirt flavor all through his head. He shakes his head at Angie. "Here's Mr. Roberts with your pants, honey." The pants so big he can pull them on without taking off the boots. He blows out his stomach to keep them up, then he just holds them bunched at the waist in his left hand. Then, like a clap, Bucky knows what's funny about the pink-quilt man. His scalp has been ripped two-thirds off his head and there it hangs. "Seventeen!" They stop attending to Bucky. His newness is fading. He's just number seventeen. Soon, between countings, he creeps away, but the dog stays behind, close to the heat of the fire. It was there that he lost the dog.

After that, he keeps hidden in the trees. Pretty soon, he knows he really is close to home, recognizes for certain the shape of the hollow floor through the tree trunks and brush. And then he begins to recognize the trees themselves, the rocks, he's played up in here, and Bucky feels, despite himself, his mouth tug up, the corners pull against the black coal crust. As he steps up his pace, his feet butchered in the boots, the pants hobbling him, he thinks he hears cracking noises. Bucky looks over his shoulder.

He sees a man, not running, but a kind of stiff hurry-walking, his arms and hands held up in front of him to break the branches and brush before his face. Elbows out, forearms up, fingers splayed, he crashes through the woods like a blind man, and Bucky can tell now he is shirtless and black-slimed. At first, he doesn't worry Bucky much, but even so, Bucky hurries up a little, the red rubber boots chafing at his heels and at the sides of the widest part of his feet. Now the crashing and snapping gets louder, and Bucky looks again, and he sees the man is gaining on him. Sees he's broke out of his quick-walk into a trot. He sees his belly, big and round and tight, jiggle, and now the man calls, "Johnny!"

Bucky begins to jog, still not truly scared, just too close to home to fool with this character right now. He grits his teeth against the tearing in his boots, stumbles into the huge pants legs, and the hand holding the waist not able to pump, that hinders him, too. "Johnny!" the belly man calls again, and Bucky gets more worried. He feels his feet bleed in the red boots, the man hollers, "Johnny! Wait there, boy!" his voice carrying a rockslide in it, and Bucky finally shouts back, "I ain't Johnny!" But the man, shocking fast despite the enormous shimmying belly and his bare busted feet, sprints a circle around Bucky, then floats in front of him, jogging from foot to foot like a football tackle, his arms spread wide, and it's all quick, quick, but Bucky somehow has time to see not only the hair all over his chest and belly black with coal slime, but the stripes and scrapes whipped into the slime by the branches, and the blood in the black, too, the man's eyes streaming white out his black face like he's coming off a shift. And Bucky, as he dodges and feints, starts to unnumb, he's thawing all over, the crust drops away, and Bucky screams, "I ain't! I ain't Johnny!" Still the man blocks him, can sidestep Bucky in any direction, Bucky is crying now, and the belly-man takes a different tack, baby-talks him, syrup in his mouth, "Johnny. C'mon, boy. It's your ole daddy, Johnny. You know it is. Johnny. You know you are," spooning, crooning, sweet candy voice, like tricking a dog so you can snatch and pen it up. "C'mon, Johnny. Johnny-boy, c'mon, Johnny-cake now," and Bucky, acting entirely out of instinct, darts, baits the belly man to the right, then spins and tears left, his sores screaming in his boots, but he is gone, the belly-man behind him in his bare feet, booming out that swelled belly-chest: "Johnny! Johnny! You know you are! You know you are now! Johnny! You know it now! Johnny! Johnny!"

Then Bucky grew up, became Avery, and learned. Dr. Livey stuck the money in the book so he'd have to open it up. Avery'd never been a reader before, grew up in a place where you do things, don't just read about them, and, besides, what books he had read had nothing to do with him, with them. But he opened this book, a study of the disaster aftermath by a sociologist, and there he was, there they were, Buffalo Creek, a little of their history, a lot of their grief, of what they carried with them past 1972, and after that, Avery never stopped learning. He never spoke to Dr. Livey again, either, after finals, and never, to his shame, returned Dr. Livey's book. But that first book made him find the second book, and the second one made him find the third, and each lesson he learned, far from glutting him, just made him lustier for the history. His greediness for learning it like alcoholism or being in a destructive kind of love.

He taught himself, because they'd never been taught their history (the first thing he learned). Sure, they'd had West Virginia history, in eighth grade, fifty minutes of free-floating information on an overhead projector. The teacher sat humpled, cozy in her fat, behind her desk in the rear of the room where she could watch them without even shifting off her seat, her mouth moving only to scream threats and order Missy Combs to crank the plastic sheeting. They copied the splintered facts, pencils pressing into greasy desks—highest point in the state (Spruce Knob), lowest point in the state (Harper's Ferry), geographic center of the state (Flatwoods)—later spat them back to pass or fail multiple choice tests, and when the bell rang, the teacher only had to waddle to the middle of the room and rewind the rollers for the next class.

They didn't learn their history. Instead they learned the Pledge of Allegiance every morning, mouthed the "Star-Spangled Banner" after that, bowed their heads for the Lord's Prayer piped over the intercom. They learned *ma'am* and *sir* and to eat all the food on their tray and how to sit and to stand absolutely still for long periods of time; they learned how to wait. They learned to follow the rules, and they were beaten if they did not, their bodies not too good for a whipping, although the poorest of the poor were whaled on hardest and most often, those children, as always, the lesson (the real poor, the poorer than you, the ones who made kids like Bucky see themselves as not poor at all (until you left out and you learned), stumbling furious defiant out the principal's office, mouths sealed, eyes a shiny blaze (*how many whacks did you get?*) rubbing violent with crusty sleeves their dirty tear-smeared cheeks). They learned not to ask questions, to do as they were told, expect little, they were raised to expect disappointment, this they absorbed from the air around them, a pessimism so pervasive, even before Buffalo Creek, that Avery never recognized it—it was temperature, weather—until he left out and realized how much the other people, at least the other white people, in this country, perceived, expected, desired. And, always, again, the poorest kids, their warning: look what will happen to you if you don't work hard, do as you're told, expect little, American poverty Appalachian-style: the shanties and decaying trailers, the retarded and the crazy, those without plumbing reeking on school buses, the ringworm and scabies and the lice, your daily meal the free one at school, your clothes somebody else's first and everyone can tell . . . and almost every one of their bodies as white-skinned as your own. That's what they learned.

But after those hours in the sunlit office of Dr. Livey, Avery learned what they never learned, and he learned why. He learned on his own, beginning at Marshall on time he didn't have, his business studies left undone so he almost didn't graduate, but he did graduate, and then he left the state. He couldn't bear to stay one week longer (and since he graduated from Marshall seventeen years ago, he has never stayed in West Virginia for longer than two weeks at a time), and through his twenties, he lived in thirteen different places, worked more than thirteen different jobs, but he couldn't stop thinking. His mind didn't leave. The history continued to ride him (this place sticky with history, history sticky in it), it was as though the interminable motion, the way he could not stay put, was an attempt to run ahead of the history, although now, looking back, it seems the only common denominator of all those shifting years was what he learned. Was the history.

He learned who could get away with what—where, when, and on whom. He learned the February 26, 1972, dam bust was not Pittston's first, wasn't even the first one they'd had on Buffalo Creek. He tunneled into the history of slagheap disasters: Letcher County, Kentucky, 1923; Crane Creek, West Virginia, 1924; Buchanan, Virginia, 1942; Aberfan, Wales, 1966 (the only one more deadly than the one he lived through). He read about explosions and cave-ins: Monongah, 1907; Eccles, 1914; Layland, 1915; Benwood, 1924; Farmington and Hominy Falls, 1968; he studied anti-union militancy and mine wars, Paint Creek and Cabin Creek in the 1910s, Blair Mountain, 1921; Matewan. He learned that over 100,000 people were killed in U.S. mines between 1906 and 1977, learned that 1.6 million were injured from 1930 to 1976. That a U.S. miner dies of black lung every six hours.

All the way across the country, Avery learned. He'd put in his shifts, then, finding the best library in the city, hide out in reading rooms, the homeless snoring alongside him. He'd check out the books, plug his ears against stereo-playing roommates and TV-addicted neighbors. At universities, he'd huddle in library carrels, completely and perversely absorbed, so desperately did he want to read it all confirmed, confirmed, confirmed, that he didn't eat, ignored his bladder, never felt his feet fall asleep. It was one morning at the University of Washington that he stumbled onto the value of a human body. Buried in fluorescent-lit stacks between yellow walls, a dripping umbrella at his feet, Avery turned a page and saw: right there, laid out in print, exactly who counted for how much where. He held his breath without knowing he was doing it. He rushed over the page, then he went back and read it three more times, slow. He learned that a body in some states can cost a killer millions of dollars. In other states, a person is beyond price. He learned that in the state of West Virginia, at the time of Buffalo Creek, a body's value was capped at $110,000. He learned that some Buffalo Creek family members got for their dead no more than a couple thousand bucks.

After Avery read this, he looked up from his book. Took several shallow breaths. Even now, thirteen years later, Avery can remember how, with those shallow breaths, he gradually became conscious of his own body. Not the twenty-seven-year-old body cramped in the carrel, but his twelve-year-old body, the memory battered into that. The disaster was carved into his body like grooves in a phonograph record, and the page about the prices, they played his skin back. Freezing, bruised, torn, naked, black, his own skin and muscle and mind and bone, how hard he fought, from Tad's crushed bedroom to his own flooded house, to save that body. The sacrifices he made in the eight hours it took. He saw Bucky's body, and Tad's, and the pink-scalp man, and the lady under the pallet, and the one hundred and twenty-three others who died that morning on Buffalo Creek, and then the thousand who lived, irreparably damaged, body and mind.

Nobody was ever the same after. Bucky grew up fast after February 26, everybody did, the adults turned old, the kids either brittled or they broke. Avery brittled. He sees right off the worst in everything, doomsday in his head. He lives in nonstop knowledge something bad's about to happen—and again today, standing under decapitated mountains, he feels that sick trickle of relief—and no matter how often it doesn't, he can't stop looking for it to come. He keeps to himself, doesn't get close to anyone much, drove his first wife crazy that way, found a second one who doesn't mind it too bad. Turned smartass, cheeky and moody, for a dozen years after the flood, although now he knows to keep that to himself, and, always, the insatiable appetite for confirmation of how bad things really are, the only comfort Avery gets. And the Clancy boy, Steve, the one Mom brought up, who lived through the flood, then died in a wreck driving too fast drunk. How people tried to tell that he risked it because he thought nothing could kill him after he beat that flood. Avery smiles. Avery knows it wasn't that, even back then he knew it. Avery knows it is the opposite. Knows it isn't a sense of invincibility, but a consciousness of your own vulnerability, of your own insignificance, an awareness so profound it shakes hands with suicide. There were lots of people, Avery learned, who didn't want to live after Buffalo Creek. And what's a body. What's a body. What's a body to do? What's a body. What's a woman, man, a girl a boy a stream a tree a hill . . .

Because of course it wasn't just people who were sacrificed. This sacrifice of land, what he stands in now, is nothing new, it has been regularly slaughtered for well over a hundred years, Avery learned that, too, the whole region had been killed at least once. Trees razed, mountains stripped, streams poisoned, and for a long time, not even any deer to speak of, no bear or turkey either, and the buffalo and panther will never come back. Although the trees have tried, and Avery looks up towards Cherryboy, though degraded, fewer-specied second- and third-growth. And the deer have come back, though adulterated, imported Michigan mule deer crossbred with the whitetail. And a few streams flushed themselves, and some of the slashed mountains are camouflaged with grass. And Avery remembers a hundred rides home, driving the state from top to bottom, Wheeling to Yellowroot, the land suspended in its fragile reincarnation, and Avery, near delirious with exhaustion and homesickness, watching how the brush tries to cover the mess. Watches the vegetation, an obscenity or grace, vining over ruined industry and failed farms, the plants lush against the machinery, the dead rusted metal. Against abandoned drift holes, barns, depots, houses, tipples, steel mills, glass factories, oil refineries, wrecked cars, chemical plants, failed theaters, packing sheds, gutted stores, chickenhouses, leaning silos, broken bridges, shut-down schools, busted dams. Only the churches fresh, it seems to him, and the Wal-Marts hacked into hillsides, and the chain convenience stores governing oft-traveled crossroads. This place not pure, and how that somehow makes him more tender for it, makes him love it deeper, for its vulnerability, for its weariness and its endurance. This place so subtly beautiful and so overlaid with doom. A haunt, a film coating all of it. Killed again and again, and each time, the place rising back on its haunches, diminished, but once more alive . . . Only this, Avery knows, will finally beat the land for good.

Avery takes a slow final look, the corpse-colored ground, the strangled creek, the lopped-off mountains, and on the edge of the mine, three spindly trees. This is a disaster less spectacular, more invisible, than Buffalo Creek. This disaster is cumulative, is governed by a different scale of time. Chronic, pressing, insistent, insidious. Kill the ground and trees by blasting out the coal, kill all the trees you don't kill the first time through acid rain, kill the water with the waste you have to dump, and then, by burning the coal—Avery smirks, he's on a roll—heat up

the climate and kill everything left. Because Avery has come to understand (not learn, but understand, confirming) that the end times his
mother obsesses about won't arrive with a trumpet and Jesus come
back all of a sudden and everybody jump out of their graves. No. It
is a glacial-pace apocalypse. The end of the world in slow motion. A
de-evolution, like the making of creation in reverse. The End Times
are in progress right now, Avery is walking on them . . .

And "What do you remember?"

*"I don't remember nothing before I woke up on the mountain with that
dog beside me."*

"What do you remember?"

"Don't remember nothing before I woke up on the mountain."

"What do you . . ?"

"Don't remember nothing before I woke . . ."

"What?"

"Don't remember nothing" Don't remember

Tad's mother screaming, and at first Bucky, thought-fumbling,
couldn't place where he was, but the scream pulled him far enough
out of sleep to hear a roar like a hurricane happening in his ear, its
volume shooting louder by the second, and in that roar, the *pops* and
cracks and *whush*. Then Tad's father screaming back at his mother, and
then an enormous grating noise, closer than the screams, and Bucky
saw out the window opposite the bed—again, him thought-fumbling,
he saw and he heard, but he could not understand—that the house
next door was coming into Tad's room.

The window shattered. Tad sprang off the floor and into bed with
Bucky, and now Bucky could tell Tad's parents were screaming Tad's
name, but he couldn't tell where they were, inside, outside. He felt the
house shift a little, it clenched its teeth against the pressure, it tried, but
he felt it give, and he and Tad bounded off the bed and to the top of
the stairs, saw black water torrenting through the first-story rooms.

The house groaned and swayed. Still clinging to each other, they ran into a bedroom on the downstream side of the upstairs, away from where the neighbor's house was coming in, Bucky reaching for a chair to break out the window but Tad already had the pane up, and then there was the screen, Bucky socking at it, butting his body into it, and he popped out enough of it that they could struggle through onto the roof over the side porch. Now the house is truly moving, the roar so deafening they can't hear each other unless they pull up and scream in an ear, even though they are linked by their arms. Bucky whips his head to the left, glances out over the narrow bottom, sees a mountain of black water tearing through Lorado carrying big stuff all in it, sees people splashing, sees a house fall forward on its face, then he sees across the way a man in a crouch on his garage roof, suspended, his arms extended like wings, choosing whether to dive off or hang on. A car gallops down on him and knocks him into the flood. Tad's house coasts, free, and the roof begins to tilt, and they start sliding down the slick tin, at first scrabbling with fingers and nails and knees the ridges in the roofing, but finally Bucky grabs Tad's hand and they leap into the water, off to the side as far away from the path of the house as they can jump.

Bucky loses hold when they hit the thick cold greasy water, then he surfaces and spots Tad's blond head in the black slush. Tad's mouth and eyes are bawled open, he is screaming, then a wave chops into Bucky's mouth, the horrible taste to it, death and coal dirt, and Bucky realizes his own mouth had been as open as Tad's. Bucky goes under. Spinning, a pressure like pliers on his chest, he can't tell backwards from forwards, up or down either. Something bigger than he is clips his shoulder and his legs are tangled in long thin metal sheeting, and as he fights that, yet another object kicks him to the top again. Eye-level with the debris, he catches sight, between the black peaks of waves, of Tad not far away. Tad's climbed up on something, and Bucky thrashes towards Tad, they're both moving in the same direction, Tad spread-eagled on his stomach on a mattress and screaming directions to Bucky that Bucky can't hear. Bucky gains on Tad, more from the push of the torrent than through his own effort, then Tad reaches both hands to Bucky, the mattress twisting and bucking, but Tad still reaches. Then he has Bucky, jerks him towards him, and Bucky snatches hold the mattress, and the mattress buckles and lists and twists as Bucky tries to mount it, and it almost overturns and throws Tad off, but Tad somehow balances it. And then the two of them are tangled on the mattress, clinging to its edges and to each other, the mattress spinning and pitching. Tad bleeds on the fabric, but Bucky can't tell from where, Tad is too black-coated, and neither can he tell how much blood there is because of how the rain and the floodwaters have thinned it and spread it. Then Bucky is distracted from the blood by a flash of light, wild sparks, then a series of explosions—power poles toppling, a transformer blowing up, the wires hitting the water with sizzle and smoke—and then the mattress slams into something he doesn't see and he and Tad are tossed back in.

Again, the utter loss of direction, of place. Again, the crush in his chest, and Bucky flutters his eyes open and sees a black darker than air ever gets. Bucky spins, lashes his arms around for anything that floats, rams his elbows into debris, his shoulders, his knees, and finally gets his hands into a mess of chickenwire tacked to the side of a shed. And then Bucky sees—and this time it's miraculous, downright unbelievable (so much so that at times Avery continues to wonder if it happened at all (while the dead-center of him knows it did))—Bucky sees on the far side of the tar-papered shed roof the blond head, ragged full of black coal, but the blond comes through, Bucky sees Tad clawing onto the chickenhouse roof.

Then the chickenwire tears away with Bucky's weight, vanishes into the swill, and he has to hold onto the shed itself, like Tad is trying to do across from him. He tries gripping the thin eave of the roof, but there isn't enough jut for him to get a real hold. He's thrown all of himself into his hands and into a little piece of his mind that knows how to hold on, and that mind piece tells him not even to bother spreading his arms to clutch the roof by its corners, it is too wide. He is going to have to climb up on top.

Bucky screams this at Tad, what he's going to do, but Tad just stares back at him, empty-eyed, his teeth bared. He can't hear what Bucky is saying, and how in God's name is Tad holding on? Bucky cannot tell. He starts fighting his way onto the roof, first dragging himself with his elbows until he's flat on it to his waist. From there, he's able to hook up a knee. He pauses a second, and it comes to him, it seems, it does, what's going to happen next, and he screams again at Tad, Tad again gazes back, bald-eyed, and Bucky can't hold the awkward position any longer. He heaves his whole body up using his hands and the knee. Bucky's sudden full weight on the roof plunges it down on his side, pitches the other side up in the air. Bucky throws himself flat on the roof to stabilize it, and the Tad side of the roof splashes back down to the surface. But Tad is no longer there.

Some dream of water walls, Avery has learned, and some dream of logs coming at them. Some dream of scaling the hills, all alone, the last person left on earth, and some just dream of running, run all night long and wake without rest. His brother Ronald still dreams of stepping on bodies, although Ronald never did, dreams of a body turning up under his feet, and his mother still dreams the loss of Bucky. Some don't dream because they can't remember. Instead, they live in the constant horror that one day they will recall, one night they will dream. But Avery dreams this: "Bucky, grab hold my arm!" And he can't, not to save his mind nor his soul, know if Tad really screamed, or if the scream is dream, too.

Dane

ALL SUNDAY morning and into early afternoon Corey and Tommy work on Corey's bike in the road. Dane pretends to watch the races with Jimmy Make, but every once in a while, he goes to the window to check on them. Jimmy tells him to settle his butt down. NASCAR makes Dane want to fall asleep, and he used to wonder if that was because he didn't understand it or if what he was understanding was all it was. He has decided he must not understand because it casts a spell on both Jimmy Make and Baron, the two of them paralyzed on the sofa with their mouths slightly open. Finally on one of his trips to peek out the drapes, which Jimmy has drawn to make the races more vivid, Dane sees that Corey and Tommy have gone. He grabs a piece of bread while Jimmy's not looking and heads out to see what they're into now.

As he walks down the road, he squishes the soft bread into little packed balls that he sticks in his mouth and sucks, rolling them over his tongue. It seems anymore all he wants to do is eat. No threat of rain in the sky, far as he can see, but the road, the yards, too, are empty, nobody about, and Dane wonders if that is because of the races or the heat. No fish swim in him. Just the jammed logs, heavy and grating, the chock-full ride in his gut, and still, he wants to eat, pile more in.

He sees two figures trotting up the road towards him, but he knows they aren't Tommy and Corey because the two figures are exactly the same height. It's the twins, David and B-bo. Even though they're identical—each blond mallet head shaved uneven, near bald in spots, brushy in others—you can easily tell them apart. David acts normal, while B-bo acts like a car with bad brakes.

"You know where Tommy and Corey's at?" Dane asks them when they get close enough. B-bo had come up with his head lowered and his right hand jerking his gearshift. Now he jogs in place, his motor idling in his mouth.

"They're up in the Big Drain," David says. "Corey and Seth are having a bike contest."

"Idiot!" B-bo shrieks. "We wadn't supposed to tell nobody."

"Oh, idiot yourself," says David. "Ain't nobody. Just Dane."

B-bo squeals his heels in the gravel and speeds off, David following, both moving fast in the direction of the Big Drain. Dane watches. He weighs whether seeing the contest, being there with the others, is worth the dangers of the Big Drain. He sucks on his bread, the nuggets lodged between teeth and tongue a comfort in his mouth. No fish moving. Doesn't look like rain. Even if it does rain, the water probably won't come out of the Big Drain because the water always comes from where it shouldn't, and the Big Drain is where it should. Dane leans over, ties his shoe, and jogs after the twins.

The Big Drain sticks out of Yellowroot Mountain about a third of the way up its side, kind of above Mrs. Taylor's house, but of course you can't see it from there. It is hidden, deeply buried in woods and in brush, it's a secret place, despite how big it is, and the only people who even know about it are those other people have shown. Exactly why it's there, Dane does not know, he knows only that it's been there all his life. It's twice as tall or more than he is, higher than a regular room, and where it disappears into the mountain, about forty steps from its mouth, it's capped with a grate. Many people have tried to get through this grate, including Bant one afternoon a few years ago while Dane squatted on the concrete side, watching. Praying that she wouldn't make it, but the grate is a thick rusted criss-crossed steel and nobody has ever managed to get past it. On its other side, the grate is hung up with shale and slate and rocks and coal, mountain guts, and the guts wash onto the floor of the culvert now and then, the water behind them coming from who knows where.

Dane hauls himself up to its mouth, huffing and stumbling, him made even clumsier than usual by the slice of bread remnant he still carries in one hand, and he passes the NO TRESPASSING signs. *How come they can do what they please with my property, destroy it however they want, and I can't set a foot on theirs?* Mrs. Taylor again. He pauses at the opening, taking in the scent, a heavy odor of cool dirt and old concrete and get-in-the-ground. *We worked for our house. They can destroy my property we worked for, but I set foot on theirs, they'll arrest me and haul me off to jail.* He rolls his bread in his mouth, peering into the Drain. Up overhead, the grind of the machinery, them working on Sunday. It is hard to see from light into dark, and although Dane squints and strains, he still makes out only the boys' drain-distorted voices and their shape. A mucky ankle-deep spit crawls out of the Drain and dribbles from its mouth, and *who knows what all's in that water,* but the want to see is strong in him, the rain far away, so he steps up inside.

The temperature drops as soon as he enters the tunnel, and now he's surrounded by the smell. He likes the smell, he hangs his mouth open to taste it, careful not to lose the bread ball in his gums. He walks the culvert spread-legged, straddling the gooey water, his tennis shoes slanting awkward down the concrete walls. His eyes slot open to the dark like a cat's, and he sees it is Corey and Tommy and B-bo and David, and also Clyde McCaffey, Seth not here yet. They have to know Dane has come in, but they act like they don't. This is what they always do, even Tommy ignores him, here where he can afford to, when he doesn't need Dane to listen. B-bo is trying to climb the drain wall by reversing up one side of the tunnel as far as his tennis shoes will take him, then barreling down through the bottom and sprinting up the other side until he crashes to his knees. The drain rocks and booms with the muffler noises from his mouth. Clyde, a boy about fourteen, catches on and starts shouting his own voice through the drain. His voice is changing, he can holler from low moany *hooooos* all the way up into whistle-pitched shrieks, the concrete rolling and largening his voice, and that sets off David, who sings a commercial tune at the top of his lungs, and Tommy, who makes like a fire whistle, and B-bo, who simply screams. Dane shrinks. He feels the crotch of his pants stretch from the pressure of the straddle, and he wills it not to split. The noise sluices back and forth along the drain walls, deafening and crazy, *and it ricocheted down that hollow. Didn't shoot straight down. It would bounce from one side to the other. That's how it completely missed some houses on one side set even lower than houses it hit on the other side,* and he wants to slap his hands over his ears, but he'll lose his bread.

Only Corey doesn't holler. Corey stands near the grate to the side of the water, up the wall a little, his arms crossed over his chest, his bike leaning against his hip. His heavy bangs shield the top part of his face like a visor. Dane's stomach logs grind. Corey wears his camouflage pants and an army green T-shirt, its sleeves pushed up to his shoulder nubs to show off the chamois rag he has tied around his bicep.

Suddenly, they all shut up. They're watching something behind Dane. Dane turns and sees Seth pushing his bike to the drain mouth. What has shut up the others is not so much Seth's approach as it is

Seth's clothes. He wears some sort of racing getup, maybe moto-cross, and, true, he has outgrown it, the waxy groundhog blubber popping through so the shirt can't stay tucked, but, still, it is a racing uniform, neon colors and a big black 44. For a moment, it strikes everybody silent.

Tommy is the first to crack it. "Coor-EE! Coor-EE! Coor-EE!" He chants his loyalty, which triggers Clyde again, and then David and B-bo, and Dane, caught off guard, claps his hands over his ears and loses the last of the bread slice to the poison water trickle.

"What's the winner get?" Clyde asks.

"Ten bucks," Seth says. Something Dane knows Corey doesn't have.

"That's if he wins," says Corey. "I win, I get to ride his four-wheeler." B-bo revs the engine in his mouth.

"Clyde'll mark it," Corey tells Seth. "Three tries." Seth nods. Everyone knows Clyde is impartial and has shown up only to see somebody get hurt.

Corey pulls his bike as high as he can up one side of the culvert. Lace bought the bike last summer at the IGA lot off some man from McDowell County, a mock mountain bike with no gears, and it was rusted, so Corey and Tommy have sanded it down and repainted it with some old paint they found that didn't stick good to metal, which turned the bike into a kind of mess that Corey has convinced himself and Tommy looks tough. Dane watches Corey climb the wall.

Once Corey gets the bike as high as he can up the side of the twelve-foot-tall drain, he pauses and gauges where he's headed on the far wall. He pounces on the bike. Then he's pedaling as hard as he can down the face of the wall, Corey so close to the bike it's like he's melted to it, and he sprays through the slime in the drain bottom, still pedaling, B-bo shrieking when he gets splashed, and Corey sails up the opposite wall, pedaling still, as high as he can until he has to spring off the bike to keep from wrecking. The bike crashes back down to the floor of the drain, but Corey lands like a fly on his hands and feet on the curve of the wall. Clyde jumps up with a piece of coal in his hand and scratches a black scrape to mark how high Corey has gone. Corey slides back down, brushes off his hands and knees, and picks up his bike. With an I-don't-give-a-shit air, just short of a strut, he saunters to a spectating position.

Seth's bike matches the motocross outfit, a neonish grasshopper green with jet black piping, and Seth claims the bike has twenty-one gears. He clambers up the culvert wall, trying for the offhandedness Corey carried. He doesn't start quite as high as Corey did, and although he begins pedaling, by the time he hits the bottom the pedals get ahead of his feet so he has to throw his legs out and away from the bike, the pedals spinning free, and he has barely mounted the opposite wall before the bike, not moving fast enough to keep its balance on the incline, starts to sway. Seth slams a shoe to the ground and catches himself before he tips.

"Coor-EE! Coor-EE! Coor-EE!" hollers Tommy.

"I didn't get a decent start on that one," Seth says. It's a mutter, but the culvert swells it to where they all hear.

"You can't be worried about hurting your bike," says David.

B-bo and Tommy scream, "Coor-EE! Coor-EE! Coor-EE! Coor-EE!"

Corey sidles back into view. Dane feels himself shrinking, and then there comes to Dane a picture of Corey as a toddler in Pampers, half Dane's size, Dane holding Corey's hand, Lace's voice: "Now you keep an eye on your charge." Dane looks at Corey climbing up the Big Drain wall and hunkers tighter in his squat.

Corey leaps on his bike. This time he rises a good five inches higher than the last time because this time he will let himself wreck harder. He splits from the bike at the last second, tumbling into a deliberate roll like a stuntman, his arms wrapped around his head as a helmet, and just before he strikes the water, he springs to his feet. The bike, in the meantime, has slammed to the drain floor with more force than earlier. When Corey pulls it up, they see the fender is so badly bent Corey has to twist it back with both hands to get the tire to turn free. Tommy and B-bo and David and now Clyde drop the name Corey altogether, chanting instead a massive animal grunt—"*HOO! HOO! HOO! HOO!*"—and the *HOOs* spiral the drain walls, ricochet and loop, until they overlap with one another. Dane hunches his shoulders up around his ears.

This time it looks for a little while like Seth might actually forget the bike and try. He manages to drag it to a starting point even farther up than Corey has reached either time, and he pounces onto the bike after it's already in motion, and he keeps up with his pedals. But, then, again, the hesitation. The second thought. And Seth, in the process of trying not to wreck the bike, turns it over anyway, gently, without damage, far, far short of Corey's marks.

"Corey won!" screams B-bo.

"COOOREEEE!" shrieks Tommy.

"He did not," says Seth. "We get three turns."

"That's two outta three," says David. "Ain't no way you can win."

Then they hear Corey's voice, cool, from down the tunnel. "Let's just erase the two earlier and do er sudden death. Don't matter to me."

The confidence in Corey's voice, the offhand charity he grants Seth—all of this moves in Dane. A mixed-up moving. Dane sees Seth nod at Corey's offer, but there's not enough light to see how Seth feels about it. Corey snatches his bike back up the concrete wall, the wheel under the just-bashed fender making a peculiar click. He climbs so high he has to tip his head to keep it from grazing the drain ceiling, it seems he's too high to even mount the bike without overturning the moment he does, and Dane flares up in his chest, a hot-chill panic that has nothing to do with the fish and the logs. But Corey does mount the bike, and he does not turn over, and, again, molded against the frame like a movie Indian on a war pony, he swoops down the wall, hits the water so hard it parts more than splashes, and then catapults up the other side, by some miracle still managing to pedal. Too awed to feel fear anymore, Dane watches with his neck craned back from his squat, his mouth gaping open, as Corey shoots up the other side, passing both his old marks, and then, Dane sees, Corey is flying. He is not pedaling anymore, but the bike's still going, it's like the bike is coasting, but up, not down, and all five boys realize that Corey's going for a 360, a complete circuit of the tunnel, marble in a tube, Corey has busted gravity, and every face is upturned, every mouth sprawled wide, while Corey flies.

He's maybe ten feet short of where he began the circuit, so upside-down his hair streams straight down off the top of his head, when gravity remembers. Dane's breath makes a quick moan-suck. Corey is coming down first, because by this point, Corey is underneath the bike, and Dane springs to his feet in time to see Corey slam into the bad water, the bike close after him, landing partly on top of his legs. Corey cringes into a crumple, his knees pulled to his chest, his hands cupping his face, and the other boys rush to huddle around him, Tommy dropping on his knees, David pulling at the bike. But Dane cannot move. Rigid leaning forward, straining after Corey with his chest but not moving, his stomach chock-full with the horror of a dead Corey, his face aflame. When he sees Seth sneaking out.

Not blatantly sneaking, he's too proud for that, he's making it look like he's just quietly waddling home, but Dane knows what he's doing. And he knows, too, that he has to stop Seth, no one else sees, he can make up for not being able to run to Corey by stopping Seth, and as Seth passes him, Dane tries. He reaches out and takes Seth's thick soft arm without really clamping down on it, without a real grab, and he is surprised at how taut is the skin stretched over the flesh. Seth snatches the arm away, the fat popping out of Dane's fingers, and snarls, "Get your goddamned hands offa me."

Corey is not dead. From his heap in the putrid water, Corey has already sensed what Seth will try. He tosses the bike off his legs, it clattering against the wall, the four-boy huddle scattering in surprise, and Corey vaults up on his one good leg, half of his body soaked in that who-knows-what-all's-in-it water, and he screams after Seth, "You damn well better get me that four-wheeler ride!"

Seth stops right there in the entrance to the Big Drain and casually turns around. So backlit by daylight he is, Dane can't see any particulars of him, can't see the look on his face. He sees only his sloppy silhouette, a box with bulges. Seth, so smug he doesn't even bother to raise his voice, speaks into the amplifier of the Big Drain: "Soor-ee. My dad says can't no kids ride that four-wheeler but me." He pauses. "Liability."

Dane swings his face back towards Corey in time to see Corey's mouth drop, the first nondeliberate emotion he has let slip. Then it snaps shut, and his loose hands seize into fists. The mouth bawls back open, and Corey is yelling, "You sonofabitch! You promised, you sonofabitch! You lyin sackashit!"

Seth has stepped clear down out of the drain so Dane sees him only from his thighs up, but he turns, and in the light like Seth is now, Dane can see his face lifted in a sneer, again, casual. "At least I ain't got a faggot for a brother," Seth tosses back. He sinks away down the bank, until Dane's seeing only the back of his pinkish head, and then nothing at all.

Corey has started after him, forgetting his hurt leg, and when he comes down on it with his second step, he screams, "Fuck!" in pain and falls again. At the "faggot," Dane's face shoots full of warmth and he shuts his eyes to hide himself. But he's been called faggot more than once, and coming from the defeated Seth, it doesn't mean as much as it might have, means mostly the embarrassment that the others heard, and the faggot humiliation is dampened by Dane's worry over what he should do now that Corey is hurt. The others have pulled in around Corey again, stunned by his sudden vulnerability, and finally Dane is moving towards Corey, Corey is his little brother and he is hurt. Dane is moving to see how bad it is, then run down and fetch Jimmy Make, this is Dane's plan, and he creeps into the collar of boys around the fallen Corey and leans down to get a better look. Dane can see the bright water in Corey's eyes from the anger and the pain, and Dane knows Corey has his mind jammed down on keeping those tears tight in their sockets. Corey stares right back at Dane, hard.

"You," Corey hisses. "You goddamned homo."

For several seconds, they are all quiet in a new way. A quiet that waits, nose poised, ear raised, for its own end.

Then David steps away from Dane, a delayed flinch. And B-bo states, at a normal volume, like he's just trying it on for the fit in his mouth: "Homo." Then, deciding he likes it, a candy fireball on his tongue, he calls, "Homo! Homo!"

"Homo!" Clyde echoes with a crooked snicker. He cackles. "Homo! Homo!"

And then it's all five of them at the same time, even Tommy, who has only the vaguest notion what the word means. "Homo! Homo! Homo!" Homo-hollering and homo-hooting and homo-squealing, they slosh the tunnel to its brim with the word, they ricochet it side to side. At first they shout at cross-purposes, one voice's word overlapping the end of another's, the *homos* knocking against each other, but soon they hit it in unison, a harmonized cheer, the *homo* sluicing from concrete wall to concrete wall, the drain doubling the word's volume and size, tripling it, quadrupling *homo*, and Dane turns and runs.

He jumps out of the Big Drain and tears off in the opposite direction from where Seth has gone; he doesn't want to reach the road too soon, cannot bear to be seen. Smashes through third-growth trees and scrub and vines, angling the steep thick-weeded bank, slipping and picking himself up before he full hits ground, his hands and arms beating a way in front of him. Then, before he sees it, he's crashed into an immense thicket of blackberries. He's snared deep before he even knows where he is, their canes whipping at him, thorns ripping, they snag in his oversized pants, Dane swims and wheels. Writhing and twisting, little animal noises from his mouth, Dane thrashes through the confusion of bloody bushes, but on the inside of his eyes, he's fighting the boys. He's beating them silly. He's already kicked Tommy, B-bo, David, and Clyde into weepy balls curled at the end of the Drain like wadded hamburger wrappers, he hears the Drain echo-swirling with their groans and sobs, and now he's turned to take on Corey. Dane turns to Corey and slams the heel of his hand into Corey's chin, Corey springs back. Dane fights Corey with fingernails and fists, feet and teeth, he punches, pinches, pulls hair, bites. He kicks, slaps, trips, rolls, the blackberry patch continuing far past where he thought it would end, he is in it forever now, canes pricking and tearing, Corey coming at him, Dane hammering back.

Suddenly, he finds himself at the brink of the four-foot drop to the road fifty yards from his house. His momentum carries him right over it, and he hits the road so hard his shins ring, but he does not fall. He hears his tennis shoes smack through the broken asphalt, the chunky gravel, and he is just starting to ease off because he is almost home, when he spots the black Ford Explorer parked at the far side of the house. Jimmy Make has company. Bill Bozer, who comes around only when Lace is gone. So Dane veers through the yard, Chancey surging out from under the porch to follow him, and Dane sprints to where the footbridge used to be and tries to jump the creek, but lands not just inches, but feet, shy of the far side, and, wet to his shins, he scrambles up the eroded bank, Chancey right with him, both of them using all fours, and then Dane is loping up the old road towards the Ricker Place.

His breath's worn thin, tearing in his throat. The bones in his legs wobbly as grass stalks. When he's far enough up the draw to lose sight of their house, he drops from a lope to a trot, and, finally, Dane walks.

He stiff-walks. His legs trembling, his hands on his hips now. Him shuddering for breath. Greasy with sweat, it's running down the middle of his chest, the small of his back, and the strange new smell that sweat carries these days. His face is down-turned, and the old road under his feet has gone to grass, kind of grass calls you lie down on it. Rank and pillowy. He passes the old pigpen, wooden slats atumble, empty now even of pig odor. The old chickenhouse, an exhausted slump. Finally, he does drop down into the fine humped grass, at a spot where he can see the trailer stain, the TV. But it doesn't even occur to him to enter his boxes. And he sits with his head on his knees, heaving after his breath, but he doesn't cry. Dane never cries. "Corey does," Dane whispers. And although his belly grates chock-full of hard stuff, grinding, he almost never throws up. "Almost never," Dane whispers out loud.

Once Dane sits down, Chancey turns back, tempted by him lowered like that. He pads over and noses Dane's ear, then he notices the blood on his arms and starts licking it. Dane lets him. "Dogs got stuff in their mouths can heal cuts," Jimmy Make will say. Chancey licks the blood down, the smears and the runs. Licks the blood back to where Dane can see the exact holes the thorns have made, each hole with a little blood bead hard on it. Lined pricks of blood beads Chancey leaves all over his arms. Then he realizes the front of his T-shirt, too, has been ripped, and he lifts it to get a look at the cut on his stomach.

The *homo* ringing in his ears, once he's lifted the shirt, he has to see more, so he pulls it over his head. He stands up to where he can see himself better. *Homo.* The blocky ill-fitting yard-sale pants—Dane has outgrown his pants, but not his shirts—soggy with sweat over his thick lower parts. Hips and thighs, womanish, mismatched. The stomach and the chest still a little boy's, a softness to both. The slack fatness in the belly drooping down, the slight droop around his nipples, them peaking out, just barely, and Dane wonders if this is how a homo looks, and he feels pretty sure, yes, he thinks.

Quick, he slips the shirt back over his head and looks up the road to the old house. He never enters the old house, rarely even approaches it. He sticks to the trailer stain. In the house there's too much chance of running into the ghosts of Grandma and Pap. The trailer box isn't capable of ghosts, but the house feels fertile with them, even though Lace has told him, "You know your grandma wouldn't come back and scare you like that." But now, Dane, still pumped full of the Corey-hate, the homo-shame, something draws Dane to the house. No room left in him for fear, and he's drawn to it. Dane finds himself walking right up and stepping into the ruin of the porch. Dane stands on the slant of boards in the stale odor of abandoned house, kudzu snarling up the Insulite walls on either side of him, and he stares at the front door knob. He knows it is not locked.

Chancey snuffles the porch rubble. Thunder rumbles, distant, but thunder, even though it hasn't looked like rain all day. The fish wake up in Dane. Flash and flicker, hateful busy fish with steak-knife fins, *I try to stay off the nerve medicine.* Mrs. Taylor's mouth a dark hole in her batter-colored face. *But this has turned into one nervous place,* moany. Moany in their mouths. Dane takes a step backwards, off the boards, but then he hears Corey's voice, twisted steel: *Goddamned homo.* Dane reaches out, touches the knob, turns it. He pushes open the door.

At first his eyes won't focus, and it has nothing to do with dark. It's how what he expected to find just isn't, and there's too much of what is and in the wrong places. All that's left from his grandma's day is the stern coal stove, the Naugahyde couch foaming with burst stuffing, the wallpaper dangling in tongues, but Dane just barely sees that. He mostly sees nothing but metal. Rusted metal, mud-crusted metal, broken metal, Dane cannot right away even separate it into things, and less than the metal, but still everywhere, plastic and wiring and cable and rope lengths and tires. Dane steps up onto the floor, his anger gone for the moment. It's pushed out by surprise. But then he understands, and the anger rushes hot right back. This is Corey's doing. It's where he's been storing his parts. The trash they've been pulling out of the creek and along the road for their plan, Dane has many times come up on them when they're talking of it, they bait him to eavesdrop, then shut up fast in an obvious way when he gets close and stare knowingly at each other, it's sheer meanness is all it is. And here now they've turned his grandma's house into a genuine dump with their mean secret mess, and the anger doubles in him, thickens, heats. But at the same time, mixed up and way down under, he feels for a moment a little bit of scared.

His arms and hands tingling, he weaves through the junk to the kitchen, and there he sees that they've been hauling in the parts not through the living room door, but through a hole in the kitchen wall. They may or may not have made the hole, but for sure, they've torn it up bigger, and Dane's fists clench. The kitchen is completely crammed with metal parts, it even smells of old metal, a rust smell like you taste when you bite blood in your mouth. A rusted sorrel-colored barrel, looking crunchy to the touch, wire screens off kerosene heaters and the heaters themselves, aluminum poles, a car battery, a car hood. There is junk piled on the floor and stacked on the old knock-kneed table, junk even wedged on top of the refrigerator, screws and bolts lined up in the windowsills. The only untrashed part of the kitchen a crooked path they've made for dragging the most recent stuff to the living room.

Dane stares. Dimly, he recalls, so dimly he can't even remember if it's true or if he's making it up, his grandma standing at the stove, her back to him. Apron strings. The white socks in black shoes. Her dress color, an overwashed kind of lilac gray. He feels a new kind of ripping. Not in the stomach, but higher up. Then, like a gift, Dane spies what he's been wanting, although he doesn't know he wanted it until he sees. A metal bar leaning against the refrigerator. Maybe part of an axle, it's hard to tell, but it looks hand-fitting, the heft looks right, and suddenly, Dane's mouth actually waters.

He picks it up. It feels unnatural in his hands. He lifts the bar over his head and brings it down, a practice stroke, and it jerks his arm down faster and harder than he expected. Dane scans the junk and picks a tin bucket, mucked inside with some kind of dried tar. He raises the bar with both hands and heaves down on the bucket, following through with all his weight. The bar glances off the bucket, it topples and rolls rattly away, and Dane almost loses his balance and falls, but catches himself. He steadies his legs and inhales. He hefts the bar again, swings it into an iron pulley-looking thing with dirt-clogged teeth, and again, the bar just bangs and bounces off, leaving no mark on the pulley. Now his breath comes quicker and lighter. Dane hears it at a distance from himself. He whams at a hubcap on the table, sends the hubcap sailing, it ricochets off the wall and wobbles to rest on the floor without so much as a dent, and then Dane is just swinging. Wildman blind, both fists around the metal, he is hammering, he is whaling, he is slamming everything the bar can reach. Metal, tires, empty milk jugs, even Grandma's old refrigerator, the noise in his ears at first a crashing but soon narrowing to a high hurt whine, until he bashes the sorrel-colored barrel, and this time something happens, the bar does go through the crunchy rotted shell. But then it gets stuck. It somehow gets wedged in the barrel's side, and Dane jerks and twists and wrenches, but no matter what he does, he cannot pull it out.

Panting, sore in his arms, he looks around himself. As far as he can see, besides the barrel, he hasn't damaged one single thing.

He climbs outside through the hole in the wall. He hears fresh the machinery working overhead. And suddenly Dane understands, in a wave that washes all his anger away, just how pathetic the junk is. How it's not even worth destroying. Then he knows Corey will never have a speedwagon, sees for the first time the childishness of the scheme. And after that, he understands that the house is entirely unhaunted. That the old house contains nothing but gone.

Once more, he hears a far-off thunder. *Open your Bibles, please, and read.* "I'm twelve years old," Dane says out loud. "I'm twelve years old, and I'm going to see it." But this time it comes without panic. This time it comes with grief.

He stands in the old yard and "Dane," he says to himself. "Dane. Dane. Dane." He bows his head. "Dane. Dane. Dane, Dane, Dane, Dane Dane Dane DaneDaneDaneDaneDaneDanedanedanedane." Until the word loses all its meaning, snaps off, and careens into the dark. Where, still, it keeps ringing. Ringing.

Bant

THE SECOND time he touched, it was just my hair. He picked up the long of it and smelled it there. Me thinking nothing but gasoline.

The third time he touched, it was my elbows and wrists. Me squatting, the backs of my thighs sweating on the backs of my calves, and he rested a hand on each of my arms. He cooled me to my shoulders and down into my hands. And it stopped my brush for as long as he held.

The fourth time he touched, I was painting around a corner, where Hobart couldn't see. I was standing, and he came behind me again and just barely laid his whole body on mine, his body nearly matching me there. This time it made not cool, but heat. He stepped back. I heard his breath lift into his throat. He pressed again, but now it was hard, it was full. I felt a hot streak from my belly button down. I'd never known about that before.

Then, during lunch, I saw Sharon less often. I'd have to kneel on the floor of his cab so nobody'd see me leaving with him, me against the door on the passenger side, watching. The dirt on his boots, his hard hand pulling gears. At first all he did was kiss me. At first, kissing was enough for us both. When he'd come back in the mornings, before he showered, he wore dirt like a snakeskin ready to shed, but under that, I felt what was in him. Not many people you could do that way, feel what was in them like that, and even if you told yourself you didn't like what was in them, it was a thing you were feeling and not with many you did. I never asked him, "Some hills in Ohio look like these here, how can you?" And I could not stop. Like getting up on a high place and the ground down under calling you to jump off.

I wasn't scared of it anymore. It wouldn't have happened the summer before. Just a year and a half ago, me standing on the outside of the school steps, waiting for the bus, my hand up on the railing at about the second stair, when someone came and pushed up against my fingers with the zipper of his jeans. Donald Glen. I felt a hardness also spongy, hardness with a give, and I knew what it was, but I could not move. He had his jacket spread open so it was hard for other people to see, and me, shamed to tell it, shamed to think it now. Me frozen there. It was like I feared if I jerked my hand away everyone would notice then, or maybe I was thinking if I didn't jerk my hand away, Donald would think not even I was noticing, it would be like it wasn't happening at all. His teeth bared in this gone-away grin, him looking off and his eyes all glass. Then the buses finally pulled in, and I snatched my fingers away and grabbed my books. I wanted to spit on the back of my hand. I wanted to raw it past the skin clean.

But R.L. made me want to touch him even when he wasn't trying to make me, and me not wanting to and at the same time wanting to so bad it was like the not wanting made the wanting worse. And he wanted me back, he did, me, this bony body, this bony face. Before, it had only been the Donalds and only in the Donald ways, dirty and sneaky and low snicker voices spoken in huddles. But this one, along with the bad he brought in me, the shame, the guilt, he also softened my bones. He cleared up my face.

I rode on the floor, no secrets in this town. Jimmy Make dropped me off a minute before my shift started, picked me up right after it ended. Hobart always got his money's worth, he watched me close, and R.L. shared a room with an older guy named Ray who slept all day. We didn't talk much when we were together. We were always lying low. It was grope and touch and rub, hand skin mouth, it comes natural when you're always only hiding together, to take advantage of your bodies there. When you are fifteen years old and there is nobody to see.

Hover of gasoline. Something about to flame.

Noon sun in a thicket of willows, little thrashy close-together things down along the creek. Rocks hard under your back, and it was very bright. Too much to see. Or the cab of the truck pulled up some dirt road and nosed into brush, leaf shadows and a shiver across my back, the somebody's coming, the getting-caught fear. Soon, I did want more than the kissing, but he was already way ahead. Some things he did I didn't even understand until later—his hand pushing my head towards his lap, his fingers searching for places I just barely knew—but I understood where to stop. Push his hands away. We didn't talk, not ever, it was all by touch. And I'd mark him, later you could see. Blue wrists.

When we did talk, eventually I asked him about Yellowroot. "Shit," he'd say. "I don't know what's behind that fill. I don't even go near there. That's not what I do, that part of the site." Southeast Ohio boy. Talked more like West Virginia than the workers from other states did, walked more like West Virginia, motioned his hands like men here did. Familiar, it would lull you. Make you trust. Then I'd go home, hear the destructing overhead, Lace talking, and I'd come back to myself. I'd come back full to myself, it wouldn't be just the him parts ruling me, and I'd think, how can you? *Now, Bant, you know bettern that.* Sometimes, lying in bed at night, I'd punch myself. Sock my right fist into the muscle of my other arm. Feel it. Ohio scab-boy. He's up there right now. You know he is.

The first few times I pushed his hands off, he was gentle about it. He'd just go back to what he was doing before, not even open his eyes. I would open mine, I'd see. But after not too long, all I'd do was take hold of his wrists, and he'd jerk clear away. Heave his back against the truck seat if we were in there, flop over on the rocks at the creek, always with a pissed-off grunt (*you know how they are, it's the same with them all. Babified.* You go on and want them anyway). And when he did that, he would open his eyes, but he wouldn't look at me. He wouldn't any longer see. Then, without me thinking, my fingers would go to my face.

"I'm just fifteen," I'd tell him.

"So? I was doing it at twelve," he'd say.

I knew, do it and get a baby and you'll never be your own self again. Like Lace did with Jimmy Make. Like Lace got with me.

"I'll use something, darlin," sometimes he tried to reach me sweet, but then I knew it wasn't just the baby. It was partly that I didn't need to do it no further, I'd had enough before anything between my legs. But also it was something beyond that that I needed to keep. That had nothing to do with my body.

I'd taste that dust on him no matter how hard he washed. Far too many times I savored Yellowroot grit in my mouth. *I don't even go near there.* I thought he was lying, how could he work up there every night and some days and not see? Along the creek one time, while he lay beside me after I'd had him in my hand. The blanket messed up, me sickish in my stomach, wiping with leaves. The narrow little willow leaves that did no good, the bigger dead leaves swept down by the creek, them falling apart and sticking in crunchy bits to my skin. Even then, I felt the pull. Boy like the way a thunderstorm before it happens sizzles invisible in air. How can you, Bant. How can. This different Bant the boy made.

Scab. How one called you to pick it. Until the pink hurt under the crust.

Lace

A MONTH after we came home, I got on at the Dairy Queen. Jimmy Make wouldn't take a job like that, and I knew it was my fault we'd come home, so I got on. Still, I believed if Jimmy Make would just lower himself to do something regular along with me, we'd get by okay, it was a whole lot easier to be poor up Yellowroot than in Raleigh, North Carolina. But, no. If he couldn't find a "real job," he had to "work for himself," so he started cutting grass and doing handyman jobs. Problem was, most people around here know how to fix their own stuff and couldn't afford a handyman even if they needed one. I didn't say much, though. Didn't feel I could, not then, not yet.

Even though I was working thirty-five, thirty-seven hours a week, I tried to get up into the woods that summer as much as I could, and I made sure to take with me what kids would go. City'd made me understand again how little else I had to give them, but city'd also made me see how woods were almost enough. Tommy was old enough to go by then, and Dane'd come most of the time. I'd leave Bant to look after Corey, Corey never took much interest in woods for woods' sake, and Bant, going on fourteen, wouldn't do anything with me anymore unless I made her. The boys and me'd blackberry some, but mostly we just walked, or sat and listened, or played in the Ricker Run. And it was only in the woods I felt less lonesomeness for Mom. I tried to feel her in the cemetery, but there it never came, I felt her only in the woods, so I'd lead the boys to certain places without telling them why. Feel Mom's seat on logs where she'd rest. Lay my hand on trees where I knew Mom'd laid hers. But I stuck to Cherryboy during those roamings, I almost never took the boys up on Yellowroot or even up Yellowroot Creek. That's how I knew later that I knew then, I just had to keep it still a secret from myself.

I was already hearing a few things at the Dairy Queen, though. And in truth, I was already seeing it in the creek. I tried to fool myself about that too, said, *well, maybe you just remember the water as clearer than it really was, memory does that kind of thing.* But nothing could cover that day in August Corey and Tommy brought back two of those big margarine tubs full of rotting crawdads. Or the afternoon a week later when I looked out the back window and saw what Tommy had in his hands.

I was rushing around getting ready for work and arguing with Jimmy Make at the same time—"Me working a full shift, and you can't take twenty minutes to pick up this place?" "I'm working, too! Just because I'm not out there cutting grass don't mean I'm not working, I'm working just as hard drumming up business, it's an investment, what I'm doing now"—when something caught my eye out a window I was passing. Tommy standing in the creek in nothing but a pair of shorts, mud smeared over his belly, and studying something he held in each hand. I stopped and squinted. It was full-sized dead fish that he held.

"Drop em!" I heard myself scream.

His face snapped up towards the window in surprise, and he did, the fish sliding out of his hands. Then I was rushing out, I was jerking him up over the bank to the outside spigot, and then I was scrubbing his hands, "Bant!" I heard me hollering. "Get me some soap!" Then Bant was there, handing me the dishwashing stuff off the sink and saying, "What's wrong, Mom? They're just dead fish."

I couldn't help telling my work friend Rhondell about it as soon as I clocked in. She was busy refilling the soft serve machine, on her tippy-toes hefting the sloppy mix bag over the machine's mouth—"Well, my god. My god. Uh-uh-uh. Uh-uh-uh"—I wasn't real sure how close Rhondell was even listening. Then all of a sudden there came a voice right behind me: "Poisons in the runoff got em."

I wheeled around, and here of all people, it was Dunky talking. This girl no more than nineteen, came from farther than anybody else to work, from clear over in Boone County. And I'd tried to be friendly with her at the beginning, but Dunky always acted real nervous, so I gave up. Now I looked at her behind her big purplish glasses, and said, "What poisons?"

"Mercury." Dunky took one finger and pushed her glasses back up her nose. "Lead, arsenic, cadmium, copper, selenium, chromium, nickel." She stopped and swallowed, got this look on her face like she'd just realized we might think she was showing off, and that's not what she meant at all. "At least that's what's in the slurry," she said kind of apologetically. "Do you know what's over top you-all?"

Rhondell actually busted out laughing. I just stared at Dunky, her round cheeks under her cheek-shaped glasses, her skin completely without lines, unlived, I'd thought that skin said, but now I saw I was wrong. I'd never even heard the word "selenium" before. "How do you know?"

"My mother-in-law learned about it." She looked down at her feet now. "You should see what all they're doing back in where we live at."

Now we all knew who Dunky's mother-in-law was. Loretta Hughes, the woman Rhondell was convinced was having an affair with Charlie Blizzard. Sometimes Dunky drove herself to work, but often Loretta dropped her off, and usually during those drop-offs, Loretta and Charlie Blizzard would hole up in a hard red booth in the corner farthest from the counter, kind of behind the trash cans, each of them nursing a small black coffee or maybe nothing at all. They'd crouch forward there towards each other, talking furious and shoving papers back and forth, Loretta sometimes getting so worked up she'd throw her hands around, but always, always, keeping it low enough that you couldn't exactly hear her words. Rhondell had it in her head it was an affair, and up to that day Dunky spoke, I'd played along, it helped to pass the time. Even though I knew it was no affair, not with Dunky right there watching and the way Loretta and Charlie would get so mad, but not at each other.

The next day when Loretta came in, I watched her and Charlie in a different way. I even made a point to empty the trash can near them, and although I couldn't tell exactly what they were up to, I thought I overheard Loretta saying something about blasting. The time after that, I thought about getting Dunky to introduce us, but part of me still didn't really want yet to know. A week later, though, I asked Dunky, and she said sure.

We walked up to them during my break. I saw they were working with a magnifying glass on something that looked like newspaper classifieds. Charlie was on the far side of the table facing us, but we could see only Loretta's back, and as we got close, he glanced up, nodded sharp and quick, then brought his arm around the paper to shield what was there. Then Loretta swung her head around, and Dunky said, "She's the one's just got the fish kill behind her house," and when Dunky said that, Loretta Hughes's face sprung wide open. I saw Loretta's face wasn't scared of nothing.

"Well, you just set right down here, buddy," Loretta said, "you just set yourself down." She scooted over and slapped the seat beside her. "What's going on up above you all?"

After that, I learned fast. Loretta and Charlie had educated themselves, they were two of the first, but there were other people too, like Patty McComas, and Jim Corbin and his wife Mavis, and Jeannie Thurst. They were ahead of people like me because their places were already being destroyed, and the Dairy Queen was their main gathering place. Most other restaurants around had closed except for Fox's, and Fox's didn't allow that kind of talk. It was a permit they'd been studying that day I first met them, they'd learned how to interpret them, and they'd taught themselves chemistry, geology, hydrology, biology, politics, law. It was amazing what all they'd taught themselves, Loretta with nothing but a high school diploma and Charlie without even that, but when I mentioned it once to Charlie, he just grunted, "You'd be surprised how quick you can learn about something that's on the verge of killing you."

At first I didn't believe everything they said—how nearly a thousand miles of streams had been filled with the rock and dirt that used to be mountaintops, and how the fill had killed everything there. How what soil was left on the flattened tops was compacted so hard that if anything ever came back besides the grasses and shrubs the company sprayed on, it wouldn't be for at least several hundred more years. How over fifty percent of the electricity in the United States came from coal. But Loretta would bring in newspaper articles to back up what she said, and materials she'd picked up from the environmental group just starting over in her county, and she had a computer, too, she'd print stuff off the Internet. Charlie would sit there and quote statistics without a shadow of emotion crossing his face, and I knew Charlie was too practical to exaggerate.

I couldn't help but come home talking about it, and there at the beginning Jimmy Make didn't say much when I did. The little bit of trying Jimmy Make'd done with me in North Carolina had vanished the day we moved home, and after only a week or two, my smallness faded. I was my whole self again. Now we were back to how it'd been before. I can't say, though, that I gave it a whole lot of attention. Things'd been neutral or worse for so long I didn't expect any better, and besides, I was so busy with working and learning and looking after the kids, Jimmy Make was more an annoyance than anything else. Something in your family you just have to put up with, like a surly teenage kid who gets on your nerves but doesn't do real harm. The phone had hardly rung all summer for his "business," and now that we were getting into fall, it was going to ring even less. But instead of looking for a regular job, Jimmy Make started talking about buying a snowplow for his truck. Although he half tried to hide it from me, he wasn't doing much of anything but watching TV, not only in the evenings, but in the daytime, too, even though with the old satellite dish scrambled, we picked up only that one channel we'd gotten when I was a kid. I'd walk in in the middle of the afternoon, from work or from the store, and there Jimmy Make'd be flopped out on that sagging sofa with his shoes off and his sock bottoms black, putting away Dr Peppers and Mountain Dews. I'd go so far as to open my mouth, but then I'd make myself shut it. I was the one made us come home. I still didn't feel I could say anything yet.

Charlie took a lot longer than Loretta to warm up to me, and those first couple of weeks, he'd often just go quiet after I came around. Eventually, though, he opened a crack. Loretta, she knew the facts, but she'd also talk about exactly what was going on behind her house and how that made her feel. Charlie would mostly talk information. Talking to Loretta was like reading a story, while Charlie was a newspaper article. I gathered that he lived over in Tout, a little town at the other end of the county I'd only visited once in my life, and somehow his home had been badly damaged, too, but I couldn't yet tell how. The first time Charlie talked to me by himself was an evening in October, and it wasn't his own troubles he was worried about.

I clocked out about nine and stepped outside for a cigarette while I waited for Connie to let Rhondell off, too. Rhondell was my ride home. It was just starting to get honestly cold, and I hadn't brought a heavy enough coat, so I sheltered between the Dumpsters, turning to the wall to keep the lighter lit. Then I heard the door open, and I looked and saw Charlie bowlegging out. But instead of heading for his car, he surprised me by coming my way.

"Hi, Charlie," I said, kind of soft so not to scare him. He mumbled back. He had this full shock of white hair like a bowl upside down on his head, and that head only came to about my shoulder. His ears, his nose, his eyes, them small, too, like a shrunken Santa Claus with no beard and no joy. He eased in between the Dumpsters and stood there looking out on the dark hill behind us, not facing me.

"I finally got into some records, Lace," he said. Then he stopped.

"Yeah?" Right away, a badness coiled up in my stomach.

"Couldn't figure out what's killing your fish, but I found out something else." He went still again.

"What?" I said.

"They've got the permit for Yellowroot Mountain."

A boot heel in my chest. "You're sure?"

He nodded. "Yeah. I saw the permit myself."

I took a deep drag on my cigarette, and that's when I felt how my hands were trembling. Filter jogging against my lip. "Who is it?" I said, steadying my voice.

"Lyon. An extension of Bitex 4. Started all the way over at Slatybank a couple years ago." He shook his head. "They must have already blasted to bits every ridge between there and you-all." He took one hand out of his pocket. And although I'd never seen Charlie touch a soul, right then he touched my arm. "I'm real sorry, Lace. You-all be careful."

I got off the next day around three, I remember. The older kids weren't quite home from school, and Jimmy Make was watching Tommy. I walked up on Yellowroot that time. Right up the creek behind the house, facing it head-on after a summer of fooling myself. Past the places where me and Daddy used to fish, past the pools where you used to could drink, and I felt nothing but numb as I passed them. Almost as high as the Hemlock Hole I went, but before I reached that, I veered away from the creek to the high steep bank, going all the way down on my hands and knees to climb it. And then, maybe how low to the ground I got, maybe the hurt of the rocks under my bare hands, the numb dropped away. It cracked off, and my mind and my heart were working hard as my body, and this is why, mind was thinking, heart was knowing, this is why we feel for it like we do—the long, long loss of it. This is why. Its gradual being taken away for the past hundred years, by timber, by coal, and now, outright killed, and the little you have left, mind thinking, heart knowing, a constant reminder of what you've lost and are about to lose. So you never get a chance to heal. Then I heaved myself on up to the bench, and I dropped down onto a log, and *Mom,* I heard myself say in my head. "Mom." I said it out loud. I looked up, towards Yellowroot's top, through limb and falling leaf and, past those, crisscrossed sky. I didn't hear nothing back.

Not a month later, I was in Dunky's husband Nathan's old Blazer, bumping up the road back to their place. "Wanna see what you-all got to look forward to, huh?" Nathan had said when he picked me and Dunky up. We pulled a slow mile, following the creek, crossing it twice on low-water bridges, wiggling along between close wooded hills, when the road finally breathed out into a big open clearing.

Many times Loretta told me how beautiful it had been, and I saw now that it used to be. Three houses tucked quiet in a broad cleared hollow, the pastured hills mounding behind them, and I could imagine it in May, when the ground would be a soft bright almost glowy green, and from a distance, all you'd want to do was to lay your cheek against it. Up against one hill was the white frame house that Loretta'd told me had started as a log cabin, and her husband's family had lived in that place for a hundred and fifty years. Against the opposite hill set the modular home where I knew Loretta's older son, Tike, and his wife Janie and son lived, then a little below it, Nathan and Dunky's trailer, all of the places prettily kept with shrubs around them.

But now it was a beautiful painting that had been ripped in two. Between the white house and the others slashed a clawed-out gulch choked with big rocks, that gulch about as deep as Dunky was tall and wide across as a riverbed, the rocks thrown out all around it even farther, eating up the yard, and at the upper end of the slash, you could see a barn caving down into it. "And I'd always thought they couldn't steal the land right out from under you," Loretta'd said the first time she told me about it. "But turns out they can rob you that way, too." You couldn't any longer pull a car all the way to the white house because of the gash in the ground, so Nathan parked at his trailer, and when I got out and looked towards the house, Loretta was leaning over the railing. "Hey, buddy!" she called. "Welcome to our mess!"

"Yeah, we felt the blasting, of course, but we didn't understand exactly what was going on—couldn't get up there, you know, the guards and gates and all—until that '96 summer flood." That was Tike talking, him and Loretta leading me up the rim of the gash to where I could get a good view of the fill. "Dad's family's been right here since the mid-1800s, and there ain't never, ever, been water through here like came that day." We had to pick our way careful over the rocks and logs, and now that we were getting closer to the barn, I saw how the flood had just plowed the ground out from under half of it. "And now we've got it three times since."

"So after the water went down that first time," Loretta said, "me and Tike took his four-wheeler back in there, snuck past the guards to see it." She took my elbow and guided me around the safe side of the sucked-down barn, and then we were standing behind it where we could see how the gulch ran clear up the hollow. "But that was two years ago, and you don't have to go far now."

There it was. This monster gray plateau, not a landscape ever had or ever would belong in our mountains, it was like it had been dropped out of the sky from some other place on earth, and running down off it, these lord-god-huge gullies cut vertically all across the face of it, and I understood, the force of the water to have carved such canyons in it. We all three stood quiet then, even Loretta stopped talking, and a November wind was stinging down that gorge. I pulled my coat tighter to me. My ears were ringing, but the ringing had nothing to do with the wind. I recalled what I'd said to Loretta when she'd told me about it back at the Dairy Queen, how naive I'd been just a month before. I'd said, "What'd the DEP say when you complained about the damage?"

Loretta snorted. "Act of God. Normal weather event. Mining didn't contribute at all."

I still stood hypnotized when Loretta was turning away, Tike behind, and they'd gone ahead several feet before I jerked my eyes loose and brought up the rear. Single-file we went along the rim, silent this time, and Loretta slipped once on a sharp-sided rock, caught herself before Tike got her arm. The wind was at my back now, pushing my coat ahead of me. Then I noticed what must have been the goat pen. Part of the fence still standing, part shredded in the rock. I knew Loretta hadn't pointed it out coming up, Dunky had told me this months ago, because the goats were the single thing Loretta couldn't bring herself to speak about. How when that first big flood hit, the nanny and her kids had been latched in their pen. And with the water crashing down so quick, no warning, by the time they knew what was happening, the current was too strong for anybody to rescue them, although Nathan tried, and nearly drowned himself doing it. As we passed the pen, I couldn't help touching one upright fence post. I rubbed my scarf across my eyes, then dropped it and jammed my hands back in my pockets, scolding myself, how much easier it is to cry for goats, why is it easier to cry for goats? And then I understood it was because a goat death was possible to imagine. It was possible to imagine a goat dying that way.

Then we were warming up in Loretta's living room, pumpkin bread and coffee, Loretta's husband, who they all called "Dad" and who looked fifteen years older than Loretta, laid up in a recliner wrapped in a blanket from the waist down. Tike and Janie's four-year-old, Zeke, was bumping up against Tike's knees—I already knew they were holding off on having another one and Dunky and Nathan were waiting on their first until they got a better grip on their future here—and Tike was showing me a spiral notebook where they'd recorded all their incidents since the first flood. The blasts, and the smaller floods, and the dead fish, and the fly rock, the number of times they'd had to pressure-wash the blasting dirt off their house, the outbuildings they'd lost, all of it written neat in marker, date and description of event, and Loretta was saying, "Did you know the explosives they use are exactly the same as the ones Tim McVeigh used in Oklahoma City? Only most of the blasts here are ten times stronger than what blew up that building."

"Oh, yeah, we'll get real large shakes," Tike went on, "see how that ceiling's cracked? I could show you all over the house. The walls are splitting off from the floors."

And me, so full up by then it was like listening from under water, and over top it all, over top all they were telling me, *this can't be, can't be, can't be, us.* Me sitting there on the edge of the couch, the coffee going cold in my hands, nodding at what they said and reading and rereading, reading and rereading, the needlepoint hanging on the opposite wall. "They're out of their minds," Nathan was saying. "You don't shit where you get your water. Any animal knows that." "Watch your language," said Dunky, nodding at Zeke, and that needlepoint, "In His hands are the deep places of the earth. The strength of the hills are His also. Psalm 95:4." "And all of em scared they'll lose their jobs, and I say, lose jobs? Lose jobs?" Loretta talking, "Why should a few people, most of em from out-of-state, get $60,000 a year while the rest of us got nothing but dust and floods and stress and poison and never knowing when that water's gonna take your house with it?"

Then all of a sudden, although he hadn't made a sound past his "good to meet you," Dad cleared his throat. I heard the phlegm in it. When he did, everybody shut up quick and turned to the recliner in surprise. Dad sat forward a little bit, and when he spoke, it started in a croak but then it ran clear. "It's like having a gun held on you with the hammer back." He raised his hand, he pointed at his head. "And not knowing when the man's gonna pull the trigger."

I wrote my first letters shortly after that, to Jay Rockefeller and Senator Robert Byrd. I'd never had any use for politicians before, around here you learn very young where a West Virginia politician's loyalties lay, but Loretta and Charlie and the others said we had to speak our piece. I listened even harder to the people who had already educated themselves, I stayed late at work, came early, to do it, and I learned fierce. It hurt to learn it, it did. It was easier to half-ignore it, pretend it wasn't that bad anyway, or if it was, couldn't do nothing about it so why get worked up, that's how a lot of people lived. But I realized to at least know part of what was going on made you feel like you had a particle of control instead of none at all.

By spring of '99, when the dozers first went up the creek to dig the sediment ponds, I'd started making phone calls to agencies. Loretta had given me the job of combing the Beckley classifieds for permit applications. The companies tried to slip those past you and wrote them in such a way you couldn't understand them unless you were trained.

Charlie trained me. I even went to a permit hearing, and although I was too backwards then to speak at the mike, I was there.

Jimmy Make'd spent the winter of '98–'99 looking for any deep mine or construction outfit that might be hiring, but nobody was. He acted like he wouldn't work for a mountaintop job, but truth was, even if he'd wanted to, he couldn't have gotten on, most of them passed over workers with union experience, and, besides, the skills you needed on those operations were different from what you learned underground. When I got home, I still told Jimmy some of what I'd learned, I had to tell somebody, but while he'd asked a few questions back at the beginning, now he said nothing at all. And I could feel it start to grind in him. I was familiar with that in him, the way he could push back without actually opening his mouth. In April, when a few days were getting warmer, he spried up and started tinkering with his lawnmower and weedeater. He made flyers by hand for his "business" and went to the Madison library to photocopy them, then he drove all over the county putting them up, he even put an ad in the paper, now that wasn't cheap. And with all that, the cockiness came back in him, the swagger in his limp. Then he did start talking back.

"Nothing to do but get used to it or move," he shrugged, not taking his eyes off the TV to prove how deep he didn't care. "Why'd you think I wanted to stay in North Carolina?"

I knew he knew that'd make me mad, and I wanted to ignore it, but I couldn't leave it be. "This is my homeplace, Jimmy Make," I said. "What about the kids? What do they got to look forward to if we don't fight?"

"Fight?" he snorted, and then he turned from the screen to face me, this know-it-all how-stupid-can-you-be look. "Honey, you won't never beat coal. It's who has the money, the rich people always win, that's how it's always been, especially in the state of West Virginia. That's why the smart people get out."

Then after we ran through that tired give-and-take for about a month, I finally said, kind of quiet and calm, "Well, some people are fighting."

I said it to test Jimmy Make a little, see what he'd do, although I mostly figured he wouldn't even know what I was talking about. So I was surprised when I saw he right away did.

"You stay out of it, hear me?" He sat up and swung his feet to the floor, and I saw his eyes lit live for a change. "You stay clear of the shit-stirrers."

"I'll do what I damn well please, just like I've always done."

Jimmy Make swallowed, he ran his tongue inside his mouth to wet it, and I saw he'd gone past mad to scared, and that surprised me a second time. It even scared me a little. "You keep the hell away from the shit-stirrers." He said it snaky, between his teeth. Then he stopped and dropped his voice even lower, Tommy and Corey coming up on the porch. "You can't do a thing about this here, and you'll just turn people against us. End up making it even worse for me and the kids."

By July of our second summer back, we were hearing the blasting, still distant, not enough to shake the house, but there it was. And by August, it was clear Jimmy Make wasn't going to get any more "handy-man" work this summer than he had the summer before. I blamed that on him. He blamed it on me. He still wouldn't apply for what few minimum wage jobs there were, even though that would have doubled our income and been easier on his back. We were in a terrible tight for money, I worried about it just all the time, and going into that fall, I couldn't even get the kids school clothes, it was all we could do to eat, and a lot of that we did on credit. Thank god the house was paid off. Tommy turned five that year, and in August he started kindergarten. It was just a couple weeks after that I got the visit from Bell Kerwin.

Late morning, nobody home but Jimmy Make and me, and I re-member I was out back hanging laundry when I heard Bell calling from the front of the house. I went around and there she stood, her hands balled down into the single pocket of the apron she wore, grinding. A friendly and calm type of person she'd been when I was a kid, but that was before her middle boy'd got bad into drugs, and since then—it'd been years by now—Bell'd moved deep into herself. But today she looked even more nervous than she usually did, those half-hidden hands kneading, her not meeting my eye. I invited her in, but she said no, she didn't have time to sit and visit, she'd just had to come up and tell me, at the head of the hollow like we were.

"Tell me what?" I said.

She pulled her hands out of her pockets then. She had a watch on, and she went to turning it back and forth on her wrist, her still looking at the ground. "Ralph heard it at work. Now, Lace, you know there's so many rumors going around anymore I don't know if it's true or not, but up here like you all are, I had to tell you." She finally stopped her hands then, and she looked directly at me. "Ralph heard they're putting in a slurry impoundment at the top of Yellowroot Creek."

Corey

THERE IS nothing to do but to tie Tommy up. So that's what Corey does. He sneaks the clothesline under the house while Tommy's eating his cereal, then he lures Tommy under by calling, "Hey, looky what I found." Mom has already left for work, she's opening today. Dad's supposed to be watching them, but truth is, Dad doesn't much care what they do as long as they're not too noisy. Once Corey gets Tommy under the house, he pins him down and ties him to the plumbing. Threatens to take Tommy's tricycle apart and throw the wheels up in the holding ponds if he screams before Corey's out of sight. Then Corey is out of sight.

Every few days over the last couple weeks, Corey has dropped in on Rabbit's yard, copycat Tommy tagging behind. Rabbit, if he was outside at all, was always buried to his belt in the freezer, and he never told them to leave, but he never paid them much mind either. Corey might have given up, but what choice did he have? The ruin of the bike, the cheat of the ride . . . then, like a miracle, it seemed Rabbit was getting used to them. How a real rabbit might if you were patient and fed it carrots and grass, *like when we found the possum, patience, like I been saying, see? patience.* He was getting used to them. Then, last Monday Rabbit pulled out of the freezer and stood sideways to him and Tommy, wiping his hands in a black rag. He had never done something like that before, standing beside them like men, and it made Corey brave, so Corey went on and said, gruffing his voice, "Think you'll get that thing running?"

And Rabbit said right back, like somebody'd shot a hole where his voice came out, "Honey, I could make run a no-legged man."

A couple days after that, Corey got his guts up again—the desperation helped, and also Rabbit's confidence about the no-legged man—and he squatted down to the freezer and he called inside, "Hey, after you get done with this projeck, think you could give me a hand with something?"

And after some very long minutes—that's how Rabbit usually answered, not like a shot in his face, but like there was a gap between the words floating out your mouth and injecting into Rabbit's head—Rabbit said, "Why the hell not?"

And finally, yesterday, the biggest miracle of all. Him and Tommy walked up on Rabbit's hind end hanging out the freezer, and Corey said, "Hi, Rabbit," and Rabbit grunted back, like usual—he wasn't so backwards he couldn't grunt—the grunt kind of pinging the metal inside. Then, lo and behold, Rabbit crawled out again. He crawled out, stood up, wiped his hands in his rag, and said, right to Corey, "You wanna give me a hand with something?"

And Corey, too stun-thrilled to control his voice, chirped "Yeah!" looking around for what might need it.

Rabbit said, "You come down here tomorrow morning." He flipped his rag at Tommy. "Leave that one at home."

Corey runs as fast as he can as far as he can so Tommy won't be able to catch up after Dad hears him screaming and turns him loose. Corey was careful to tricky up the knots. It will take a while.

It's about a mile to Rabbit's house, but Corey does not tire. After he puts decent distance between him and Tommy, he eases into a trot, unless he sees somebody out who might notice him, then he speeds up. He's worn the right clothes for helping Rabbit—the oil-splattered jeans, the camouflage T-shirt, the chamois rag—and he carries a pair of Jimmy Make's White Mule work gloves, them flapping huge-handed as Corey pumps his arms.

But when he reaches Rabbit's house, Rabbit's not in the yard. Corey hadn't thought of that. The freezer just sits there, all coffined up, the end where Rabbit usually sticks out covered by the metal panel. Corey's not sure what to do. He stands in the front yard a while, hoping Rabbit will see him, then, *Hey, Rabbit,* he calls inside his head. A mind message. He waits. He waits a good while. But soon Corey knows there is nothing but to knock on Rabbit's door, and Corey has never done that. He's not sure anyone has.

The house is a very dark green, like it wants to disappear into the hill, the brush. The particleboard porch is heaped with trash bags. Corey takes a breath and sidles past the station wagon, peeking in to make double-sure he didn't just overlook the DUI contraption last time, then he climbs up on the porch, straddling trash bags, and waits again, hopeful that Rabbit heard his feet. Something in the trash moves. He reaches up and knocks, the door with a punky give to it, like your knuckles might leave dents. The thing in the trash bags moves. Then the door swings open. Rabbit peers from behind it. An odor solid as stone rolls onto the porch—stale hamburger grease, months-old woodsmoke, and very dead cigarettes—and in the middle of that odor hangs the more compact and immediate smell of Rabbit. Rabbit's yellow smell that he carries always, soaked-up liquor leaking out his skin, but today the smell is the purest Corey has ever smelled, and it pours straight from his mouth. Corey realizes from Rabbit's look that Rabbit has no idea why he's knocked.

"Member?" Corey says. "You told me come down this morning." Corey flaps the gloves a little. "Give you a hand."

Rabbit breathes out the smell, so pure it's more amber than yellow.

"Oh. Yeah."

Rabbit looks away, out over top Corey's head. The trash bag thing flops free and drops over the side of the porch into the weeds.

"You wait out here on the porch for me."

Corey waits in the yard instead of on the porch. He flashthinks ahead to him and Rabbit stealing up the run to the old house while Dad watches TV and Mom's at work. He sees Rabbit step through the hole, then kind of reel back in wonder at what all Corey's got. Hears Rabbit say, "Well, look here, Corey. You're closer'n you thought. If we just take this and hook it up to them things . . . yeah, it'll take some fooling with. But I'd say, in a week, we got it, buddy."

Rabbit slams out the door and stumbles past Corey, carrying a flashlight and a coil of rope. To Corey's surprise, he opens the station wagon's tailgate and hurls the stuff in. Rabbit wears a tight pair of double-knit pants with teeny-tiny checks and a blue Dad's Dog Food T-shirt. He climbs in the front seat, and right before he shuts the door, he stops, looks at Corey, and says, "You comin?"

Rabbit hunkers down into some serious key-turning and gas-stomping. The interior of the car is kind of falling in all around, and although some places have been stapled back up, they aren't holding real good. Behind Corey, there are no more seats, just a gutted-out space covered by carpet with a bad rash. Rabbit finally jerks out the radio, reaches behind it, and fools with something there while alcohol rises off him like a speech balloon over a cartoon character. The engine catches for good. As they back out, Corey studies the steering column again, pondering where they might have attached the DUI contraption, but then his eyes get snagged by Rabbit's hands on the wheel. The hands are pure black. Not creased, not smeared. They are black-dipped like a DQ cone, only blacker than chocolate, the very blackest at their tips, grading off a little as you look farther down his hands to his wrists. A working man's hands. Corey nods.

Now they are pulling out Yellowroot Hollow Road, they have rolled to a half-stop at the stop sign, and Rabbit is turning right, away from town. Corey's insides brighten, ha, riding with a drunk you don't hardly know, and *I ain't scared. Don't care what Mom and Dad do if they find out, either.* Rabbit accelerates, and the car talks back with a series of sharp smacks, sounds like that old-timey Jacob's ladder toy of Dane's, and Corey sits forward, alert. Rabbit doesn't talk with his voice, though his breath talks, in little grunts, and he holds a steady thirty-five—Corey can see it on that big speedometer curving across the dash—and Rabbit's reared back like he's in a recliner, his head slumped nearly level with the steering wheel, but far, far away from it. Finally, Corey asks, "What do you need me for?"

The Rabbit gap again, the space between the words leaving your mouth and hitting his head. Then. "Oh," Rabbit says. "We're goin up in here to pick up a part."

From behind, a monster engine comes bearing down, and Corey spins around in his seat to watch, *will it get us this time?* like he always does when a coal truck's coming, at Dad's truck, at the school bus, and it is always thrill Corey feels, never fear. The truck stampedes them like a steel hurricane, the grille surging enormous in Rabbit's rear window, Corey grinning back, he can feel the truck in his teeth, and the millisecond before it crashes them to kingdom come it lunges over the double yellow line and explodes past, its dirty wake lifting the station wagon off its tires. At least a little, seems to Corey. Rabbit doesn't even seem to notice that something went by. And, ha, Route 9, who would think this sorry-ass narrow road could even hold a coal truck and a car at the same time, sometimes it's like the truck casts a spell and swells the pavement for a second just so it can get by. Corey faces front to watch it disappear, his hands on the dash, and then he notices how his hands are dirty even on their tops. He opens them and admires the grime creased into them, unwashable dirt from the hours he's spent trying to fix the bike.

Now they're turning off onto a paved road back up a hollow. Corey has passed the road many a time, but he's never been up it or given it a second thought. It's a short hollow, only six or eight houses on either side before the road starts climbing, steep. The road narrows, gets tunnelly in the heavy green brush, but stays weirdly paved. Down below, you can occasionally see an overgrown railroad spur, covered with the kind of plants grow over and around old clinker beds. Lot of rabbit tobacco. Then they round a bend, and boom, Corey insucks: right smack in front of them the world turns to tipple.

This humongous old tipple. It is one of the biggest tipples Corey has ever seen, ain't nothing in the windshield but tipple, nothing out the windows, either, and overhead, the chutes and belts, some of them having broke off sudden and just hanging out there in midair, and wires and cables dangling all over like dead snakes, the tipple bleeding rust down its corrugated walls and aluminum pieces of it having shuffled loose and flapping there, and Corey, his chest hardening, he bounces higher in his seat. The flashlight, the rope, the NO TRESPASS-ING signs all over with their tongues sticking out, but him and Rabbit will just throw a fuck-you finger back, they'll be strutting in after that part . . .

But Rabbit does not stop. He drives right under the tipple, past more NO TRESPASSING signs, and Corey is left turned around in his seat on his knees, until the tipple is shut out by how the road curves.

Then the asphalt starts breaking down here and there, dipping, in places it's completely caved in and the station wagon seems almost like it's driving on its side, Corey expects to hear a scrape. He knows they are mine breaks, a long-ago deep mine under them and the road caving into the tunnels, and what would you see if you fell all the way through? And Corey pictures Paul Franz and them in the back of the station wagon, real nervous about these mine breaks, while Corey rides at ease with one arm out the window. They pass a jeep wrecked in a gully right off one of the worst dips, the kudzu moving to bury it, and if you look hard, under the plants, there is metal all around, cables and truck parts and big pipes and rusted square things. The green stuff rising quick and pressing through that metal to where you can't tell what the metal was, poison ivy, Virginia creeper, a million just plain weeds. Strangling and pushing, in-growing there, birthing a new kind of species, this crossbred vegetable metal. Rabbit cruises along in a cool slouch, his pint bottle upright between his checkered thighs. "Oh," he mentions as they nosedive into a road buckle so sharp-angled seems it might take the headlights out, "this here mountain is just chock-full of deep mines."

They shake clear of the brush a little, pull a rise, and down below, Corey can see an unfenced cemetery, gravestones kind of scattered on it. When he looks closer, he sees several graves have fallen clear through. Just a chute of earth dropped down like a plug gone, and he's never seen anything like that. Rabbit's taking a gulp from his bottle as they hit another big crack, and a hefty slog spills on his checkered pants, but Rabbit just brushes at it. Then the plants close back in again, shouldering on you, the humping and heaving green, pressing, and the sky pressing, too, towards rain, the air heavy with it. Bust-ready. Corey cannot wait.

The paved road peters out in a broadish flattened place under a hillside that has been sliced straight up and down to make a sheer orange cliff a couple stories high. The face of this cliff is drilled at neat intervals with augur holes the size of garage doors, like a row of garage doors straight back into the mountain, and, shit, forget the tipple, an augur hole would beat the tipple all to hell. Corey gets his bounce back, but tamped down so that Rabbit will not notice, and now Corey is seeing shadowy metal stuff, and rubber and wires, and *like passing that grate at the end of the Big Drain,* and . . .

But Rabbit has already got his flashlight and rope and is staggering off into the overgrown field away from the augur holes, his little bottle stuck in the elastic stretch waistband of his double-knit pants. Corey swings out and follows through the bad brush there, coarse tan grass and nasty locust saplings and mountain olive. He carries his work gloves, the locust thorns ripping at his jeans legs, and it starts to sprinkle finally, the rain seeming to fall from far, far away, the sky so far above the high augered cliff. Then Rabbit draws up sudden and stops.

Corey almost walks right past him, then gulps an "ah!" despite himself. They stand on the edge of a mine break so camouflaged with grass there is no way you could have seen it ahead of time unless you were circling directly over it, like a bee. The hole is biggish, two, three feet across, and it falls in on itself soft, the grass still growing down its sides where it collapses in, and below that, you can see nothing but dark.

"There ya go," says Rabbit. He begins uncoiling his rope. Right then, Corey understands.

"You wanna put me down there?" Corey meant to ask it steady, but it comes out cheepish. He wants to bite himself.

"Yeppur," Rabbit says. "Won't work the other way. You ain't strong enough to lower me." Rabbit is already ringing rope around Corey's chest, snugging it under his arms.

Corey steps backwards a few steps. Inside his ribs, a little mouse begins to run at slippery steel walls. "What for?" he asks.

"Well, there's an ole panel off a breaker box down there. I think it'll do the trick."

"How do you know it's down there?" Corey asks.

Now Rabbit is tying knots, and Corey's never been this close to him before. Rabbit is fumbling around him, the yellow smell in rings, urine, then last week's liquor, then today's. "Oh, me and my cousins been all through these tunnels. We seen that breaker box and knew it was near this hole because of the daylight coming through. But it was too much to drag it all the way back to where we come in." The bristled face, the unnameable color, and on top his hatless head, the oily copper coils. Rabbit finishes his knotting, steps back, and studies his work. "Once you get hold of it, untie yourself, fasten the rope around the panel good, and I'll haul er up out of there."

Corey notices Rabbit doesn't say anything about hauling him back up.

It takes a good bit to scare Corey, but being dropped in a hole he can't see the bottom of by a drunk man, well, that comes close. The mouse, now mice, skittle at those slippery walls. But Corey is no chickenshit. Then it occurs to him (*just a little low-to-the-ground speedwagon*) what kind of payback this should get him. Just how big Rabbit is going to owe. "Whereabouts is it?" Corey says.

"Once you get down there, I'm pretty sure it's back that way." Rabbit tips his head to the left. The rain is falling harder.

"What's it look like?"

"Oh, it's like a big metal box. You'll know it. Ain't nothing else like that down there."

Corey sits on the grassy-sloped edge of the mine break. *It'll sound like a chainsaw starting up, that engine in it.* He feeds the flashlight Rabbit hands him into his camouflage shirt and tucks the shirt tight in his jeans, carries it that way to free up his hands. Then he looks up at Rabbit, and Rabbit looks at him, and Corey scoots straight off before his brain can think.

Despite being drunk, Rabbit manages to get the rope snubbed short

287

and taut, and he even pays it out proper, so Corey doesn't freefall. Corey's clinging to the rope with his gloves, he swings his feet to feel around, and he hits dirt for a while. *I'm going in a mine,* he has never been in a mine before. Used to be, when he was little, he would say, "I'm gonna be a miner." And Dad would say, "Won't be no coal left for you to mine," and now Mom says, "Won't be no mountains left for you to work," and Dad has always said, "No, boy, you ain't working in no mine." *They're right,* Corey thinks, *I won't have to go in no holes. I'll work er on top.* And scabs, Dad calls em, ditch diggers, *that ain't no mining,* but Corey doesn't care, he would run that shovel easy as handling his bike. The rope grinds up under his armpits, it hurts, forces his arms to splay out in an angle they don't want to go. But also Dad will say, when Mom is not around, *we won't be here by the time you're big enough to get a job. We'll be in North Carolina then.*

Corey has heard Rabbit begin to pant, and now Rabbit kind of giggles and calls, "Buddy, you're stouter'n I thought!" Corey tightens, his body's growing cooler and cooler, and he tells himself not to think, think instead, *North Carolina. North Carolina.* But Bant said they ain't got no four-wheelers in North Carolina. *You remember seeing any down there?* she said, and, well, no, Corey didn't, but he was littler then, didn't remember anything real well. *That's a city,* Bant says. *You can't ride a four-wheeler in a city, it's against the law, it's not street-legal down there.* Corey told Dad what Bant said. *Well, that's a lie,* Dad said, but like he wasn't paying real close attention to what Corey had said.

Then, quicker than he can think, Corey drops. He doesn't fall far, but he hits ground in a kind of squat-crumble on his bad ankle, and he screams "Shit!"

Rabbit calls, "Where the hell'd you go to?"

Corey runs his hand along the rope. "Knots gave." He stands up, wincing on the ankle, then swagger-staggers a few short steps. Light spills down the hole, and even with the rain in it, it lights this part of the shaft surprisingly clear, even though you couldn't see jack from up there in the daylight. The floor is puddled with water, the ceiling in places dripping with it, cool, and the ceiling is right down low to him, like a ceiling made to fit him. Standing underneath it makes him feel tall. He looks as far as he can see up and down the tunnel in both directions, but he doesn't see any metal panel. And because of how he fell, he can't get his bearings, doesn't know which way Rabbit pointed, so he backs up against a rumply uneven wall, tries to see up to where Rabbit is. He hollers, "Show me yourself!"

The tiny-checked knees plop down on where the grass caves in.

"Now which way do you think it is?"

"That way," calls Rabbit.

"I can't see what you're talking about."

"That way!" and now the rope is kind of swinging around, like Rabbit thinks he's waving it towards the box.

"That don't tell me nothing!"

The checkered knees disappear. Next thing Corey knows, a rock is skipping past his head towards the part of the shaft on his right.

"That way!" Rabbit hollers.

"All right," Corey mutters. *Speedwagon*, he tells himself. *Speedwagon speedwagon speedwagon* he chants in his head to drive down the other. He can hear the mine drip drip. He already has the flashlight out of his shirt, and he thumbs the switch, but nothing happens. Flicks it off, tries again. Nothing. He slaps it in the palm of his hand, nothing changes, *speedwagonspeedwagonspeedwagon buddy will he owe me* he unscrews the end, spills the batteries on the ground, turns them around, wedges them back in. Now he's scared to even try again, but he does, and, there it is. No light. "Son. Of. A. Bitch," Corey says.

He lifts his face up to the hole. "Rabbit! Your light don't work!"

"What?"

"I said, your light don't work!"

Silence. "Oh. You sure?"

"Yeah, I'm sure."

A shuffling around the rim of the hole. "Didja check the batteries was pointing right?"

"I tried everything."

"Well, now." Silence. *Speedwagonspeedwagonspeedwagon,* to drown out, what is coming, no, *monkey monkey monkey* and Rabbit calls, "Well, just walk that way feeling with your feet. It's there on the floor somewheres."

"How big is it?"

"Shit, it's near big as a air conditioner. You can't miss it."

Corey cusses, loud, *monkey.* Then he just charges at the tunnel. He bows his legs a little and swaggers on the bad ankle, cussing, and he just charges along under that low roof, over the bumpy earth floor, but the harder he tries not to think (monkey), the more he does think (monkey), it's there all along right under the cusswords (monkey), the light from the hole melting fast, and Corey decides *sonofabitch* isn't powerful enough, so he switches to *fuck* (monkey), but *fuck* is really too short, so he tries *goddamn motherfucker* (monkey). He sees nothing metal at all, he feels nothing metal at all, the light narrowing behind him like a funnel closing, and him sloshing through cold water, his tennis shoes soaked, and the shaft is wide enough that he has to zigzag it to have any chance at all of hitting that breaker box. He keeps cracking into blunt objects, then he has to strip off his gloves, and feel with his naked hands, but they are always rocks, and it occurs to him, what if one of them coffins fell in here, and, then. He's somehow turned a bend, and there is no light at all.

Corey stands stock-still. Without light, he is no place. First he was there. Then he is nowhere. And now, he's not just no place, but he starts to lose himself.

All of a sudden, he's not knowing where his parts stop. He cannot tell where he ends. His hands, his feet, fading, then his skin, too, fading, and then he's not even knowing about his head, he is not he is losing Corey. He panics, flails, he grabs. He goes after Corey, he snatches at him, tries to bundle him back, but he finds himself swimming at air, and finally, on frantic instinct, he wheels and plunges towards where the light should be. He's not thinking *Rabbit* or *speedwagon* or *motherfucker* or even *monkey*, Corey's not thinking at all. The black starts to gray and then starts to shape, puddlewater splashing up and the rough tunnel sides he can finally see. Corey is still plunging after himself when he hits it, the metal stubbing his tennis-shoed toe. It's in the dead middle of the floor.

He reaches down. He takes off a glove and feels of it, the metal. He pings it with a nail, makes sure. Then he strokes it. And with that, he is himself again. He is Corey, and sonofabitch if he hasn't found the goddamned breaker box, and is Rabbit *I can make run a no-legged man* gonna owe him now.

The panel is too awkward, too bulky, for him to pick up, even if it weren't heavy, which it is. He has to walk it end over end to the hole, and he is very careful with it, rocking it gentle, straining his biceps, feeling the good muscle there each time he catches it before it falls on its side. The hardness in the breaker box, like the hardness in Corey's body, to touch the breaker box is to feel its return. He hears deep inside him the way the speedwagon will start. He ties the box good with the rope, and Rabbit hauls it back up, and Corey can hear the pleasure in Rabbit's grunts, and *is Rabbit going to.* The pressure of the taut rope erodes the mine break edges so they give a little, dirt and shale peppering Corey's head. Him with his gloved hands on his hips watching the panel dangle, rise and spin, his knots holding, and his speedwagon, the way it will start like a chainsaw, you'll jerk its rope to start it, and then buddy, will it wail.

After he hauls Corey back up—a couple iffy moments at the crumbly edge, then Corey claws his way out—Rabbit backs the station wagon as far as he can over the bad brush, and the two of them load the panel in the rear. Corey bears the same weight Rabbit does. It is outright raining now, the rain with a chill to it, more November than August. Rabbit slams the tailgate shut, then swigs a victory drink, a swallow as long as his neck. Then he offers it to Corey. Corey has tasted whiskey before. He knows how it will ram, then fire, his throat, so he is careful, he doesn't cough or gag. He just wipes his lips with his bare arm and says, "Ahhhgg. Oom."

During the trip back on Route 9, Rabbit doesn't crack thirty-five again, so more cars and trucks whip and barrel around them on the endless double yellow lines. Again, Rabbit is reclined in his seat, slouched with his head thrown back, one windshield wiper cranking a rhythmic shriek. Cory slouches, too, full of what he has done. Him and Rabbit up at the old house, he sees, working, Rabbit showing him how to put things together, Rabbit letting Corey use his tools, Corey saying, *Well, now, I don't want to mess your stuff up,* and Rabbit saying, *Hell, you're not gonna mess nothing up, I can tell you know how to handle tools,* and Rabbit just about to show Corey exactly what part they need to make the engine fire when Corey hears the siren and then notices the lights.

He turns to look behind them, hopeful it's the rescue squad. It is not. Now Rabbit, with a long-suffering exhale, is pulling off on the shoulder. He pitches the pint bottle under his seat and cusses.

It's not even the deputy. It is Pinky McCutcheon himself at Rabbit's window. Pinky looks right over Rabbit to Corey, and says, "Who do you belong to?"

Bant

I DIDN'T have an alarm clock, but I could tell myself what time to get up before I fell asleep at night, and then I would. I decided this time I'd try before it was even light at all, figuring the nosers wouldn't roam too far in the dark. I woke when I wanted, and I saw the boys' door was open, and I snuck out careful not to make a noise, but I wondered if Corey couldn't smell gasoline from a deep sleep. Baron pranced up from where he slept between the chair and couch, the strangeness of me leaving at that hour. I'd been planning to tie Chancey, but when I got outside, I saw he was up and gone.

Dew lay heavy as rainwater on the metal gate, and on above, those holding ponds outbreathed a steam like winter mouths. Smoking nastiness. It was lighter up in there than it had been down at the house because of the trees and ridges gone. I hadn't guessed the light right. At first I stuck close to what was left of the creek, now knocked to a trickle and poison-filled.

I climbed up to walk along the ponds, on the grass, out of the rock. At the toe of each pond, a gummy outlet drained into the next one over rocks chickenwired together, the water a green-gray spew with fuzzy stuff in it. As I walked, the water pulled at me. I knew from Lace what might be in that water, the chemicals, the metals, and how would they do your skin? Plunge my arm in and skin rapid-shrink away? Saran Wrap thrown in a fire? And then the muscle, that'd go, too, snap, crackle, pop. And finally the poison would hit bone, and, true, the bone would slow it, the poison would have to work harder, but before too long, the bone would be pocked all over with little burned-out pores. Something like my face. Up over the mine rose a cloudpile strange for the morning, more like something you'd see in the afternoon. Clouds bumping along the bald level rim, clouds busy, stepping back and forth in front of each other, jostling for space.

There'd been a second flood, a little flood, two nights ago. The clouds made all afternoon and evening, sun shining at the same time, the sun just boiled the clouds up fuller. I watched the clouds build as I painted, and by the time I got home, the sun was finally covered, and Lace and Dane were worried. Jimmy Make was not, and I understood why. The May flood still seemed maybe a fluke, and the week before, we'd had a false alarm, we'd moved the cars and Lace made Jimmy stay up, but nothing happened. Now Jimmy Make and Lace argued over it, Lace talking about camping up at the Ricker Place, Jimmy saying that was stupid and we had nothing to "camp" with anyway. Finally Jimmy did move the truck with the mower and weedeater in it up on the above-the-hollow road. Because Lace had to work the next day, Jimmy said he'd stay up and watch.

I didn't hear the cloudburst. Wasn't any thunder to it. What woke me was something big and heavy slamming the base of the house, that and Baron yipping. I sprung up and into the living room where Lace was hollering at Jimmy Make, what had he been doing, why hadn't he warned us? and I could tell by looking at him he'd been out of a deep sleep no more than a few minutes longer than I had. Lace yelling, "Let's get the kids out now!" and Jimmy yelling back, "Get em out where? It'll knock em down. It's dark. We're safest in here," and Baron on the back of the couch, barking at the waters out the window. Jimmy Make yelled, "It'll only rise so high, there's less rain this time than there was in May," and Lace screamed, "How the hell do you know? You weren't even here," while Tommy in his pajama bottoms clawed at my arm, "Where's Chancey at? Where's Chancey at?" and more stuff hammering and slapping along the underpinning. "When it moves. When I feel this house move. When it shifts. What do we do then, Jimmy? When it starts to go?" Lace had gone beyond hollering, she was speaking hard cold little sentences now, and Jimmy screaming back, "You're the one wants to live in the middle of this mess!"

That goddamned Corey had already sailed out of bed and jerked open the kitchen cabinet for the big high-powered flashlight Jimmy used to spotlight deer. While Jimmy Make stood in the living room window with his face pressed against the pane and his hands framed around his face, trying to see, Corey knelt in the broad sill of the push-out window in the end of the house, the glass cranked open to kill the reflection and the light shining out on the water. I was still standing at the end of the hall, right before the living room, I couldn't figure out where to move, and I could hear Dane in the bathroom dry-heaving, and I felt for him. I knew he wouldn't bring nothing up. But then my feet felt wet, and at first I thought I was imagining it, but then I felt it on the tender parts, the instep, between the toes, and I understood it was high enough this time to seep up through the floor. I ran to where Jimmy Make was, thrust my face against the window like him. Out front, the leaping water, no moon on it, all you could see were darker angled objects studding up out of it and the foam glittering white. Then Corey was hollering, "She's dropping! She's dropping!" And Corey was right. That was all the higher it got.

I found Tommy crouched on top of that old high-boy dresser in Lace and Jimmy Make's room. It was the highest place in the house he could have got except the refrigerator. Some kind of instinct in him. Lace and Jimmy began to fight again.

By the time I hit the boulder field at the foot of the fill, the hollow was full of light. The rocks, they shook me up like they always did. Hard to put a word to it, but it was like the middle of the world showing itself where it shouldn't. When it should stay a private secret place. I dropped over and fast-crawled them, making myself not think. Then I crossed over to the side of the fill, back to the earth wall I'd tried to climb last time. It was easier this time, that little practice helped, and I think I got four or five body lengths up.

What I thought first was that I'd misstepped and somehow set it off myself. The ground started rolling, and then I heard the boom, and I understood it was a blast, and the second I understood that, I was skidding on my side down the earth wall. My arms still flung above my head, grabbing, and me brown-blinded, pelted and battered, the air full, my eyes full, my mouth, dirt dust gravel fly rock, and beside me, the fill seethed and rolled more rapid than the wall, one long skinny channel of rocks in the fill, it was avalanching. And then rocks the size of baseballs were hitting me, and I couldn't tell where I was, but I heard Lace, *protect your head*, and I threw my arms around my head and balled up.

Then the boom drew back into itself, away up on the mine, and I was at the bottom, in the big raw rocks, my arms still around my head, some stones still hailing a little. My arm and leg a long scrape from sliding down, and they stung, and although the big boom was gone, my heart echoed it inside me, while the fill still shifted and rolled, trying to resteady itself. I opened my eyes and raised up, and I could see, despite the dust in the hollow like a fine brown blizzard, the blast cloud up over the mountain, slow-shrinking now.

Then I looked back over the boulder field and saw in the dust clouds a spot of bright blue. Beyond the blue, some creature bolting back down the hollow, too small for a deer and too big for anything else wild, and I realized it was Chancey. Which meant, I understood next, the blue was Corey or Tommy.

Then I was hurtling over those bad rocks. Leaping from one surface to the next hardly slipping, something inside me knew how to go, and when I got right up on the blue, the dust settling, I saw it was Tommy, and I yelled his name, but he didn't raise up. The back of his T-shirt was still heaving, and I reached down, jerked him up, pulled him to me. The beat of his heart I felt both in his ribcage and under his spine, he was completely full of it, heart, and he was coated with pea-sized pebbles and dirt and dust, and of course he was crying, and I said, "I should beat your butt for following me up here." I meant it to sound mean, but it came out like a sob. He said something back through all the snot in his head, I couldn't tell what, but then he turned to look at me, his face moving from scared to stubborn to insulted, and when I finally heard him sniffle, "Corey got to go," I realized he was talking about the snake ditches.

Dane

DANE WAKES in the air between the bottom bunk and the floor, he comes to in that second he spends in the air, then he slams on the floor, still wearing the boots, and the boots are tangled in the sheet, so the sheet comes with him. And Lace is hollering, and then Dane thinks how much farther Tommy had to fall, and he reaches out and across the floor, patting for Tommy, but Tommy is not on the floor. So Dane gets on his feet and stretches up and reaches in the top bunk, pats again, Tommy not there, either, and Lace is in the room, her arms and legs stiffened, her hands open, her face yelling for Tommy, and Dane throws back all the covers, but Tommy's not there. While Corey just lies on his couch, perched on one elbow, watching. He hasn't even been knocked off the couch by the blast, even though he is smaller and lighter than Dane is. Then Lace wheels away so fast from the empty bunk and back to the hall that Dane gets knocked down one more time.

Corey vaults out of bed after Lace, smashing down on Dane's arm as he goes, and the front screen slams twice. Dane wobbles to his feet, the logs high in his chest, heaving, and then he is climbing into the top bunk. He pulls himself into the top bunk, his hands mushy like they've lost their bones, and there he sits rigid on Tommy's mattress, his legs crossed, the bottoms of his boots in his hands.

He's sat there, not moving, for a long time, when he hears them again in the yard. Lace still yelling, although you can hear the loudest of it is over, and Tommy still bawling, Dane listens. He doesn't hear Bant.

The logs lunge. "Move," he tells his body. His body does not. He swallows, the logs right under his throat. "Move," he says again, he makes it sound harsh, and this time his hands let loose his boots. His legs unfold, and Dane swings down low enough that he can peek out the window behind Corey's couch.

Bant is stalking away from Lace, towards the Ricker Run, her shoulders hunched forward, her hair hiding her face. Dirt all over her clothes. Lace is hollering, "You hadn't gone up there—you get back here!—he wouldn't't've followed—Bantella See, right now! Old as you are, you know better!" and Bant disappears around the back of the house.

Lace

EVEN BEFORE that visit from Bell Kerwin, we'd been hearing the heavy equipment. Muffled distant at first, but by October, exactly a year after Charlie told me about the permit, we were hearing it right up over our heads. Killing the trees, I knew that's what they did first, and I knew it didn't necessarily mean an impoundment was going in. But it for certain meant the death of Yellowroot. If I'd looked at it head-on, I don't think I could have borne it. Because through all those hard, hard years, I understood now, as I'd lost my self, my dream, my dad, my mom—it was place crept in and filled the lack.

The other thing, though, I'd learned through that loss, is that anger is easier than grief.

By then, I wasn't any longer just listening at the Dairy Queen. I was talking. I spread the word whenever I could, lots of people didn't really understand what was happening, just like I hadn't, because of how the industry kept it hidden up over our heads. And my manager, ole Connie Peters, didn't like it one bit, but Connie didn't like to confront anybody but kids, so mostly she just gave dirty looks. I'd tell people the truth, too, say I wasn't against coal mines, "my dad and granddad and husband were all miners. I just believe they can do it a better way, a way that would actually give us more jobs and not ruin everything we have." Some people would laugh at me, and some would wave me away with their hand, and a few would get mad. But the more people I talked to, the more I came to understand that most people, they thought just like me. True, there were some who'd admit it wasn't pretty, but then say we had no choice, coal is all this place has ever had and ever will. But that bunch, I figured out, was one way or another making a living off it. Then there were a few who actually called it a good thing, said knocking off the mountaintops provided flat land and cheap coal. "Cheap coal!" Loretta would say. "Look what we're paying for their cheap coal—for somebody in Ohio, Virginia, New York, Michigan, Iowa, Europe, even, to have their lights, we're losing everything we got." And I knew the ones who said that about the cheap coal were the few at the very top, the ones sick and crazy from greed.

Charlie always said if we'd have a vote on it, the majority of people would be against it. But around here, majority had never ruled. And the majority was scared to speak out. Sometimes I'd get almost as mad at them as I was at the companies, but several times, Loretta or Dunky sat me down, talked sense to me, and if I got myself calm, I heard. I already knew. How some were scared a family member would lose a job, and they were right, they were right. Those companies would blackball a person quicker than you could spit. Some were scared if they went against it, their neighbors would look down on them—a lot of people don't want to cause a stir and stick out, all that raising we had against showing ourselves. I understood that, too, I knew I'd always been considered outlandish exactly because I didn't mind sticking out.

They put in that new gate real early in the spring, but long before then, I'd walked up the hollow. I put a shell around me, armor on my heart, that's how I did it. Anger, not sad. I'd seen the sediment ponds, then I'd seen the trees coming down. I watched the fill grow. I'd seen the impossibility of climbing it to check what was behind. It scared me to death that the kids would get up in there, and I threatened them to keep them out. Corey and Bant were the ones least likely to mind, so I warned Corey I'd take away his bike for a year if I heard he'd gone up there, and I cautioned Bant about the guards, said she might get arrested. It seemed mean to tell her that, but I wasn't lying. I imagine Corey snuck up anyway.

I wrote more letters, made more calls—for the first time in fifteen years, I didn't have a little one at home to watch, that made a difference, too—and I marched in a couple rallies in Boone County while Jimmy Make thought I was at work. I spoke out at a permit hearing. Then at a second one. It turned out I was good at that. By the time I got to that big protest in Charleston, the one with the TV cameras, Loretta and them were nudging me to the front of things, coaching me to talk.

It was outside a Lyon stockholders meeting at the Marriott, and the rich men in their khakis and golf shirts passing in and out those glass doors didn't lower themselves to look at us, waving our signs from across the street, but Lyon'd also brought in their workers. They did that all the time, paid their workers to counterprotest or to speak at the permit hearings against us, their guys wearing those bizarre orange stripes up and down their pants legs and sleeves, "Lyon stripes," they called them, like they were in some kind of brainwashed zombie army. Some of them even marched in step. A couple started antagonizing us, calling us out-of-state agitators. One hollered, "You're takin food outta my kids' mouths," and I just hollered right back, "You're taking the life outta my kids' bodies," and by the time the WSAZ camera got to me and asked me what I was doing there, I was mad way past stage fright. I had my say.

Somehow Jimmy Make never learned about the TV thing. Yeah, we didn't get WSAZ at the house, but you'd have thought he'd hear it from somebody else, but little as he went out anymore, I guess that saved me. He'd more or less took up living on the couch by then, had got down from Mountain Dew and Pepsi to Wal-Mart pop, dressing in nothing but boxers or sweats, the weight layering on him, the slack. The less paying work he got, the less unpaid he'd do at home. I couldn't hardly get him to even keep an eye on Tommy anymore. And I remember how we slept together that year. I remember. He'd have already been in bed for an hour or more, separate on his own side, and I'd got practiced at undressing without a light. I'd climb in careful, keeping to my territory, I knew just how far to slide in, the halfway mark. The smell of Jimmy Make. The difference from how he used to smell. The old mattress with a bow in it and you had to balance yourself up on one side of that dip. I'd lay there for a while on my back, my whole body stiff, listening to the rhythm of his breathing, the quality of his breaths, trying to tell if he was sleeping. Usually he was not. But he said nothing, and I didn't either. Each of our breaths moving against the other.

Some days he ignored me. Others he just wouldn't lay off. Sneering about how I didn't know what the hell I was talking about, ordering me away from the treehuggers. But even Jimmy Make had sense enough to know that telling me what to do would just provoke the opposite. So he started pulling out his wild card. His big gun.

"What if somebody hears you're in with the shit-stirrers and does something to one of the kids? Huh? Ever thought of that?"

"I'll kill em," I hissed back.

Jimmy Make choked a short sarcastic laugh. "You'll kill em? You'll kill em? Ha. You have no fucking idea. You wait. You just wait."

"It's the kids I'm fighting for," I'd say. "Their future. So they'll have something of their own to grow up for."

303

He'd snuff. "Whatever. Future don't matter when you're dead."

Of course, I'd never admit it to him, but what he said did scare me. I questioned the kids in private, had anybody said or done anything to them? The three youngest didn't seem to know what I was talking about, and Bant would say only that it didn't matter. But I still did worry, and although I kept fighting, I did not join the environmental group, no matter how hard Loretta and Charlie, and eventually, even Mogey, who wasn't well enough to go himself, urged me to. Because regardless of what Jimmy Make believed, I did know the real reasons to be scared. Like how a year or two before, over in Logan, they hung effigies of environmentalists. How just that past summer, '99, the Logan County Commission hired school bus drivers and other county employees to attack people reenacting the historic unionizing march on Blair, and they even beat up Secretary of State Ken Hechler, eighty-five years old, they bloodied him good. You'd hear about people like that Chapman woman over in Willette who brought a lawsuit against a mine, and somebody cut her brake lines, and the sheriff told her she better buy a handgun, carry it all the time. Guy in Kanawha County who spoke out against it on national television, they snuck in of a night and slashed the throats of his dogs. At first, I thought some of the stories about the intimidation were exaggeration or rumors. But then somebody threw a rock through Loretta's car window when it was parked outside the environmental office over in Boone County. Then there was me, small-time as I was.

I never told anybody but Loretta about it. Thank God I was alone. I was heading back from Danville after getting groceries, we had to drive all the way over there now that the Prater IGA had shut down, and I'd stopped at the big convenience store in Riley to get gas and use the bathroom. The restrooms were off in the corner and down this short hallway, kind of hidden past the pop and beer coolers, and when I came out, a man was standing in that little passageway like he was waiting to get in the men's room. I noticed him right away because he looked out of place, dressed up like he had an office job, tie and all, suit coat. He was blocking my way out, and I figured he didn't see me, so I gave him this kind of how you doing? half-smile and said, "Excuse me."

He didn't move. "I know you," he said, and, stupid as I feel looking back now, I thought he was coming on to me. I half-smiled again, this time with a yeah, whatever, leave me alone look, and I tried to ease past. He had his hand in his pants pocket, big loose dress pants. I felt his hand move in the pocket and press against my leg, his hand still behind the cloth, and, lord help me if I didn't think at first it was his dick, and I just pushed harder to bust past and get away. But then he blocked me with his whole leg and pulled out enough of the gun that I could tell what it was. Then he dropped his leg and let me go.

People don't do stuff like that around here. I'd never had a gun pulled on me in my life, never seen a gun pulled on anybody else, even though in this state, there are guns all over the place. I got myself back in the truck, and by the time I did, my whole body had gone to shivering. Even my teeth were chattering, I bit down but couldn't make them stop. I had to sit there and wait before I was even safe to drive, I don't know how many minutes went by. And I was shaken for several more days, but after that, I tell you what—it just made me fight even harder.

One day in February 2000, Charlie all of a sudden asked me if I'd like to take an afternoon and ride out with him to Tout. I glanced across the table at Loretta sitting beside him, and she raised an eyebrow he couldn't see, so I knew she was surprised, too. A week later I lied to Jimmy Make I had to work a day I didn't, and Charlie picked me up in the Dairy Queen lot.

It was snowing but not laying, flurries spiraling into the wipers, and us closed up there in the tight space of the cab, it made me a little nervous. I tried to small talk for a while, but Charlie never had gone for that. So we sat quiet for maybe thirty minutes, listening to the heater fan, the road tracing the narrows between creek and hill. Then, as we got farther from my side of the county and deeper into Charlie's territory, he started.

"I was born and raised in Tout," he told me. "My daddy moved off the mountain and down into the camp to work the mine when him and Mom first got married. That was 1922, and I was born a little after. So I seen the changes in Tout." We hit a Y in the road, and Charlie took the left. Slant-falling snow, leafless black trees, no color anywhere. "During my boyhood, it was a company town. Company store, company doc, company preacher, ball team, scrip, whole nine yards. Me and Anita got married in 1945 soon as I got back from the war, and I worked Prince George Number 7 most of my young man's life. Automation come in the '50s, half the town left out, but I got lucky, they kept me on. Company sold off the houses, and I bought ours and fixed er up. But then Number 7 shut down completely, and I was out of work like everybody else." We were pulling a steep rise then, and Charlie stopped talking as he shifted down. In three minutes, he'd told me more about himself than he'd let out in the past eighteen months. Then he began another sentence, stopped, and tried it a different way.

"I'll tell you this, but I ain't told Loretta, you keep it to yourself—after that, I worked several strip jobs. I did. Country needed the coal, I needed the work, I didn't have any problem with that. And even when these big jobs first started coming in, yeah, the mountaintop mines, if I'd been younger, I probably would have tried to get on one of them. Didn't know any better yet."

Now we were passing the Tout sign, and Charlie went still again. I'd only been over here once, when I was a little kid, and at first, passing through, it looked to me like all the other gutted-out cast-behind mining towns I'd seen through my life. A big paintless boarded-up store still plastered with faded ads going clear back to the '50s. The collapsing houses, some held standing only by kudzu vines, and the concrete steps leading to concrete foundations with nothing on top.

Then Charlie reached the end of the town, turned around, and started driving back. It was then I noticed how Tout was different. Because in those sad thrown-away towns I was familiar with, yeah, you would often see a place or two burned to the ground. But in Tout, I was seeing house after house after house had been torched. And most of the burned houses, I realized now, didn't look like they'd been too old. And the fires themselves, I saw that now, too, had happened recently. Melted and charred aluminum siding peeling off the houses that hadn't burned all the way to the ground. Floors covered with blackened rubble that the weather hadn't smoothed down yet. Charlie pulled into the little gravel lot of the closed-down post office and turned us so we faced out, and two dogs on a ramble jogged through a ditch, but otherwise, not a soul moved anywhere. And directly above this whole eerie scene loomed a broad level hump covered with long yellow grass.

Charlie turned off his truck. We sat in total silence now, snow still sifting, afternoon sinking quick towards dark. I looked at Charlie's hands on the wheel, his big swolled-up knuckles, all out of proportion to the rest of his body.

"They started coming in here late in '94 trying to buy people out. They're doing the same thing now in Omar, Four Oaks, Medlay. But us here in Tout, we were the first I know of. They come into your community that they've already started destroying, then they start making little side deals with people. Brewing suspicion and pitting neighbors and friends and family members against each other, make it harder for people to stick together and fight, oh, they're great dividers, the industry is, they mastered that way back during the union drives. And that makes people even less want to stay, which brings the property prices down even lower. Not that a home under a mountaintop mine is worth much anyway.

"I'll tell you something else, too, Lace. Anita and me thought about it. Thought about selling out, even after me living my whole life here and Anita most of hers, not to mention all the family I got going who knows how far back on what used to be that mountain there." He paused for a second, looking at the broad blunt mound. "Why not just clear out of this mess, I was better off than a lot of the people here, I had some savings, go buy a little place in Putnam County or somewhere like that where you can ignore all this if you want to. So they brought the papers to the house, we was that close. That's when I found out you had to sign a form that said you'd never protest a mine again and would never move back within twenty-five miles of Tout."

I looked quick at his face then. I'd never heard nothing about that. He chuckled real low. "Now that's illegal. I suspicioned it was, and I researched it, and I was right. But my neighbors and all, they didn't know any better. They just went on and signed." He shook his head. "What else could you do? If you didn't, they'd just refuse to buy. But I refused to sign, not necessarily because I wanted to stay within twenty-five miles. Not even because, at that time, I wanted to protest a mine. But because a coal company wasn't going to tell me where I could live and what I could say."

He sat quiet for a few more minutes. Pulled his gloves on and turned the ignition back over for the heat. Then he passed his hand, I could see those big knuckles knobbing up even through the glove, across the dusk-dimming houses. "Not too long after they bought the places, lo and behold, the houses started burning down. Wake up in the middle of the night, there goes another one. Couldn't catch nobody doing it, but of course, nobody official tried too hard. The company said they knew nothing about it, claimed vandals must be the ones. But it seems awful coincidental to me, even though it also seems senseless as hell. Unless it's to intimidate those of us left to get out."

He cocked his head, looking up past his visors towards the hump.

Then he slumped down a ways in his seat to see better, and I did the same. The hump not much more than long broad shadow now, level along the edge, rolling a little way back. You couldn't any longer see the thin grass.

"There she is. Tout Mountain. 'Reclaimed.' They knocked er down by at least half." He brought his gloved hand to his mouth, bit down for a few seconds on his thumb. "And I'll tell you something interesting, something I wouldn't have thought." His voice went gentler then, almost tender, like I had never heard it before. But instead of being a comfort, it raised the flesh on my arms. "The hardest thing of all about living through this, hasn't been the blasting or the dust or the flooding or the fires or how they broke the community. It's looking up there each morning, at a landscape you had around you every day of your life. And seeing your horizon gone."

I ended up spending that whole evening with Charlie and Anita. When he drove me back and dropped me off outside Mrs. Taylor's so I could slip into our house, it was later than I'd expected to be, but not later than if I'd just pulled a shift. All the lights in the house were off but the porch, and I figured everybody was in bed. But soon as I opened the door, the porch light caught the white of Jimmy Make's shirt on the couch in the dark.

I stopped in the doorway to get my bearings. My eyes adjusted slowly, and I saw he was in his boxers, and a long-john shirt too small to hold his belly, a band of skin pushing out at the bottom, and, for some reason, his big work boots. There wasn't enough light that I could read his face, but his body was crouched forward on the cushions. I could feel the coil in him.

"I know where you were."

I pulled the door to behind me. I waited.

"Kids n me stopped at the Dairy Queen. Connie said you'd gone to a rally in Charleston." He'd had his head hunkered down between his shoulders a little, and now he raised it up so his face was pointed at mine, but still I couldn't see his eyes. I said nothing. I wasn't sure if it was worse to be at a protest in Charleston or at Tout with Charlie, but right after I thought that, I didn't care. And then I felt a surge of hate for Connie, but then that went away, too. And all I felt was hate for Jimmy Make.

Hate for his ridiculous boots that he needed on him to make him a man, and for his empty know-it-all-ness, and his spinelessness, and most of all, his I-don't-care, while there sat Charlie and Anita in the ghost ruin of Tout, having lost almost everything except their will to fight, and Loretta and her family battling for their hollow, every rainfall that passed through a death threat, and still they never left. And so many other people I'd met in the past year and a half who were standing up against it, too, and my hate for Jimmy Make at that moment was the purest it had ever been, not a thimbleful of love to dilute it. And all I wanted was to throw something at him, something heavy and throw it hard, not even so much to hurt him as to see it break against him, the relief that would come with that shatter, and then he said, "Sometimes I think you're more married to that mountain than you are to me." And the hate rushed out of me like a hole'd opened in my back.

He had named it. The marriage, it had been understood without either of us saying, we never spoke about. We fought about everything around it, but I realized right then neither of us had ever dared to name the marriage, but now Jimmy Make had. And when he did, me still standing in the door, the cold on my back, I suddenly saw that what tied us together wasn't any longer that clench of thick harsh rope. That wasn't it at all. What held us together now was a sinewy tangled-together nerve. A long stretched nerve that had never been tied right, had just been clapped together and then ingrown tight. And that nerve had been fraying for a very long time, but now it was on the outer verge of snap.

By that spring, 2000, the only reason Jimmy and I'd talk at all was to arrange practical stuff, mostly around the kids, and to argue. We weren't ever touching, either. Us dodging through the narrow house all balled in on ourselves, and some days, we were polite, we treated each other like company. Other days, we shot silent hate at each other, off our bodies, out of our eyes. In the meantime, it'd been a year and a half since I'd started that other kind of fighting, and already, even though I wasn't fighting nearly as hard as many, I understood why people were as tired and frustrated as they were. If I got an answer to a letter, it was a form, usually only barely related to what I'd written. If I got an answer to a phone call, and that almost never happened, they blamed another agency, another department, they told me call somebody else. No matter what evidence people brought to permit hearings, seemed ninety-nine percent of the permits went through. If the DEP did come out and find a violation, they just wrote a little citation, demanded some diddly-squat fee that it was easier for the company to pay, and pay, and pay, than it was to fix the problem. "If there's a legislator in this state not owned by coal," Loretta would say, "I ain't never heard of him or her, and I know coal lives upstairs in the governor's mansion because no matter who a man takes in with him, he ends up in bed with coal." You could bring a lawsuit, and some did, but most people didn't have the money for that, and even those good lawyers couldn't always work for free. Besides, coal ran most judges, too.

So people were just plain worn out. Most of the ones who had suffered enough to start fighting were already tired when they began, and after a year or so, they'd get dragout beatdown exhausted, if they weren't outright sick from the stress. And many people were sick from the stress, and not just the people fighting it, many people just living in it were sick from it. And what the hell? I'd ask myself again. What the hell is it? Because even if everybody had money to leave, I knew most of us would stay. And if those who'd left had any choice, most of them would run right back. Then I started thinking, especially of a night, standing in the black yard after Rhondell'd dropped me off, the unseen land close around me—maybe it was something about the mountains' layers. Something about everything layered in them dead. All that once-live stuff, strange animals and plants, giant ferns and ancient trees, trapped down there for 250 million years, captured, crushed, and hard-squeezed into—power. That secret power underground, that sleepy force lying all around, contagious somehow, catching, setting off the power pulls on top, the trickery and thievery, the violence and the loss, the way power will fight for power. The power under here, I told myself, if it can cause all that, it must also put a hold on us. Not greed for coal, not that kind of hold, we'd never got the profits from that. No. But just the pull, the draw, of so much power in the ground, and the kind of hold that makes.

When was it I first started seeing the assumption that me and Jimmy Make'd just always be together? Looking back, I know I'd got a glimpse of it during the first year back home. But the first time I saw it naked, bold-lit, was that night in February when Jimmy Make named the marriage. Then once you see the assumption, you can't any longer not see it. And then it's not an assumption anymore. It's no longer that invisible brace under your marriage, and after that was gone, well, I realized not much else was left besides that sinewy nerve. And gradually I was able to imagine how to just cut it, suffer that sudden terrible sharp pain, might actually be better. Fast, quick, terrible. Because how could I endure both the slow loss of the place and on top of that the slow loss of him?

As I began to see all that, I started to shed a little of my Jimmy Make anger, some of my hate. I even started to feel, for the first time in years, a little tenderness, if not for Jimmy Make, and maybe it was, at least for us. For that third thing we'd been together. We still went at it vicious, same fight so many times we had it memorized, me screaming, *stand up to them with me, have a spine,* him bellowing, *I worked in the goddamned industry, you cannot fight them. You'll never win.* But I was coming to see that what he considered fighting and winning was different from what I did. And the other difference was, he wasn't raised on one little piece of ground like I was, and he'd never had to use that place to fill in for something he'd lost.

Then we had the May flood, and that changed the fight between us, that raised the stakes, and then the July night flood, it forced my hand again in the most terrible way. I told Jimmy Make, I made my voice reasonable, "Let's move back up in the Ricker Place, the water can't get in there."

"We don't got the money to fix up that place, and we won't never have it long as we stay here because I won't never find work."

So I said, "Then move the house to where Mom's trailer was."

"And where would we get the money to do that? Besides, you know well as I do they'll take Cherryboy next, and then what do you think might wash down in that cove there?"

I had come to believe what Loretta and Charlie did, that people would have to die for the government to step in and do anything. "So how can you leave your kids live here?" Jimmy Make would say, and of course, that was it. That was it. Even though Jimmy Make didn't honestly believe we'd ever get killed and just said that to get me to move. But I knew we would get washed out. I knew that in my heart.

I can't lose my kids. I can't leave my place. One more time, the terrible choices. Sometimes it seems I've spent my whole life choosing between bad and bad—stay at college or leave, have the baby or die, marry Jimmy Make or not, stay in Raleigh with a decent job or come home with none, fight to keep the land or give in and keep Jimmy—only now the bad choices are three. Stay here without my kids. Leave the place with them. Or keep my kids here with me and risk losing them altogether.

What I do know, after almost two years of not even getting any-body to listen, much less take action, is this: the best way to fight them is to refuse to leave. Stay in their way—that's the only language they can hear. We are from here, it says. This is our place, it says. Listen here, it says. We exist.

Bant

"COULDN'T you say you were going over there for something? Sneak over and see?"

"They don't let us wander around wherever we want." R.L. giggled then, at the foolishness of me, and me thinking, you know how they are, and here you go on anyway.

"Or ask somebody."

"I done asked, I told you that. They said ain't nothing over there to worry about."

"And you believe em?"

He rolled over hard on the creek rocks to steel those eyes at me. "Listen, you-all wanna stay in here, you want your brothers to have jobs, your husband, you better just get used to this here. Or go on and move out. You don't want that, do you?"

The rocks chunky and mean in my back, sun showing too much, I could feel the places on my face shining out. And it wasn't just what I knew of North Carolina, it was also the other people who moved and then came back, I'd heard them. *Why, they don't treat each other no bettern animals. Got to where I wouldn't even open my mouth in public.*

315

I'd heard. *And that Stanley boy, he just disappeared. Yeah, up there in Dayton. They never did find that boy.*

"Why don't your daddy put in an application?" He was trying to make up a little now.

"That ain't the kind of mining he knows how to do." I thought a second before adding what came next. "And he wouldn't do it if he did know how."

"Oh, wouldn't, would he? Rather be down in a hole all day?"

Skinny-ass Ohio boy, his boots bigger than his legs, how can . . . how can you hate what you hunger so for?

"You know all those deep mines are shutting down anyway. No future there. This is the future, what I'm doing."

"He's gonna move back to North Carolina, get work down there, if he can't get on at this place over Mingo."

"Well, you-all won't be able to get much for that house."

Like we didn't know.

"You-all could go down there, save up your money, come back here, and open you up a small business. Like I'm gonna do in Ohio."

Blown all over with rock dust when he comes off each shift. Ashes, not coal, looks gone to ghost, he does. Dust ashes ghost.

"I still think you could get up in there and find out for me."

"You're talking a lot today, ain't ya?" He rolled to his back, laced his fingers under his head. Fox-grinned. "Well, you do me a favor, I'll do you one. Maybe."

A cold spot made in the base of my throat. I pulled myself farther from him, although I didn't move my body, didn't let him see.

"You hear me?"

I said nothing.

"Ain't talking now, are you?" He pushed his face closer. "You do me, I'll do you."

"You said they'd never let you up there."

"Oh, I'd find a way if I wanted it bad enough."

The end of something. It just always was. And what was it to grow up in this ending place, butting always against that, what? All those little half-ghosts, hovering. Glaze out the thinking part of your mind and you can see them all over the hills.

"I'm only fifteen."

"Yeah, and I'm twenty and running out of patience."

Corey

B-BO AND David swear Seth and them have gone to Myrtle Beach for two weeks. They say Seth was bragging about it, which he would. That part sounds right. Bragging about what all they'd get to do down there in Myrtle Beach, not counting the beach—and even the beach is something Corey has not ever seen—but also about how they'd play miniature golf and do bumper cars. And, David says, Seth told about this speedtrack down there. You pay a couple dollars and race around the loop in this low-to-the-ground racecar. Corey feels his face harden up when David tells him this. David swears he saw Seth and them leave out of here two days ago with their Suburban loaded with so much stuff they had to carry this white box on top, and B-bo swears he saw the same thing.

But Corey doesn't trust them—he doesn't think they're deliberately lying, just isn't sure they're bright enough to really know—so he checks on the house for two days from the creek before he decides David is right. At least about them being gone. Who knows about the two weeks part, which means Corey and Tommy need to act fast. Although it's not like they're doing something wrong or bad. It's just Corey picking up his prize.

Because this is where things have got to: Corey's bike is totaled, he's tried for hours to fix that wheel, but all he's done is make it worse. And Bant says he can have hers, but Bant's is a girl's. Rabbit in jail for who knows how long, could be years, and Dad more cranky and hateful-acting than ever, him and Mom fighting day and night, and Corey's not exactly on his good side either, after getting a DUI with Rabbit while under Dad's watch. Mom didn't like that at all. Not a snowball's chance in hell Dad will help Corey now, and there in the old house the parts sit, oh, all that time and muscle and brain Corey put into gathering them together. Because of all that, Corey is being watched close these days, it won't be easy to pick up his prize, even with Tommy's help. He was whupped on good, both for going with Rabbit and for tying Tommy up, but ha, *don't care. Just pretended like it hurt.* The real punishment is how close he's watched.

So on the third day, when Corey leaves the creek and sneaks through the yard to the shed, it's after Bill Bozer showed up to see Jimmy and Mom's long gone at work. Because of the high redwood-colored walls, no one can see him from the road. The shed is one of those portable aluminum things you buy someplace like Lowe's in a couple pieces, then haul home in your truck and put back together. It doesn't have a floor. It just sits on these wooden struts and the floor is ground. The double doors in the front of the shed that swing open to let out the four-wheeler are locked, but not with a padlock, although there is a part of Corey that would have liked a padlock, because then him and Tommy could have busted it off with a blowtorch and hacksaw like Dad and Bant did up the hollow. The double doors are locked with a deadbolt you can open from the outside with a key or from the inside with a lever. Corey has a plan.

The next day, after Mom leaves, Corey makes a lot of noise under the house with toy trucks he doesn't even like anymore, and just when he figures Dad can't stand it a second longer, he asks can him and Tommy go to David and B-bo's house. Dad says go.

At the shed, Corey and Tommy work fast because who knows how long Seth and them will really be away. The bigger the hole grows, and the achier and sweatier Corey gets, the more he not only doesn't see it as stealing—he'll put it back after he rides—but the more he sees it as coming to his own rescue. *Righting a wrong,* and Tommy agrees, Tommy was there. They have just the one shovel, and when Corey gets tired, he has Tommy spell him, but it becomes clear fast that Tommy isn't much of a digger. He gets bored too easily, and he whines. Still, Corey must stay nice to Tommy, both to keep him from telling and because to make a hole big enough for Corey might take extra days. It turns out the ground is not as easy to dig as Corey had thought. And it turns out that Tommy is a lot thicker than you'd think by looking at him, which Corey discovers each new time he makes Tommy try the hole. Ole Chancey is much more taken with the digging than Tommy is. He lies on his stomach with his ears cocked and in his eyes a look similar to the one he uses on squirrels, and now and again, Chancey sails in and helps, but he doesn't understand how to throw the dirt in the right pile. This is not the first time Corey has wished that Chancey had hands.

It's late afternoon when Corey decides the hole is big enough for Tommy to squeeze through. His head goes through easy, but right away his shoulders get stuck. Tommy is on his belly in the hole with his head in the shed trying to pull his shoulders and arms after him, and he looks like a dying fish, his spine scooped out the wrong way, squirming his knees to drive himself on through. Corey squats behind him and pushes.

"Don't poosh!" yells Tommy.

"We gotta get you through, boy. I want this done by supper." Corey is thinking ahead.

"Let me back out! I'm gonna put my hands in first this time."

Corey heaves his own shoulder against Tommy's butt and Tommy kind of squirts ahead and screams at the same time—"Keep it down!" snaps Corey—and then Tommy is through the hole to his waist, and Corey can hear that he is crying, and then Tommy drags his hips on through.

"You scraped my back! You scraped my back!" Tommy has already worked up an abundance of snot, you can hear it in his throat.

Corey hisses, "Tommy! Ain't you a little man?"

Almost immediately, Tommy quiets. Corey can hear him snuffling and swallowing back the snot. In the meantime, Chancey has tunneled right after him, Chancey and Tommy are both in the shed, and Corey, who has felt the anticipation building in his bladder for some minutes now, has to pee. Desperately.

"It's dark in here," calls Tommy.

"I know it's dark in there. Just walk to the front of the four-wheeler, then feel around the door for the lock." Corey is jogging from foot to foot.

"Where's the front of the four-wheeler?"

"Feel for the handlebars, stupid." Now he's gripping himself with his hand. He turns towards the back of the shed, pulls down the elastic waist of his shorts just far enough—they don't have a fly—and pees against the aluminum.

"What's that noise?" Tommy says. Then, "Oh, here it is," and just like that, long before Corey expected Tommy to find the lock, he hears the metal doors open with a kind of crack and wump. Corey wheels around towards the front, some pee still coming, it wets his shoes, and he dashes to the shed doors pushing his wet self back in his shorts as he runs.

"They're in there," Tommy says with a kind of awe, and Corey knows he means the keys are in the ignition.

"Yes!" Corey whoops. He leaps up in the air and smacks a high five at Tommy's hand, which he misses.

He dashes to the four-wheeler, touches the ignition, makes sure for himself. Then he climbs the footrests, straddles the machine, and leans his whole body forward over the front, drapes the metal with himself. He half lies there, his stomach gouged by the steering wheel, in the brutal aluminum-soaked shed heat, inhaling the good gas and oil, and Corey feels, for the first time in months, the hard want dissolve away.

It won't be a problem to start it or drive it. Corey has driven one before, over at the ATV rodeo last year, Dad paid for him to ride around the track, any dummy could drive this here, and Corey is no dummy. But they're not going to ride it right now, no, he's already thought through the best plan. They can't be seen running around on it on a Saturday afternoon. They'll do it tomorrow, Sunday morning. Not at the crack of dawn, when the engine would draw too much attention. And not in the afternoon, when too many people would be out. But around ten o'clock, when three-quarters of the hollow will be at church and the ones left won't think nothing of a four-wheeler starting because everybody's used to engine noise. Four-wheelers, chainsaws, tractor lawnmowers, drills, monster machines working overhead. Everybody's used to it.

Bant

ON WHITE shorts it's going to show, you know that it will. I hadn't known about the blood, I'd brought nothing for it. Had nothing with me but my lunch in a Kroger bag which now I wouldn't eat, and he dropped me off behind the funeral home so the motel people wouldn't see me leave his truck. I came out from Scott's parking lot and hobbled up the street, not from pain, but to keep what I thought was more blood from dripping out. To use the bathroom, I had to pass through Hobart's office, so most days I held my pee a long long time. He was watching some show about men fishing in a swamp, the little office reeking its Hobart smell, crushed stale crackers and old man body. Made me want to spit. I shuffled through with my legs together, wondering what he could see on the seat of my pants, and then I was thankful for the fishing show, the air conditioner. It would have been past bearing if on top of everything else, Hobart could hear me in the bathroom too.

Once I got my shorts down, I saw most of the stickiness was not blood. I had to take toilet paper, ball it up, hope it stayed steady in my pants. Back outside, I took my brush from the gasoline jar, dipped it into paint, pulled it out, and watched it spray blue across my thigh. That was the first I knew I was shaking.

We'd argued for some time, which would come first, me giving it to him or him showing it to me. Finally I gave in because I thought I had way more to lose than he did, and if I'd give up all that, why wouldn't he do his little bit to help me out with the other? What reason would he have not to?

His finger first, a hurt both dull and sharp. Raggedy nail edge. He decided he didn't want it along the creek, didn't want it on the rocks, so he'd scouted out a secret daytime place where he could park his truck. Then he wanted it in the truck bed, not the cab, he wanted it stretched out on a blanket on the ridges there, but I couldn't do it out in the open like that, up some dirt road just one hill over from Left Fork. There were for me no secret places here. And he said if they can see us in the bed, they'll see us in the cab. But I needed around me at least that steel.

In the movies, it was always dark, or close to it. In the real, the windshield blew up the sun like a magnifying glass. We were undressed only where it mattered, his jeans peeled off his hips, no underwear, my shorts dangling off one ankle. We wore our shirts and we wore our shoes. Me forced up against the passenger door, the window handle in my back, the armrest, too, and he felt like a muscle between my legs. The sweat helped, the slickness there. The slickness, the glare of the cab, and a pounding that had nothing to do with any way I'd ever moved or'd want to. That dull pounding after the hurt, my back against the door, my spine crunched up, jammed again and again. Against that door. The sun was in my eyes, and I closed them and saw red, but what happened had nothing to do with fire. Something smelled like rain in loam. Something smelled like fish thawing. The cab rocked to where I heard his thermos rolling a little on the mat below me, and after, he picked his cap off the floor and twirled it on one finger. I saw blue paint on his face. "God, girl," he said. "You're tough." Like for the first time he respected me now.

The strange cool had left out of here and the weather had gone back to how it knew it should be in August, and then it went even past that. Making up for the other. Hard to sleep at night, me skimming along, a heatwet with a weight, a push, a push you awake, my jammed-window room glaring with the bright gas smell, and some nights I would end up like an animal would figure out, down on the floor, the little coolness there, and a few nights I got all the way out to the porch, if the heat was worse than the bugs. I figured Jimmy Make would think that was where I was going, if he noticed me slipping out at all, on the night I was supposed to get my half of the deal. I would leave before Lace got home. It was just Tommy and Dane she'd check on when she got in, Corey only because he was in the same room with them. Nobody worried about Corey and me.

Three days after we did it, R.L. said he'd take me up. Saturday night he had off that week, and he figured Saturday would be safest anyway, they were working a skeleton crew. The hollow screaming with locusts and all the other little things, the way they'd scream loudest in the hottest heat. I felt that green all around me, even in the dark it was green, you knew, it was a wrapping green, overpowering the houses, their puny lights, that green pressing, cradle or stall. Those heavy plants making up for the other, and the hills under plants, and the blackness inside the hills, beating, so you were five times layered, you knew, five layers held, heat, scream, green, hills, and the black inside. Pressing. I'd told him to pick me up in front of Seth and them's because they didn't talk to no one and Mrs. Taylor across the road slept early in the back room. He had his headlights off, but his engine idling. When I opened the door, the cool air shocked my skin and the dome light cut on and he smiled.

325

I liked to ride in the dark with the windows down, night pouring over me, but I knew he wanted the AC. When he wasn't shifting gears, he drove with one hand reached over on my thigh, and once I looked down to the nail there. I knew what had happened had moved him in the direction opposite from where it had moved me. He'd already said something about me visiting his family in Ohio. I'd said nothing back. I knew by this time you could measure in inches how far this boy went down. I'd got there now.

Before the guard shack, I ducked on the floor, covered myself with a nubbly motel blanket, the stink of old cigarettes in it. I felt those truck guts working right under my knees, the metal surge, and I couldn't hear what lie he made up for the guard. Then we were in, I felt us powering up the hill, and I climbed back in the seat. Looked out on that wide company road, we were flying, and it was gravel, yes, but it was still smoother and broader than the paved county and state roads the trucks busted all to pieces down where regular people drove. Since we'd done it, I'd only seen him once, while I was painting. We hadn't yet been alone in this way, and now that we were, I knew for sure. There was no place else in him to go. It was like how me and Dane came up that one time on an electrified fence, and Dane was scared to go through it, and one of us needed to touch it, to make sure. And all I did was walk near the line, I didn't even touch it, without touching it I knew there was no current there, and I was right. The road got steeper, two coal trucks hammered past us, R.L. gunned the pickup harder, and then we lost all the trees. We were rising up out of the hills. *Out of the holding, out of the holding hills,* I said a little song in my head.

Then I realized we'd come out on the mine top. There was no moon overhead, and I tried to remember if there'd been moon down home because here, of course, there'd be no moon overhead, here moon was underfoot. The bald ground prickled sharp all over with artificial lights, and far beyond those, a few dulled stars. He banged the truck behind and away from where they were working, away from the brightest lights, him dodging dirt knobs like mini-mountaintops and weird little plateaus, and even though we hadn't been close to that sky-high dragline to begin with and were now heading away from it, I still couldn't see to the top of it out the truck window. Could see mostly only the horrible big block of its base. R.L. was swinging and banking through tracks and trenches, the dead land silvered, strangely shadowed, and with the land as tore up as it was, he had to shift often, and I thought, good. Get that raggedy nailed hand off me.

We hadn't hardly spoke a word the whole way up, but now I felt a tight flutter in his quiet, and I knew he was scared. I was past scared, I had got that way once what had happened happened. I had in me a few streaks of hope, but more than anything else I felt numb unbelief. I was finally here, so close, but most of me still couldn't believe I would at last see, at last know. It was like when I was little and waiting for Christmas, waiting so hard for so long that by the time we got within days of it, I no longer believed it would come at all. So that when it really did come, it had already been stolen by the unbelief. He stopped the truck behind a rise that would hide it.

We were on a part of the mine they must have already worked out, and we stepped out in a big shadow there, beyond the reach of the lights. The machines destructing right alongside of us sounded different than they did destructing overhead. I craned my neck and my back to take in the dragline, its own neck swinging. All lit up along itself like a ski lift I'd seen on TV ads for Snowshoe. He started off with my hand in his, but I hung back enough so that our fingers slipped apart. I was looking around, trying to figure out in what direction Cherryboy might be, the impoundment, but nothing has no direction. Upside-down peel of moon, *skin you alive,* she'd tell us in second grade, and I'd see that inside-out kid, bloody snagged in a barbed wire fence. Ohio boy, Scab-boy, sorry scared boy, I followed him, still straining for where the top of the valley fill might be, and the unbelief in me knew he didn't know where he was going.

I followed him, the dark tank top, floating, the Skoal can scar in his right hip pocket, and over that killed ground, I'm telling you, you didn't walk so much as coast, there was nothing in such ground to hold you, only the dead crunch under your feet. And lying naked to sun like the ground had all day, it had sopped up heat, and now the day heat fogged up off the surface, rising around us. He moved quick, keeping to trenches, behind mounds and rock piles. At times, he crouched to listen, tugging me down with him when he did. The layers that had pulled me to him had dropped away like snakeskin, and then he was stark to me, normal to me. Finally he was less than that.

Then it wasn't just distance and direction I lost track of, it was time, too. I could mark a few places by things that happened—the time we were all of a sudden to our shins in some nasty muck-filled pond; the time a truck passed not far away, and he outright dove into a ditch and knocked me down with him; the time we almost walked off a high wall. R.L. first, him catching his feet like he was slamming on brakes, throwing out his arms to his sides, and when I crept up to see, I was peeking over a sheer rock drop some twenty feet high. Sometimes I could see clear where we were walking, in the foil-colored fake light. Other times I moved by foot feel. I did it without fear while feeling all along the fear off him, and he didn't talk to me, and I didn't talk to him because I didn't want to know for sure that he didn't know at all. What I had lost for it. What I had paid.

Then we came around a high dozed-up mound of dirt, and there sat a pickup truck. First thing I thought was it was somebody else's truck. Then my stomach turned and dropped, and I knew it was his truck, and anger tears almost flashed hot in my eyes, and the near tears made me even angrier. And I heard him say, "I told you there wasn't no impoundment up here."

My chest surged, and I felt my arms stiffen, and I heard myself say, "You tricked me. God*damn* you."

He stepped back, hackled his shoulders a little, and if I could have seen his face, I knew it would hold some self-righteous glare. "I did not trick you. I got you up here, didn't I? It just ain't here."

"You have no fucking idea whether it's up here or not. You had no fucking idea where you were going the whole goddamned time." I heard myself almost sob, and it made me hate myself, I held my breath to make it stop, and the next thing he said, he didn't sound mad so much as confused.

"Listen, baby, I wouldn't trick you. I love you." He paused there, like he was giving me time to take that good news in. "It just ain't here." He reached out his arm, like he was going to comfort me, but that just made me harden. I backed off to where he couldn't touch me, and I said, "I'm going on. See for myself," and I turned and walked away.

I walked away, and he came after me, snatching at my bare arm, he accidentally scratched me with the nail, and I about hauled off and punched him, but something held me back, him rambling, "Are you crazy? You ain't gonna find nothing. If I couldn't of found it, how the hell will you?" Me still walking, faster now, jerking away when he touched me. "You'll just get stuck up here and they'll arrest you. If you don't kill yourself first."

I started trotting. I was to myself enough by then that I was careful where I laid my feet, but I trotted. He kept right with me, then he started talking something else, I should've known he wasn't really worried about me getting arrested or killed. "And what if they catch you? And they find out I brung you up here?" He was huffing a little, trying to keep up. "I'll lose my job, quicker'n that. They'll fire me." Now I heard a wobble in his voice, and it made me hate him harder. "I have to have this job. You know that. Where else am I gonna find work pays anywhere near this?"

"I won't tell them." I turned and faced him, still moving.

"Even if you don't, they'll figure it out. Guys at the motel know I'm fooling with you." He was just this side of crying now, babified, and I hardened so deep I wasn't even mad, I kept moving, and he whined, "I done what I said I would, I got you up here, it just ain't here. I love you, baby." He snuffled, little gulping noises coming out of him. "C'mon, let's just get offa here. I can't lose my job. Look at what I already risked for you. I done did. Look." He reached out for me. "I love you."

All I know about what happened next was I fell. Don't know if he tripped me or knocked me down, don't know if I stumbled myself trotting backwards over ragged ground, I only know I was moving in a blackness that was inside me more than outside me, and then I know I fell. And the land. Under me, dead, gone, buried, me thinking, crucified, dead, and buried, the end of something, it just always was, and on the third day; no ma'am. And my grandma said, *You Bant, you're different.*

And I said, *Grandma, I can't feel any longer for it.*

And she said, *Now Bant. You know bettern that.*

And I said, *You have to let go of it to keep going ahead.*

And she said, *You know what's right.*

And I said, *I'm too young to have nothing but past to believe in.*

Then I found myself back in the truck. I didn't know how I'd got there, but I knew I'd done it myself. The boy was nowhere to be seen. Me bleeding from the heel of my hand, right there above the pulse, and what if that kind of dirt got in? I ground it against my jeans despite the hurt. Then R.L. opened his door, swung in, and slammed it harder than he needed to. I didn't look at him after that.

Lace

I WAKE with the taste of Jimmy Make's shoulder in my mouth. Not the real taste of it, because Jimmy left early this morning after I fought him. And not the recent taste of it, because it is only the memory taste that can bring water under my tongue. I wake tasting the memory of Jimmy Make's shoulder with sun in it, freckles on top the brown and sun in the skin. But I never taste the sun in Jimmy Make anymore.

We fought me into tears, fought me into a knot on my knees, but we fought him until he wasn't angry anymore. Fought him past mad. Started fighting the minute I got home, house hollow-blacked and the light of the TV, and finally, no light at all. We fought to cigarette breaks, to whiskey shots, to try to sleeps, then we'd remember something and fight again. We fought til the little cool came, crack of the night, fought til the gray pushed the black out the land. We fought til he picked up his keys.

He'd shower at the mine, but the places he'd miss, shadows lurking on skin. Shadow Jimmy. Never got to make a man. Him boy, then middle-aged, no in-between, the boy in the middle-aged body, and how much did I take from him? That slow low ruin. Down in a hole.

Sunless skin, coal taste in it, swallow memory back. Linoleum floor and coal stove, smoke in my little girl throat. The soft clot it makes there.

I tell you, each of my kids I love in a different way. Tommy, my baby. Hold him against my body here. Feeling I get with Tommy, with him it's all feel, yearn to nustle, boy-squirm under my breasts, then the slow settle. Finally the tuck. Sweet nut. Tommy growing up poorer than the others had to, Tommy growing up poorest of us all, and him not even knowing any different. When I'd always thought by the baby we'd be doing better, for your children, how things are supposed to be. Tommy I love from my belly. From the center of me.

Corey. They call him little Jimmy Make. But he's half little me. The hard want in Corey, thrusting, the anger and envy, open mouth, reach down your hands and him crash right through, Corey. A go, go, go, while everything around here hollers at you *stop*, and I know there is no way we can fill that crave, no way we ever will, and I want to catch Corey, shake him, show him, look at me. Look at me. And if all you're going to do is want, at least want life. Starving even when you're full. Because also in Corey is the Jimmy Make part, the hot wet, Corey a flame, a push, a glow, and although of course I love Corey different than I loved Jimmy Make, the same force in Corey draws me still.

I knelt in the dog-smelling carpet, head smashed in my arms, he hadn't hit me, I wasn't trying to beg. My body quivering under me, me swabbing the soak of my face—then I heard the ring of his keys. My shaking stopped. I lifted my face. It was undark enough to see. His bare pale feet. The stains on his jeans. The glut of stomach, flesh under his chin. The limp when he turned to leave.

See him heave, the bow of his back, arch over me. Big cat. Wet horse. A swimming through air, catch me there, I needed that then. Hard rolling beauty and the tight of his skin, and I thought I'd lost all memory of how love felt, lost it so far back unnoticed I didn't even have enough to copy by, had no pattern, that's what I'd thought. Hard rolling beauty in that boy, rolling, burst drain. Shadow Jimmy. Out of a thousand fights, he'd never driven away, and this one him not even angry, there was light enough to see. And how much did I take? My mouth on his skin. Taste it there.

Sad dark Dane. All that he carries quiet in him and how he feels too much, how he pulls into him everything, then closes like a mussel. Mussel soft inside. Way he'd just sit on my lap as a little one and watch, how he wouldn't cry for food. Then he wouldn't cry for pain. Dane will never have an easy time of it, I've known that since he was tiny, and I used to believe I could do some of his hurting for him, soak it away. But now I know different. I want to take Dane's shoulders between my hands, press my eyes to the crown of his head. I want to cover him.

Bant I love most different from the rest. Little sister, little friend. Bant's dear face, and the skin will scar, but it is a luxury to heal a face. A luxury to heal. What the two of us went through together beginning that dark January, her growing her life while I was growing up, us moving over ground. Ground moving up into us. The years it was just the two of us, before Jimmy and the boys, Bant my side, my echo, Bant my death and then my borning, and if Tommy's my stomach, Corey through my hands, Dane in my tears, then Bant is fused to my ribs. Feel her there.

I raised up when I heard him take the keys, there was light enough that I could see. I raised, and I called his name. Jimmy turned around. There was light, I could see his face. It wasn't mad. Jimmy Make had started feeling sorry for me.

We flashed, glistened, we glowed. Him heaving through water, and the sun on his skin, water drops glisten flash, brown flecks spun gold. Spun gold. Creek trees and rocks and weeds, me riding his shoulders, my feet tucked behind his hips, a new animal made. Him never wanting past now, never thinking past real, the way he filled me and made me forget me, animal wetness, hotbody catheat. Needed, I loved, I took from him then.

I wake this morning at ten o'clock, my skin already sticky where it touches skin. Too much raw sun in the room, the ripped sheer curtains, the bent rod, and I wake with in my mouth the taste of Jimmy Make's shoulder. And I wake knowing that although today he will be home, Jimmy is not waiting on me any longer. This time, Jimmy will choose. And I know, at thirty-one years old, Jimmy Make has finally grown up.

Dane

IT'S TEN fifteen on a Sunday morning, and although the house is never empty at that time on a Sunday morning, it is almost empty now. Dane stands in the living room door looking at where Jimmy Make's truck is not, while the logs grind tight in his gut. So little room to move. Corey and Tommy left half an hour ago, taking care not to wake Dane, which means they are up to something because otherwise they would have deliberately bothered him. Bant was out until after two in the morning, Dane heard her sneak back in, and with her sneaking came a bad feeling in Dane, a feeling with colors, an animal smell, but a feeling he cannot name.

But what worries Dane most is when he passed Jimmy and Lace's room a few minutes ago and he saw Lace alone in their bed. He paused there in the hall, looking harder to make sure Jimmy Make wasn't hidden somewhere in the covers, but it was only Lace, awake, her eyes open, but not seeing Dane. Now Dane realizes Jimmy's truck is gone and he never heard it leave, which makes him think it's been gone a good while, and for Jimmy to leave in the middle of the night like that . . . Then there's what Dane saw at the end of the hall last night.

335

He pours Foodland Frosted Flakes into a cereal bowl, stops a minute, decides to trade up for a mixing bowl. He stays so hungry lately, despite his stomach being always more than full. It is not a good hunger, not appetite, it is just an order to keep applying pressure. *What's goin on, you got worms?* Jimmy Make talking. Dane turns towards the porch, Baron at his feet, back-pedaling, bug-eyed alert for something to drop, and when Dane opens the front door, he tips the bowl, loses his spoon, and slops milk on Baron's head. Baron's tongue happy. Dane picks up the spoon and carries his cereal to the edge of the porch, where he sits with his legs dangling and the railing right over his head. Feels the sting of air on the piece of his little toenail he ripped off last night. Sunday morning. Almost nobody home. Would things be different if they still went to church? No. Dane knows they would not. *Things are gettin awful. Just awful, things are gettin.* What's coming. What's coming next. Open your Bibles, please. Read.

He spoons the cereal into his mouth like a duty. Mrs. Taylor is at church. Mrs. Taylor has finally decided. Before very long, her house will be empty, too, she is just too worn out to stay. *If we all last til then.* He likes Mrs. Taylor, but if she leaves, she'll take the stories with her, but then how much does it matter anyway, with the stories in him already? *Turrible. It's just turrible.* He'd be going to school anyway, he'd be working way less hours even if she stayed. Him going to the new middle school. New kids to discover new meannesses for Dane.

They fought hard last night, fought nasty. Lace was very late getting home from the Dairy Queen, but Jimmy Make was mad enough to sit up for her, Bant slipping in the back door while they were at it in the living room. The fight had been a bad one, but Dane hadn't thought it that much different from most of them. Until later when he had to pee.

He had woken up, and often when this happens, he tries to hold the pee, wills himself back to sleep, but there is always also the very real risk he will pee the bed. He hasn't for over a year now, Dane believes he's outgrown it. But last night, the fear of backsliding and bed-pissing outweighed his fear of the dark. He could feel the almost morning in the dark, it was graying a little, but it was still dark enough to threat. So Dane ventured out on his nighttime bathroom ritual, screwing his eyes tight shut in the dark down the hall—he runs his hand along the wall, he knows exactly where to stop—until he hits the bathroom doorjamb, reaches inside, and flicks the light. Only then does he open his eyes. He'd done all this last night, and after he peed, he turned the light back off like Lace made them do, clamped his eyes closed, and began groping his way back to the bedroom. Then something happened.

He felt a pull on him from behind. Something down the hall magneted his back, it commanded *look and see,* the command deeper than voice or tap or clutch, even more insistent than the pamphlet pull, and Dane clenched his jaw against it; he stiffened his back. But it would not ease up. It yanked. It ordered. It forced. Until finally it was worse not to look than it was to look, finally this Dane knew, so without turning his whole body, without exposing his front to it, at least he could hold onto that, he craned his neck around over his shoulder. And saw.

At the end of the hall, at the entrance to the living room, lay the monkey. Even though it was too dark to see that far, even though there was no way his eyes could have adjusted that fast, Dane could see. The monkey wasn't sitting up looking at him, no. It wasn't alive. The pull had come off it dead. It lay crumpled in its usual death pose, Dane recognized the way it lay even though he has never actually seen the monkey, still Dane recognized that pose. He knew. Limp on the carpet, twisted funny unlike any live thing would lie, and its dirty fur swished a little, Dane saw it move, the way it swishes when water passes over it. That was the only thing about it that moved. At Dane it cocked its empty dead eye.

Then, abruptly, it let Dane go. He was suddenly turned loose and tearing back to his bed, slamming his arm in the bedroom doorframe and stubbing brutally his little toe on the leg of Corey's couch. Corey didn't twitch. Dane shot under his covers, snatching them all the way over his head, and he lay trying to hold the outside of his body rigid as ice while inside his whole self was abeat. He grasped after prayer. Felt it air in his heart. Then he heard the whispers. End-of-the-world mutter, voices soft-chutter, moany. Moooany in their mouths. He heard.

This morning, he'd had no fear about walking back into the hall. He knew, even though it hadn't been a dream, that the monkey would be gone. Knew that with the same recognition he'd had of how the monkey always lay.

Baron scratches the screen door, wanting out. Dane ignores him, reaches his hands up to stretch his arms on the rail. He hears a motor start down the hollow; a motorcycle or ride mower or four-wheeler. Then he realizes it's coming all the way up into their part of the hollow, where nobody has much reason to come, especially with the gate locked back up. Dane looks towards the bend in the road to see who it is.

The first thing he can tell is that it's two kids on a four-wheeler, and the next thing he can tell is that it's Tommy and Corey—the chamois rag fluttering—but then he reminds himself that's not possible. But then it's clear that it is. They aren't going very fast, just kind of sput-tering along, and Dane knows they're trying not to draw attention to themselves. That's the only reason Corey wouldn't be gunning it. Chancey trots along at a safe distance behind.

Dane has risen up on his haunches by now, clutching the rail over his head with both hands, tensed, and now they're putting right past the house. Dane sees they're none too glad to spy him spying on them, which he can tell by the way Corey ignores him so hard it turns inside out and becomes the opposite and the way Tommy's mouth *ohs* in frightened and disappointed surprise before he buries his whole face in Corey's back. Now Dane is standing, paralyzed by three cross-pulling feels: the temptation to get revenge on Corey's meanness by running inside and telling Lace; a jaw-drop awe that Corey has managed not only to steal Seth's four-wheeler but knows how to drive it; and, louder than anything else, curiosity over what Corey will do next.

They jiggle past and on up the hollow, the camouflage fenders rocking with the bumps in the road, their legs spraddled over the big engine, the chamois rag flagging. Dane hits the ground in his bare feet and sprints to the road to see whether they're heading for the valley fill or the snake ditches, then Corey takes the hairpin turn that doubles back up to the above-the-hollow road. The moment the four-wheeler's out of his sight, Dane hears it explode into speed. The snake ditches.

He springs back up on the porch and snatches his tennis shoes from just inside the front door. Then he's across the yard and road and clawing straight up the hill to the above-the-hollow road where Corey and Tommy will have to pass on their way back down the hollow to the snake ditches. But the bank is steep and viney, and Dane slips two times, three times, four, he tangles himself, cussing without words his awkwardness, his broadish woman hips, these he blames, and while he's thrashing around to regain lost ground, he hears the four-wheeler barrel by above him. Then he busts free and finds himself staggering out into the higher road before he expected to, and over the noise of his own breath, he can hear that they are idling now, no doubt looking for the turnoff to the snake ditches.

The snake ditches are not a place Dane would ever choose to go, and would never go alone, even though snakes, like dreams, are the least of his problems now (him little, and Jimmy Make bringing them up on the dirt bike, and Dane scared *skeered* of snakes while Bant was not, Jimmy was quick to point out, although later Bant told him not to feel bad, she had been scared, too, but still later, Dane wondered if she just said that to make him feel better). The snake ditches are a bad place, but, like the Big Drain, Dane's need to watch mutes the dangers of the snake ditches. As does, although he would never think it to himself, his want to be a part of the others.

He runs down the road after them, but not in the middle. He sticks to the sides in case they should look back and see him. The reaching sides, overgrown and heavy green, the road in August a tunnel of plant. Balancing on the top of a rut, he tries to keep clear of puddle, water, mud, but he slides into it a time or two anyway, and over top his own gasping, over top the swish his side makes against branches and weed, he hears the four-wheeler engine holler and strain off-road. He hears Corey yell something at Tommy.

Then he's left the road and is creeping through the underbrush on the side of the track they have begun to tear to the snake ditches, Dane terrified that if they see him, they'll abandon the ditches altogether and speed off somewhere he can't follow. Sweat slicks up and down his back, spills between his two little breasts, he feels it tickle, he smacks at it to go away. Suddenly Corey comes into full view, and Dane ducks behind an umbrella magnolia to watch from behind. Chancey has already spotted him, but Chancey doesn't care. Still mounted on the four-wheeler, Corey forces it forward, then gentles and coaxes it, forces, then coaxes, alternating like that, while Tommy sweeps back and forth in front dragging away bigger obstacles.

Dane burrows deeper into the understory, away from the makeshift track, prowling ahead until he is no longer behind Tommy and Corey, but parallel to them, hidden in leaf. Then, from the side of his eye, he realizes he can see the snake ditches. They are there. And they always come at you like that, he remembers, a crack in the natural. Creepy concrete unexpect. The snake ditches see you before you see them, and the sight of them shrinks him a little, and in his mind, quick then gone, he sees again the monkey. The four-wheeler has already reached the base of one of the ditches, and Tommy is scrambling back up behind Corey. But Dane sees Corey has miscalculated. The snake ditches are too narrow for a four-wheeler. The tires completely straddle the concrete span. You cannot drive a four-wheeler up a snake ditch.

Corey pulls the throttle back, softens the motor a little, and he and Tommy consult. Dane is huddled behind a log, gnats in a loose globe around his head, but he is afraid to reach up and wave them away. He dips and shakes his head instead. He's sweating heavily, Dane nearly nauseated with his own just-adolescent stink, and inside him, along with all the other fullness, the contraries running: the black-red hate, a bite-your-lip-to-keep-from-crying I feel so much hate. Then, tightly twined around the hate, a desperation to be part of this thing so hated. And, finally, fitting with the hate snug as a puzzle piece, the tenderness for what you know is younger and weaker and blood. Love.

Dane knows what they'll try next. The concrete spillway between catchment ponds. Dane knows they are full of wet summer's runoff, and he can see the spillway—putrid algae-colored and slimed. But today no water flows over it. They are arguing now, Tommy cocking, then ducking, his head, his elbows flapping in powerless indignation. Finally Tommy gets off the four-wheeler, stomping his feet as he does, and Dane knows Corey has had to promise him a ride the second time around in order to get rid of him now.

Corey rams the machine at the steep ground alongside the spillway while Dane crawls behind kudzu to sneak a better view, and twice Corey stalls the machine while climbing the bank, both times slipping backwards some before he gets it restarted, but he does get it restarted, and he does climb the hill. And there rises in Dane, again, entangled with the hate and the love, an admiration very close to pride, of Corey and his talent with machines. Man-talent. Metal-made.

Reaching the top of the spillway, Corey turns the wheel to the left and eases out along the concrete. Apparently, there is a ledge there, or the edge of the top pond is shallow enough that he can drive in it, Dane can't tell. The spillway is steep, maybe as steep as a sliding board, but it is higher than even the tallest sliding board they took down at school because it was too dangerous. Of course, it's far bigger across than a sliding board, about as big across, Dane figures, as five four-wheelers parked end-to-end. And when Corey pauses there on top, Dane understands, instantly and precisely, what he will try to do. He's going to chute down the spillway, rip into a turn before he hits the water, then gun his way back up to the top. A U-turn on a steep slant slicked with algae.

The first time, he doesn't go all the way to the bottom, doesn't get real close to the water—unusual for Corey, but there it is. Corey swoops down the concrete with the rag flagging, his oil-colored hair streaming in air, that hard little body moving with his machine the way other people move with horses, like his body is welded to it. And then, about two-thirds of the way down, he jams the wheel, his torso torqued from the hips, and whizzes back up, Dane can even hear the tires spit in the wet algae, in the tiny concrete grooves. Tommy is yelling and bouncing up and down in triumph, having completely forgiven Corey's kicking him off, and then he begins clambering up the side of the spillway to claim his own turn. But Tommy's not going to make it. Corey is already revving for a second run.

Dane is standing now. He no longer needs to hide because it no longer matters if Corey knows. Corey is plunging down the spillway, it's happening very fast, and like in the Big Drain, he ups the ante. He deliberately dips under his tracks from the last trip, flirting with the water. Taunting. Then, an instant before he touches the poisoned-looking pond, he leans into the machine and jerks the front wheels, his face set serious as cast iron. Then it happens. Either the turn angle is too sharp, or Corey wrenches the handlebars too quick, or he's simply gone too far down for the four-wheeler to recover. The machine flips over backwards with Corey under it and crashes into the catchment pond.

A blurb and sucking in the water. The empty in the air where the engine used to be. The slime already drawing back over, and in Dane's mind, a high-speed repeat, *he'll come up, he'll come up, he'll come up, he'll come up, come up come up come up,* while Tommy slides violently down the hill, falling but not bothering to pick himself up, still moving, his mouth making whooping noises that match no feeling at all. Chancey races up and down the pond edge, head lowered, ears cocked, Dane's head swelling with a pressure that feels like a tire pump tapped into his skull *come up come up come up come up,* and he can hear all his blood moving in him, the flood roar to it, like fluid rushing between his bones and his skin, and he hears his breaths as something apart from him, rapid blasting *huhs* as though he's started running again.

When he has not. When he cannot, when he should be, he should be running into the water, pushing the machine off his little brother, *got to listen for a rumble* kiddie pool spinning *you young people can run for the hills* Corey's biceps, rag fluttering, stink of the slop bucket *open your Bible, please,* and. Dane cannot move.

Now Tommy is screaming in a way Dane has never heard before, deeper and louder than any little kid should be able to scream, moan in it, and Dane, still not moving, strains his eyes into the surface of the pond, clouded and boiling—and Dane's insides finally go. The fish rip a hole and the logs spew free, the water torrenting after them, let-go loose loss pain, and Dane falls on his knees *him shit himself, him did, him did. Him shit himself, him did,* Tommy screaming—

Then he hears different yells. He snaps his head around, sees Jimmy Make stumbling through the fresh track in the brush. The look on Jimmy Make's face so unfamiliar that at first Dane knows it's Jimmy Make only by the stagger.

Bant

SEPTEMBER came like it always did, that no-season month between summer and fall. The woods still green, but exhausted from the heat, you could see it in the leaves if you pulled them close. They looked ready for the change. We waited, too.

Two weeks after Labor Day, I turned sixteen. I'd been looking forward to that birthday for a couple years, but now I didn't want anything made of it. Only thing I had to celebrate was not missing my period in late August, and that was relief, not happiness. Lace tried anyway, brought home a Dairy Queen cake nobody but Tommy could enjoy. Me, Lace, and Dane just filling our places at the table while Tommy ate up on his knees leaning forward. Lace let him have all of our pieces.

Past my candles, I watched Dane across from me, in that old army jacket of Avery's that he'd taken to wearing all the time since Mrs. Taylor moved to Cleveland, a little before Jimmy Make left. He'd grown over the summer, now he was near tall as me, but he was always trying to hide the growth under the jacket like it was a tarp. I watched him. His face marring up with pimples right when mine was finally starting to clear. I was scared to think what might become of Dane. He never cried over Corey. Tommy did, and I did, and Lace did, and Jimmy Make did, too. Dane just tighter shut. Since Corey's funeral, Lace had gone to the cemetery on the edge of town a couple times a week, and usually she took me and Tommy with her. Dane, seemed he'd know when she was going before she did, shut himself up in his room and not answer back even when she opened the door and spoke right to him.

The fall stayed unseasonable, just like the summer had been, and a strange skiff of snow fell that first weekend of October, cold setting down like a lid that lifted three days later. Uncle Mogey said in his life he couldn't remember a snow early as that. Then, a week after, we heard an enormous slurry impoundment had busted over in Martin County, Kentucky.

That was on the West Virginia border, not far from us, and the first few days we couldn't get any real news on the disaster, only word of mouth. Then when Lace finally got hold of a *Gazette* with the official story, it was even worse than the rumors had been. It said the impoundment had been sitting on top of a mountain just honeycombed with abandoned deep mines, and finally its bottom simply gave out. The sludge lake dropped into the shafts, shot through the mine tunnels and out through the blocked-up drift mouths, and 306 million gallons of poison muck killed everything in the waterways for a hundred miles. Didn't kill any people (and that was the real act of God, Uncle Mogey said, because, of course, an act of God was where Lyon blamed it), but it buried their properties in what they said was a toxic black pudding some places seven feet deep. And nights after that, I'd wake and taste it. Toxic black pudding. The way the sounds cut sharp, then stick gobby and bitter on your tongue.

That put the fear into even the holdouts, the ones who said it would never happen, at least not that bad. For a little while, people kind of came together like they used to back when I was small. Uncle Mogey's turned into a gathering place. Loretta and some of her people came, Charlie too, and Maxie and the Williams, Bell Kerwin and the Hills, and other people I'd never even met. I saw in the way Mogey moved he was feeling worse than he ever had, but he turned nobody away. We sat under the Jesus poems and the blast cracks in the walls, and they told memories and hearsay of Buffalo Creek. They named to each other the slurry impoundments we knew about around here—the ones behind Deer Lick, the one at Mayton that people said was 900 feet high, the one behind the elementary school in Raleigh County—and when they got done talking about that, they'd wonder on the ones we didn't know about, the ones that we'd just heard tales about—like Yellowroot—and the ones so deep hidden we didn't have any idea. No one knew where all those impoundments might be.

You'd have thought Martin County would make me want worse to find out what was behind our own fill. And I did wait a little for that want. But the want never came. I hadn't been up the hollow since before Corey's accident, hadn't seen the mine site since the night with R.L. Yeah, the impoundment bust scared me, scared me bad, but worse, it made me even more helpless than before. And from helpless, I had learned, what a short step it was to I don't care. How else could you grow up, how you could walk around in your body every day, unless you learned not to care. And by that standard, I realized, I'd been wrong when I was younger. By that standard, it was Jimmy Make, not Lace, who'd been grown up all along.

Corey could have made Lace give up, too, but I wasn't surprised when it did the opposite. Lace got heavier and heavier into the environmental group, especially once Jimmy Make left, which meant now she was telling me not only stuff she picked up at the Dairy Queen but stuff from the meetings, too. She heard that the Martin County spill was twenty times bigger than the Exxon Valdez—then she explained what that was to me—"and some scientists are calling it the biggest environmental disaster in the history of the eastern United States."

But all the news died down real quick, like it always did when something happened around here, if the news got out at all. Who matters and where. On the other hand, it turned out somebody did think we mattered, only in a different way, because that was the last months of the election campaign, and a second Bush was campaigning in our state harder than anybody had, people said, since John F. Kennedy.

Another thing that changed after Corey died was that Lace started going to church again, even though before she'd been mad at the churches. I heard Loretta and Charlie Blizzard get into it over the church-going up at Mogey's one evening, Charlie asking Loretta how she could still stand it with so many preachers preaching, "God gave man dominion over the earth" and "The good Lord put this coal under the ground for us to use."

"Bullcrap and foolishness!" Loretta snapped back. "Them preachers are the ones have always spoke for the companies, you know that, you were raised in a coal camp. Anybody with a grain of sense can see we're destroying what God made. 'The Earth is the Lord's, and everything in it,' Psalm 24. He wants us to fight for it, and I pray every day for God's help in this fight." As she said that, I knew she was right, I heard Grandma's voice deeper under hers. But I still couldn't go myself.

In the middle of all this, Jimmy Make came back. In October, a month after he left, and October'd always been the month I loved the best. The mountains blooming good-bye, and how the sky pulls away to show you itself in October. Beautiful blue like we don't often get around here, and it no longer crouching down on you as it sometimes does. He came back late on a Saturday morning, when he knew we'd all be home, and afterwards, I'd wonder how careful he'd planned it.

Whether he'd spent the night before at Hobart's, waiting. We were eating lunch, and I heard a vehicle, but I didn't think much of it because it didn't sound familiar. But then Chancey and Baron ran to the door, Baron yipping, but not in a watchdog way, more like I-can't-wait, and I guess we all suspicioned it then, but Tommy said it for sure. "There's Dad!" Then looked like he'd be in trouble for naming it.

Dane was sitting right across from me, and I saw his eyes change. Tommy dropped his sandwich and ran to the window. I watched Lace without turning my head, but her face wasn't telling me nothing. Jimmy waited for us to come out on the porch, too scared or too proud to come to the door, and when we did—and we all did, Lace too—I saw he was in a gray minivan with a crumple in the front fender and a long pair of scratches down that side.

He swung out with his head lowered or hung, I'm not sure which, and Chancey and Baron ran to him, and I thought Tommy would, too, but Tommy stayed back. Jimmy wore a navy blue windbreaker I'd never seen and had his hair cut real close. He swung out, flinched at the weight on his leg, and looked at us. Then he called across, his voice pitched a little higher than it normally was, "I got me a good job in Raleigh." I saw him swallow. "I come to take down there anybody wants to go."

The screen door slammed. It was Dane going back in. Tommy walked down the steps into the yard, but he stopped there. Chancey was sniffing the North Carolina tires, and you could hear the minivan's radio playing low, raspy and tough, Jimmy Make's favorite. Classic rock. The radio playing, and things speeding up now, and in my ears I heard the damped-down roar. Roar that'd come first at the funeral, and now at the cemetery, it came every time, and these days I was always at a distance, even without the roar, but when the roar did come, I'd start watching from even further away. And I heard Tommy say, at that distance, "Why don't you stay here, Daddy?"

And Jimmy say, "You know staying here's a bad thing for us all."

I saw that Tommy didn't move.

Now Dane was coming back out carrying a box piled with his clothes. I couldn't even think where he got that box until later we saw how he'd dumped out the Christmas decorations. He walked right past Lace and me without looking at us, his head turtled down in that army jacket, and when he got to Jimmy Make, he didn't look at him, either. He slid open the van door, set his box on the seat, climbed up beside it, and slammed the door shut. The sun bounced off the closed windows. I couldn't see him anymore.

Tommy had not moved. Him in a too-big Marshall sweatshirt all four of us had worn, the cuffs hanging loose, partway ripped from the sleeves. I was watching his back quiver, hard enough that you could see it even under the big shirt, and from my distance, I heard Jimmy Make say, "Tommy, it's up to you to decide."

And Lace say, "He's too young to decide."

And Jimmy, "You say that because he won't pick you."

Now Tommy was outright crying. A new kind of Tommy crying, not crying because he was mad or'd been done a wrong or wanted attention or'd busted something. I saw Lace drop down beside him, and I watched her turn him towards her and pull him against Jimmy's old flannel shirt that she wore. She said something in his ear. Tommy bawled louder, clung tighter to her neck. I saw her kiss him, then gentle pull his arms loose. She held his hands down with hers and kissed him again. Lace was crying, too.

When she stood, Tommy looked behind at her one time. Then he went. Stumbled across that scraggly yard with his hands over his eyes and his elbows cocked out, his back gone from that high quiver to a full-length shudder with the sobs. The roar in my ears so loud, me so far, everything moving but me. Jimmy Make stepped forward and picked him up and kissed the top of his head, and I'm not sure I'd ever seen him do that. Then he carried Tommy around to the passenger seat, Tommy kind of pulling away from him, his back arched and his face in his hands. But he didn't try to climb down. Jimmy slammed the door and came back to the front bumper. He had his head down, like he was going to scuff his feet. But then he looked at me.

"You coming, Cissy?"

Even far away from the van as I stood, I saw he knew my answer already. And once again, I realized Jimmy Make wasn't nearly as dumb, as young, as I used to believe. I saw the hurt in his face before I said anything back, and I saw at the same time, but not even as part of the hurt, the boy in the face, too. I saw the boy behind the face made man too soon. And right then, it came to me: I was older now than he'd been when he had me.

I felt myself shake my head. The dull roar in my ears. Then something told me that, serious as this was, I should speak to him, too.

"I'm staying here, Daddy."

That was when he finally crossed the yard. To get to where I was on the porch, if he'd used the steps, he would've had to pass Lace. So he crawled up under the railing and pulled me against him. It felt not right, my head turned funny, crunched up in his arms. We'd had no practice at this here. But he hugged me close. And even at my distance, even though I could not catch up, I smelled the sleepy sweat smell.

Jimmy Make idled the van while Lace fetched Tommy's clothes. Somehow they knew to do that—him to wait, her to get them—without speaking. When Lace carried them out in one of the two suitcases we owned, she passed them through Jimmy's window. Then she stepped away from it and said something to Jimmy Make I couldn't hear.

Near as I could tell, Jimmy Make and Dane didn't look back when they pulled out. Jimmy had to turn the van around, so it was Tommy facing us as they left, most of his face blurred behind the half-rolled-down window. I thought I saw his eyes still screwed up, crying. I know for sure he didn't wave.

Soon as we couldn't see them anymore, I dropped down under the porch railing, same way Jimmy had come up, and I headed up the hollow.

I hadn't been past the gate since before Corey. I kept my head down and thought nothing but walk. Butchered hollow shocking full of that October sky, so few trees left to block it, I was completely exposed, anyone could see. But I no longer cared. When I hit the rockpile at the toe of the fill, I took it like Jimmy Make had, upright, my arms spread, and I kept perfect balance because I did not care. I didn't stop when I reached the skun-out slope, I just clamped on and spidered up. I climbed steady without thinking, without feeling, there was no other way to climb it, I knew that now. Time passed funny when I stayed at that distance, roar still in my ears, but before I realized it, I was near the top, and the bank I was depending on was running out.

I saw I'd have to move over onto the fill, and then I did feel a twitch of fear, but I just picked my self up. Carried my self even further away. No sooner did I step onto the fill than it did go loose under me, I couldn't get any ground, everything sifting out from under my feet, and the day of the blast avalanche came back to me, and, again, I got scared, but I just picked my self up. And again moved away. I swam dirt fast enough to outrun the landslide, and finally I had my arms on a big rock where I figured I could rest before the very last piece, and I pulled at the rock, and it seemed to be setting steady, so I climbed on up.

I was about a body length and a half from the very top of the fill. I was sweating, my lungs tearing after air, and I spat out the Yellowroot dirt in my mouth. I saw how I'd ripped the knee of my jeans, how I'd scraped the underneath of my bare arms, all without feeling it. One thumbnail torn in a nasty way. I looked to the bottom of the fill where so often I'd stood looking up, but I couldn't any longer remember me there. I strained my eyes through the trees and brush left in the lower part of the hollow, trying to see the house. But from up here, it looked like in Yellowroot Hollow, there wasn't nobody living at all.

Then I looked above me. Earlier, I'd started to see the fill really had two tops. You couldn't tell for certain from the bottom, but now, from my rock shelf, I saw for sure. The valley fill I'd climbed didn't come directly off the mine. There was another fill, another top, behind this one. Which meant there was something between the two.

I did the final part on my hands and knees, just threw myself onto that dry quicksand and scrabbled quick enough to stay ahead of the suck. When I reached the rim, it right away crumbled under me, but, still crouching, I shifted, and it settled to where I could squat and not fall. Then I saw.

Lace had been wrong. And Lace had been right.

A smaller, fresher fill rose up behind my fill. Between the two fills lay a kind of bowl, big enough to hold three houses the size of Uncle Mogey's. But even big as that bowl was, I was almost sure it was too small for a slurry impoundment. I couldn't tell for sure, though, because I couldn't see its bottom. All I could see were the trees.

That bowl was jumbled solid with dead trees. Bulldozed trees, hundreds of them, still holding their branches, their root balls, their crowns, some still clung to with brown leaves, those trees colored like the trees in the fill, dull colors that had nothing to do with the woods. A tree slaughter maybe fifteen feet deep, and because the top of the fill I'd climbed was lower than the top of the second fill, the highest part of the logjam was almost flush with the rim of the fill where I squatted. I duckwalked a ways along the sinking rim, looking for a place to see bottom. And finally, I thought I saw, through all that layered mess, a little sunlight flashing off water.

I eased my body down the inside of the fill. Gentle as I could, I crawled out on the top skein of logs. The moment I touched them, they shifted, groaning and knocking, and I held my breath, crouched low and light, until they reshuffled and seemed to catch. I shimmied down into them. Waited. They held. I dropped a little further. Waited. They held. Then I was threading limb, trunk, root, like being inside some muck-caked woven basket, the odor of dried mud not like mud should smell and their bad grit all over me. Then I saw clearly a pond below me, and I seized tight inside, but one more time, I pushed me away. I bellied over the top of the pond to a log that led to the ground, and I crawled that one with my feet and hands. Then I dropped to the firmest ground I'd felt since I'd left the hollow. Although I knew this, too, wasn't real ground.

I saw that there were at least four good-sized sediment ponds under the logjam. Bigger than any of the ones in the hollow. You couldn't see into these ponds any better than you could see into the ones down below, so I reached over my head for a stick to check how deep they were. But the branch wouldn't snap from the tree, I had to twist the branch until it tore off, and then, sudden, it came to me how green those trees were, and that put a hurt in me. A hurt for those pitiful trees, how short they'd been dead. Then that hurt started pulling after it the other ones. They started, I felt my self coming back to me, and I inbreathed quick and deep, bit my lip, and back-stepped my self away. I thrust my stick in that poison pond. Didn't hit any bottom *all those lessons in losing, Bant, how good you are getting, practice makes perfect and be sure to start young.* I pushed down deeper, stirring, poking, and, still, I felt nothing solid *first Pap, then Grandma, then woods mountains places, then Corey, and now today, how many lessons in let-go?* Don't care. I leaned over the pond as far as I dared, stretched my arm as far as it would go. *Then why didn't you go with Jimmy Make, you don't care?* Still no bottom. I understood.

The runoff from the mine site, miles and miles of compacted dirt, no soak to it, and when it rained hard enough—it would split off slick as water on tin. Gush full these sediment ponds, then overflow, and this huge raft of trees would lift. The trees would lift, swirl a little bit, butt and jostle, crammed tight like they were. Start to surge and ram against that crumbly dirt lip where I'd just been squatting, until pretty soon, the lip would blow.

The lip explodes. The fill buckles under itself, collapses, water and logs and rock and dirt, sluicing down the face of the fill. Sucking up more stuff as they go. Biggening, swelling, fill turning half water, water turning half fill, the whole monster slamming into the hollow and the blocked-up sediment ponds there, the flood inhaling into itself what the lower ponds hold, too—more water, muck, and poisons, more trees and trash—until finally all of it crashes the gate and roars right down Yellowroot Road. Our house would be the first to go.

I dropped my branch in the dirty water. I sidled along the pond to the back of the bowl, climbed through the dead trees there, and crawled up the smaller fill to the mine.

I hadn't seen the site in daylight since the day of the snake ditches with Corey, over three months ago. Now Yellowroot was completely gone. I'd figured that's how it would be. But for some reason, I hadn't let myself think how if Yellowroot was finished, they'd be taking Cherryboy next. And they were. They'd made their first big blast into Cherryboy. They'd sheared part of it away to leave a tall flat naked face. I looked at it. I looked at the dead man-made cliff, and at first I felt nothing for that cut on Cherryboy. Then I felt nothing except I had to get into the woods.

The machines were running between me and them, but I wasn't scared. Not of the men, not of the equipment, not of a blast. I stayed to the edge of the site, and I didn't watch them working, watched only that raw bone edge of Cherryboy. It was a long ways I had to walk, and eventually, the men did see me, I heard at least one of the machines cut off and then some shouting. I didn't care. By then, I was almost to the woods, and I broke into a jog. I ran, feeling the men at my back, but not caring, hearing the crunch of dead ground, and *I don't care.* I heard myself say it out loud this time. I ran faster, stumbled, caught myself in mid-fall and pushed on, it was hard to get air, until, finally, under my feet there came softness. Overhead, there came shade.

Then I was moving the way I used to in the woods, before the distance came between me and it, the way I moved in woods and woods only. All the clumsy I felt around people, and buildings and pavement and flat, it used to fall away from me in the woods, and it fell away now. I could feel what was nearby, its size, its closeness, its give, beech, poplar, oak, holly hickory hemlock laurel, touching nothing, tripping nowhere, what Mogey always said about the hum. October smell in my head, and me and Grandma, sassafras and pawpaw and beechnut, like sunflower seeds under your feet, I pushed myself harder, *don't care,* and yellowroot, too, after the sap went down *Some folks, they use yellowroot for just about everything.* They brought me up here before I was born, and I do remember, smell of November wetter-leaved than October smell *don't care* me and Lace and Sheila in the little room, me and Lace in the little bed, yellow linoleum floors. Grandma showing me what to chew for the good taste in it *Now that was our chewing gum,* me carrying my little sack, head weed-high, *Close to the ground like you are, Bant, you can see stuff bettern me. Red berries is what you're looking for.* Senging. Sanging. Sing, sang, sung, *You can live off these mountains. Put you in a little garden, and you can live off these here.*

It caught my eye. Strange that it did, fast as I was moving. But there it was, just off the path I'd started following, I had to turn back to go to it. A fresh-dug spot. The yellow-red dirt bared, and then I saw how the dead leaves had been turned up and cleared away, and I knew it was very recent.

I drew in closer. Somebody had placed around the filled hole's edge little rocks, sparkling with quartz, careful chosen and neat. Making like a little grave. I stood there for some time, quieting my breathing.

At first I used a stick, but fresh and loose as that dirt was, I ended up just using my hands. The hole was shallow, and I hit metal fast, and I recognized it as soon as I saw the orange. Lace's old lunchbox from grade school. Then I knew it was Dane.

I pulled it out of the hole, and when I shook it to clear the dirt, it gave a loose rattle. I sat back on my heels and brushed it off. The soothing pictures, I'd forgotten—the boy riding his friendly bear. The father bandaging a deer's leg. In the background, the smiling mother with a broom. I thumbed open the buckle.

Inside lay an acorn, a tiny hoof from a toy horse, a scrap of magazine paper. And the chamois rag.

My heart heaved once in my chest. I felt it roll. I turned over on my side in the leaves.

Was it worse to lose the mountain or the feelings that you had for it? Now that I'd lost this much, I realized that to not care wasn't to save yourself at all. It was only another loss. Then I remembered something Uncle Mogey told me, back when things were just starting to get truly bad. It was right after Grandma's funeral, and people were all over the house and the yard, visiting and eating chicken and coleslaw off paper plates. I was sitting on a cable spool a distance away, mad at them for eating at such a time, mad at the quiet laughs. Mogey walked over to me, but I didn't even want Uncle Mogey near. And Mogey, he sensed that, the way he had of knowing such things, and he stayed only a second, didn't squat down. He said just one thing. Standing over and a little behind me, so I saw mostly his narrow Sunday shoes looking wrong on his feet, and he said it like he didn't want to be pushy, like maybe it wasn't worth saying at all.

He said, "Bant, I've learned something about times like these. In times like these, you have to grow big enough inside to hold both the loss and the hope."

It had meant little to me then, which was why I'd forgotten it. But now I saw. It was what Lace already knew. What Grandma knew. What a lot of people around here had to have known for a very long time.

I reburied Dane's box. I set back careful each glittery rock. I stood up and wiped my hands on my jeans, pushed my hair away from my face. Then I headed towards home to tell Lace what I'd found.

Acknowledgments

This book was born from interviews and conversations with people in the southern West Virginia and eastern Kentucky coalfields. Some of them are living in the middle of mountaintop removal, others are fighting it, and many are doing both. I wouldn't have written a word without the stories, passion, grief, terror, and courage of the following people: Gayla, Ray, Dustin, and Johnny Aliff; Joe and Judy Barnett; Teri Blanton; Julia Bonds; Moss Burgess; Pauline Canterberry; Dave Cooper; Gail Ferrell; Michael Foley; Laura Forman; Denise Giardina; Larry Gibson; Maria Gunnoe; Donna Halstead; Joann Hammond; Lavoris Harris; John Holston; Willard Kelly; Lenny Kohm; Bryan McNeill; Mary Miller; Denver Mitchell; Carlene Mowery; Janice Nease; Jimmy Prater; Bill and Donna Price; Cindy Rank; Jewel Rohrer; Patty and Butch Seebok; Vivian Stockman; Bertie Vance; and Freeda Williams. Special thanks to the Ohio Valley Environmental Coalition and Coal River Mountain Watch.

William Maxie and Rick Eades contributed valuable factual information. I am also indebted to the outstanding articles on contemporary mining by Ken Ward of the *Charleston Gazette*. Details about the

Buffalo Creek disaster came from Kai T. Erikson's *Everything In Its Path,* and Gerald M. Stern's *The Buffalo Disaster.* Richard Fauss of the West Virginia State Archives was tirelessly helpful. Jackson Connor, Frankie and Lori McDonald, and James Pancake provided necessary material not related to mining. Paula Clendenin always had a room when I needed one. Pauline Canterberry and Mary Miller assiduously collected newspaper articles for me and kept me abreast of new developments after I left West Virginia. To all of you, my heartfelt thanks.

I am inexpressibly grateful to those who read the manuscript in earlier versions and offered their feedback and, perhaps even more important, their encouragement: Caitlin Sullivan, Jackson Connor, Wendy Somerson, Phil Terman, Judith Kitchen, Anneliese Truame, traci oberg-connor, Mark Guarino, Diana Hume George, Philip Sullivan, Steve Snyder, and Emily Forland. Roxanna Aliaga and Trish Hoard are the kind of editors I didn't think existed anymore. I still can't believe my good fortune in finding them. I thank Jack Shoemaker, my publisher, for his vision and his commitment to my book.

My deep appreciation to the Pennsylvania Council of the Arts, the West Virginia Commission on the Arts, the Washington State Artist Trust, the Whiting Foundation, and the Christopher Isherwood Foundation for their financial support during my writing of this novel.

I want to thank my sister, Catherine Pancake, without whom I wouldn't have started the book and with whom I discovered many of the seeds for it. My parents, Joe S. Pancake and Robbie Pancake, made me aware of the environmental costs of strip mining by the time I was six years old. Finally, my greatest gratitude to Caitlin Sullivan, for her wisdom, her patience, and her uncompromising faith in me and this project.

To find out more about mountaintop removal mining, please go to www.ohvec.org; www.appvoices.org; www.kftc.org; www.ilovemountains .org; www.crmw.net.

PHOTO BY ANITA NOWACKA

ANN PANCAKE grew up in Summersville and Romney, West Virginia. She is the author of the short story collection *Given Ground,* for which she won the 2000 Katharine Bakeless Nason Fiction Prize. She holds a BA from West Virginia University, an MA from the University of North Carolina at Chapel Hill, and a PhD from the University of Washington. Her work has appeared in publications such as *Glimmer Train, Five Points, Quarterly West, Shenandoah, Virginia Quarterly Review,* and the *Journal of Appalachian Studies.* She is the recipient of many awards, including a Pushcart Prize, the Whiting Writers Award, the Thomas Wolfe Fiction Prize, and a National Endowment for the Arts Creative Writers' Fellowship Grant. She lives in Seattle.